# PLOWED FIELDS

## TRILOGY EDITION

# BOOK ONE

For Jacki Lowe,
One of the great women at
AbrahPower. I am honored
by your presence today.
With love,

Jon Barber
1-20-20

# PLOWED FIELDS
## TRILOGY EDITION

# BOOK ONE


# THE WHITE CHRISTMAS
# AND
# THE TRAIN

————————

## JIM BARBER

Copyright © 2019 by Jim Barber
First Printing: 2019
Published by Morgan Bay Books™
Library of Congress Control Number 2019901845
ISBN 978-1-7327845-3-6
ISBN 978-1-7327845-4-3 (Ebook)

Printed in the United States of America

Cover design by Jane Hill
Cover photo by Krivosheev Vitaly
Author photo by Brandi Williams

Morgan Bay Books
432 Princeton Way
Suite 101
Lawrenceville, GA 30044
www.plowedfields.com
www.jimbarber.me

# ACKNOWLEDGMENTS

I've always loved to write, but writing a novel was never one of my big goals in life. And then, on a beautiful spring day when I was traveling between two small towns in middle Georgia as a young newspaper reporter in 1985, the idea for *Plowed Fields* came fully alive to me, and I felt compelled to write the story. I wanted to preserve a time and place that had shaped my life and positioned me to achieve my dreams. So, first, I must acknowledge my family, friends and many others whose presence influenced my growing-up years.

Specifically, I credit my parents—my daddy Elmo who died in 1991 and my mama Marie who remains eternally young; my sister Caye Robinson and brother-in-law Charles Robinson, who really lived the era I wrote about; my grandmothers Flossie Lee Willis Barber and Carrie Elizabeth Weaver Baker who loved unconditionally and worked as hard as anyone I've ever known; my uncles Jake Baker and Bug Baker who managed to raise crops and earn livings—though Lord knows how—with help from a bunch of young'uns like me and my cousins, Greg, Don and Chipp Griner, and Mike and Regina Baker; my uncles Virgil Barber (a World War II hero) and LA Barber, who shared their knowledge of the old days and farming before my time; my cousin Faith Barber Noles; one of my oldest friends, Jerry Moore, with whom I shared the only real experience recorded in this book; and the best friend ever, Greg Harrell. I also must pay homage to the amazing teachers at West Berrien Elementary School and Berrien High School—particularly Wanda Vickers, Gail Danforth, Linda Davis Brooks and Calva Gill McDaniel—who gave me far more than I gave them through my efforts in the classroom. And to the late S.T. and Clarice Hamilton, who gave me my first newspaper job at *The Berrien Press*.

I populated this book with names and places near and dear to my heart, but the characters are completely fictional. The Taylor family may be villains in this story, but the real Taylors are lifelong family friends and nothing like their namesakes in this book. Not to mention some of the most amazing gospel singers God ever put on this earth!

It is no easy task to turn an idea into a book, and many people read my manuscript, offered ideas and encouragement, and helped make *Plowed Fields* a reality through their criticism, proofing and insights into the publishing industry. In alphabetical order, they were Betty Bell, Becky Blalock, Janice Daugharty, Sam Heys, Jane Hill, Maggie Johnsen, Joey Ledford, Cindy Theiler and Emelyne Williams. In addition, I would be remiss not to mention the late Jim Kilgo and Conrad Fink, two extraordinary professors at the University of Georgia who gave me confidence to believe in my talent; and the late Duane Riner, press secretary for Georgia Governor George Busbee and an *Atlanta Journal-Constitution* editor. Duane once gave me a byline above the masthead in the AJC, but more importantly, he believed in me from the beginning and proved to be an extraordinary mentor and more. Rarely a day passes when I do not recall his influence and I hope I give back a small measure of what he gave me.

No doubt, I have overlooked someone worthy of mentioning, so to all who helped make this dream a reality, I offer my sincere thanks and gratitude.

Grateful acknowledgement is made to the publishers of the following for permission to quote from material in copyright or the public domain:

*The Holy Bible*
Luke 2:1-5, King James Version.

*Putting in the Seed*
Frost, Robert. *Mountain Interval.* New York: Henry Holt, 1916. *1st in Poetry and Drama*, December 1914.

*The publisher has made every effort to secure the necessary permissions to reprint any quoted material and to make full acknowledgment for its use. In the event of any question arising as to the right to use any material, the publisher, while expressing regret for any inadvertent error, will be happy to make the necessary correction in any future printings, provided notification is sent to the publisher.*

# PRAISE FOR PLOWED FIELDS

"If Pat Conroy had been raised on a tobacco farm in South Georgia, this is the novel he would have written. *Plowed Fields* is a powerful story about a time in history that left more scars than we care to remember. With his rich detail of farm life, complex characters and sure sense of storytelling, Jim Barber has captured a time and place in Americana with lyrical precision and stunning beauty. Amid the darkness and evil, he has infused this story with warmth, heart and hope as promising as a newly plowed field."

– Becky Blalock, author of *Dare*

"Not since Larry McMurtry's *Lonesome Dove* have I read such a solid, unembellished, detail-rich portrayal of rural life lived out in fiction. In fact, while reading *Plowed Fields*, it seemed I was watching an intriguing TV miniseries. *Plowed Fields* is all that a family saga should be—natural, endearing, superbly written and enchanting. Add to that fresh and exact! The characters come alive under Jim Barber's control. Jim Barber is a master storyteller; so by definition, that makes *Plowed Fields* a masterpiece. Readers are in for a glad experience."

– Janice Daugharty, author of *Earl in the Yellow Shirt* and
*The Paw-Paw Patch*

"Set in the recent past this is the perfect novel for our time of national uncertainty, cynicism and corruption of values emanating from the very top. In nine episodes, *Plowed Fields* gives us the turbulent 1960s as lived in Georgia by the Baker family. Their haunting saga of desire and responsibility—of revolution and resolution—has a great deal to say to us today. In the words of the aphorism often attributed to Mark Twain, 'History doesn't repeat itself, but it often rhymes.'"

– Alan Axelrod, author of
*The Gilded Age, 1876-1912: Overture to the American Century* and
*How America Won World War I*

# PRAISE FOR PLOWED FIELDS

"*Plowed Fields* explores the hard choices we make, the love we give and the joy, sorrow and hope that shape our lives. It is a deeply moving story of "ordinary people" navigating through extraordinary times. Ultimately, *Plowed Fields* paints a portrait of faith lost and found. Joe Baker and his family will resonate with you long after the last page is read. I hope there's a sequel."

— Sam Heys, author of *The Winecoff Fire* and *Big Bets*

"Imagine a family like TV's The Waltons living and loving on a tobacco farm in South Georgia during the 1960s, and you will have a strong sense of *Plowed Fields*. The story certainly has a wholesome quality— some might even say sentimental—but it's also 'glazed with the sorrow of a devastating truth.' Jim Barber has captured a time and place with exquisite detail and superb storytelling *Plowed Fields* will break your heart, but it's the warmth and tenderness of the people and the story that will stay with you."

— Emelyne Williams, editor of *Atlanta Women Speak*

"Jim Barber's extraordinary *Plowed Fields* is reminiscent of Laura Ingalls Wilder's masterpiece series of Little House books. Barber's canvas is hardscrabble Cookville, Georgia, of 1960 rather than Ingalls Wilder's 1870s Minnesota. And rather than focus on a daughter, *Plowed Fields* centers on Joe Baker, the oldest of Matt and Caroline Baker's six children. The family saga tracks the Bakers over a tumultuous decade in which they weather struggles with drought, fire, a family feud, loss of faith, death and the cultural changes shaking the rural South of the civil rights era. Barber is an exciting new voice who defines family and coming of age with an engaging style."

— Joey Ledford, author of *Speed Trap* and
*Elkmont: The Smoky Mountain Massacre*

For Pearl, my bride

# PLOWED FIELDS
## TRILOGY EDITION

# BOOK ONE

---

And go along with you
ere you lose sight

Of what you came for
and become like me.

Slave to a springtime
passion for the earth.

---

*Putting in the Seed*
~ Robert Frost

# THE WHITE CHRISTMAS

## 1960

# CHAPTER 1

JOE BAKER PUSHED THE throttle forward, easing the tractor to a crawl as the row-end neared. In one clumsy motion, he pulled up the machine's hydraulic lift, raising the plow from the ground, and dropped his casted leg onto the brake pedal. The back tire froze, pivoting the tractor and aligning the wheel perfectly into the furrow of the previously plowed row. Dropping the turning plow back into the dirt, he pulled the throttle down to top speed and headed the tractor up another row, leaving a wake of ripped earth, dark and moist.

Blatant self-satisfaction betrayed the boy's usual stoic approach to farm work, emerging as a smirk to the plaster mold encasing his right leg from knee to toes. Such delight was uncommon for Joe, who had negotiated more tractor turns at row-ends than he cared to count. But then again, so was the state of clumsiness that stamped the youngster's every move these days, prodding his ego on an endless effort to prove his worth, his usefulness.

Joe checked the back wheel's position against the furrow, adjusted the plow's depth and relaxed as the tractor lumbered up another row. Just a few more passes and this field, the largest of six on the Baker farm, would be plowed and settled for the winter's rest.

The boy looked across the field, which was framed against a ruby sea of late evening sunset, and surveyed his handiwork. Picture-perfect layers of earth lay end over end, concealing like a grave every trace of the fluffy white cotton that had lived in this ground a short time ago. But Joe knew instinctively that the land held no deathly quality.

The plowed field was a dazzling sight to behold, lying in wait for the springtime seed that would turn fallow land once more into a festival of life. Every year at this time—his favorite, when the air became crisp, nipped with the approaching winter chill, and the pace of the days relaxed like a sweet-flowing melody—the boy became aware of the sacred trust placed in the land. A freshly plowed field held promise and radiated beauty. Joe respected the promise, he saw the beauty; but somehow any real attachment to the land always escaped his grasp.

Nevertheless, he had volunteered—or more accurately, insisted—for the task of plowing this large field, relegating his father and grandfather to the toil of relaxing and taking care of less pressing matters. He had accomplished the job by spending the hours after school perched on the tractor, working until the evening shadows disappeared and failing daylight forced him to attend his regular chores. Now, as he surveyed the results of his labor, he permitted himself another smug glare at the cast. And, experienced a twinge of guilt over the praise the effort would reap from his family. They mistakenly saw the endeavor as another example of a good boy's dedication to the virtues of hard work, when in reality, far more than he dreaded the tedium of farm life, Joe despised any signs of uselessness in himself.

This last thought had been revealed to Joe early in a journey of self-discovery, a voyage plotted by the startling course of his sophomore year of high school. Other people had undertaken grander journeys of the mind and made more important discoveries about themselves, he felt sure. But the value of his own journey was worth more, or so thought Joe, who tended to qualify his words and thoughts as products solely of himself.

While admitting a farmer's life held no great joy for him, the overwhelming finding of this personal journey had been an acknowledgment that he needed a sense of normalcy and purpose in life. In his mind, normalcy meant daily routines, obligations and expectations that were carried out, met and fulfilled without fuss or fanfare; and a purpose was any task to accomplish, from plowing a field to doing homework.

Early in his convalescence from the broken leg, there had been too much fussing and fanfare over Joe. He had felt like an invalid, a burden to the family, which suddenly seemed to neither want nor need anything from him. Feeling weak and inadequate, he had determined to restore a semblance of normalcy to life. He tolerated the good intentions of his family for several days, then pronounced himself recuperated and set out to prove the point. Whether he had proved it to the family was a matter of debate, but the boy felt more like a man.

Still, he was not whole. While his strength had returned quickly, the splintered bone required time to heal. Until that healing occurred, Joe would seek normalcy in his own way, and he would permit himself absurd pleasures such as taking delight in the accomplishment of any task that defied the will of the broken leg.

Joe owed his handicap to the perils of high school football. He had been a member of the Cookville High School Rebels, primarily because only thirty boys attended tryouts and every available body was needed for the varsity team.

Cookville was a football doormat in South Georgia, where enthusiasm for the sport verged on religious fervor. Joe had held no illusions about his ability to elevate Cookville to unscaled heights, which a break-even season would have accomplished. Yet, in the span of two games, he had recorded one of the team's more memorable careers.

He had combined minimal talent with maximum luck to occupy a moment in the spotlight and a place in the suppertime conversations of the Cookville community. Such notoriety might have been heady stuff for some high school sophomores, but Joe was immune to fool's gold. Luck, if there was such a thing, was a two-sided coin, evidenced by the brevity of his football career.

Even before the accident, Joe had borne little resemblance to a football player. In full uniform on a full stomach, he barely weighed one hundred thirty-five pounds. Still, he carried more weight than most people realized. His grandfather described Joe as a sturdy sapling, conditioned by his environment like a tree adapted to the elements. The boy possessed strength and stamina, both physical and inner, honed on his family's farm.

His talent for the game lay in his hands. They were work-hardened, oversized paws, with long, grasping fingers and wide, bony knuckles.

Those hands had caught the eye of Coach Ben Simmons on Joe's first day of football practice during an exercise known as Milking the Cow, which was also a chore that brought Joe into intimate contact with the family milk cow virtually every day.

As an exercise, milking the cow involved stretching the arms to full length at shoulder level and repeatedly squeezing the hands open and closed. Long after the majority of his teammates tired of the exercise, arms sagging and hands cramping, Joe had stood perfectly postured, his fingers flexing at a steady pace.

Coach Simmons had approached Joe, regarded his hands with mild curiosity and asked, "Can you catch a football, son?"

"Yes, sir."

The coach had acknowledged the answer with a casual nod, but a week later, Joe was the starting tight end for Cookville.

The boy's football knowledge extended little beyond what had been learned in rough, high-spirited games on the playground of New River Elementary School. It was limited experience, but typical of rookie Rebels because Cookville was a rural community. There was no spring football practice because most team members were busy helping their families plant crops. And while fall football practice officially opened two weeks before the start of school, most of the team, including Joe, staggered in sometime during the second week.

Coach Simmons could not expect otherwise, and thus kept the game simple. The Rebels offense consisted of twenty plays, the vast majority of them designed to send the running backs into the waiting grasp of swarming defenders. There had been an element of surprise then, when—in the 1960 season opener against the Valdosta High School Wildcats—Cookville quarterback Dale Bennett took one step back after the snap and fired a quick pass over the middle on the first play from scrimmage.

Valdosta was a perennial powerhouse on the football field, four times larger than Cookville and embarrassed to have the Rebels on their schedule. Cookville was the perennial patsy, having never scored against the Wildcats in seven previous games and downright intimidated on their eighth and most likely final try.

Joe had caught the ball on a dead run, with outstretched fingers between two Valdosta linebackers, then raced seventy-seven yards for his life to the end zone for a touchdown. The Cookville bench and stands promptly erupted into frenzied exhilaration. Players rushed onto the field and hoisted Joe to their shoulders. He became an instant star. When the pandemonium calmed, Valdosta proceeded to block the extra point kick, then scored the game's last sixty-three points, chalking up the first win of a state championship season.

The 63-6 shellacking did little to dampen optimism for Cookville's second game against the Cook High School Hornets. Cookville and Cook were archrivals, but beyond their neighboring locations, name similarity and good-natured ribbing, there was little in dispute between the two schools on the football field. Cook reigned supreme. In the fourteen-year history of the rivalry, Cookville had tallied a dozen defeats and salvaged ties on the other two occasions.

The game was played under a steady drizzle. It was a head-busting, hard-hitting slugfest between two mediocre teams playing with more heart than talent. Midway through the third quarter of the scoreless game, Joe ran a sideline pattern near mid-field. Dale Bennett's pass was wobbly and overthrown, forcing Joe to cut sharply back across the slippery field.

At the last second before the ball sailed over his head for an incompletion, Joe leapt into the air, snagging the leather spiral with the outstretched fingers of one hand. As he hauled in the ball with both hands, two opposing players collided in mid-air against his right leg, striking from opposite directions with bone-crushing force. One helmet rammed Joe right beneath the kneecap; the second drove through his hamstring.

In the ensuing fall from grace, when he realized the sickening snap reverberating across the field came from his body, the boy had known his football career was finished. He had banished the game to a dead place in the mind, where memories of what might have been rarely mingled with what never was.

He landed flat on his back, the ball rolling casually from his hands onto the wet grass. A mad scramble ensued around him, and a Cook player recovered the fumble, but Joe never even realized he had dropped the ball.

His knee exploded like a conflagration. He struggled to sit, fighting for consciousness. When his eyes focused on the injured knee, absorbed the splintered bone sticking through the bloodied pants leg of his uniform, Joe promptly, and smartly, gave up the fight.

He had woken sometime later on a hospital stretcher, enduring a series of X-rays before a doctor finally injected a merciful dose of morphine. The next time he woke, Joe was in a hospital bed with his leg encased in a heavy plaster cast, attached to a pulley contraption suspended from the ceiling.

From his parents, Joe had learned about the surgery necessary to set the bone back in its proper position and reattach torn ligaments and tendons. From his brothers and sisters, he heard the gorier details: how the loud crack of his leg hushed the crowd instantly; the awestruck silence inspired by the ambulance driving onto the field and off again with his limp body; the hero's standing ovation given when the sirens blared to life.

People often picked strange heroes, Joe believed, and the boy harbored not a single delusion of grandeur. At his best on the football field, he had demonstrated average talent. Lady luck had been the divining rod of his football fortunes, and he had prospered and perished with her whims—another conclusion Joe had reached on his journey of self-discovery, along with the realization that he was destined to be one of those masses of men who led a solid life of averages.

Joe could live with the averages, but the boy had made another discovery about himself on the solitary journey. It was frightening, an idea he did not fully understand but one that shared equal billing with his need for normalcy and purpose.

The boy looked out across the field once more, gazed across treetops into the sunset and acknowledged the well of restlessness running deep inside him. This restlessness scared Joe because he could not define it in exact terms, and because it provoked anxious feelings that he was destined to remain solid and would never soar as long as he was here on this place, this farm that meant so much to his family.

Joe wanted to force these thoughts from his mind, but he could not deny that his most memorable moments occurred when his actions or circumstances scraped against the grain of his character. And he could not help wondering where that grain was headed, and the scars it might sustain along the way.

The boy's thoughts ran fast these days—no doubt compensating for his legs, Joe figured—though not always so deep. In one moment, he was likely to ponder a pretty girl; the next, the approaching Christmas season; and then, this kind of brooding reflection and speculation that cluttered his head with more questions than answers, invariably leaving him confused and glum.

Confusion bothered Joe like a gnat in the dog days of summer. He preferred simplicity, which was probably why he thrived on the familiarity of routine obligations and patterns. Normalcy kept his head uncluttered, restrained him from thinking deeply and warded off confusion. When normalcy failed him, as it did now, Joe had learned to seek distractions. They were easy to find when a boy's thoughts ran as fast as his did these days. And then, without his appreciation, a distraction presented itself in the form of the last row to plow.

Joe wheeled the tractor into another perfect turn at the far end of the field and dropped the plow once more into the dirt. But instead of speeding up the last row, he idled down the engine, pausing to fish a cigarette from the pocket of his jeans.

He lit it and took a long drag, looking out across the field once more, thinking deeply about nothing in particular. Dusk had settled over the farm, leaving only a faint reddish hue over the treetops. A rustling breeze chilled him through the red flannel shirt, hinting of a hard freeze sweeping in from the Arctic hinterlands.

Joe took another drag on the cigarette, then accelerated the engine once more and headed the tractor alongside the fencerow. The boy guided the tractor with more caution on this row, ever mindful of a time long ago when he had tangled the plow in a fence and required his father's help to extract it. He passed a small meadow, where cattle grazed on light brown clumps of dried grass, and then edged his grandfather's prized blackberry bramble, now reduced to a dormant skeleton of vines woven through the fence. Finally, the tractor skirted the edge of the pecan orchard, its barren branches affording Joe the comforting sight of smoke curling away from the chimney of his home. A sudden rush of anticipation for a job well done and the hearty supper to come turned the boy's head toward the end of the row.

And waiting there was his daddy.

------

Matt Baker stood at the edge of the field with his hands shoved into the pockets of faded dungarees, searching for warmth against the evening's chill. A slight smile crossed his face as he witnessed his oldest son's smooth attempt to discard the cigarette. Joe made a quick turn to his left, leaned over the wheel shield as if checking the plow and allowed the cigarette to fall into the ground as fertilizer for next year's crop. But not before Matt, who possessed eagle eyes, saw the red glow and trail of smoke.

He'd always assumed Joe would take up smoking. But not so soon. Matt had resisted the leaf's lure until well past his nineteenth birthday, and he'd started smoking to combat the tension of war. Of course, his son had waged a war of his own these past few months, a private war carried out despite, or perhaps in spite of, the family's best efforts. The boy had endured the pain of a shattered leg and a lost dream with valor and resolve. If Joe found solace in a cigarette or two, Matt would neither begrudge him nor read the riot act over it.

No one had ever questioned Joe's perseverance and stubbornness. But equally so, the magnitude of those qualities had never rivaled the likes of that shining through in the weeks and months gone by since the boy had been carried off the football field on a stretcher. Once home from the hospital, Joe had refused their coddling, cordially but in definite terms telling the family he could take care of himself. Then he'd set out to prove his word, making a mockery of the doctors who believed the recovery process would leave him a temporary invalid.

The doctors predicted a difficult adjustment to the heavy cast; Joe was moving with athletic grace, albeit on crutches, within a week. The doctors predicted a minimum three-week absence from school; Joe was roaming the halls of Cookville High School after just eight days of lessons from the county's truant officer. The doctors predicted months of crutches; Joe was wearing a walking cast within eight weeks.

The pace of recovery was so alarming that once Matt had dreamed his son was racing down the football field, on crutches, intent on catching an overthrown ball. The dream had seemed so real that he had woken his wife with the suggestion that Joe probably should stay off the football field awhile longer.

Matt smiled in memory of that stuporous expression of concern, but was instantly sobered. In reality, Joe would never step on another football field—at least not as a player. His knee and two other bones shattered in that freak accident were now held together by steel pins, and while the boy would recover without a limp, the leg would never be the same. His son's spirit and courage, however, remained unbroken.

Matt peered across the fresh folds of earth, acutely mindful of the skill and dedication his son brought to the farm work—and achingly aware that the boy's destiny lay elsewhere.

Long ago, Matt had sensed Joe saw life differently than he did. That despite the boy's down-to-earth demeanor, he possessed vision of breadth and depth. That when Joe looked out across these fields, he saw more than treetops and a faraway horizon. A few weeks ago, though, Matt had realized with startling clarity just how differently Joe and he looked at life.

They had been butchering hogs one crisp Saturday morning. It was a messy job from the moment Matt shot the two barrows. Working in companionable silence, they had split, gutted and sliced the shoats from end to end, tapping every edible scrap of meat. The chitlins and lights had been that night's supper, the feet pickled, the head made into souse and the brains frozen for the family's traditional Christmas Eve supper.

When they were winding up the job, dumping the last wash-tubs of bloodied water and wiping down knives, Matt had turned to Joe and suggested, "Son, how 'bout next time we let the butcher in Cookville do this?"

Matt had expected an answer of either lighthearted agreement or a teasing scoff. Instead, without breaking stride for even a side-ways glance at his father, Joe said sharply, "Beats the heck of out me why you didn't do that this time."

The quick retort struck Matt like a slap in the face. He resisted an impulse to reprimand the boy, sensing Joe was unaware of his sassy tone. In truth, Matt had intended to send the shoats to the abattoir, changing his mind only because Joe had volunteered to help with the butchering. "Wait a minute," Matt had said. "I thought you wanted to do the butcheren."

Joe looked perplexed. "What on earth gave you that idea?"

"You did," Matt answered stoutly. "The other night when I mentioned we had two hogs ready to butcher. You volunteered for the job almost before I got it out of my mouth. Hell, son, I was all for senden them to the abattoir in the first place. I didn't, only be-cause you seemed so surefire ready to do the job yourself."

"Uh-oh," Joe groaned, rolling his eyes. "I assumed we'd be doen it at home like always. I was just offeren to help. Butcheren hogs is the last thing I wanted to do."

Matt had known then, inexplicably or perhaps from something in the way Joe uttered those words, but he had understood with certainty that father and son would never tend this farm as equals in a partnership. He had realized that Joe looked across the treetops surrounding these fields and saw a horizon beckoning with unfa-miliar and infinitely interesting places, people and experiences. And Matt had understood that, like his father before him, he, too, would surrender a son to dreams different from those he dreamed.

Standing on the field's edge, Matt felt a sudden need to find out if he would be up to the task of letting go when the time came. He had an even stranger feeling that the answer would soon come to him.

As he waited for the tractor to arrive at the row-end, Matt considered anew the difficult months Joe had come through. If the boy's pace of recovery had been extraordinarily quick, then the intensity of it had been downright exhausting. In those first days home from the hospital, Joe had needed help to get from the bed to the bathroom, and his stubborn demand for no concessions on his behalf had bordered on the absurd.

Once, in particular, he'd insisted on a full-fledged bath, refusing a washbowl and cloth in favor of the tub. So Matt had carried the boy into the bathroom and left him on his own to climb into the tall claw-foot tub. There had been a loud thud and a few muffled curses from time to time, but all had gone well until Joe finished bathing and discovered he could not climb out of the tub. At that point, he'd put pride aside, calling for "a little help and cooperation."

Matt had found him stuck in the deep tub, prone on his back, with the encased leg draped over the edge, unable to right himself without wetting the plaster mold. Matt had hauled him up, offered the boy a towel and walked out without a word said between them.

Joe had suffered a few other indignities, but mostly, he was successful in compensating for the handicap. In fact, too often he overcompensated, rushing headlong to tackle any chore or task that needed doing, working like a mercenary to earn not the almighty dollar but a measure of respect. At first, Matt had tried to rein in the boy. In quick order, however, he'd turned Joe loose, allowing him to gallop a breathtaking pace on a journey for peace of mind. Whether Joe had found peace remained unclear, but certainly the harvest season had never run smoother or easier for Matt.

Apart from his regular chores, Joe had taken over the daily grind for his father and grandfather, providing the men additional daylight to work in the fields. He'd replaced Matt on the combine at times, hauled trailers back and forth between the fields and unloaded and stacked a truckload of fifty-pound bags of hog feed in the barn. Just when Matt had figured Joe to reach his limits, the boy—cast and all—had climbed into the tops of pecan trees to shake loose the nuts. Now Joe was winding up another self-appointed task, and as he brought the tractor to a stop, a rush of pride swelled Matt.

Joe cut off the engine, then swung his good leg over the steering wheel and dismounted the tractor.

"That's a fine piece of plowen, son," Matt said. "You've got the fields looken real good."

"Fields always look good this time of year, Daddy," Joe replied, smiling slyly. "I just hope they'll look good come next fall."

"Me, too," Matt agreed. "That's what I always hope for; it's why I keep doen the same thing year after year."

"Yes, sir."

"Are you glad to get a vacation from school?" Matt asked.

Joe looked quickly past his father in the direction of Cookville High School, where a few hours ago he had taken the final algebra test and history exam before the start of Christmas vacation. He enjoyed school and the separate identity it provided him from the family. The days he'd missed after breaking his leg had seemed like an eternity, leading him to believe he would never wish for another school vacation. And yet, the rigors of catching up on missed work and the spirit of the Christmas season had changed his mind, leaving him eager for the two-week vacation—just as the arrival of the new year would make him ready to return to his studies. Everything in its time, Joe thought.

"I was ready," he answered.

"I was always ready for a vacation from school," Matt said, squatting to pick up a handful of the nutrient-rich earth, sifting it through his fingers. "We only went about seven months of the year back then, but even that seemed too long to me. I always wanted to be right out here."

Joe, watching the dirt fall from his daddy's hand, said suddenly, "A boundless moment."

Matt peered up at his son, puzzled.

"*A Boundless Moment*," Joe repeated with an embarrassed shrug. "It's the name of a poem by Robert Frost. I can't think of how it goes, but you reminded me of it just now."

"Oh," Matt said, staring as if he expected a more forthcoming explanation. When none came, Matt scooped up another handful of dirt. Standing, he gestured for Joe to do the same.

Joe quickly obeyed, the black soil cool and heavy with moisture against his palm. He righted himself and faced his father.

"This dirt may not seem significant to most people, but it means an awful lot to me," Matt said evenly. "I make a liven from it. I depend on this dirt to provide for your mama and you children. I take care of it. I feed it. I understand it, and I know how to use this dirt to get what I need in life. You might even say I control it, leastways as much as a man can control a piece of earth without bowen to the will of nature."

Matt paused, measuring his words with a sweeping gaze across the field and back to Joe. "Strange as it may sound, son, you're kind of in the same position as this dirt. Right now, Joe, you're pretty much compelled to do what I tell you—whether it's plowen a field, sloppen hogs or milken a cow. But there's bound to come a day when I tell you to do somethen and what I'm really doen is asken you to do it. When that day comes—and you and I will both know when it's time—you're not gonna be compelled to do what I say anymore. And I hope very much that when you make your decision, Joe, you'll follow your heart and do what's right for you."

Matt searched the boy's eyes at length, then asked earnestly, "Do you understand, son?"

Joe wanted to tell his daddy that his heart would always urge him to do whatever Matt wanted, even if it meant lying down across a railroad track in front of a fast-coming train. He wanted to tell Matt that loyalty was the most important expression in the world, except possibly for love and making love, the latter of which he could only guess about at the moment. But instead, the boy replied simply, "Yes, sir."

Matt regarded his son carefully, concerned about the thoughts behind the boy's unreadable expression. He didn't doubt for one second that Joe understood him. But in Matt's experience, the difference in understanding and doing was as wide as the gap between winning and losing.

Joe was a natural helper, someone who could be counted on to stick around as long as help was needed. He had a knack for making the people around him not only comfortable but also increasingly willing to accept that level of comfort. When Joe faced that moment of truth—the choice between will and obligation—Matt suspected it would take a mighty shove or supreme inspiration to push the boy toward the gateway of his heart. He hoped inspiration would rule the moment.

"Do you know the whole story about how you got your name?" Matt asked suddenly.

"After your brother, my uncle," Joe recited automatically. "He was killed at Pearl Harbor."

"That's not the whole story," Matt said coyly. "We almost named you Mark. From the day your mama found out she was expecten, she planned to name the baby Mark if it was a boy. I thought it was a fine name until a few weeks before you were born, when she finally got around to tellen me the reason she wanted to name you Mark. She was married to a Matthew, you see, and her intentions were to name our sons Mark, Luke and John. Matthew, Mark, Luke and John—your mama wanted the four gospels right in the family."

"Really?" Joe asked skeptically, with a bemused expression. "Are you pullen my leg, Daddy?"

"I swear to God it's the truth," Matt laughed, spreading his hands. "Needless to say, I put my foot down. Declared once and for all that we'd name the baby after my brother if it were a boy. I thought your mama was carryen religion a little too far."

Joe nodded tepid agreement. His father's disdain for the church warranted no comment.

"Well," Matt continued, sounding more serious. "It was a good thing we named you after your uncle, son, because you're a lot like him. Both of you born with a wanderlust."

He paused, allowing Joe to consider the thought. "As far back as I can remember, your uncle was always runnen off somewhere else."

"The prodigal son," Joe interrupted, quoting his grandmother.

"Not at all," Matt shot back. "My brother loved home, but his heart tugged him elsewhere. I'm glad he followed it and don't doubt for one minute that your grandma ain't, either. It was the right thing for him to do. In those few years with the Navy, your uncle saw more of the world than most men see in a lifetime. He truly lived the life he wanted."

Matt paused again to choose his words, then looked hard at Joe. "I'm tellen you all this, son, because I want you to know that it's okay if your heart leads you elsewhere," he said soberly. "There's no law that says a boy has to follow in his daddy's footsteps. I've got everything I need right here in Cookville, and I farm because it's the right thing for me to do. But wherever you go and whatever you do will be the right thing for you, Joe, and it'll be fine by your mama and me."

Matt allowed the dirt to trickle from his hand, watching it fall back to the ground. "But regardless, whatever you do, wherever you go," he said, returning his gaze to Joe, "remember this farm and your family will always be here for you, son. No matter what."

Joe stood dazed, stricken with disbelief, muted by the moment.

Matt smiled, slow and serious until his face dissolved into a spitfire grin. "Well, hell, I'm on a roll," he said, dusting off his hands. "I probably should tell you all about the birds and the bees, but you already know that stuff."

Joe shrugged modestly. "Did Mama mind too much about not getten a Mark in the family," he asked as Matt mounted the tractor and settled on the seat.

"Nah," Matt answered, leaning against the steering wheel. "Turned out Mark was her least favorite of the four gospels—at least name-wise. I don't rightly know how she feels about the scripture."

Joe nodded, still bewildered.

"You feed the hogs, son," Matt said a moment later, "and I'll milk the cow. Then, we'll see 'bout getten us some supper."

"Sure thing, Daddy. And thanks, for the talk."

Matt gave his son a gruff smile as the tractor roared to life. He waved a hand, then drove off along the rutted field lane running through the pecan orchard and alongside the house.

Joe stood there—transfixed as he tried to absorb the meaning of this moment with his father—until somehow his legs began moving him toward the house. Gradually, he realized his hands still held the dirt. He stopped in his tracks, unclenched his fist and allowed the black soil to fall away. Brown stains remained on his palm, and the hand suddenly felt withered and bone dry. His teeth gritted, and the same dry, lifeless feeling filled his mouth. He began moving toward the house, quickly, purposefully this time, not stopping until he reached the well, where he rinsed his hands clean in clear, cold water from the spigot. Then, he fed the hogs.

---

Later, with night settled over the farm, Joe sat around the kitchen table with the family, listening to his brother deliver a lengthy, if somewhat overblown, blessing of the evening meal. Supper was waiting and everyone was hungry, but mealtime prayers took precedence over the food and the appetites. Joe's mother and grandmother did not abide religion by rote. The two women wanted prayers from the heart, believing words of simplicity and honesty far more valuable than eloquence or superficiality.

Joe was thinking about those unchanging values, the rituals of home and the ties that bound him, when he felt the heavy weight of eyes upon him. He raised his head and found his father staring back at him. They acknowledged each other with brief smiles and nods before Matt closed his eyes and bowed his head.

Joe lowered his gaze once more, but his eyes stayed open, staring at the reflection in the plate.

As a boy, he had followed his daddy's footsteps, worshipping the man who helped give him life and expecting to work the farm with Matt one day, just as Matt now did with his father. As he'd grown older, Joe had continued to worship his father but not the man's way of life. He'd tried and tried to understand where their two paths quit running parallel, why his had crossed into uncharted territory. He had brooded over the differences, the seeming inability to reconcile his own desire and ambition with loyalty and responsibility to his family.

Suddenly, the dilemma no longer mattered. His father had granted Joe a license for the future. Matt had freed him from the tightfisted chains of the farm. No longer would Joe try to smother the fire of ambition smoldering within or quench the thirst pulling him away from his family. He was free to ponder and pursue another kind of life, a different set of responsibilities.

Joe had an inkling of the future then, a sense about the way life worked—of freeing yourself from one set of chains in order to be yoked to even tighter bonds. And in a way, the boy was glad just to be sitting at the supper table, belonging to this family, with nothing more than hunger pains to satisfy.

# CHAPTER 2

CAROLINE LAY SNUG IN bed, buried beneath covers with one leg draped over the warm body beside her. Even without looking at the ticking brass clock on the nightstand, she knew it was time to begin another day. Her free foot burrowed through the pile of blankets and quilts, found the bed's edge and lifted the covers. A frigid draft rushed up her flannel gown, and she dropped the covers, wanting to savor the warmth awhile longer. She snuggled closer to Matt, listening to his rhythmic breathing and feeling the steady rise and fall of his chest.

On another cold morning nineteen years ago this day, she'd woken early as well—a little fearful, yet excited over the prospect of a moment exactly like this one. She had been sixteen, driven by the impetuosity of youth and tempered by the wisdom of maturity beyond her years. Two days later, Caroline had married Matt. He had been not much older, but equally sure of his wedding vows. Even God had been certain of their union, sending a white Christmas as a blessing.

Caroline forced herself to roll away from Matt and got out of bed to face the cold morning. She dressed quickly, pulling on an everyday yellow cotton dress with long sleeves, then began her ritualistic morning inspection of the house.

In 1934, long before Caroline knew Matt, fire had destroyed the original Baker home. The family had lived in the corncrib across the road, while Matt's father, Sam Baker, hurriedly rebuilt the house. His construction skills had been marginal, but Sam had tackled the job with pride and dedication. The result was a rectangular building, with an A-frame roof and an expansive front porch pointing due east.

The front door opened into a wide hall stretching deep into the house and leading straight into the bathroom. Three bedrooms lined the left side of the hall, with the living room, dining room and kitchen on the right. A fourth bedroom—Sam and Rachel's—

jutted off one side of the kitchen, with a large pantry and closed porch on the other.

The rooms were all large and spacious, with twelve-foot ceilings and long windows. Their decor was a hodgepodge collection of heavy furniture pieces destined to become antiques and flimsy articles picked up at bargain prices. Without a doubt, the front two rooms were Caroline's favorites.

The living room contained a Victorian sofa, burgundy-red velvet with brocaded black roses. Two matching chairs—one in the same shade of burgundy and another royal blue—accompanied the sofa, all sitting on a decorative rose-colored floor rug inlaid with various shades of flower patterns. The room also contained a Queen Anne sofa with worn mint green cushions, a similarly colored sturdy recliner and various tables built from cypress knots taken from a grove of the ancient trees that grew on the farm in a bog of mud and pitch-black water.

Matt and Caroline's bedroom suite was made of dark Spanish oak. A rare tiger oak mantle framed the redbrick fireplace, which stood between two closets made of pure cedar. A cedar trunk, once Caroline's hope chest, set at the foot of the bed.

A curio shelf, an upright piano, two sea captain's trunks and a mirrored dresser with a homemade curtain covering its open bottom lined the wide hallway.

Stopping at the door between the trunks, Caroline checked the girls' room, then moved on to the boys' room, which had a lopsided appearance due to a jutting corner space on the far end of the house.

Joe had claimed the corner space for himself, setting up a small desk and his ladder-backed chair with the cowhide seat. He was badgering his father to seal off the corner with a wall, so that he could have a room of his own. Caroline had resisted the idea so far. After Christmas, she intended to relent. Joe was the oldest of her six children by several years, and she agreed with Matt that the boy deserved some privacy.

The dining room contained an aging table, buffet and china cabinet, all made from black walnut. A silver coffee and tea set adorned the buffet, giving the room a sense of elegance. Unfortunately, that distinction was marred by the presence of a large chest freezer, one of two required to store the enormous amounts of vegetables and meat necessary to feed the large family.

A honey-colored oaken cupboard, along with the fireplace, dominated the comfortable kitchen, while a varnished rocking chair and church deacon's bench provided ample sitting space. The table, its side benches and two end chairs had been hewn by Matt and Sam from pine trees. Though well sanded, these homemade pieces yield the occasional splinter, interrupting meals with a howl when someone acquired one in the backside.

Her tour completed in the kitchen, Caroline built a fire, using the last piece of resin to start the blaze. She made a mental note to ask Joe to bring in more from the barrels outside, then turned her attention to preparing breakfast for the hungry brood that would soon overrun the kitchen.

Caroline appreciated these rare moments of solitude, almost as much as she enjoyed her busy days, the result of six children who, she liked to believe, required her constant attention, but were quite capable of fending for themselves.

She cracked a dozen eggs into a mixing bowl, poured in a hefty amount of canned milk and added a dash of salt and pepper. Using a wooden spoon to beat the eggs, she crossed over to the one kitchen window that afforded an unobstructed view of the horizon. Gray clouds hung heavy and low over the fields and pecan orchard, once again reminding Caroline of that December nineteen years ago.

In any other year, a snowy Christmas Eve would have been cause for celebration in Cookville, where the chance for a white Christmas was only slightly better than snow on the Fourth of July. But it had been 1941 and residents of the sleepy South Georgia community did their best to ignore the white fleece covering their flat lands. Snow nor anything else seemed special that Christmas because the community feared what they would lose in the coming years and grieved for that already lost.

As it had for so many Americans, December 7, 1941, brought tragedy to the Bakers. Among those killed when the Japanese unleashed their bombs on Pearl Harbor was Joseph Samuel Baker, the oldest of Sam and Rachel's three children. It took three days for the heartless telegram to arrive, notifying the Bakers of their son's death aboard the USS Arizona and his unaccounted burial in a watery grave.

A taxi driver brought the telegraph to Sam and Rachel and then returned to Cookville, spreading word that the backwoods county had lost its first son in the fight for freedom. There would be others, of course, but Joseph had been the first casualty and the community responded with an outpouring of respect. The county honored the fallen soldier with a memorial service in the high school auditorium two weeks after Pearl Harbor and later erected a commemorative bronze plaque on the courthouse square when it was discovered his body would remain forever lost in the sea of Honolulu.

Pearl Harbor staggered the good citizens of Cookville, but Matt's surprise wedding to Caroline three days after the memorial service socked them in the gut. Matt was just eighteen, a rakish young man with a footloose and fancy-free reputation. Caroline was a stranger, the orphaned daughter of a preacher who lived with her spinster aunt in Tifton.

There had been talk about the quick wedding, but Caroline had not minded the gossip. She and Matt had married for love and nothing else. And thanks to the war, they had proved their sudden nuptials were no shotgun arrangement.

Caroline never regretted becoming a bride at such an early age—though she figured to pitch a fit should any daughter of hers come up with a similar notion. She and Matt had been one of those blessed couples, the lucky ones for whom it was love at first sight. While she couldn't say positively that she expected to marry Matt from the moment she laid eyes on him, the idea had taken hold in short order.

Matt, of course, did claim to have decided to marry Caroline on first sight. He'd courted her shamelessly, stealing kisses and camping out on the doorstep of the home she shared with fussy Aunt Evelyn. Her aunt was mortified, but Caroline threw caution to the wind and embarked on a torrid romance. Stolen kisses quickly led to stronger feelings, and when the passion grew too ardent, they fell apart and talked.

Caroline carried conversations effortlessly, but in all her life she'd never found anyone easier to talk with than Matt. Words came naturally between them as they discovered each other. He proposed within two months of meeting her, promising the wedding could wait until she finished high school in the spring. Caroline accepted and began wishing for springtime.

Then Pearl Harbor happened. Matt proposed again, and they were married three days later—to the chagrin of the community but to the pleasure of Sam, Rachel and even Aunt Evelyn.

The Christmas Eve wedding had been a simple affair. Caroline wore a white velvet dress, and Matt donned the dark blue suit purchased a few days earlier for the memorial service honoring his brother. They had married beside the French doors between the living and dining rooms of the Baker home. It was a small service attended only by Rachel, Sam, Aunt Evelyn and Matt's best friend, Paul Berrien, along with Paul's two older sisters, April and June. Preacher Fred Cook performed the ceremony, and Caroline had promised to love, honor, cherish and obey her new husband. They honeymooned for a single night in a small guest cottage on the Berrien estate, and there Caroline had discovered the joy of unbridled passion. The next day, she had helped Rachel cook Christmas dinner, while exchanging the sly smiles of new lovers with her husband.

She had never ever once had any regrets.

----

Matt padded down the hallway, his worn socks doing little to warm his feet against the cold that had seeped into the wooden floor overnight. He did a double turn at the end of the hall—first right, then left—and caught himself in the kitchen doorway, captivated by a vision of his wife. Caroline was peering out the window, whipping a bowl of eggs with purpose, yet, undoubtedly lost in her thoughts. On countless times, Matt had come into the kitchen to find his wife gazing out the window as she handled some simple task. He never tired of this vision, the reality of his dreams.

Caroline seemed so much at home here, as well she should have been, but he was amazed, as always, at how thoroughly she had become a part of the place. Even Matt, who had expected she would adapt to his family without much fuss, never could have guessed way back when about the sense of belonging that would develop between her and his parents. But he had hoped, of course, because Caroline had come into the family at its darkest hour.

Not only had his brother Joe died in 1941, but a few weeks before Pearl Harbor, his fifteen-year-old sister, Ruth, had broken his parents' hearts by running off and eloping with a fighter pilot stationed at nearby Moody Air Field. Knowing he must soon follow his brother into the military, hurting over the twin loss suffered by his parents, Matt had broken a promise to himself and asked

Caroline to marry him before she finished high school the following spring. Three days later, he'd been a married man at the age of
eighteen. And he'd given his parents another child, a daughter to
comfort them and take away the heartbreak of things gone terribly
wrong.

Caroline had indeed become another child to Sam and Rachel,
and they had become the parents she'd lost to a freak automobile
accident at the age of twelve.

She had been a town girl when she came to the Baker farm, used
to conveniences like electricity and indoor plumbing, luxuries like
drugstore sodas and telephones. But what she lacked in farm-life
know-how, Caroline made up for with a pioneer's character. She
learned their ways—absorbing the knowledge that would make her
a good wife to Matt when he came home from the war—and added
her own special touches to the family recipe. Now, they were so
akin to each other that it sometimes reminded Matt of the prover-
bial chicken and egg: Had he not been there from the beginning,
he never would have known which came first.

Matt suspected his father came closest to the truth of explaining
the special bond between Caroline and his parents. Sam maintained
the Bakers were a family haunted by "the orphan spirit," which he
defined as a longing for the kind of completion in life that only a
family can give.

Caroline certainly had an orphan's credentials, as did Sam and
Rachel to a lesser extent. Sam was comfortably estranged from his
family, while Rachel's was spread far and wide across South Georgia
and Florida. Caroline had been an only child, whose closest relative
had been a spinster aunt when her parents died. And Aunt Evelyn
herself, whom Matt had come to know and love as his wife did, had
died back in 1957, leaving Caroline bereft of any family except for
a smattering of cousins so far removed they hardly counted as kin.

If an orphan spirit was the culprit that linked Caroline so closely
to Matt and his family, then so be it. Though his own childhood
had been ideal and he could not fathom a feeling of incomplete-
ness, Matt certainly appreciated the opportunity to fulfill that
longing or any other yearning Caroline might have.

Smiling, he walked softly to his wife, put his arms around her
and kissed her lightly on the neck.

The sensation brought Caroline pleasantly back to the present.
"Mornen," she said.

"What's so special out there?" Matt asked by way of greeting, nuzzling her neck as he spoke.

"Most everything," Caroline replied, yielding her neck to the tender assault, the bowl of eggs temporarily forgotten.

"Such as?"

Caroline peered out the window once more, her gaze sweeping through the pecan orchard to the horizon beyond and the small outbuilding a few yards behind the house. "Oh, I see a beautiful field, newly plowed," she said respectfully. "A syrup house stocked with probably the finest cane syrup in the state and a smokehouse with a nice fat ham that will water your mouth on Christmas Day.

"And you," she added softly, turning in his arms to look at Matt, "made it all possible."

"I had a lot of help," Matt grinned, pulling her closer.

Caroline kissed him passionately, despite the bowl of eggs wedged between them.

"An almost proper way to start the day," Matt said seductively when the kiss ended. "You let that brood of young'uns eat cold cereal for breakfast and we could make it entirely proper."

Caroline cocked an eyebrow at him. "That's how we got this brood in the first place," she teased, gently breaking the embrace. "I should start the coffee," she continued, sounding suddenly practical. "Ma and Pa will be in here anytime now, and the children should be up soon."

Matt watched her purposeful stride to the stove, where she set the bowl down and turned her attention to the coffee pot. He lowered himself to the deacon's bench, retrieved a pair of work boots from beneath and began pulling them on, his gaze still fixed on Caroline.

His wife was a beautiful woman, tall and firmly built with a mane of ash brown hair and a sense of unaffected elegance. Matt loved the whole of her body, not only for the way she looked and carried herself but also in the way she fit against and meshed with him. Their bodies were the perfect blend, balanced in the right places with a few incongruities thrown in to keep the mix interesting.

Caroline nearly matched her husband in height, coming in a shade under two inches shorter than Matt, who stood exactly two inches shy of six feet in bare feet. She was the more strong-boned of the two, though both of them had medium builds. Her hair—which she pinned up during the day and spent several minutes brushing at night before coming to bed, and to Matt—was long and wavy, contrasting sharply with his straight, black crown. They both had brown eyes, but again, hers were light and shining and his dark and smoldering. Her skin tone was pure peaches and cream, tanned healthy rather than damaged by hard days of work in the sun, whereas Matt's natural swarthiness had a coppery tint baked by the sun and etched by a full-blooded Cherokee ancestor.

Caroline may not have been a classic beauty with her oval-shaped face, but her complexion was flawless, fresh and possessed of an aura that radiated generosity and caring. Her countenance adorned Caroline with the kind of beauty that Matt cherished.

If pressed to single out one bodily feature of his wife that stood out among all others, Matt would have picked her legs. *Without doubt.* They were long and shapely, the kind of legs that Betty Grable had used to forge a career in show business. Those legs gave Caroline an indelible stamp of grace, a sureness of movement that had been bred into their children with equal measure.

Matt considered himself a lucky man to have Caroline as a wife and the mother of his children. And from time to time he marveled as well that his love for her continued to grow day after day.

She was, of course, a different woman from the girl he had married. He remembered the girl being too thin and coltish, but she had worn her hair long almost all the time back then and Matt had made her promise never to cut it short. Somewhere along the way, probably when he was in Europe during the war, she had taken to pulling it up during the day. Matt didn't mind. His wife let her hair hang loose and long when it mattered. Giving birth to six children had changed her girlish figure, thickening the waist he once held between his fingers, but Matt preferred the womanly look of the present.

Caroline was a treasure, no doubt, deserving of more than he'd ever been able to give her, yet satisfied beyond question with the life they had carved for themselves in this piney wood community.

This last thought occurred to Matt as he spied the golden band on Caroline's left hand, wondering for the umpteenth time whether he could afford a diamond engagement ring for her. Money was already stretched too thin for Christmas, but Matt had his heart set on surprising her with a ring.

He knew buying the ring this year would amount to a foolish waste of money, dollars they didn't really have. Next year, perhaps, the farm would do better and the money would be available. Then, too, their twentieth anniversary would present a special occasion for an extravagant gift. But Matt was tired of waiting around for a special occasion to give his wife the ring she should have had before they married. He'd been doing that all his life it seemed, always managing to find some excuse to buy the ring next time. This once, he hoped to thumb his nose at fortune and do what he wanted.

Deep down, however, Matt knew more pressing matters were at hand than buying an engagement ring for the woman who had shared his life for nearly nineteen years. Like finding the money to buy Christmas gifts for six children. And on a more down-to-earth basis, feeding those children and having enough money to plant next year's crop. Still, he determined to give some serious thought to the ring on the hunting expedition planned for later this morning.

Rising, Matt crossed to the window, scanning the gray horizon for an indication of when the rain might come, wondering whether the hunting trip would be wet and cold, or just cold. Though slung low across the sky, the clouds seemed light for rain. He figured the wet stuff was still a day or two away, but the heavy overcast on this cold morning harkened him back again to the past.

"Do you remember how you felt this time nineteen years ago?" he asked suddenly, turning to look across the room at Caroline.

She glanced up at him from the table, where she was slicing pieces of streaked meat for frying. "Scared to death," she smiled coyly. "I wanted to be a good wife, to please you, and I was afraid to at the same time."

"Not me," Matt shook his head. "Guess I was too young to be scared—or too dumb. I wanted to get married and start maken babies." His brow furrowed. "Or at least practicen at it."

"You obviously were good at it," Caroline said with a wink. "You were real potent."

Matt shrugged. "You were just real fertile," he teased, finishing the private joke between them.

Matt moved in front of the fireplace, lacing his fingers behind his back to soak up warmth from the roaring blaze. "This weather reminds me of that time," he said, reminiscing while Caroline poured grits into a pot of boiling water. "The way it snowed that Christmas Eve was sure special. My whole life I'd never seen more than a few flakes and then on my wedden day, it snowed and snowed. Do you remember the drift that piled high beside the front porch?"

"By the swing," Caroline answered, taking over the story. "We sat there, swingen back and forth, draggen our feet through the snow. I remember thinken back then that the snow was God's way of blessen our marriage."

Matt shrugged his head, neither agreeing nor disagreeing with this last suggestion.

Caroline brought him a cup of steaming hot coffee, black, kissed him lightly on the cheek and moved again to the window, observing the cold, leaden sky once more. "Do you think we might get another Christmas snow?" she asked hopefully.

"I doubt it," Matt said, sipping the coffee. "Temperature's supposed to climb into the fifties this afternoon, and I tend to think those clouds look a lot worse than they are. Course, the weatherman on TV last night said a cold wave is on its way south, so you never know. It might just happen."

"A big snowfall sure would bring back a lot of pleasant memories," Caroline said wistfully.

"A big snowfall might take a few minds off Santa Claus, and what he may or may not bring for Christmas," Matt said ruefully, turning the conversation to more pressing matters.

"We'll do the best we can," Caroline reassured him, returning to the stove. "Ma's made a few clothes for the children, and we can buy candy and fruit and maybe some small toys to stuff the stockens. They're smart kids, Matt. They understand Santa Claus has his good years and bad years."

"That won't make it any easier," Matt grumbled. "Hell, they're kids, honey. They don't page through that Sears catalog day after day for nothen."

"You'd be surprised," Caroline said briskly. "Sometimes the anticipation, the wishen, is better than the real thing. Besides, I don't want the gift-getten to take away from the real meanen of Christmas."

"Well, I don't think there's much chance of that happenen 'round here," Matt muttered dryly.

"Oh, hush up," she admonished, "and let me finish maken breakfast."

Matt set the empty coffee cup on the table and sauntered over, wrapping his arms around her once more. "You're some woman," he murmured, leaning around to peck her on the cheek.

Caroline gave him a sidelong glance, which meant either she knew what he said was true or wasn't in the mood for his charming. Either way, she was telling him to get lost and let her finish cooking breakfast.

"Guess I'd best get to the milken," he laughed.

"Guess so," she shrugged.

Matt released her.

"Lucas is comen over this mornen," he said, plucking a lined denim jacket off the back of the chair in his place at the head of the kitchen table and shrugging into it. "We're gonna do a little hunten after breakfast and then cut some wood. I probably won't be around for dinner."

"We're goen into Cookville this afternoon," Caroline reminded him.

"It's a date," Matt nodded, heading for the back-porch door. He stopped by the refrigerator, glancing back at her. "By the way, ask Joe if he wants to go hunten with us. He's missed most of the season so far, but he's getten around well enough on the leg that he might enjoy it."

Caroline nodded agreement, and Matt was gone to begin the day in earnest.

---

As the aroma of scrambled eggs, fried pork and perking coffee drifted through the house, Caroline heard the first stirrings of her waking brood. She finished the eggs, dishing them onto a plate and setting it on the stove to keep warm. She gave the grits a quick stir, then began setting the table. She set out the ten plates and was retrieving flatware from the cupboard when a truck needing a new muffler pulled into the yard.

Hurrying, she laid the forks and spoons on the table in a tangled pile, crossed over to the small window beside the kitchen sink and pulled back the yellow curtain in time to see Lucas Bartholomew pull up to the barn in his ancient pickup. Lucas climbed out of the truck and ambled over to the barn gate, where Matt was on the other side milking the Guernsey cow, which the children had named Brindy. Caroline let the curtain fall back in place and went to fetch a cup of coffee for him.

She shared a history with Lucas, too, begun on the day she had married Matt and woven intermittently ever since.

She'd watched Lucas grow from a small, playful child to a rangy, serious young man. She recalled Sam once saying that Lucas had the backbone of two men, prophesying his willingness to take on hard work would carry the black man beyond the wrong side of the tracks in Cookville. Sam had been correct in a manner of speaking, but Lucas struggled for everything, more than most people did anyway.

His father had loved liquor too much, dying when Lucas was just fifteen and straddling the boy with a sickly mother. Two years away from a high school diploma—a rarity for colored men in these parts—Lucas had been forced to quit his formal education to care for the ailing Merrilee Bartholomew. He had gone door-to-door, doing odd jobs, working long, hard hours, most times for fair wages but sometimes not.

Lucas never complained. He just went quietly about his business, earning the reputation of a go-getter and winning the respect of the people willing to give him a fair shake in life.

His mother—a frail woman whose bedridden posture never diminished her spirit—had died a few years back, freeing Lucas from the burden of medical expenses. His response had been seemingly unpredictable and abrupt. He'd bought the pickup, packed up lock, stock and barrel and headed to nowhere in particular, intent only on seeing whether a colored man stood a better chance of improving his lot in life up North. He'd returned to Cookville in the late spring of this year, in time for the summer's work, saying simply that city life did not agree with him.

Matt had taken Lucas under his wing even before the boy's father died, offering work and steering him toward other opportunities when the Bakers had no need for an extra hand on the farm. Matt paid better than fair wages, but more than that, he instilled confidence and pride in Lucas. Actually, Matt was one of two mentors who showed Lucas the virtue of the straight and narrow. The other was Paul Berrien, and he was perhaps closer to Lucas than Matt because his mother had worked as a maid for the Berrien family many years before failing health forced her to the sick bed.

Since returning to his roots, Lucas had worked almost exclusively for Matt and Paul. He had taken up the slack on the Baker farm when Sam suffered a heart attack at the start of the tobacco season, and even now, when his service was needed little, Matt continued to find odd jobs for him. Paul also kept him busy with various projects on the Berrien estate, maintaining a vegetable garden and flowerbeds and other odds and ends. In his spare time, when neither Matt nor Paul could justify working him, Lucas hustled to keep busy.

He was no slouch and highly regarded by all but the most of hateful of their community.

Bobby Taylor belonged to this latter group.

When civil rights-minded Yankees conjured up visions of racist Southerners, Caroline felt sure someone such as Bobby Taylor sprang to mind. Bobby—the mere thought of his name brought a bad taste to her mouth—was the embodiment of everything wrong with the South's attitude toward colored folk, and then some. He was wickedness personified, guided by bonds of hatred, spite and prejudice. Bobby did not stand alone with his views in the Cookville community but he stood apart, even in the crowd.

Ironically, Caroline shared a history with Bobby that also began on her wedding day but had long since withered, except for occasional happenstance and her own strong memories.

On the morning of her wedding, shortly after arriving at the Baker house, Caroline had set out on a brisk walk to the Carter's Mercantile. The store stood at the crossroads of the unincorporated New River community where the Bakers lived, serving as a beacon for social life much like the area churches and elementary school. It was, then and now, a tidy store, stocking groceries, hardware, clothing and most any other item a body might need.

Caroline had made the long trek through the snow to fetch several cans of jellied cranberry sauce for the next day's Christmas dinner. Arriving at the mercantile, she found Lucas playing in the snow while his parents shopped. He was a thin child, with a dimpled smile and a spark of sunshine in his eyes.

Enchanted, Caroline approached the little boy and tried to strike up a conversation. Lucas promptly hid behind the red and white gas tank.

"Are you playen possum?" Caroline coaxed.

He did not answer, but instead peered from behind the tank. Caroline smiled, earning the same in response, and Lucas placed small hands across his eyes, peeking through the slits of his fingers.

"Peep-eye," Caroline said, playing the game. "Can you tell me your name?"

Lucas hesitated as the store door jingled. He seemed on the verge of answering when a black-gloved hand appeared from nowhere, shoving the little boy aside. His balance altered, Lucas tried to catch himself but stumbled and fell.

"Get out of my way, kid," a mean voice shouted.

Shocked, Caroline shifted her gaze from Lucas to the young man standing over the boy. She estimated his age about the same as hers. He was almost handsome, of average height and wiry build, with dishwater blond hair, a sculpted face and a ruddy complexion. But the face was set with a bully's sneer, and his gaze sought her approval with a lopsided, haughty smile.

"This country'd be a damn sight better off if we'd fixed his mama and castrated his daddy," Bobby Taylor declared proudly, puffing out his chest. "We oughtta send their black asses back to Africa."

Caroline found him ugly to the bone, and she faced him down with an icy glare. Bobby, who usually charmed women with his near-good looks, frowned slightly, uncertain about her attitude. So Caroline had clarified it for him.

She strode over to the cowering boy, plucked Lucas off the cold ground and cradled him in her arms. "There was no cause for that," she hissed at Bobby. "You oughtta be ashamed of yourself."

A muscle twitched in his cheek, and Bobby released a contemptuous snort. "Well ain't you high and mighty, Miss Pretty Panties," he snarled, looking her up and down. "I don't know who you are, priss, but folks 'round here don't take too kindly to nigger lovers. You'd do well to remember that before shooten off your mouth next time."

Caroline had known right then it was a useless exercise to argue with Bobby Taylor. She had leveled him with another sour glare, then stepped past him and carried Lucas into the store.

Though she found the current times confusing—fretting over the growing tension between blacks and whites, wondering whether boycotts and demonstrations proved more divisive than enlightening—Caroline despised hatemongers. Of course, when you hacked down to the meat of the issue, there was only a thin line between the blatant bias of hatemongers and the subtler prejudice of those who believed in equality for Negroes as long as it suited their own particular way of life.

People were beginning to unearth those built-in prejudices, and Caroline feared they would unleash a firestorm of wrath and unrest. She supposed her family would face the music as well, learning and struggling with the new rules of a changing society. Despite good intentions, the Bakers were virtual newcomers to the task of confronting built-in biases. It was only a short time ago, after all, that they themselves had practiced the art form of subtle discrimination.

Sighing, the waters still muddied in her mind, she slipped into Joe's denim jacket, picked up the cup of coffee and went outside to the barn.

---

"Mornen, Lucas," Caroline said, coming up behind him. The air was chilly, and her breath came out misted. "Thought you might like to warm up with some coffee," she said, offering him the steaming cup.

Lucas took the cup gingerly. "Thank you, ma'am," he nodded, smiling. "It's cold enough all right."

"We're 'bout to have breakfast," she said. "Do you want a bite to eat?"

"No'sem," Lucas shook his head. "I ate before I came out this mornen," he continued in his slow, deliberate tone of speech. "I just stopped by to see what time we was goen hunten. I'm headed over to Mr. Paul's right now. He's got a broken window pane that needs fixen."

"Okay, then," Caroline smiled as Matt stepped to the gate, carrying a pail half full of fresh cow's milk.

"I'll take that," Caroline said.

Matt handed her the bucket over the fence. "I'll be in soon."

"No rush," she said. "Everyone slept late this mornen, even Ma and Pa." Turning, she gave Lucas a quick wave. "See you later, Lucas. I hope y'all have good luck with the hunten."

"Yes'em," he answered. "So do I."

Caroline walked the short distance back to the house, leaving the two men in discussion about the best place to cut a load of wood. She picked up a lone pecan along the way, deposited it in a full bucket of nuts on the back porch and went inside, her arrival coinciding with the emergence of Rachel and Sam from their bedroom.

Sam closed the door behind his wife, smiling at Caroline above Rachel's ranting and reprimands about his heavy snoring the previous night. "Good mornen, daughter," he greeted. "I trust you slept better last night than my bride claims to have."

Rachel rolled her eyes and apologized for oversleeping. "What can I do to help?" she asked, tying a worn apron around her waist, while Sam poured them both cups of coffee.

"Everything's mostly done," Caroline replied, taking off the jacket and tossing it on the deacon's bench. "You could put the silverware out," she added, gesturing to the pile of spoons and forks on the table. "I'm gonna strain this milk. We oughtta have enough cream by tomorrow for a churn of butter."

The house came fully alive then, bolstered by the eruption of six children fighting to use one bathroom, taking out their morning grogginess on each other. One by one, they straggled into the kitchen, bringing with them different shades of brown hair and brown eyes, and personalities far more distinctive. The children had their individual routines and quirks, but there was a sameness about their morning habits that reassured Caroline.

Joe came first, as usual, kissing his mother and grandmother, questioning Sam about his state of well-being and adding wood to the fire. He then plopped down in the rocking chair by the fireplace, sipping on a cup of black coffee and contemplating the flames in silence.

Relaxing came hard for Joe, unless he was bone tired or in the mood for fishing. The boy was a mass of controlled energy, clicking from one task to the next with a metronome's precision, always aiming for a beginning rather than an end. In one way, Caroline found it odd that someone so full of vim and vigor would start the day at such an unhurried pace. It seemed a contradiction of sorts, but Joe needed a moment's peace to harness that boundless energy, to synchronize with the rhythms that would carry him through the day.

When all was said and done, Caroline had come to expect a study in contradictions from her oldest child. For such a straight arrow, the boy was remarkably flexible, able to switch gears at a moment's notice, even anticipating the dawning of such a moment.

He seemed contented with whatever came his way, never complaining, utterly free of desire for material possessions, and yet, it seemed apparent that his life was destined for adventure and new experiences. And strangest of all, though Joe was the least likely of the children to be considered a dreamer, he dreamed the biggest of them all.

He was curious and inquisitive, capable of probing someone's deepest thoughts without ever once seeming like a busybody, willing to invest the time required to listen with interest. He devoured any piece of written material, from *Progressive Farmer* and the Sunday newspaper to the Bible and any other book.

He was handsome, too, though not overwhelmingly so like his father. Joe had brown hair, the color of pecan shells, dark brown eyes and clean-cut features. He was dark complexioned, turning deep brown in the summer, while needing a few more inches in height and pounds of muscle to fill out his medium-build frame.

Just days from his fifteenth birthday, Joe was beginning to feel his oats, and Caroline could not help fretting over how he might sow them.

As the firstborn child and grandchild, he occupied an extra special place in the hearts of his parents and grandparents. For such a long time, Caroline had figured her son would be an only child. She had become pregnant soon after Matt came home from the war in 1945, delivering Joe on the last day of that historic year. Almost five years passed before she gave birth again, though not for lack of trying. Then she had turned into a virtual baby factory, delivering four more children over the next six years. It made for a busy household, and somehow in the middle of tending to those babies, Caroline feared Joe had lost part of his childhood to the weight of responsibility.

Joe carried the burden of being the oldest easily, though, never seeming to let it weigh heavy. He ruled over the other children with quiet charisma, like some benevolent dictator whose subjects obeyed him loyally because they held faith in the rightness of his edicts. He did the overwhelming share of chores on the farm and set a good example in school for his brothers and sisters. Caroline and Rachel demanded that he set a good example in church as well, while Matt and Sam expected him to be a jack-of-all-trades around the house.

Joe faced heavy expectations, but he thrived under the pressure.

He delivered on expectations. Failure was not part of his vocabulary, though he surely tasted it from time to time as everybody did.

Caroline fussed occasionally about the boy's diligent pursuit of achievement. She would have worried incessantly, but Joe seemed at ease and contented for the moment, so there seemed no reason to belabor a moot point.

Of course, Joe was more subdued and pensive lately, but the boy was due some privacy to recover from the recent turmoil. His shattered leg was merely a rousing finale, capping a summer of one heart-wrenching moment after another. No one could have come through such a summer unscathed or unchanged, without needing time to catch his breath and return to an even keel. Such moments were the stuff of life's turning points, and Joe had caught each hairpin curve on the rollicking ride. The turbulence was such that if Caroline had cursed—which she didn't—she would have deemed it one hell of a summer for her firstborn son.

---

It was the summer Sam had his heart attack. Technically, the attack occurred in late spring, but they were on the second sweep through the tobacco patch and the days were hot as blazes, making it seem like summer even if the calendar claimed otherwise.

They had been shorthanded that day in the effort to fill the tobacco barn. Joe and Sam had been alone at the barn around dinnertime, trying to catch up on the hanging before the leaf started sweating, which would discolor it in the curing process and result in lower prices on the auction floor.

Joe was straddled between the lower tiers of a room, hanging the heavy sticks in the barn as Sam passed them to him. Sam was having to lug the sticks off a trailer outside the barn door, haul them inside and then shove them up to Joe. The barn itself was like a hothouse, the air stagnant and stifling with the sour odor of overheated green tobacco.

They were halfway through the job when Sam pushed another stick toward Joe's waiting hands. He never completed the motion, gasping suddenly with the stick's top end just above his shoulder. His face contorted in pain, the stick fell out of his grip and Sam toppled backward, landing hard on the packed dirt floor.

Joe practically fell out of the barn in his haste to aid his grand-father.

Sam clutched his chest, making a throaty plea for help as Joe raised his head off the dirt. Then the pain became too intense. He lost consciousness, mumbling incoherently and slipping into silence as his eyes rolled back into their sockets, his full weight slumping against the ground.

Joe believed his grandpa had died. He slapped Sam across the face twice, then ran for help.

The family heard him coming from inside the house, yelling at the top of his lungs. Stark terror was etched across his face when Joe arrived, pleading for quick action.

Sam had revived when they reached the barn, and the doctors later termed the attack mild. He had recuperated slowly and surely, but the illness had shaken Joe to the core. It was the boy's first head-on collision with mortality. More would come that summer.

———————

It was the summer Joe acquired the voice of a man and learned how to use it as well.

The change in his voice literally occurred overnight. He went to bed with a sore throat one night and woke the next morning with a voice like deep ice. His throat got better. The voice stayed with him.

Long before the overnight change in voice, Joe had been blessed with a rich baritone, never prone to the awkward high pitches of adolescence. Even as a small child, his voice—deep, husky, spoken from the bottom of the chest—had startled friends and strangers with its heavy pitch.

The latest change in tone had been subtle maturity; Joe's discovery of the power behind the voice rang out with an ear-shattering timbre. And it had caused walls of false pretense, cloaked in a veil of self-righteousness, to come tumbling down around the Bakers.

The moment occurred on a day—rare for this particular summer—when it was raining cats and dogs. Everyone spent the morning slogging through a wet tobacco patch. At dinnertime, they returned to the house and sat down to a piping hot meal prepared by Rachel.

Paul Berrien—taking a few hours off from politicking for the sheriff's office and his regular duties as president of the Farmers and Citizens Bank of Cookville—had stopped by and was persuaded to have a bite of dinner.

Lucas, who usually ate his noontime meal under the shade of the pecan orchard or at Carter's Mercantile, was in the cab of his pickup with a bologna sandwich and his personal jar of ice water. As in Cookville, where whites and blacks used separate water fountains and bathrooms, the Baker family drank from one water jar in the fields and Lucas from another. Lucas had never set foot in the Baker house, much less used the family's bathroom.

The children were still washing their hands and changing out of wet clothes when Rachel glanced outside the side window and declared, "I feel sorry for Lucas haven to eat in his truck."

"Me, too, Ma," Matt agreed, coming to her side to peer out the window.

"I suppose we could fix a plate for him at the dinen room table," Caroline suggested hesitantly. "He never has anything but a cold sandwich. He could use a hot meal on a day like this. I imagine he'd be grateful to be inside, where he could warm up a little."

"I agree with you, daughter," Sam said. "Go tell him to come inside, Matt."

A few minutes later, Lucas was seated alone at the dining room table with a heaping plate of fried chicken, mashed potatoes with gravy, butterbeans, biscuits, a jelly glass of iced tea and a slice of pound cake, while the Bakers and Paul Berrien crowded around the kitchen table. Everyone supposed they were making a progressive statement, allowing the colored man to eat at a table in their home, and they were feeling quite proud of themselves during the blessing.

But when Sam delivered a thunderous "Amen" to the prayer, Joe piped in loudly: "Why's Lucas in the dinen room? He oughtta be in here with us."

Joe had spoken with innocent naiveté, as if it had never occurred to the boy that the mores of the times forbade Lucas from sitting down with the family at the dinner table. But silverware clattered, mouths dropped open and a few of those gathered around the kitchen table nearly fell out of their chairs as the words dishonored their token gesture to noble intentions.

"Hush up!" Rachel hissed in a whisper.

"Joe!" Caroline gasped, also whispering. "He might hear you."

Disbelief spread across Joe's face as the cause of their anxiety dawned on him. "So why is Lucas in there?" he repeated dryly.

Everyone stayed silent. Joe looked from his mother to Rachel to Sam and finally to his daddy, demanding an answer with the intensity of his gaze.

"You know why, son," Matt said finally. "White people and colored people just don't take meals together—at least not around here, not in this day and age."

"It's not proper," Rachel added softly, sounding suddenly uncertain about her admonishment.

"Why not?" Joe pressed pointedly.

Sam shrugged. Rachel frowned. Caroline dithered for an answer. "That's just the way it is," Matt said heavily.

Joe grunted softly, placing his hands flat against the table. He gazed down at his plate of food, then back to the faces around him. "Well, *the way it is* is the wrong way," he decided aloud. "It seems to me we're the ones who oughtta have the right to choose who we want to sit at our kitchen table."

Joe pushed away from the table, picked up his plate and removed himself from the kitchen. He walked casually into the dining room, joined Lucas at the table and struck up a conversation as if nothing out the ordinary had occurred.

In the kitchen, they began to eat as well, in ponderous silence. "Chicken's good, Granny," one of the children remarked, but no one paid attention.

"Oh, good Lord!" Sam snapped finally, fed up with the weighty silence. "I think we can fit another body at this table without causen too much trouble."

Everyone looked at him, then at each other, nodding vaguely, while Joe and Lucas continued talking in the dining room, chuckling, seemingly oblivious to and unconcerned with the melodrama played out in the next room. But the following day, Caroline asked Lucas to join them for the noon meal, and he did.

It became a standard practice from then on, although Lucas announced on some mornings that he would eat a sandwich under the shade of a pecan tree or grab something at the mercantile for dinner. He was not one to take advantage of an open invitation.

---

It was the summer Pal died.

Pal was a white German shepherd given to Joe a few weeks before Summer's birth. The dog had been Matt's idea, a special gift to occupy the boy in those times when everyone else was too busy, a situation that rarely happened when Joe was an only child.

The strategy worked. Joe was smitten with the dog, and Pal with the boy. They became constant companions, living the classic story of a boy and his dog.

Pal had been a horse, allowing Joe to ride on his back. The dog had delighted in taking the boy's arm into his mouth, gently wedging it between the sharp teeth of his powerful jaws, shaking his head from side to side, never once leaving a mark on the skin. Pal had gone everywhere with Joe, tagging along on hunting trips and even sharing a rowboat in the pond while Joe pursued his favorite pastime, fishing. Joe talked to the dog, sometimes in private, often in public, and Pal seemed to understand. The boy also took excellent care of his pet, never once requiring a reminder to feed and water the dog, providing him occasional treats, teaching Pal to herd cattle and chase hogs that strayed from their pens.

As far as anyone knew, only one bone of contention ever came between boy and dog, arising shortly after Pal's first Thanksgiving with the Bakers. Even that had been a misunderstanding.

Joe came around the corner of the house one day to find Pal spread out on all fours, happily devouring the last of the holiday turkey carcass, which Caroline had given the dog. For some unaccountable reason, except maybe to a five-year-old, Joe concluded Pal had gone into the house and stolen the turkey right off the table. Enraged, he stomped the dog's tail. Pal promptly turned on the boy, sinking his teeth deep into the skin of Joe's shoulder. Joe had required four stiches and a tetanus shot, and nobody ever again questioned Pal's right to the remains of a turkey feast.

Pal took ill a few weeks after Sam's heart attack. He began coughing and wheezing, refused to eat and finally holed up in his favorite winter sleeping spot—underneath the house on the east side of the double fireplace. Joe crawled under the house hour after hour, petting the animal, coaxing him to eat, but Pal grew more listless. Finally, Matt called the veterinarian.

Dr. Byrd Hutto took one look at Pal and diagnosed a terminal case of heartworms. Joe had been crushed, but Pal was ten, the ripe old age of seventy in dog years, and had avoided heartworms longer than most farm dogs. The vet administered a painkiller and promised to check on the dog's condition the following morning. But Pal died that afternoon.

Rachel found him. Pal had crawled to his customary place at the bottom of the front porch steps, standing guard over his family one last time before giving up the ghost. Rachel covered his body with a burlap sheet, then walked down to the tobacco patch to tell Joe.

The boy had taken the news with a tired nod and returned to work. That evening he wrapped Pal in the sheet, loaded the body in the bed of the pickup and drove to the back woods. He buried the dog beneath his favorite deer stand, returning home late that evening with red eyes and going to bed without supper.

When anyone attempted to console him, Joe simply shrugged, declaring, "He was old; it was his time."

Matt acquired another German shepherd a few months later, a puppy that showed every indication of being a suitable replacement for Pal. The children even named him Pal-Two.

Joe said he was a fine dog, but only with passing interest. His little brother, Luke, however, thought Pal-Two was just swell.

––––––––––

It was also the summer Stonewall Jackson was killed.

Stonewall was related to the Confederate Army hero in name only. He was a gopher tortoise that had made his home in a burrow on the Baker place for at least nine years.

Sam, Joe and Pal had found the tortoise nibbling in a collard patch across the road one dewy spring morning. They had followed him out of the field, back across the road and down to the northern edge of the Baker property where Stonewall had his den. Joe hitched a ride on the hard shell for part of the way, and the young Pal barked continuously in furious amazement.

The tortoise took it all in stride, bravely holding his head high and plodding for home with the extra weight on his back. Sam said he had a noble look, judging from his beady eyes and erstwhile determination, and deserved a proud name. He suggested Stonewall Jackson, and the name stuck.

Stonewall became a family fixture, raiding the greens and gardens every year, giving free rides to one Baker child after another and living a peaceful existence in the same burrow. They came across the gopher countless times, wrote his name on the bottom of the shell in magic marker and considered the tortoise a family pet. Even Pal hushed his barking when it became apparent that Stonewall Jackson belonged on the place.

One Sunday in late August shortly before school resumed, the entire family had been whiling away the afternoon on the front porch, with a churn of peach ice cream. A brief shower had fallen minutes earlier, and the occasional blast of rifle shot seemed to be creeping closer to the house. But there seemed no cause for alarm.

They were well into their second bowls of ice cream when a freckle-faced, husky boy came walking up the road with a rifle slung over his shoulder.

"That's icky Wayne Taylor," Summer informed them, groaning.

Wayne had started school with Summer, but he had failed the first grade. He had passed on his second try, only to fail the second grade in the most recently completed school year, which, in Summer's opinion, meant bad news for the middle Baker daughter.

"Ooh, Carrie," she squealed. "He'll be in your class this year."

"Hush up, Summer," Caroline admonished. "I don't want to hear that kind of talk. You understand?"

"Yeah," Summer sighed dramatically.

"That's not the way you answer your mama," Matt said reproachfully.

"Yes, ma'am," Summer remarked, amending her previous answer to Caroline. She sent her mother a contrite look, then dove back into the ice cream.

Joe snickered, goosing his sister in the ribs to show Summer she was not fooling anyone with her feigned sense of regret. She stuck out her tongue at him.

Caroline, eyeing the rifle Wayne was carrying, felt a tingle of apprehension. "I know the Taylors are gun fanatics, Matt, and they may know how to use them," she said, frowning. "But it makes me a little uneasy for him to come walken up here with it so casually like that."

"There's no cause for concern," Matt soothed. "The way I hear tell it, that boy's the equal of many a man around here with a gun."

"Wayne may be good with a gun, but he sure is dumb," Summer remarked, unable to keep quiet.

"You'd be dumb, too, if you'd been struck by lightnen," Joe said.

"That's probably true, Summer," Caroline added. "Maybe Wayne can't help it. He's lucky to be alive."

Lightning had struck Wayne three summers ago during a thundershower. He had been unconscious for two days and suffered burns on his hands and arms. The doctors had detected no permanent damage, however, and the boy had emerged from the coma seemingly unchanged by the incident.

"Well, I won't argue that he's lucky to be alive," Summer agreed with her mother. "But Wayne must have been pretty dumb in the first place. The boy was swingen on a steel chain wrapped around a tree during the middle of a lightnen storm. That's not exactly the smart thing to do."

No one contradicted Summer, not even Caroline, so they waited in silence until Wayne came closer.

"Howdy, Wayne," Sam called.

"Hey," the boy replied, stepping into the yard and coming to the brick walkway. "How y'all getten along?"

"We're doen just fine," Matt answered.

"We'd offer you a bowl of ice cream, Wayne, but we've just dipped up the last of it," Rachel apologized. "We put fresh peaches in it."

"I don't like peaches," Wayne said, rubbing a hand across the stubble of sandy hair on the top of his head.

"Oh," Rachel grunted, settling back in the rocking chair and returning to her bowl of ice cream. Peach was her favorite flavor.

"How's your family, Wayne?" Sam asked with diplomacy, for Wayne was the son of Bobby Taylor, and there had been ill feelings between the two families that summer. Bobby was campaigning for the sheriff's office in a heated battle with Paul Berrien.

"Good as can be," Wayne said.

"What are you out shooten for today?" Matt asked to change the subject.

"Mainly I'm practicen," Wayne replied. His face spread into a smile. "I did shoot an old gopher back down the road a piece," he boasted, gesturing toward Stonewall Jackson's abode. "Figured I'd spare him the trouble of getten mashed on the road."

Wayne snickered. But his announcement paralyzed the Bakers momentarily, their shock giving way quickly to a horrified surmising.

"You shot what?" Joe demanded, bolting upright, spilling the last of his ice cream on the porch floor.

"Just an old gopher," Wayne replied.

"It was probably our gopher, you dumb-ass," Joe yelled.

"Joe!" Caroline admonished.

"Settle down, son," Matt warned. "We don't know that it was Stonewall."

"How many other gophers have we seen down that road?" Joe asked dryly. "I'm gonna go find out," he continued, leaping off the porch. "Where is he?" he barked to Wayne.

"Down, down there," Wayne stammered, pointing, sensing he had just worn out his welcome. "I kicked him in the ditch."

Joe headed down the road in a fast trot, with his brothers and sisters in close pursuit.

"What in the world possessed you to shoot a gopher," Caroline asked bluntly a moment later, frowning at Wayne.

Wayne frowned back, searching for a reason and coming up empty-headed. He shrugged off an answer.

"You should have known better," Matt declared. "There's no reason to kill an animal for the sake of just killen. You're supposed to be a hunter, boy. Surely you know better."

Wayne's eyes widened.

"That gopher's been liven on this place since almost before you were born," Sam said bitterly. "You had no cause comen down here to disturb him, much less kill him." He paused, then added tightly, "I think it's time for you to get on home, Wayne."

"And I'm gonna make sure you get there," Matt added. "Your daddy and I need to have a talk."

"It was just a gopher," Wayne blurted out defiantly.

A muscle twitched in Matt's cheek, and Caroline steadied him with a calm hand of reason placed against the side of her husband's leg, a gentle reminder they were dealing with a ten-year-old instead of a grown man.

"Go on and get in the truck," Matt instructed, pointing to the pickup.

"Do you want me to come along, son?" Sam asked.

"I'll handle it, Pa," Matt replied, stepping off the porch as the children came back up the road, with Joe carrying an obviously dead Stonewall Jackson.

They waited in mechanical silence as the procession marched mournfully to the porch.

"It's him," Joe confirmed bluntly a few moments later. "Shot twice through the bottom of his shell." He shifted a daggered gaze to Wayne. "What did you do, Wayne? Turn him over and watch him flop around on his back awhile before you killed him?"

The question hung in brittle silence for a short eternity.

At last, Matt motioned to Wayne. "Let's go," he said.

"Where to?" Joe snapped.

"I'm taken him home to have a talk with his daddy," Matt said.

"I'm comen, too," Joe insisted.

Matt considered the wisdom of having Joe come along, but in his moment of indecision, the boy deposited the tortoise body in the bed of the pickup and vaulted over the side, staking claim to his rights.

"Okay," Matt agreed hesitantly. "But you let me do the talken when we get there."

The order went unacknowledged for a pregnant moment.

"Are we clear on that, son?" Matt asked again, firmer this time.

"Yes, sir."

As Matt told it to Caroline later, Joe held his tongue in the ensuing confrontation. "But fire came out his eyes, Caroline," her husband exclaimed. "You know how dark they are anyway. Well, they looked like polished black marbles stuck in his head, taken note of every word, every detail. I couldn't help but think that he looked like some hangen judge who'd already made up his mind and was just waiten around to pronounce the sentence, maybe even carry it out, too. Any sane man would have wilted under that glare, and Bobby did get a little tight around the collar." He hesitated, considering. "But that might have been simply because he's afraid somethen like this could hurt his chances in the election. Folks wouldn't take too kindly to some smart-aleck kid trespassen and shooten somethen that don't belong to him."

Likewise, Bobby Taylor took issue with Matt, scowling, snarling, accusing him of exaggerating something of no consequence. In the end, however, Bobby handled the incident with more tact than Matt would have given him credit for, conceding his son had made an error in judgment and promising none of the Taylors would ever again set foot on Baker property.

"But I don't know what to make of it, Caroline," Matt said with concern. "There was some bitterness to be sure. But he almost made it sound threatenen." He shook his head thoughtfully. "I know I did the right thing by goen to Bobby."

"You did," Caroline assured him.

"I don't want anybody who doesn't have a proper respect for life comen around my family with a gun, especially some smart-assed kid," Matt continued. "But still ...." He frowned, uncertain. "We may not see eye-to-eye with the Taylors, but there's never been any bad blood between us, and I'd like to keep it that way."

Matt hesitated again, tension lines creeping onto his face. "Bobby's never struck me as the type to forgive and forget," he said heavily. "I have to say I feel a little uneasy about the whole situation, Caroline. Like maybe I was there for the beginnen of a blood feud or somethen."

He shrugged. "I just don't know what will come of it."

---

Matt's concerns had proved prophetic in a manner of speaking, except the feud developed between Bobby Taylor and Paul Berrien, two total opposites who had waged the fiercest campaign in memory for the office of county sheriff. It seemed to Caroline the Bakers had been trapped into the war between Bobby and Paul, forced to take sides, caught on the fringes of something bigger than themselves. And she agreed with Matt: It was an unsettling, uneasy situation.

Caroline shook her head, pushing the thought away to concentrate on pouring the pail of warm cow's milk into a deep pan, straining it through a clean white cloth in the process.

Her mind returned to Joe and to Matt's parting request earlier in the morning. "Joe," she said, tipping the pail upside down to drain the last of the milk. "Your daddy's goen hunten with Lucas after breakfast. He thought you might like to go."

Joe grunted, something noncommittal, his eyes still skewered to the dancing flames.

Her motherly instincts growled, her wings unfurled, on guard again for danger—to her son, to her family, both of whom seemed caught up in a rising tide of misfortune. Caroline bit the inside of her lip, eyeing Joe and glancing around the kitchen in a symbolic search for the source of her worry. But wherever she looked, the waters were receding. She supposed it was the tension of the summer making her feel this way. But that tension was fading like newsprint turns yellow with old news. And then, as if reading her thoughts, Joe turned around and smiled. "I've got somethen else to do this mornen, Mama," he informed her.

Caroline returned his smile, nodding vaguely. And though it was infuriating and did not feel right, she checked her Mother Hen instincts.

It was Christmas, after all, the season of peace, and she had her faith. Caroline turned around quickly, bowed her head and uttered a silent prayer for the gift of the season.

---

Summer followed Joe, barging into the kitchen with her usual style, smiles and a word or two for anyone who cared to listen. So they humored her, allowing their oldest girl and second child to divest herself of a night and morning's worth of silence.

Summer had turned a precocious ten over the summer and she tended to have a piece of advice for everyone these days. Her tongue was sharp, witty and a tad sarcastic on occasion, but her heart was a treasure chest for good intentions. Still, in these wonder days of discovering her place in the family, Summer had a way of upsetting people. Her steady chatter wearied the best of them, and played on frayed nerves like fingernails on a chalkboard.

Caroline had given birth to her eldest daughter on the first day of summer in 1950. Naming her after the season had been a sudden impulse.

Caroline had expected a boy, to the point that she'd given scant attention to girls' names during her pregnancy. She'd had her heart set on a John, so much so that Matt had suggested Johnetta when Summer arrived. Caroline had frowned at him, then immediately dubbed her daughter after the season of her birth.

It was a perfect match. And while Summer was not exactly perfect, she possessed an inner strength rare for someone her age. She might have chattered incessantly, but the girl was more than talk. Her character matched her beauty.

Summer shared her mother's fresh complexion, but her hair, though thick and wavy like Caroline's, was the darker brown color of her father. Like all the children, she was slight of bone and muscle, but she showed signs of developing the curves of a woman, and her face was rounder and softer than the assorted collection of leaner looks that pervaded the family.

Sixteen months separated Summer from John in age, but they were miles apart in manner and habit. The second son of Matt and Caroline had inherited a love of nature from his grandfather and a silent disposition from some unknown ancestor. John was friendly, courteous and cheerful, never one for a long face, but he filled many of his hours in solitary communion with the land. He had crisscrossed the fields and woodlands countless times, inspecting plants, observing animals, seeking beauty. Once, in the late evening shadow of a towering pine, he had watched undetected as a bobcat came down to the Old Pond for a drink of water. Another time he had come upon a turf battle between a king snake and a rattlesnake. The snakes had tussled for several minutes, but gradually the king snake coiled around its opponent. Then, suddenly, the king had flexed and straightened, snapping the rattlesnake in half.

Even Sam, who had seen his share of wondrous moments in the woods, had been impressed with John's forest fortunes.

John was also the family artist, using crayons and pencils to create pictures that reflected his love of nature. Caroline herself had always been drawn to beautiful paintings, so she figured John's talents came from her side of the family. But his inspiration was truly a gift from Sam.

John definitely favored Caroline, lean in the face with hollow cheeks, tall and thin, with a mop of straight, dark brown hair, almost always too long, falling somewhere between the nearly black color of Matt's and the lighter shade of Joe's dark brown.

Carrie was their Christmas baby, born a day after the blessed event in December 1952, arriving fourteen months after John. She was easily the most enigmatic of the bunch, an awkwardly shy little girl who hid in the shadows around strangers and sometimes among friends. True to her birthright, Carrie seemed lost in the middle of the Baker brood, the one least likely to find her voice. She seemed fragile, like a sparrow, from spirit to body, which, though painfully thin, was blessed with abundant grace. Carrie had the lightest shade of brown hair in the family, but her light brown eyes sparkled in a special way.

The hard of heart dismissed Carrie as the plainest of the six Baker children, but she was not ordinary. She radiated gentleness, a quality that shown quietly in her eyes and in the way she cared for the family. Carrie would find her wings eventually and venture from the protective nest of her family.

Eighteen months separated Luke from Carrie, and another fifteen months stood between the youngest son and Bonnie.

Luke was the most rambunctious of the children, a six-year-old sparkplug waiting to ignite and often difficult to control once sprung to life. Bonnie was four, the baby of the bunch, a bit spoiled and still young enough to get away with it. Their looks and personalities were still developing, but Luke clearly favored his father while Bonnie resembled Caroline.

Different though they all were, there were obvious patterns and linkages among the six children. Most striking to Caroline was the pattern of personalities: bold and brash for Joe and Summer, turning quiet and tender for John and Carrie, to daring and engaging for Luke and Bonnie. She had no way of knowing, but Caroline felt certain that had she given birth to two more children, this double pattern of active and passive characters would have been completed.

Caroline was also struck by the rhythm of appearances. Joe and Summer were the different ones, obviously cut from the Baker mold, yet clearly distinctive from their brothers and sisters. John and Carrie favored each other the most, while Luke and Bonnie bore the closest resemblance to their parents.

As the children gathered around the table that morning, Caroline felt a keen sense of pride. She knew the Bible warned against those who would be too prideful, but God had given her this passel of children, blessing them with good looks and noble spirits. It was moments like these that caused a wellspring of grace to bubble over in Caroline, refreshing her faith and preparing her for the battles of the day.

She took a deep breath, allowing this invigoration to wash through her, cleansed like a repentant sinner on the last day of a tent revival. And then, smiling, she took her place at the table and delivered the breakfast blessing.

# CHAPTER 3

BY EIGHT O'CLOCK THAT morning, breakfast was a memory except for dirty dishes, and everyone was at work. Summer was dispatched to strip the beds and put on fresh linens. Carrie and Luke were sent outside: her to gather eggs and him to feed Pal-Two and the two barnyard cats—Tom, a wiry black male with a wide face and four white paws, and Bob, a feisty female tabby that had lost her tail as a kitten. Bonnie had done her best to stay underfoot of everyone else until Rachel put an end to the shenanigans. Now the little girl was standing on a chair beside the sink, happily rinsing the dishes her grandmother washed.

Matt was somewhere on the place with Lucas, cutting wood, hunting or goofing off if the mood struck him, while Joe and John were helping their grandfather bag pecans.

With everyone busy, temporarily settled, Caroline sat down at the kitchen table to plan Christmas dinner, poring through a small sampling of her cookbook collection. She loved to cook and spent many of her leisure hours reading and rereading cookbooks and magazines for recipes. Holiday meals were her favorites, although she and Rachel invariably wound up preparing a traditional feast. Still, every Thanksgiving and Christmas, Caroline pulled out one special recipe that would give a distinctive flavor to the dinner.

Now and then relatives ate a holiday dinner with the Bakers, but those occasions were seldom these days. Rachel's sister, Euna, and her family had spent the most recent Thanksgiving with them, but they lived in Ocala, Florida, and Euna's grown children, who had families of their own, obviously wanted to spend the holidays at home. Rachel also had a sister-in-law, niece and nephew from her brother Alton, who had drowned in a boating accident several summers ago. But they rarely visited with each other anymore, only a little more so than Caroline did with the few distant cousins on her side of the family.

Sam had three brothers, two of whom were dead, and Caleb,

who dropped in unannounced each year in late fall, bringing with him bags of grapefruit, oranges and tangerines. This year Caleb and his fourth wife had come calling the week after Thanksgiving, unexpectedly knocking on the door one afternoon with enough citrus fruit for a small army and staying only long enough to eat supper and breakfast the next morning.

Caroline sighed, recalling Sam's frequent contention that the Bakers were afflicted with the "orphan spirit," and began flipping through a worn copy of *Betty Crocker's Picture Cookbook*.

Christmas dinner this year would be an affair for the immediate family, which meant Caroline would have to curb the temptation to overindulge her culinary talents. With ten mouths to feed in one house, it was a chore to cook too much food, but Caroline was equal to the task. Her holiday meals were appreciated, too, even when they were served again on the day after the holiday. On the third day of leftovers, however, everyone complained. And on the fourth day, they mutinied and demanded something different, so perhaps her late start in planning this year's Christmas dinner would prove a blessing in disguise by keeping the feast to a bare minimum.

She began her list with the turkey, a twenty-pound bird at the least, and added the ham, which was hanging in the smokehouse for the occasion. She wrote down cornbread dressing and cranberry sauce, butterbeans, creamed corn and fresh turnip greens. Dessert necessities—pecan pie and spice cake—were added to the list, along with a loaf of pumpkin bread and sweet potato pie. Something was missing, she thought, frowning, then remembered candied sweet potatoes, another necessity for a holiday meal at the Baker table.

Caroline glanced up at Rachel. "How 'bout maken some chicken and dumplens for Christmas dinner, Ma?"

Rachel turned around, drying her hands on a towel as she considered the request. "To tell you the truth, Caroline, I don't really have a hen to spare for butcheren."

Caroline considered the quandary, then beamed. "That's no problem," she said. "Matt and I are goen into town this afternoon. I have to buy a truckload of groceries as it is, so I'll just add a hen to the list."

"Good," Rachel agreed, then asked as an afterthought, "What specialty have you got planned for us this Christmas, Caroline? It's gonna be hard to top that squash casserole from Thanksgiven."

"That's my little Christmas secret," Caroline teased.

"Mama, why are you smilen so big?" Bonnie asked suddenly, scrutinizing her mother with a scrunched face.

Caroline and Rachel laughed loudly. "Because your mama loves to cook and holiday meals are her favorite," Rachel answered, hugging the girl to her chest. She looked back to Caroline. "What's on the menu this year?"

Caroline read off the list of foods, starting to write again as soon as she finished.

"Don't forget my pear tarts and fruit cake," Rachel reminded her with a touch of indignation that her Christmas staples had been overlooked.

"I'm already putten them on the list," Caroline replied swiftly. "It wouldn't seem like Christmas without your fruit cake and pear tarts, Ma."

Rachel smiled broadly, appeased by the compliment, then turned serious. "I'll need a few things from the grocery store for the fruit cake," she said, putting a finger on her chin. "Let me think."

"Candied fruit?" Caroline started.

"Yes," Rachel agreed, taking over the list of ingredients. "Some candied cherries, pineapple and orange. Lemon peel if they have it. And the nuts, too. I thought I'd try almonds and walnuts this time, so pick up a bag of those, too."

"They're already on the list," Caroline confirmed, then added, "Grandpa'll have a fit if you don't put pecans in it."

Rachel nodded agreement. "I'm plannen to," she said. "I just mentioned the almonds and walnuts because we don't have any. I also thought I'd try fig preserves in it this year. And molasses, too. I want it a little darker than usual. What do you think?"

"Good idea," Caroline remarked. "It might spice up the flavor. That reminds me: How are we set for spices?"

"Let me see," Rachel said, walking to the cupboard. She opened the cabinet and began rummaging through its bottom shelf. "All that baken at Thanksgiven cleaned us out. We're low on everything. Nutmeg, allspice, cinnamon."

"I ordered cinnamon, pepper and vanilla extract from Amelia," Caroline said, referring to Amelia Carter, the wife of mercantile owner Dan Carter, who also sold Watkins products and Avon cosmetics. "I also ordered some butternut flavoren," Caroline continued. "Amelia showed me a butternut cake recipe in one of her catalogs, and it looks scrumptious."

"What about the liniment?" Rachel questioned. "We're completely out."

"I did," Caroline replied. "And they also had some vanilla-scented shampoo that I got for Summer. She's starten to notice her looks, and I thought it might be somethen special for Christmas."

"That's nice," Rachel agreed. "Better add ginger and baken powder to the list."

Caroline wrote on her pad, then glanced at Bonnie, who had climbed down off the chair and was stretched out on the deacon's bench. "Don't tell Summer about the shampoo, Bonnie," she urged. "I want it to be a surprise."

"Why ain't Santa Claus given it to her?" Bonnie inquired.

"He'll bring her something else," Caroline assured her young daughter. "Course, the way I hear it, Santa's elves were sickly over the winter, and Christmas is gonna be slim pickens this year, honey."

"We'll need brown sugar," Rachel interrupted to change the subject. "And eggs, too," she added regretfully. "My layers can't keep up with the holiday demand."

"A couple of dozen?" Caroline suggested.

"I'll need eight for the fruit cake alone," Rachel replied, shaking her head. "I'd make it three at least, and if we don't eat eggs for breakfast the next couple of days, we oughtta have enough to get us through."

"Three it is," Caroline concurred, again adding to her list. "I also planned on maken a couple of cakes—coconut and burnt-sugar—but that'd be too much." She hedged. "But I could make them both and then give one away," she thought aloud.

Rachel agreed, smiling at her daughter-in-law's indulgence. "We might as well have a real nice fruit salad while we're at it," she suggested, caught up in the spirit. "We got all those oranges and grapefruit from Caleb. You could pick up some apples, bananas, grapes, cherries, a can of pineapple. We've already got pears and peaches that I canned in the fall. Top it with nuts and fresh cream. I've always thought a good fruit salad was a meal in itself."

"Fruit salad it is," Caroline beamed, writing down the ingredients. "Do we need anything else?"

"I think we stopped needen back when I mentioned pear tarts

and fruit cake," Rachel answered dryly. "Probably even before that."

"You promised we could make Christmas cookies," Bonnie reminded her mother in urgent tones.

Caroline smiled. "We'll do it tonight, sweetheart."

"We're set then," Rachel said.

"For a feast fit for a king," Caroline concluded triumphantly.

---

Around mid-morning, Sam tied up the last bag of pecans and Joe hoisted it onto the scales. Sam adjusted the weights until they balanced, jotted down the poundage on his note pad and scribbled through a quick set of calculations. He grunted. "The Berriens got about nine hundred pounds per acre this year," he scowled. "That's worse than our orchard. We got nine seventy-five."

"But nut for nut, their pecans are meatier than ours," John pointed out, flopping over on one of the fifty-pound bags to rest. "They oughtta bring a better price."

"True enough," Sam replied. "I'll do some figuren tonight to see what price I need to break even."

"We've still got a deal, Grandpa," Joe said questioningly, reminding Sam of his promise to allow the boy to sell the season's final load of pecans.

"I'll make you an offer in the mornen," Sam said gruffly.

They were in a one-room barn, with a porch across the front. The barn was isolated on the southeastern side of the farm, stuck in a sheltering grove of hardwoods and pines. In summer, the barn served as a storehouse for cooked tobacco. Sam ran his pecan business from it in the fall and early winter.

The business gave Sam and Rachel an income independent of the farm, which Sam had turned over completely to Matt with the exception of the pecan orchard and half the cattle operation. Sam insisted on using the pecan money to pay taxes on the farm, and he paid the children to pick up the nuts. It was about the only money they earned all year.

Though the heart attack had curtailed his business somewhat this season, Sam was making a modest profit, and he had determined to use his success to reward Joe for the boy's hard work on the farm.

Tomorrow, Sam would make a deal with his grandson. But now he needed help from Joe and John to grind sugar cane in order to carry out his promise to the children to make one last batch of syrup. He slapped John across the rump. "If we're gonna make syrup today, I'd better make hay and grind the cane," he announced. "It just so happens that I need four strong arms to haul it out of the barn and help run the stalks through the mill. Are you boys up to it?"

"All right!" shouted John.

"Sure thing," Joe agreed.

A half hour later, Sam was pushing purple cane stalks through the electric mill, which purred softly as it pulverized the sugary shafts. The juice ran down a funnel, dripped onto a grating that strained out the bulk of impurities and finally emptied into a fifty-gallon drum.

The cane mill was set up across the road from the house, beneath one of two shelters flanking either side of the corncrib. Sam and Rachel had set up house in the one-room outbuilding years ago when their home burned to the ground. It had been cramped quarters for two adults and three children, but they had managed. Now the barn floor was piled high with the recent harvest of corn.

The last of the cane crop was in one of the front corners of the crib, and Joe and John were hauling the stalks to Sam. They were playing mostly, jostling back and forth and wrestling in the bed of kernels. As could be expected, John was on the losing side of these good-natured bouts. He was covered from head to toe with a filmy white dust but smiling broadly, and the picture reminded Sam of a time years ago when his boys had done the same thing on a cold December morning.

He took a deep breath, chasing away the melancholy, helped by the timely arrival of Amelia and Tom Carter across the way. They pulled up in a red sedan, the car hardly coming to a stop before Tom bounded out and headed across the road.

Tom was twelve, fair complexioned, thinly built, with a mop of golden hair. Though they were not related by flesh and blood, Sam felt a kinship with the boy. Tom was the son of shopkeepers and merchants, but his blood boiled for the outdoors. He spent many hours, days and nights with the Bakers, a friend to all and to Joe in particular, despite the two-year gap in their ages.

"Hey, Grandpa!" he called to Sam.

"Howdy, Tom," Sam returned. "How are you, Amelia?" he

called a little louder to the distinguished woman with a blonde bouffant who followed her son across the road at a leisurely pace.

"Good mornen, Sam," Amelia drawled in a voice that was pure Southern belle, distinguished by a no-nonsense clip. "How are you feelen today?"

"Fine and dandy," Sam replied as she reached him. "Just getten ready to make one last batch of cane syrup. I'll send along a bottle for you and Dan."

"It'd be mighty appreciated," Amelia said. "And if you have any extra, you might consider letten the mercantile sell it for you."

Another round of greetings interrupted Sam's answer as Joe and John came around the corner, each with an armload of cane. "Mornen, boys," Amelia said. "How's that leg, Joe?"

Joe stood on his good foot, shook the mending leg and smiled broadly. "Almost good as new," he told her dryly. "The best leg money can buy and steel can hold together."

Amelia laughed at the sarcasm. "The cast is comen off soon," Joe continued more seriously. "Hopefully next week before school starts back."

"Good," Amelia nodded, politely returning her gaze to Sam. "What about my offer, Sam?" she pressed him.

"You're a born deal-maker, Amelia, and a dear one at that," Sam answered. "But I don't have enough this year. We'll use all the syrup and then some around here." He gestured to the silver ladle hanging on the edge of the barrel beneath the grinder. "Would you like a sip of juice?"

"No, thank you," Amelia replied briskly. "I'm in a hurry this mornen—maken deliveries so all the fine women of this community can cook up a delicious Christmas dinner and look pretty while they're doen it." Her tone settled. "I had some stuff for y'all that Caroline ordered, and Tom's been badgeren us all mornen about comen over here to make the syrup."

Tom had joined the boys in the corncrib, retrieving more cane.

"Dan had him worken in the store this mornen," Amelia continued dryly. "You can imagine how happy Tom was about that." She looked past Sam to where the hogs were rooting beyond the fence. "I keep hopen he's gonna want to take over the business someday, but I have a feelen he won't ever take to it."

"Everybody's gotta do what they gotta do, Amelia," Sam said gently.

She nodded, shifted her gaze to him and smiled. "I suppose they do." She shook her thoughts. "I need to run, Sam. Just send Tom home when you're tired of him."

Tom heard this last comment as he came walking up with his arms full of cane. "But I'm spenden the night here, Mama," he reminded her somewhat urgently. "Remember? I'm goen with Joe to sell the pecans in Albany tomorrow."

Amelia put a hand against her forehead, feigning shock. "How could I forget?" she drawled. "That's all you've talked about for the last week." She turned to Sam. "Are you sure it's all right if he tags along, Sam?"

"I don't see why not," Sam replied easily. "They'll have a good time."

"Okay then," Amelia agreed. "But Tom, you'll have to come by the house later this afternoon and get clean clothes."

"Yes, ma'am," Tom promised.

Amelia smiled affectionately at them all. "Bye, now," she waved quickly, a round of farewells trailing her walk back across the road to deliver the much-anticipated order of Watkins products for Caroline and Rachel.

When she was out of earshot, Sam checked the level of juice in the barrel, weighing it against the stack of cane by the mill. "That's enough, boys," he told them. "Why don't y'all take the cover off the kettle, and we'll get this show on the road."

The massive kettle, which also served to make sour corn mash for the hogs from time to time, was kept kitchen clean by Sam. It was made of thick, black cast-iron, suspended in the middle of an enormous brick casing with a chimney running up the backside. On the side of the brick structure was an iron door, similar to a steel forge, a reminder of the old days when a wood fire had been used to cook the syrup. Sam had modernized the cooker a few years back, installing a gas burner that gave him better control of the heating process.

Joe and Tom removed the canvas cover from the kettle, while John went inside the house to inform his sisters and Luke that the syrup-making was ready to begin. Sam ran the last cane stalk through the mill, switched off the machine and with Joe's help pushed the boom-suspended grinder away from the barrel.

He picked up the ladle, dipped it into the ugly greenish-gray mixture and raised a sampling of the juice to his mouth. His nose crinkled, and Sam licked his lips as Joe and Tom waited for him to render judgment. "Sharp with a sickly sweet twang," Sam announced with connoisseuric flare. "A flavor that truly can be enjoyed only by those lucky enough to have acquired a taste for it." He hesitated dramatically. "Sad to say, I am still not one of those souls."

Joe and Tom broke into wide grins. It was a perfect batch. Sam had never acquired a taste for cane juice, but he loved the syrup it made. The boys on the other hand loved the juice almost as much as the syrup, and they quickly took turns with the ladle.

"Grandpa," Joe said cheerfully, taking his second sip of juice, "if the day ever comes when you sample cane juice and decide you like it, well then ...." He hesitated. "Well then, I think I might just have to give raisins another try."

Sam laughed, appreciating the inside humor. None of the Bakers liked raisins.

At that moment, John stepped out on the front porch of the house. "Grandpa!" he yelled across the way. "Granny says to come on in and eat dinner before you start the cooken."

Sam looked from Joe to Tom, smiling faintly. "We have our orders, boys."

---

Matt and Caroline left for Cookville shortly after the noon meal, promising to be home for supper, anxious for time to themselves. They were cheerful setting out, but a difficult task lay ahead of them. It had been a bad year on the farm, despite a promising start.

Spring rains had come plentiful and crops had thrived early. But then, when the crops needed rain most, the skies failed them. Corn withered in the fields, peanuts failed to mature. Decent crops of tobacco and cotton spared the Bakers a full-blown disaster, but only barely. And even the pecan crop, which Sam counted on to pay taxes and give him and Rachel spending money, had responded with its worst yield in a decade.

As usual, the Bakers were strapped for cash.

Money, money, money. It sometimes seemed the bane of their existence, and truthfully, neither Matt nor Caroline cared much for it—as long as they had enough to feed the family and keep the farm in business, meet their debts and maybe put away a few dollars for a rainy day. The problem was, they rarely did.

Sam had paid an exorbitant price for the farm's first two hundred acres way back in the 1920s. There'd been second, third and fourth mortgages along the way, and they had bought another two-hundred-forty-eight-acre parcel two decades later, again paying premium prices. Those debts were paid in full now, but the accomplishment had left their coffers empty, still struggling to get ahead of their needs.

Matt was a resourceful farmer who shunned debt whenever possible. Most of his neighbors borrowed money in the spring to plant their crops, paying off the loan later in the year with the fall receipts. But not Matt. Each fall, when receipts were totaled and debts paid, he figured out the cash amount needed to plant next year's crop and put those dollars in a separate bank account that could not be touched until the spring. They lived off what was left from the season's profit.

As resourceful as he was, however, equipment needs sometimes forced Matt to swallow his pride and call on the Farmers and Citizens Bank of Cookville for a loan. Two years ago, he had borrowed for a new pickup, replacing the worn-out Ford that had been new shortly after the war. The loan had been paid in full this year, and Matt had hoped to pad their meager savings as well.

Instead, the unexpected had occurred in the form of hospital and doctor bills—first with Sam's heart attack and then with Joe's shattered leg. There had been no insurance to cover those high bills, forcing Matt to dip into the savings, and now there were no savings to fall back on in case something else unexpected occurred.

It was the same old story—land rich and cash poor—and Matt could trace back a million times to the root of the problem. Too much of their land lay idle, not by choice but necessity. Matt was a good farmer; he worked hard and his family supported him. But the Bakers were stretched too thin for labor, despite the best efforts of Matt, Sam and Joe.

Too often in the past, they had to pay hired hands, which ate up profits like black shank wilted tobacco. But as he and Caroline drove along the newly paved black top toward Cookville, Matt saw a glimmer of hope for the future.

The children were growing up, and soon they'd be able to do the work now farmed out to hired hands. And then, too, Matt saw the possibility of clearing more land for new fields. Joe was an excellent farmer, and the boy had a few more years at home before heading off on his own. John and Luke already showed an inclination for the work, and both seemed to have considerably more interest in the job than their oldest brother. Matt suspected as well that Lucas Bartholomew would welcome a steady job from March through November.

Of course, none of that helped with the current financial dilemma. They were still poor as an Oklahoma dust bowl. But they would get by this hardship, as they had done all the others, Matt thought, just as Caroline informed in taskmaster tones:

"We have to be practical this year, Matt," she began. "Maybe we can get a doll for Bonnie because she has her heart set on one. And surely there's some little toy that'll satisfy Luke. He hasn't asked for anything in particular, anyhow. Joe, Summer and John already have a good idea that Christmas means slim pickens this year. And even Carrie realizes Santa Claus has good years and bad years."

Matt listened carefully to his wife, knowing she made sense. They had to spend their money wisely. But Matt also knew that Caroline could turn practicality into a new definition for frugality.

"We can buy them each a big bag of candy, maybe a can of mixed nuts, too," Caroline persisted, her mind churning over a whole list of practical ideas as she talked. "No, on second thought, we don't even have to do that. I can get bags of nuts in the grocery store—Brazil nuts, pistachios, almonds, English walnuts, maybe some cashews—and we can put some of each kind in the stockens. They'll have a ball cracken them. You know how hard those shells are."

His wife's plans were even grimmer than Matt had anticipated.

"Whoa, Caroline!" he said stoutly. "Now, honey, I've given this Christmas a lot of thought, and I want you to think about it, too."

It was a true statement. Matt had spent the morning considering the perfect gifts for his family while chopping wood and hunting with Lucas. He'd come home from the expedition with a load of dead wood, nary a spent shell, and a slew of ideas for Christmas presents.

"I know money's tight," he continued. "And I know the kids need clothes, shoes and all that stuff. But remember, this *is* Christmas, Caroline, and it's about the only time they get gifts all year long." He hesitated, then continued softly. "I think they deserve a

little better than the necessities, some candy and a few nuts that are
*hard to crack.*" He paused once more, looking hopefully at his wife.
"Don't you?"

Caroline reddened, embarrassed by the grim Christmas she was
ready to give her family. True, she did not want them so wrapped
up in the material side of the holiday that they failed to take heed
of the day's real meaning. But they were good children, deserving
of the kind of thoughtfulness that Matt had in mind and she had
neglected.

"You're right," she sighed.

"Now take Joe, for instance," Matt continued with not a disparaging thought about her shortsightedness. "He likes to read and
lately he's taken to quoten me poetry by Robert Frost. Surely, we
can afford a book of poetry for him. And John likes to color and
draw. Maybe we can get him a paint set. I know for a fact Luke has
his heart set on a toy tractor at the John Deere dealership, and like
you said, Bonnie wants her doll. And surely there's somethen special Summer and Carrie have in mind."

Leave it to Matt to check her practicality, Caroline thought,
proud to be married to this man who was strong and forceful when
necessary, unafraid of tenderness when the moment required a
softer touch. "Summer's talked nonstop about this pale-yellow satin
dress she saw at Bishop's in Tifton," Caroline said thoughtfully. "It's
pretty and a tad overpriced, but she could wear it for Easter, I suppose. And Carrie wants a watch. I don't know exactly why, but I
heard her tellen Summer that's what she wanted for Christmas.
That's expensive, too, but I guess since her birthday falls so near
Christmas, we oughtta get her the watch."

"Let's do it then," Matt said happily. "We got all year to be poor,
honey, so we might as well have a little bit of fun while we're at it."

Caroline rolled her eyes, but pure joy lit her face. "Might as
well," she agreed.

----------

After dinner, Sam repeated the cane-tasting ritual for the other children, having earlier sworn Joe and Tom to secrecy about the first
sampling. Joe orchestrated the moment perfectly, even reproducing
his line about raisins, drawing a chorus of gags from his brothers
and sisters. Then Sam announced grandly, "Shall we pour?"

With Sam guiding, Joe, John and Tom lifting, they tipped the drum on its side and filled the iron vat to the rim with the greenish-gray juice. Sam lit the burner, played with the flame for several minutes to adjust it, and then settled back for a long wait until the cane juice came to a slow boil, which would cause the skimmings—bits of fiber, waste and trash—to rise to the top of the kettle.

Summer and John dipped several mayonnaise jars into the vat, filling the containers with juice for sipping while the syrup cooked. The children loved cooking syrup, probably as much as eating it. Syrup-cooking days were an opportunity to idle away a few hours, listening to their grandfather weave outlandish tales. Their favorites were bodacious accounts of hook-handed pirates and fire-breathing dragons, all woven to explain how Sam had come to wear the black patch that shielded his left eye and partially covered a jagged scar stretching to the bridge of his nose.

Sam stood almost six-foot-two, solidly built but carrying little excess weight, especially since suffering the heart attack. His hair was silvery white, cropped short and high on the forehead by choice. His face was long, chiseled, with a jutting chin and sharp nose, roughened by a heavy shadow of beard. He was naturally dark, pigmentation descended from a great-grandmother who was full-blooded Cherokee. He had thick, ash-gray eyebrows, and his deep brown right eye seemed proportionally small for such an imposing man. Sam was handsome, but his face was marred by the black eye patch and wicked scar. The flawed face gave him the sinister look of a pirate who pillaged without conscience. But Sam was a gentle giant of goodness to those who knew him well.

Today, he would lose the eye while dueling with an evil knight to save a fair maiden trapped in a castle tower. Sam was set to begin his yarn when Joe broke ranks.

"I'll be back in time to help you pour up the syrup," Joe informed his grandfather.

"Just what's so important that you don't have time to sit and listen to my story?" Sam demanded to know.

Joe gestured to the woods behind them, where the hogs roamed. "There's a section of fence on the backside that Daddy wants mended before the hogs push through," Joe said naturally. "I wanted to get it done this afternoon since I won't be around tomorrow."

It was an honest answer to a degree. In truth, Joe knew the real reason Sam wore the eye patch. He had seen behind the patch. And while he still enjoyed the outrageous stories spun by his grandfather, sometimes his mood preferred to forego those tales of white-knight heroes and dark-souled villains.

"The fence could wait," Sam grumbled.

"Maybe," Joe agreed. "But then again, we could spend Christmas chasen hogs all over creation."

Sam huffed.

"Do you want to come with me, Tom?" Joe asked his blond-headed friend.

Tom was stricken with a look of disbelief. He gulped, then found his voice. "To tell you the truth, Joe, I'll stay here," he said sheepishly. "I'd rather cook syrup than fix fence."

Joe nodded his understanding. "Okeydokey," he remarked cheerfully, turning away from them. "See y'all later," he called over his shoulder.

Sam frowned, wishing Joe would learn to relax, wondering what drove the boy urgently forward. But he did not dally long with such musing because he had an eager audience for a story and a kettle of syrup to cook.

The children sprawled around him, finding seats where they could under the shelter. Summer grabbed the tractor seat, and Bonnie stretched out on the machine's hood. Luke and Tom settled on opposite sides of the front wheel axle, while John and Carrie hoisted themselves into clear spaces on the workbench. Sam took his usual spot, on a fat plug of firewood tucked against the back wall of the shelter. They passed around the jars of cane juice like bottles of whiskey, everyone taking a sip at their turn, even those who had not acquired a taste for the tangy mixture.

Sam was an adroit storyteller, weaving intricate plots of love and beauty, hate and war, action and adventure, good and evil. Today, he launched into a tale of evil knights and damsels in distress. The cane juice began to bubble like a witch's caldron, the impurities rising, covering the surface with a dirty white foam, and Sam horrified his audience by allowing the hero of the story to suffer the ignominy of having hot oil poured into his face from a castle tower. The children gasped, and Sam paused to tend the syrup, skimming away the dirty foam with a white net and then turning up the heat.

His tale went fast after that, recounting the hero's tortuous recovery, the climatic jousting battle to the death between the two knights and the good knight's rescue of a fair maiden. When the tale was finished, the children were drained from the tension, so they stared hypnotically into the boiling kettle, savoring the story.

In a while, Luke broke the spell. "Grandpa," he said seriously. "Have you ever gone to merry old England really?"

"Of course, he hasn't," Summer barked. "But you went to Paris, didn't you, Grandpa?" she continued smartly, giving Luke a hopeless look. "Don't you know anything, Luke?"

Sam shushed her, then turned to Luke, who was glaring with contempt at his sister. "Summer's right," Sam admitted. "I've never gone to merry old England, but I was in France during the Great War. I saw Paris, and one day I intend on goen there again with your grandmother.

"Paris is a beautiful city," he continued, launching into another story, this tale real and mellowed in his mind over the years.

He told the children about the Eiffel Tower, the Arc de Triomphe and the Louvre, about Notre Dame, Sacré Coeur and the Latin Quarter. He told them how the Seine River cut through the city and how a grotesquely masked man haunted the Paris Opera House. He told them about French wine, French bread and French women, whom he swore could not hold a candle to Rachel. The one thing Sam did not mention was the war, the reason he'd had an opportunity to walk the streets of Paris.

"Can I go with you the next time?" John asked eventually, dazed, sighing in a voice that broke the silence of another spellbound audience. "I'd like to go someplace besides Cookville, and Paris sure sounds nice."

Sam smiled at the boy.

"You're goen to Tifton the day after tomorrow," Bonnie reminded her brother, a little testily to show her dismay over John's apparent forgetfulness about their traditional Christmas Eve trip to town.

John rolled his eyes. "Anybody can go to Tifton, Bonnie," he said dryly.

"Well I bet the people in Paris don't even know where Tifton is," Carrie interjected defensively, for Bonnie's sake.

"She's got a point, John," Summer remarked pointedly, playing referee.

John shook his head, casting a disparaging gaze upon his sisters.

Tom changed his position on the tractor wheel and drained the last drops of cane juice from one of the mayonnaise jars. He wiped his mouth with the back of a hand. "Adventures sound fun," he commented, "but if I lived on a farm, I'd never go anywhere. I'd just stay put and be happy." He looked around at his friends. "Y'all are the luckiest people in the world to live here. I wish my folks had a farm."

"Oh, shut up, Tom," Summer remarked bluntly, sending him a withering glance. "That has absolutely nothen to do with what we're talken about." She caught a breath. "Besides, you're here on this farm almost all the time as it is. And besides that, your folks have a store. A store beats a farm by a long shot."

Tom bit his lip. Sometimes he wanted to slug Summer across the face. But he reminded himself that he was a guest and had to mind his manners.

"Nope, Summer, you're wrong," he said firmly but nicely. "A farm is loads more fun than a stuffy old store." He looked at Sam for confirmation. "Don't you think so, Grandpa?"

Sam sidestepped the question. "It really depends on the person," he said diplomatically. "Personally, I prefer the outdoors, but I can see where others might find that runnen a store has its advantages."

Summer and Tom put their feud on hold, temporarily at least, though neither one seemed satisfied with the answer. Still, the children launched into another round of bantering, and it soon became obvious to Sam that his storytelling skills were no longer needed.

From their chatter, the children moved on to games of touch football, tag and dodgeball, the time flying by in a whirl of fun. They were playing hide-and-seek when Joe came silently out of the woods, emerging at the gate a few yards from where Sam watched over the syrup.

"What happened to the troops?" Joe called from the gate, surprising his grandfather.

Sam glanced behind him, watching Joe unlatch the gate and step into the yard. "They got bored with the battle," he replied. "But they'll be back for the finale."

Joe pushed the gate closed. "Is it safe around here?" he asked teasingly, his eyes shifting from side to side. "Are the dragons slain and the maidens saved?"

Sam smiled. "We battled evil knights today," he replied. "And toured Paris." He returned to the syrup, giving it a quick stir with a long stick. "I suppose you're getten too old for my stories."

"Not at all, Grandpa," Joe said sincerely, hobbling over to the shelter. He leaned against a support pole. "I just really wanted to get that fence fixed today."

Sam sighed. "I suppose I sound like my feelens are hurt because you didn't want to hear my stories?" he said questioningly. "But they're not."

"You sure?" Joe asked.

"Absolutely," Sam replied lightheartedly. He gestured to the woods and asked, "Are you finished back there?"

"I had to come back for a few more staple nails and a shovel," Joe answered. "It was pretty ragged in a few spots, and there's a washed-out place that needs some dirt thrown over it before those hogs start tryen to root their way under the fence. We probably oughtta string some barbwire across the bottom to make them think twice about goen under instead of through it. What we really need is a brand-new fence, but I don't guess there's much chance of that with money be'en the way it is around here."

"'Fraid not," Sam agreed, staring hard at Joe, then turning back to the syrup. "You better get on and finish it up," he suggested tiredly. "It's turnen awful cold out here."

Joe blew a cloud of frosty breath. "Sure is," he agreed. "I'll be back in a jiffy."

His grandson headed across the road to retrieve the needed tools, and Sam watched him, wondering when their little boy had grown so tall and so old. Joe had been a carefree child, a smiling wonder, full of wholesome anticipation, bent on a bit of merry devilment. In one way, he was still the same boy. But there was some strong force lurking within him, something guarded and intense, hell-bent on achievement and responsibility. It bothered Sam, and he made up his mind to ....

"To do what?" he asked himself, aloud.

"Sir?"

Sam shook off the cobwebs and turned to the voice behind him, finding Joe already returned with the bag of nails and shovel in hand. "That was quick," he muttered. "You goen or comen?"

"Comen." Joe stepped closer, piercing his grandfather with a concerned gaze. "Are you okay, Grandpa?" he asked worriedly.

Sam nodded quickly, reassuringly. "I was just thinken," he re- marked candidly. "About you, to tell the truth."

"What?" Joe inquired.

Sam shrugged. "There's somethen I've been wanten to tell you, Joe, ever since you went off earlier to fix that fence," he said pur- posefully. "Now, I don't want you to think hard on what I'm goen to say because that probably would defeat the purpose. But, son, you've got a whole life ahead of you to mend fences. And if the truth be told, Joe, no matter how hard you work at it, keepen up with the patchwork is a lifelong chore. So slow down a little and enjoy, son, because those fences are gonna always be waiten. And sometimes, chasen hogs can be fun—if you know what I mean."

Joe pursed his lips in serious contemplation, then grinned. "Stop and smell the roses—is that what you're tellen me, Grandpa?"

Sam considered the inference. "To steal a phrase—yes," he said emphatically. "It's good advice."

Joe smiled again, looking away, nodding. "Grandpa, I know I've been a little intense lately," he remarked frankly. "But when you get right down to it, most everything 'round here's been pretty intense for a while now. Once this cast comes off, though, things'll get back to normal. And I promise to be my old self." Joe paused, changing his tone to lighthearted humor. "Whomever or whatever he was."

He hesitated slightly once more. "But right now, Grandpa, with all due respect to your good advice and duly noting that roses are nowhere to be seen on this brittle December day, I am taken leave of this conversation and returnen to my fence. Because as Mr. Rob- ert Frost says: 'Good fences make good neighbors.'"

"You're missen the point of the poem," Sam replied dryly.

"Yes, sir, I probably am," Joe shot back goodheartedly. "But it's not open for argument right now because I'm cold." He affected a pout. "And I want to finish menden my fence."

Sam waved him off. "Go on then," he muttered pleasantly.

"Thank you, sir," Joe said, pushing the gate open, turning back to Sam as he closed it. "How long till you're finished here?" he asked.

Sam looked at the boiling kettle. "It's ready for the floppen," he remarked. "I'd say about thirty, maybe forty minutes at the most."

"I'll be back in time to help you pour it up," Joe offered.

Sam nodded. "I rather figured you would."

Joe saluted and disappeared into the woods, leaving Sam in a better mood.

He increased the furnace heat again, bringing the thickened mixture up to flop on—but never over—the kettle's rim. Stepping from beneath the shelter, he called across the way to the children, who were now building tunnels in the hayloft.

"It's floppen time," he hollered.

Flopping was the final stage, the children's favorite part of the syrup-making process, except possibly for Sam's stories. Sam cooked the juice another thirty minutes until the gooey mixture turned a smooth, honey-brown color, and then extinguished the flame—about the time Joe came walking up to the gate for the final time.

"We're ready to pour it up, Joe," Summer told him, motioning to her brother with a syrup bottle. "Come on and give us a hand."

Joe considered the request, then shook his head in the negative. "Y'all don't need me," he assured her, walking toward the house, muttering something incoherent about roses to smell and things to do, leaving behind a confused bunch of young'uns and a smiling grandfather.

They watched him for a while, and then funneled the syrup into an odd collection of long-necked and wide-bottomed jugs. Afterward, they cleaned the kettle, reattached its canvas cover and carried a baker's dozen of bottles to the syrup house. When Sam closed the door, wedging the wooden block in the empty space between two logs, syrup-making was finished for another year.

———

Cookville was anchored by a red brick courthouse in the middle of the town square, surrounded by neat rows of prosperous shops on all four sides. There were Top Dollar, Super Dollar and General Dollar, all dime stores; two women's dress shops, two drugstores and two restaurants; four department stores, of which Coverdale's and Moore's were considered more exclusive than Kenwin and Allied; the Majestic Theater, the Farmers and Citizens Bank of Cookville, *The Cookville Herald* offices and a pair of rival law firms. A feed-and-seed also occupied the square, along with the furniture and hardware stores. Sitting off the square, in the four corners, were a gas station, a car dealership, a combined liquor store and pool hall, and the county jail.

Two grocery stores lay behind the south end of the square, and an assortment of other small businesses flanked out in any direction. The railroad—north-south and east-west lines—intersected at a depot on the east side of town, and beyond that intersection lay the quarters, where almost all of Cookville's colored population lived. The high school and hospital were on the north side of town; the funeral home on the west side; and the Farmer's Market on the south end. There were three sprawling tobacco warehouses, numerous churches and a myriad of housing styles intertwined amid the quiet streets.

Nearly everyone knew everyone else in Cookville. Gossip and other devilishness were rampant, as were neighborliness, good deeds and general caring.

All in all, Caroline felt she lived in a progressive community. The 1960 Census showed a slight decline in population for the county, but the General Telephone Company had just last Sunday hooked up service to the north end of the county, where the Bakers lived. A man had died from a rattlesnake bite at the Holiness Church a few months earlier, suggesting a backwoods character to some, but Cookville had voted overwhelmingly in favor of a female congressman a few weeks later, electing Iris Blitch to her fourth term.

Most important to Caroline, however, was that Matt stood solidly behind his community. He believed in shopping at home. The Bakers did most of their business in Cookville, a lot at the Carter's Mercantile in their own New River community and the rest on occasional trips to Tifton or Valdosta.

On this day, Matt and Caroline did business with reckless abandon, jingling the till of store after store, cramming their packages into the cab of the pickup before assaulting the next shop, sometimes together, other times by themselves. Their last stop was the grocery store, where Caroline spent a solid hour filling her holiday shopping list, which contained the staples such as flour, sugar and tea, in addition to the items needed for Christmas dinner. They spent a small fortune there, but lady luck smiled on Caroline and her name was one of three pulled from a hat in a chamber of commerce raffle for twenty-five-dollar gift certificates.

She and Matt were in the truck, ready to go home, when her husband suggested they stop by the fish market.

"Ma's cooken up those spareribs tonight," Caroline told him.

"That's okay," Matt said. "Anything we buy tonight will still be fresh tomorrow. And besides, I got an urge for oyster stew and fish roe. Maybe even a mess of mullet to go with it."

Caroline bit her lip and conceded her point. After the extravagance of the day, a few more dollars spent at the fish store would hardly matter. "Okay," she relented. "But don't get mullet. I'd rather have perch."

Matt grinned, caressing her shoulder as they drove. "We'll get both," he decided.

"Oh, brother," Caroline muttered with feigned sarcasm. But a few minutes later, they were on their way home with two pints of oysters, a pound of roe and enough mullet and perch to feed the family and then some.

It was dark as they drove, and Caroline was tired from the shopping and addled by the amount of money they had spent. She drifted into silence, staring out the window into the darkness of the passing woods.

"Come over here and sit next to me, woman," Matt demanded playfully, startling her from the silence.

She turned to him and found her husband wearing a grin bright enough to light up the truck. "What's got into you?" she asked.

"I'm feelen feisty and wanna nibble on your ear," he teased. "So come on over," he said again, gesturing to his side.

Caroline cleared a path through the packages between them and scooted beside Matt. She put one arm around his neck and ran a finger softly down the length of a sideburn.

"Wow!" Matt moaned. "You sure weren't doen anything like that nineteen years ago tonight."

Caroline pressed her lips against his temple. "I was tryen my best to be a proper young lady," she purred, allowing her free hand to rest high on his thigh.

"You were proper all right," Matt teased. "I love you better now that you're not so proper."

Caroline smiled and laid her head against his shoulder.

"How 'bout a Christmas carol?" Matt suggested at length, sensing her concern about the shopping spree. "I'll start."

"Okay," she agreed.

He started *Jingle Bells*, his deep voice ringing true and clear in the truck cab, and Caroline joined in on the opening verse. Before long, she sang with her heart. The Christmas spirit had come.

# CHAPTER 4

A WHITE SEDAN WAS parked in the front yard when Matt and Caroline arrived home from the shopping expedition. The new car belonged to Paul Berrien.

The house itself looked homey and inviting. Bright lights lit one of the side bedrooms, while the Christmas tree emanated a pale glow from the living room.

The tree was a shapely cedar, cut from the Baker timber on an outing that Sam, Luke and Bonnie had undertaken in mid-December. Sam was responsible for procuring the family Christmas tree each year, and he turned the effort into a memorable day for the children. Most years, he took the entire brood. Sometimes, like this year, he picked a select group. For the children, the anticipation of whom their grandfather would select for the outing was more fun than being picked. There were never hard feelings because everyone understood their time would come—though Caroline suspected Sam had picked Bonnie this year because her young mind might have been unable to grasp the concept of waiting until next year.

Regardless, Sam and the two youngest Baker children had set out one chilly morning after breakfast, armed with a picnic basket full of fried chicken, deviled eggs, eggnog and five seedling trees. They had traipsed across most of the farm, with Sam pointing out a variety of evergreens—cedars and Virginia pines, all planted by him over the years for just such an occasion. The cedar—nine feet of standing fragrance with a busy spread—had been the unanimous choice. They had chopped it down, stopped for lunch; then pegged the five seedlings and came marching home with the prize and any number of scratches from the tree's prickly needles.

Matt drove the truck around to the side porch entrance and killed the engine. "I guess Paul's trained to be sheriff now," he said, referencing his friend's just-completed orientation for newly elected sheriffs. "Do you think he's up to it?"

"It's not a job I'd want," Caroline replied, "but I imagine Paul's up to the task. Why do you ask? Surely you think so, too."

"I do," Matt confirmed. "It's just that you and I talked about a lot of things duren the campaign—whether Paul could win, what a jackass Bobby Taylor was, how ugly everything turned. But you never said flat-out whether you thought Paul was qualified for the job."

Caroline considered the notion. "I admit to haven a few doubts," she said. "It's quite a jump, goen from banker to sheriff. There's probably people more qualified, but I suspect Paul will do a crackerjack job of runnen things. Nothen much ever happens around here anyway. Right?"

"Not very often, that's for sure," Matt agreed. "And for Paul's sake, let's hope for peace and quiet over the next four years."

Matt and Paul were childhood best friends, and Caroline respected the privacy of their companionship. *Even now*, after she and everyone else had discovered the most terrible secret of their friendship.

The two men were an odd pair: Matt, a poor farmer struggling to make ends meet and thriving amid the battle; Paul, an unmarried heir to a small fortune and living proof that money could not buy peace. Matt was the commoner, Paul the aristocrat. But their friendship cut through the distinctions of rank and privilege and forged on basic instincts like trust and faith.

It was not unusual to see them walking the streets of Cookville—Matt in dungarees and work shirt, Paul in a tailored suit—caught up in conversation, laughing and solemnizing, cajoling and counseling, supporting and cautioning. They hunted together and, many years ago, had drunk liquor together as well, until the early morning Matt had stumbled home one time too many with whiskey on his breath. Caroline had met him at the door, holding a young Joe in her arms, and told Matt to choose between booze and his family. Her husband had never required another reminder of his priorities, and she had come to tolerate that once-in-a-blue-moon pool game that lasted deep into a winter's night.

The friendship had survived despite long odds, because of bonds formed in childhood. Paul's overbearing father, Britt Berrien, had hunted with Sam, and eventually their sons had joined them on the outings. Paul was older by two months, but they had been in the same classes at school, first at New River Elementary and later at the high school in Cookville—every year but the eighth and tenth grades when Britt had shunted his son off to military academies in Atlanta and Tennessee. World War II had carried Matt to Europe and Paul to the Pacific. Returning home after the war, Matt had joined his father on the farm, and Paul had embarked on a seven-year tour of duty at the University of Georgia, pledging a fraternity and earning degrees in finance and law.

Paul had returned to Cookville, engaged, bringing home a young sophisticate from Atlanta, a woman named Paige whose beauty was matched by her flippancy. He had taken one look at his bride-to-be in the vista of Cookville and promptly sent Paige home to Atlanta, the engagement broken.

Paul had floundered a few years, working in the bank under the tutelage of his domineering father. When Britt died, Paul had assumed the presidency of the Farmers and Citizens Bank of Cookville. He ran a tight ship, increasing the bank's assets, but never seeming to enjoy the task.

And then, the county's sheriff for twenty-eight years, Marvin McClelland, announced he would not seek re-election. The citizens thought it a good idea since Marvin had been bedridden for the past year, paralyzed from a massive stroke. And Paul seemingly found a purpose.

Seven men had coveted the sheriff's job, and the voters divided sharply in the Democratic primary, with Bobby Taylor and Paul winning spots in the runoff. The runoff campaign was sharp and bitter, carried out in late August over the three hottest weeks of the year, waged on racial overtones so crass and vulgar that Caroline still blanched when she recalled the harshness of it all.

Bobby had staked his position without mincing words, vowing "to keep niggers in their place" regardless of the yellow-bellied Supreme Court of the United States, ridiculing Paul as a member of the Kennedy crowd bent on the death and destruction of this great country. Paul had taken the high road, refusing to criticize his opponent, promising only to administer justice fairly and equally. Bobby had campaigned like a bull in passion, with hell-raising stump speeches and driving determination. Paul had relied on understated charm, toying with passion, falling back on the issues.

In the end, Paul emerged victoriously, earning the sheriff's badge and a blood-sworn enemy by a margin of ninety-eight votes.

In November, Kennedy had carried the county by the slightly larger margin of one hundred fifteen votes.

All this played out in Caroline's mind as she carried the Christmas purchases into the house through the back door to Sam and Rachel's room, while Matt toted in the bags of groceries through the back porch. She needed three trips to complete the task, planning to move the packages to hers and Matt's room later in the night, then stuck her head in the kitchen, greeting Paul and her in-laws, before finally cutting through the bathroom to check on the children.

She found Luke and Bonnie planted on the living room floor in front of the TV, too engrossed in a Christmas special to acknowledge her greeting. The other children were in the girls' room, with Summer leading everyone through the paces of a new dance called the *Twist*. Caroline stuck her head in the door, intending to quiet them, but backed away from the commotion at the last second and simply pulled the door closed behind her.

Paul was recapping his two weeks of sheriff's training when she arrived in the kitchen. He sat in the tiny rocker with his back to the fireplace, long legs stretched comfortably in front, hands wrapped easily behind the chair. He was tall and muscular, an imposing man with carefully groomed black hair, striking emerald green eyes and the face of an aristocrat. He had the swarthy look of an Italian count and spoke with a cultured Southern accent. Dressed in charcoal slacks and a white button-down shirt with a black leather bomber jacket, Paul presented a vision of irresistible manliness.

Caroline noticed all this as she hurried around the kitchen, putting away groceries and completing the supper preparations.

She often wondered why Paul had never settled down with a wife. He'd had opportunities besides Paige. Women had flung themselves at Paul with regularity for years, but he'd given them only fleeting notice. Now it seemed all the good ones were married, raising families, and Paul was still a bachelor, spending what should have been the prime of life devoted only to his aging sisters.

Caroline shook her head in dismay. It seemed like the waste of a fine man. But some situations were never as straightforward as they seemed, and she knew it was wrong to cast doubt on lives she had no reason to judge—just because they differed from her idea of fulfillment.

She put those thoughts out of mind then, stuck a pan of biscuits in the oven and began to fill glasses with ice. "Paul, have some supper with us," she suggested.

"No, thank you, Caroline," he replied, sitting up straight in the rocker. "I got in late this afternoon from Atlanta, and June and April were already in the midst of preparen a homecomen dinner for me, so I'd better get on back. I just stopped by to give you folks a personal invitation to the swearen-in ceremony."

"We're plannen to be there," Matt smiled.

"With guns blazen," Sam teased.

Paul grimaced. "Just don't shoot the sheriff," he deadpanned. "I have it on good authority that while he's a man of impeccable character, his shooten skills are suspect."

He stood, telling them, "The ceremony's scheduled for three o'clock on New Year's Eve at the courthouse. My adoren sisters have planned a little celebration back at the house afterward, and we thought it might be fun to make it a New Year's Eve party. They're gonna grill steaks and make eggnog, and I think they've even concocted some kind of pâté made with black-eyed peas." He paused. "For luck," he added, shrugging. "Anyway, we'll just have a good old time. And make sure y'all bring the children, too, because April and June are plannen a party for the ages."

"Sounds wonderful," Caroline said. "We haven't done anything special on New Year's Eve for years."

Rachel cleared her throat. "There is church, Caroline," she reminded her daughter-in-law. "It's kind of become a tradition to see the old year out and the new year in with prayer."

Caroline put a finger to her lips. "I completely forgot about that," she frowned.

"It's no problem," Paul said. "My sisters always attend the watch service, too. They're plannen our get-together for right after the swearen-in ceremony. That way, anybody who wants can attend church. Besides, I plan to be worken at midnight. It probably wouldn't look too good for the sheriff to be whoopen it up at a party his first night on the job."

"We'll be there," Matt announced.

"Good," Paul replied, stretching a kink out of his neck. "Well then, I should get on home and let you folks eat supper."

Caroline made an impulsive decision. She should have consulted Rachel first, but there wasn't time. "Paul?" she called as he eased toward the dining room. "Since y'all are goen to treat us on New

Year's Eve, we'd be honored if you, April and June would join us for dinner on Christmas Day. Ma and I are cooken enough food for a small army, and it's just goen to be the family. We'd appreciate the company, if y'all don't have anything special already planned."

Paul considered the invitation. "That's kind of you, Caroline," he replied. "I'll have to check with my sisters, but it's safe to say we'll accept." He paused, then added warmly. "It's a nice thing, folks, haven good friends like y'all."

---

The Berriens lived in a stately Georgian mansion, secluded at the end of a private lane cut through the middle of a pecan orchard. The house sat far enough off the main dirt road that even in winter when the tree branches were bare, passersby could not glimpse it. Its isolation aside, both the house and its occupants were sources of great admiration and awe, of envy and jealousy, and all other of the noble and despicable feelings that the rich and privileged inspire in those of lesser means and position.

The rank and file took for granted that the Berrien estate was a safe haven from everyday problems. Matt knew differently. He was privy to the truth concealed behind the gracious contours of that red brick facade with its brilliant black shutters. He felt the tension mixed in with the mortar and knew better than most just which closets held which skeletons and which doors were best left closed.

Berrien roots stretched deeply into the history of Cookville, beyond the town itself to the days when this part of South Georgia had been wild and pristine, untamed by civilization, ripe for exploitation by men with means and vision.

James Berrien had been such a man, possessed of only moderate means but a cunning mind fertile for opportunity. James was a distant cousin of John McPherson Berrien, the "American Cicero," who rose to leadership in the Whig Party and had a Georgia county named in his honor. He settled in South Georgia in 1817, taking advantage of the Georgia Legislature's decision to sell four-hundred-ninety-acre lots for the bargain price of eighteen dollars. Within seven years, James had acquired more than ten thousand acres of land, planting the seeds for the vast family fortune now controlled four generations later by Paul Berrien and his two sisters, April and June.

Land ownership had been merely the edge of a goldmine for a savvy prospector like James Berrien. In the 1820s, he established government-chartered ferry services across the Withlacoochee and Little rivers, using the profits to set up trading posts on the Old Coffee and Union roads, the principle routes from the heart of Georgia to either side of the Florida coast. Those businesses thrived, and James expanded his empire into cotton farming and construction. He owned about one hundred slaves before the Civil War, and convinced county leaders of the need for a new courthouse and school, acquiring the building contracts for both.

His business acumen was bounded only by the venture's limit for profit, and, ultimately, his ability to cut his losses allowed the Berrien fortune to survive the Civil War intact.

In 1858, James got himself elected to the Legislature. Sensing the coming rift between North and South, correctly concluding the South would lose, James began divesting himself of slaves and sold off some four thousand acres of land for a bargain price of four dollars and twenty-five cents an acre. The land would be worth less than three dollars an acre after the War Between the States.

On January 9, 1861, James Berrien cast a "yea" vote as Georgia declared itself a free and sovereign state. But more important was a decision he had made a few years earlier to convert the bulk of his fortune into gold and other secure investments that would hold value regardless of the war. James and his son, Alexander, buried the gold in the middle of a vast grove of young live oak trees, and then Alexander went off to war, where he was killed at Gettysburg. When the war was over, James, then seventy-five, led his grandson, twenty-one-year-old Thomas, whose arm had been shot off in the Battle of Atlanta, to the oak grove and forced the young man to dig up the gold.

It was tortured work for a one-armed man, carried out while James lectured his grandson about the virtues of hard work and the toil necessary to sustain wealth, repeating over and over, "The price of success is high, but the reward is solid gold."

When an exhausted Thomas finally retrieved the cache of gold, hoarded away in a pirate's chest, James promptly buried it again and then dug it up by himself. "Loyalty to your own flesh and blood comes without cost," he told Thomas. "Beyond flesh and blood, it's wise to count."

James Berrien was ruthless and overbearing, driven by steel

wheels of greed and profit. He required loyalty, he tolerated ambition, and he trampled ill-conceived dreams. Thomas Berrien learned those lessons well from his grandfather.

In those first few years of Reconstruction, James and Thomas overhauled the family empire. They planted depleted cotton fields with vast acreage of pine trees, setting the roots for another fortune to be made in sawmills and naval stores. Of more importance, however, they used the gold to open a bank in Cookville.

James Berrien had come to the South from New Jersey, and the banking venture showed his carpetbagger colors. The Berrien bank extended credit to small farmers at criminally high interest rates, placed liens on money crops and then acquired ownership of the mortgaged lands when the crops failed to bring in the cash needed to make the payments. Within a short time, the Berrien estate totaled more than twelve thousand acres of land and an untold fortune.

In 1870, Thomas Berrien fathered a son, Littleton Albrighton, whom his wife called Britt for short. A short time later, James Berrien passed away at the age of eighty.

———

All these things ran through Matt's mind a few hours after Paul Berrien had taken his leave from the Baker home. A more detailed account of the Berrien family history could be found in the leather-bound volumes of journals tucked away on solid mahogany shelves in Britt Berrien's old study in the family mansion. The journals had been penned almost daily by four generations of Berrien patriarchs.

Matt had read some of the books with Paul, he'd heard other stories from June and April and from Britt himself. He had no idea whether Paul or his sisters continued to record the family history in the journals. Matt did know the records were incomplete, however, because he himself had stripped two pages from one of the books, history that revealed a secret Matt had sworn to keep hidden.

Like his father, Britt had learned well the lessons of greed and ambition. He had learned when to cut his losses, when to count the costs; and he had humbled a family of immense wealth, power and prestige to its knees, leading them to search for treasures more lasting and rewarding.

Britt cultivated the role of a blue-blood Southern aristocrat. Armed with a degree from the University of Georgia, he assumed control of the family fortune when his father died. He mined the pine trees like panning for gold, harvesting the first yields of timber to put his sawmills in business and tapping the naval stores for tar, rosin and turpentine. He also recoined the reputation of the Berrien bank, changing its name to the Farmers and Citizens Bank of Cookville and bringing a sense of fairness to its profiteering practices.

The banking moves proved popular with the forgiving citizens of Cookville, as did his philanthropic gesture to pay for the construction of a new library in the growing town. In appreciation, county leaders voted to build new schools with Berrien timber, and voters elected Britt to the Georgia Legislature. In between, Britt hemmed his way deeper into the commerce of the community, establishing hardware and farm supply businesses that prospered like all the other Berrien ventures, until the family wealth multiplied with almost every cash exchange in the community.

By then, with his parents dead and no siblings to share the wealth, the family fortune belonged entirely to Britt. So he set out to acquire a family.

He began by building the family home, erecting a three-story mansion in the middle of the oak grove where the Berrien fortune had resided during the Civil War. He spared no expense on the house, importing the finest construction materials and hiring the best architects, builders and landscapers. The house contained six spacious bedrooms, a sitting parlor and formal living room, a library and sewing room, an eat-in dining room and formal ballroom, and an enormous kitchen with two pantries. There were Greek archways and tapestries on the walls, an expansive marble staircase swirling up three flights and elegant chandeliers hanging from the ceilings.

The grounds mirrored the magnificence of the house, which was designed to accommodate the natural beauty of the site. Sitting in the middle of a lush three-acre carpet of grass, the house was framed on its right side by a majestic live oak that anchored the grove of trees swirling away in all directions on the backside. The left side and front of the house were free to soak up the sunlight, spaciously landscaped with flower gardens and dotted sparsely with hardwoods. The guest cottage set off the left corner of the entrance lane, where the road split into a circular drive around the house.

In his thirtieth year, when the house was ready to be decorated, Britt made his annual pilgrimage to Atlanta to represent his constituents in the Legislature and, in the course of duty, plucked up one of the city's leading debutantes as his bride. Britt simply swept young Alice McMillian off her pretty feet. After a brief courtship, they married in a grand ceremony at the First Baptist Church on Peachtree Street and then whisked away to a month-long honeymoon at The Cloisters on Sea Island, followed by a two-month tour of Europe to satisfy a lifelong desire of the new bride.

When the honeymoon was officially over, Britt carried Alice back to Cookville and installed her as the lady of his grand house. Two days shy of their first anniversary, Alice gave birth to the first of two daughters. They named the child April. Two years later when their second daughter was born, she likewise was christened for the month of her birth, June.

Alice McMillian Berrien played the role of doting wife to a Southern aristocrat with skilled perfection. She opened her heart and home to the backwater community, throwing fabulous parties, organizing hunting expeditions, creating an atmosphere of dignity and respect. Invitations to these grand parties and vaunted hunts became highly sought prizes, with governors, congressmen and diplomats dancing in the elegant ballroom, sipping expensive wines and feasting on the most succulent foods.

In those first years of marriage, Britt and Alice combined deep affection for one another with a sense for style to create a state of wedded bliss. They enjoyed each other's company and found common ground in the care of their two young daughters. Then, for whatever reasons, they drifted apart as their daughters grew older. Alice tired of the constant entertaining, while Britt threw himself deeper into the pursuit of fortune. It was both shocking and pleasantly surprising when Alice Berrien became pregnant for a third time late in life.

April and June were away at college, and Britt had high hopes the new baby would restore zest to the marriage. It was not to be. The pregnancy proved torturous for Alice, and she died shortly after giving birth to Paul, the son Britt had wanted so badly.

Everyone grieved over the loss of the splendid woman, but they took solace from little Paul. There would be a man to carry on the family name.

With their mother dead, April and June abandoned their gay college life at the University of Georgia and returned home to care for their newborn brother. After a proper period of mourning, the Berriens once again opened the doors to their home and resumed the festive lifestyle that Alice had pioneered with sophisticated elegance.

April and June tried valiantly to return a halo of greatness to the Berrien mansion, but their mother's ghost doomed the effort. The luster was diminished, and the Berrien sisters simply lacked the polish necessary to restore it. Matters were not helped any by their father, who became abrasive, reclusive and more domineering than ever of his family, and increasingly ruthless in his business dealings.

Neither April nor June were beautiful like their parents, but a fair share of suitors called on both women. In turn, Britt rejected each and every one, some with calculated indifference, others more rudely. He seemed determined that his daughters would spend their youth locked inside the beautiful house, caring for the child whose life had exacted such a heavy price from the family.

April and June harbored no resentment toward Paul. They loved their brother, caring for him as if he was their own child, protecting and nourishing the little boy with tender hearts and patient skills. Mutual bonds of devotion developed between the siblings over the years as they dwelled under the heavy hand of Britt Berrien. But in her twenty-eighth year, June grew weary of the isolation.

Headstrong and smart, June stood up to her father, informing Britt that she could no longer tolerate the life of the idle rich. Against her father's wishes, she obtained a teaching position at New River Elementary School, where she met Calvin Moore. He was a robust man, six years her junior, who taught history and science to the upper grade students, and passion and romance to June. They fell in love and Calvin asked June to marry him at the end of the school term. Britt was livid when June announced her engagement. He condemned Calvin as a money-grubber in search of a quick fortune and vowed to disown his youngest daughter if she went through with the wedding.

June thumbed her nose, defying her father once more, and married the man she loved. They rented a tiny house in Cookville and lived happily off the poor salaries of schoolteachers. She and

Calvin had three wonderful years together before one fall night, after working late at school, Calvin drove his car off the sharp curve below the Carter Mercantile. The car slammed into a pine tree and burst into flames. By the time a passerby came upon the wreckage, Calvin had crawled from the car. But he was burned severely and died before help could be summoned.

June was shattered by the loss of her beloved, and Britt immediately pulled his daughter back under the protective family wing. He resigned her teaching position, renewed her maiden name and sent her to an Atlanta sanitarium to recuperate from the shock. June returned home a few months later, resigned to her fate, fully devoted once more to her family, and contented with positions in social clubs and occasional stints as a substitute teacher.

April also rebelled against her father. She married on a whim to a traveling encyclopedia salesman, a man who did indeed see her as an opportunity to gain a fortune. It happened at the beginning of the Great Depression, and the marriage lasted only a few weeks before April realized her mistake. Embarrassed by her poor judgment but not enough to spend her life with the miserable man, April sought her father's help to have the union annulled. The ensuing gossip had lasted slightly longer than the marriage. Now few people remembered the man.

By the time the Great Depression took hold, gloom hung as heavy over the Berrien home as it did on Wall Street. The festivities and frivolity that once had transformed the house into a beacon for the socially prominent were retired to a bygone day and in their place, arose a prim and proper politeness. In time, the world began to think of the Berriens as reclusive and standoffish.

It was his friendship with Paul that allowed Matt into the house where others seldom went in those days.

On a muggy evening in August 1941, Matt came to the mansion in search of his friend. Unable to summon anyone to the front door, he strolled around back and came upon Britt Berrien. Britt was standing on the verandah, staring vacantly off into the darkened grove of ancient live oaks behind the house, oblivious to the visitor to his home.

The massive oaks—a few with crown spreads of more than one hundred fifty feet and trunks exceeding thirty feet in girth—provided a buffer between the house and the gentle-flowing New River. The back of the mansion—antebellum in style with six towering Greek pillars and a balcony, painted dazzling white with black shutters—contrasted sharply with the graceful lines and red brick facades on the front and sides of the house.

It was about eight o'clock when Matt arrived, and a full moon bathed the grounds. Matt noticed a half-empty bottle of Scotch on the porch railing, and ice rattled in a glass, which the old man lifted to his mouth and drank from greedily. A chill ran through Matt that not even the hot evening could warm.

It had been a brutally hot day, the kind that made dust lazy and baked the countryside to a point where even nightfall failed to bring cool relief. Crickets chirped wearily, a whippoorwill cried its lonesome tune in the distance and fireflies darted beneath the canopy of towering oaks, streaking the evening with their reddish glow.

Matt stood perfectly still for a moment.

Ice clinked again as Britt drank deeply once more, then set the empty glass beside the Scotch bottle. The old man unbuttoned his shirt, a clumsy attempt to seek relief from the heat, and Matt realized Britt had consumed more liquor than usual. He turned away, intent on leaving, but Britt sensed the movement.

"Who's there?" he demanded to know, bracing a hand on the porch rail to steady himself. "What do you want?"

Matt detected a slur in the questioning voice, concluding with certainty that Britt was drunk. "It's just me, Mr. Berrien—Matt Baker," he answered. "I stopped by to see Paul. Didn't mean to disturb you."

"Oh," Britt mumbled. "Paul's not here, Matt. He went with April and June to prayer meeten over at the church." He paused, then exhaled a short bitter laugh. "Imagine that," he muttered with a touch of sarcasm. "Prayer meeten. I don't have much use for prayer meeten myself. Matter of fact, I don't have much use for church at all."

Britt had not always held such a low opinion of church. He and Alice had attended Benevolence Missionary Baptist Church faithfully until she died. But after her death, Britt's church appearances became increasingly rare until he finally stopped attending. Still, he insisted April and June attend Sunday services, and he made sure Paul accompanied them. Although his absence puzzled the congregation, church members consoled themselves with the gratitude that his contribution to the collection plate remained intact.

"How do you regard church?" Britt asked a moment later.

"Can't say I have anything against it," Matt answered quickly, stepping to the edge of the verandah. "I try to make Sunday services. That keeps Ma happy."

"Yes, indeed," Britt replied, forcing a laugh. "Children must keep their parents happy."

He picked up the Scotch bottle, then stumbled across the porch, fell into a wicker rocking chair and motioned Matt to sit in a duplicate rocker beside him.

Matt wasn't sure whether he felt compelled to accept the invitation or just downright curious to see where the unexpected encounter would lead. Regardless, he covered the distance across the verandah and took a place in the comfortable rocker.

"Would you like a drink?" Britt inquired, offering the bottle of Scotch. "I'm out of glasses and ice, but you're welcome to tip the bottle."

Though partial to Scotch, having sampled it with Paul on several occasions, Matt shook his head. "No, sir—none for me."

Britt frowned, then withdrew the bottle. "Well, I'm goen to have another one," he decided, pouring the tumbler half full of liquor.

Sweat glistened on the glass, and the warm liquor melted the last shivers of ice as it ran into the tumbler. Britt sipped from the glass, and some of the Scotch spilled over the rim, dripping onto his chin while watery beads from the glass trickled down his chest.

Matt turned away in disgust, frowning over his decision to stay, fixing his gaze straight ahead into the monolithic grove of oak trees. The whippoorwill was still calling its lonesome song in the distance. Somewhere closer by, an owl hooted an answer. Matt scanned the trees in search of the owl, and in that single moment, his perception of the Berriens changed forever.

"He's not really my son," Britt Berrien mumbled.

Matt shot his gaze over to the man beside him. "Sir?" he asked, certain he had misunderstood the intended message.

Britt glared back at Matt. "Paul is not my boy. I raised him, but he's not mine."

Britt looked away, dazed by his admission, once again seemingly oblivious of Matt.

"Maybe I should go, sir," Matt said after a moment, rising from the rocker. "I'd appreciate it if you'd tell Paul I stopped by to see him."

"Don't go!" Britt commanded, cutting his gaze to Matt. "I've just told you that Paul came from another man's loins. That's quite a secret to share, Matt. Give me the courtesy of hearen whatever else I might have to say about the situation."

His better judgment warned Matt to walk away from the drunken man and forget this moment. Curiosity again swayed him to stay. Matt sat down rigidly, his hands locked on the arms of the rocker. Then Britt told a story that had bound Matt to a secret only slightly less sacred than his marriage vows.

Britt explained to Matt that he had decided to marry Alice McMillian before falling in love with her. They met at a fashionable party in Atlanta, where he had gone purposefully in search of a wife. Alice had been the belle of the ball—a perky young woman schooled in the social graces, yet sarcastic enough toward her high society lifestyle to appeal to Britt's basic instincts. Britt cut in during the first dance, and they married a few months later.

"She was the genuine thing back then," Britt told Matt. "Unlike any woman I'd ever known, and quite a step up from the whores I saw. For the first time in my life, there was a person I felt at ease with, someone I didn't have to put on airs for. Hell, I couldn't even do that with my own mama and daddy."

As partners in marriage, Britt and Alice lived the high life for several years. Each grand party, every organized hunt, even the ladies' luncheons added another element to their happiness, and the birth of two adorable daughters raised the heights of marriage to yet another dimension. There should have been a fairy-tale ending to the story, but gradually, Britt and Alice became bored with the bliss. He reverted to his petulant self, she tired from the strain of trying. Within a few years, the couple had little in common beyond their children. For the sake of their daughters, Britt and Alice kept up appearances. But when first April and later June went away to college, their parents stopped pretending and retreated to their own worlds.

"We barely took meals together, much less shared a bed," Britt explained to Matt. "To say I was shocked when she told me of her pregnancy would be a gross understatement. I was positively stunned. I was fifty-three-years old, she was past forty and we slept together maybe once in a blue moon. After the shock wore off, however, I got excited about haven a new baby. I'd always wanted a son to carry on the family name, and somethen told me this baby would be my boy. I did my best to make Alice a part of my life again. But the more I tried, the colder she grew toward me. Finally, I chalked up her attitude to the pregnancy. She had a hard, hard time carryen Paul. She vomited constantly and when she wasn't throwen up her guts, she felt on the verge of it."

About a month before the baby was born, Britt returned home late one night and found his wife sprawled on the parlor floor. He first thought she was unconscious, rushing to her side only to spot an overturned bottle of bourbon beside the sofa. He smelled her breath, which reeked of alcohol, then promptly shook her awake. Groggy at first, Alice soon snapped to attention as Britt berated her.

In the midst of Britt's tirade, Alice grabbed the empty liquor bottle and hurled it at her husband. The bottle glanced off Britt's temple, then crashed and broke against a marble-topped table.

"I could have killed her at that moment," Britt told Matt in emotionless tones. "Just wrapped my hands around that delicate throat and choked the life out of her. But in a way, that knock on the head brought me back to my senses, made me realize somethen serious was wrong and Alice needed my help."

Britt forced down his anger, tried to reason with his wife and explained he was concerned for her well-being and their unborn child. "Maybe I haven't been a good husband," he told her patiently. "But I want to make you happy again, Alice. I want our baby very much. I'd like a son, but another girl would please me to no end."

His admission seemed to shock Alice back to her senses. She looked at him curiously. "This child really does matter to you?" she remarked questioningly.

"It means the world to me," Britt replied sincerely.

Alice smiled sweetly. "Well Britt," she said, speaking slowly. "I'm delighted to hear you feel such tenderness for this baby, especially when it isn't even yours. It's my fondest hope that you'll feel the same way as the child grows up under your protective care, with not even an ounce of precious Berrien blood coursen through its veins."

Britt glared at her, refusing to believe the admission. "What do you mean, Alice?" he demanded harshly.

"It's quite simple," she said flippantly. "Affairs, Britt, darlen. You didn't really think all that fun outside the marriage bed was yours exclusively, did you? I had myself one, too. A humdinger. And now

I'm haven another man's child. What about you, Britt? Do you have any bastard children that I should be aware of?"

Britt slapped her then, hard across the face, the force of the blow tumbling Alice across the floor.

"I started to beat her senseless," Britt told Matt, "but I'd never been the kind of man who hit women, certainly not one who was pregnant. And too, that one slap brought Alice back to her senses. She got scared then, realized she'd made the mistake of her life. She apologized, got right down on her hands and knees and begged my forgiveness." He paused, then added in a whisper, "But I didn't forgive her. Then or now."

Britt hesitated, remembering, collecting his thoughts, then took another drink, this time straight from the bottle.

"I was never an easy man," he continued. "But I never knew just how cruel I could be until that moment." He snorted, a bitter laugh. "I had this woman on her knees, beggen me for forgiveness, sayen I could have any woman I wanted whenever I wanted, promisen she'd be good, be at my beck and call. Just to please let her live out the rest of her days in peace, and she'd do anything I asked.

"It was pitiful," Britt sneered. "Truly pitiful. A disgrace to the way she was raised. But I promised anyway to raise her bastard as my child. And I made a vow that our daughters would never take up her whorish ways or become the despised woman she had become. Then I told her to pack her bags because as soon as she had the baby, I planned to send her to a sanitarium for a long stay.

"Just the slightest mention of a sanitarium sent her over the edge," Britt recalled, now speaking in monotone. "Alice had an aunt who was sent away to some mental hospital, where she went from be'en merely loony to crazy as a bat. That the same thing might happen to her was Alice's worst fear comen true."

With his pregnant wife collapsed in a heap in the middle of the parlor floor, Britt simply walked away from Alice and retired to his room. Over the next few weeks, Alice tried to atone for her mistakes, but Britt rebuffed his wife. He continued dropping cruel hints about a sanitarium, going so far as to falsify a court order committing Alice to the state hospital in Milledgeville. He presented the document to her along with breakfast in bed one morning a few weeks before the baby was due; Alice went into labor a short time later.

The labor was tortuous, life-threatening, a sharp contrast to the ease of her first two deliveries. But Alice gave birth to a perfectly healthy son, which the doctor presented to Britt as "a chip off the old block." Sometime later that night, Alice Berrien began to hemorrhage. By morning, she was dead.

"I should have felt *somethen* when Alice died," Britt told Matt in a wistful tone. "But really I didn't. Unless maybe it was for the best. I don't think I would have sent her to a sanitarium, although she was surely certifiable. But it would have been almost impossible to live with her.

"Anyway, I raised Paul as my son. Promised I would, and I did. It's not his fault he's a bastard—and I'm proud of him in a way, even though he's soft just like his real father was."

Britt hesitated, then laughed contemptuously. "It's ironic, though," he commented. "Paul believes I resent him because his mother died given birth to him." He shook his head, marveling at the thought. "He truly believes I loved her that much."

Britt leaned forward in the chair and shook away this last thought. "My daughters are very much like their mother was when I first met her," he remarked proudly. "They are kind and gentle and sympathetic. Happy souls." He paused to ponder. "But they are not innocent," he continued in a sad tone. "I made them anything but innocent. Made sure the children paid for the sins of the parents."

Exhausted, Britt stood, shuffled forward to the porch edge and leaned against one of the massive white columns, staring up at the white moon hanging low over the oak grove.

Matt rose as well, crossed slowly to the end of the verandah and stopped, sensing something else must be said on this night.

"Matt, you be a good friend to Paul," Britt added quietly, still gazing up into the nighttime sky. "He needs good friends."

Matt nodded in silent agreement, but his answer went unacknowledged. He walked away from the house, carrying with him the one secret he would never share with anyone, leaving behind its teller, a man who continued to stare into the darkness for many nights to come.

———————

Matt heard Caroline call his name and roused himself from the battered recliner. He crossed the living room to stand beside the space heater, soaking up the warmth, thinking of another secret involving Britt Berrien.

Matt had taken this second secret into confidence seven years ago, on the cold night that Britt stuck a pistol into his mouth and pulled the trigger.

Paul had found the body, stiff from rigor mortis, still sitting in the white wicker rocker on the verandah. He had sought out Matt a short time later, and they had calmly, carefully, taken every possible step to conceal the cause of the death. They had loaded the body into the back of Matt's pickup, scrubbed away the blood stains on the verandah and dumped the ruined rocker into the depths of New River.

Next, Paul had placed a call to an old friend, Arch Adams, the county coroner and owner of the local funeral home. Reluctant to go along with the scheme at first, Arch finally agreed to rule the death a heart attack, falling prey to Paul's persuasive argument to spare his sisters the trauma of knowing their father had committed suicide.

The three conspirators had guarded the secret closely over the years, but ultimately, they had been powerless to conceal the true nature of Britt's death. Now everyone knew. And with the knowledge came stained reputations and painful reconciliation with the past. Still, they had all survived the accusations, outlasted the innuendo and perhaps learned a lesson as well.

Of course, Matt himself carried another secret from that night, the final thoughts of Britt Berrien, which the man had entered into one of the leather-bound journals a short time before taking his own life. Matt had found the book in the grass beside the verandah. Those last two pages had contained a soulless account of the circumstances surrounding Paul's birth and Alice's death. The words made for harsh reading, and, at the time, Matt had deemed it pointless to expose his friends to anymore unnecessary pain. Uncharacteristically, he had taken it upon himself to shield his friends from the truth, ripping out the last two pages and returning the journal to Britt's study. The next morning, in the comfort of his own home, with Caroline and Rachel preparing breakfast, while Sam sat at the table reminiscing about their dead neighbor, Matt had stood in front of the kitchen fireplace with his back to them and tossed those two pages into the roaring fire.

He and Paul had never talked about that night. And Matt had discussed it with Caroline, his parents and the children only once, back in the summer when circumstances compelled him to give them answers to the gaggle of questions that cropped up in the heat of the moment. They had listened to his explanation, believed him and put the incident in the past where it surely belonged.

From time to time, Matt questioned the wisdom of his decision to conceal Britt's last words, fretting he had overstepped the bounds of friendship with censorship of the truth. Occasionally, he even wondered whether Paul somehow knew the truth about his heritage. But when those moments occurred, Matt tried to follow the sage advice of his mother and leave the past in the past, which was what he did now as Caroline called him again to join his family in the kitchen.

He stepped away from the heater, warmed to the bone, and went into the kitchen, where the delicious smells of fresh baking assaulted his senses.

The kitchen table was covered with an assortment of merry Christmas cookies, smelling of cinnamon, oatmeal and peanut butter, shaped as wreaths, bells, stockings, Christmas trees, reindeer and Santa Clauses. There were plates of molasses cookies and gingerbread men, along with a tray of frosted, nut-filled bonbons.

Matt stood at the door, inhaling the aroma, basking in a moment of fulfillment. Summer handed him a gingerbread man, and Matt bit into the spicy brown bread, savoring every mouth-watering morsel. He rubbed his stomach to show his appreciation, then began a round of sampling. Eventually, he made his way to the side of the kitchen where Caroline was beating a bowl of cookie batter.

"I'm in my element here," she told him.

Matt nodded in agreement, wrapping his arms around her waist, kissing the nape of her neck and pressing against her. "Tonight," he whispered, as his wife pushed gently back against him.

# CHAPTER 5

JOE RESTED AGAINST A stack of empty burlap bags in the pecan barn, vaguely aware of the dull ache in his knee. He supposed he had overworked the leg, but the thought, like the pain, was not at the center of his mind. He watched intently as his grandfather scribbled calculations on a notepad, waiting for the deal that Sam would offer.

Outside, the rear of the pickup sagged under the weight of the pecans, sacked and bound for the trip to Levine's Pecan Warehouse in Albany. Joe, Lucas and Tom had loaded the pecans and the trio would make the journey—Lucas to drive, Joe to negotiate the sale and Tom to offer support. Once the pecans were loaded and Sam began his calculations, Lucas and Tom had retreated outside to allow the dealmakers privacy. Joe could hear them talking, though, and he knew they were eager to be on the way to Albany. So was he.

Joe saw this venture as an opportunity to prove—if not his manhood—then his capability. And while money rarely mattered to him, he needed the cash as well.

Sam cleared his throat, circling three figures on the paper. He fiddled with his eye patch and looked at Joe. "Here's the deal," he announced as Joe straightened and pushed away from the burlap stack.

"I need twenty-five cents a pound to cover my expenses and make a slight profit on the side," Sam said briskly. "These nuts ought to sell for at least twenty-eight or twenty-nine cents a pound. My offer is that we split fifty-fifty anything above twenty-five cents. Anything you sell above twenty-nine cents is all yours."

Joe ran a set of calculations in his head, deducing he should earn a minimum of forty-eight dollars from the deal if the pecans sold for twenty-nine cents a pound.

"You also pay Lucas for his time," Sam added.

"How much is that?" Joe asked.

"Your daddy pays him seven dollars a day," Sam answered,

pausing to watch Joe rub his jaw and mull over the offer. "Fair enough?" he finally questioned.

Joe stuck out his hand, smiling broadly. "Deal," he answered as they shook hands. "And thanks, Grandpa."

---

It was a ninety-minute trip to Albany in the pickup, and the warehouse was packed with sellers when they arrived. "Everybody wants some Christmas jingle," observed Lucas, watching as young and old alike stood in line with various shapes of buckets, pails and sacks waiting to have their pecans weighed.

Joe, who was using the crutches to ease the pressure on his knee, took a place in line, watching as the warehousemen weighed pecans and dumped the nuts in various bins marked for improved varieties and seedlings. Other workers bagged and tied one-hundred-pound sacks of pecans, which were stacked to the rafters in piles across the warehouse floor. In a nearby corner, four machines worked methodically cracking the nuts. His attention glued to the commotion, Joe failed to hear the first summons for his pecans until, finally, the warehouseman tugged on his crutch.

"Hey, buddy, I ain't got all day, and neither do all those folks behind you."

Joe turned to find the speaker was a sandy-haired boy not much older than himself.

"So?" the boy pressed impatiently, sneering. "You got any nuts or not?"

A few feet away, Lucas and Tom snickered at the remark's snide implications. Joe shot them a withering glance, then turned to the business at hand. "Yeah," he said lazily. "I got a ton's worth. Probably more."

A quick retort appeared on the worker's lips, but he flashed a grin instead, slapped Joe on the shoulder and whistled down two co-workers to unload the pickup. "It's been a long day, buddy," he remarked to Joe. "You'll need to see Mr. Levine personally with a load like that."

"Where do I find him?"

"Over yonder," the boy said, pointing to a corner door.

A few minutes later Joe was standing with Joel Levine, a rotund man about the same age as Sam. Levine was bald, about two inches taller than Joe, with a pleasant demeanor and a booming voice. He exchanged greetings with Joe, then began inspecting the pecans, examining nuts from several bags, using a pair of massive hands to crush open the hard shells and sample the meat.

"I'll give you twenty-seven cents a pound," Levine declared.

Joe had come prepared to barter, and he quickly dismissed the offer. "Sir, I might consider twenty-seven cents if these were seedlings," he replied smoothly, "but these nuts are pure Stuart. I was expecten thirty-three cents."

"Thirty-three!"

"I'm willen to negotiate," Joe announced.

"Twenty-eight cents," Levine snapped.

"Maybe thirty-two," Joe said reluctantly. "These are quality nuts, Mr. Levine. They're heavy and they're tasty."

The pecan broker seemed to reconsider. He reached in a bag, pulled out two more nuts and cracked them against each other, producing a perfectly shaped morsel of brownish red meat from the shell. "They are tasty," he admitted. "Okay, son, I'll give you twenty-nine cents for them."

"Thirty-one and a half," Joe said firmly.

"Thirty," the pecan dealer snapped back impatiently.

"I can get thirty-one and half, probably more in Florida," Joe shot back.

"It's a long way from here to Florida, son, and you're gonna have to go down as far as Orlando or Ocala before you get much more than thirty-one cents a pound," Levine replied formally. Joe stood stiffly, afraid the portly businessman was about to call his bluff. "But I like your spunk, boy, so I'll pay your price. Come inside my office. We'll tally up and write you a check."

Joe took a deep breath. "I need part of it in cash," he said quickly.

Levine nodded. "I figured as much," he mumbled.

---

A short time later, Joe emerged from Joel Levine's cluttered office with a fat check for his grandfather and one hundred eight dollars in cold cash for himself. He whistled a jolly tune. And was frozen in his tracks by a voice, melodiously savage and dripping with animosity.

"I don't know where you come from, boy, but 'round here, niggers know their place. And we kick the asses of those that don't."

Ahead, a crowd of men gathered in a semi-circle around Lucas and Tom. The voice belonged to a barrel-chested, evil-eyed bully, a sawed-off shotgun whose lifelong destiny was to prove that his tough attitude made up for his short stature. He stood a few feet from Lucas, stretched to full height and glaring at the black man. Beside him stood another paragon of brawn and menace, this one packaged head and shoulders taller than his short companion.

Joe quickly sized up the two men as the chief troublemakers, but the crowd had a lynch-mob mentality. A shattered soda bottle and its spilt contents lay on the concrete floor between Lucas and the troublemakers.

The short man edged closer to Lucas, who stood motionless, knowing any move toward a defensive posture was tantamount to throwing the first punch as well as an exercise in futility given the odds of a fight.

"Your ass is ours, boy," he spat at Lucas.

"You ever seen black turn blue," the tall one growled.

A thin sheen of sweat broke across Lucas' forehead, Tom took an unconscious half step backward and Joe appeared between them like a ghost, unannounced and unexpected.

Joe stepped forward, brandishing his left crutch as a protective guard between Lucas and the two troublemakers. "If you mess with him, you'll have to go through me," he said evenly. "And him, too," he added, pointing the other crutch at the bewildered Tom, who again made another unconscious movement, this time forward.

The moment froze as the two men comprehended the turn of events. Finally, Shorty grunted. "Oh, Lord," he muttered in disbelief. "We've got us a crippled white boy full of righteous indignation." He looked at his tall companion. "Whataya make of it, Perry?"

"The boy must be a nigger lover, Bert," replied Perry. "Plain and simple."

"That true, crip?" Bert asked Joe. "Are you a nigger lover?"

"I'm a friend," Joe said firmly.

The short Bert shook his head, cursing under his breath. "Well, friend," he said sarcastically. "This ain't got nothen to do with you. We want the nigger."

Joe dropped the crutch in his left hand, the wooden brace clattering on the floor of the silent warehouse as he brandished the other crutch as a weapon. "Like I said," he replied stiffly, "if it's got somethen to do with one of us, it's got somethen to do with all of us because we're here together."

Bert stood an inch shorter than Joe, but likely could have ripped him apart with his bare hands. The shorter man cursed. "Stand aside, boy, or you're liable to get hurt," he snapped impatiently.

"Maybe so," Joe shrugged calmly. "But I'll get a lick or two in first."

A test of patience began, carried out over brittle silence. Joe and Bert glared at each other; Lucas stood with his arms by his sides, the original source of animosity now the forgotten man in this fight; and Tom stared with glazed eyes.

Bert made a slight move, a disbelieving shrug more or less, and Joe choked on his weapon. The hair on his neck straightened, his heart pounded and he came alive with animal instincts. He waited breathlessly for the next move, which came pregnant seconds later, with ear-splitting ferocity in the form of Joel Levine's booming voice.

"What in tarnation is goen on here?" the pecan broker demanded to know.

Levine moved with lightning speed despite his rotund shape. He charged between Joe and Bert like a bull picking a target. His fat neck strained against the collar of a heavily starched shirt, and his flabby jowls bristled as he came to a skidding halt in the middle of the shattered soda bottle. His hard-soled shoes crunched against the broken glass. He cast an indignant look downward, then kicked away the offending glass.

"Somebody better start talken!" he declared violently.

"Aw shucks, Joel," Perry muttered, hunching over his tall form. "Just a little friendly disagreement. Nothen for you to fret over."

"I don't fret," Levine growled, glaring at the taller of the two troublemakers. Finally, he turned his black scowl to Bert. "What kind of disagreement you got with these boys?" he asked the shorter man.

The stocky Bert pointed a fat finger at Lucas. "This nigger stepped out of line," he said contemptuously before flipping his finger to Joe. "And when we tried to put him back in place, this one got all riled up and righteous." Bert shook his head and searched for words. "Another self-righteous, nigger-loven kid," he hissed finally. "Ain't that just what the world needs."

"I couldn't care less what the world needs," Levine snorted, "but I don't tolerate these kinds of shenanigans in my warehouse." He looked from Lucas to Tom before fixing a stern gaze on Joe. "Boy," he said. "You're Sam Baker's grandson, ain't you?"

"Yes, sir," Joe answered. "How'd you know that?"

Joel Levine ignored the question and turned his fury back on Bert and Perry as Joe allowed his crutch to fall back into its rightful place.

"Listen up and listen good," Levine shouted. "This is my place of business. I treat my customers with the respect they deserve and I expect the same from them." He put a hand on his hip. "I don't know what happened here, I don't care what happened. But Bert, Perry, these people belong to one of my best suppliers. I can't imagine it's in their character to start a fuss. Even if they did, though, my warehouse ain't the place to settle it. Now, men, I want you to get your butts out of here and let these people finish their business. And if you plan on bringen an attitude back next time you come, don't bother comen. It ain't welcome here."

"Jesus, Joel," Bert grumbled.

"We're goen," Perry said contritely.

"Yeah, we're goen all right," Bert sneered. He turned slightly, then seemed to reconsider and pointed a finger once more at Joe. "Better watch your back, boy," he warned quickly. "You, too, darkie," he added, nodding at Lucas.

"Go!" bellowed Levine in a voice that shook the warehouse rafters, causing a sweet old lady to drop a pail full of nuts and sending Bert and Perry scurrying out the door without another backward glance.

"Idle threats," Levine said when the troublemakers were gone. "They're basically good old boys with short memories. They won't be bothern you anymore."

"Maybe not," Lucas mused. "But I'll feel better when we're out of this county and closer to home."

"That's where y'all oughtta be headed," Levine agreed. "It's a long drive home for you boys. Y'all best be getten to it."

He started to move away, barking orders for someone to clean up the mess of broken glass and spilt soda. "Sorry, ma'am," he said to the elderly woman, who was stooped over picking up her scattered pecans. "Vernon!" he yelled to the sandy-haired youth who had assisted Joe at the weigh-in. "Get over here and help pick up these nuts."

"Wait a second, Mr. Levine," Joe said suddenly amid the furor.

Unaccustomed to taking orders, Joel Levine stopped in his tracks, glancing back at Joe. "Y'all still here," he said reproachfully.

"How did you know who I was?" Joe asked for the second time.

Levine considered the question. "Your grandpa gave me a call this mornen and said you'd be comen my way."

"Why?" Joe asked curiously.

"He just wanted to make sure I knew who you were, so there'd be no misunderstanden between us in case we had trouble reachen a fair deal," the pecan broker answered.

Joe shook his head in disbelief. "You discussed our deal?"

"Sure we did," Levine replied. "That's a big load of nuts you were sellen. It was worth a lot of money."

Joe rubbed the back of his head, putting two and two together and coming up with betrayal at his grandfather's hands. He felt cheated of a chance at manhood. He had thought he did an outstanding job of bargaining, permitting himself a good measure of pride as the pecan dealer's secretary wrote out the check for Sam and counted out the cash for Joe. Now he felt played like a fool. "If you made a deal with my grandfather, sir," he said bitterly, "then what was the point of all that hagglen between us? Seems to me you could have saved both of us a lot of time."

"Whoa there," Levine interrupted. "I'm not gonna lie to you, son. Your grandpa and me did talk price. But you and I struck a deal fair and square."

"What if I'd accepted your first offer?" Joe asked. "Twenty-seven cents ... I believe that's what you said. I know my grandpa said not to take anything less than twenty-eight."

"I would ... I would've," the older man stammered. Finally, he inhaled uncomfortably. "Listen, son," he smiled faintly. "All I can say is that you and I struck a deal fair and square and it was a bargain different than the one I made with your grandfather. Now if that answer don't satisfy you, then I'm sorry. But you're gonna have to get Sam to fill in the particulars." He shrugged. "Now I've got business to tend to, and you've got a long drive home," he said pleasantly. "Let's both be getten to it. Okay?"

A muscle twitched in Joe's cheek, registering his displeasure, but he nodded agreement. "Sure enough," he mumbled.

---

Tom and Lucas were silent on the trip home, partly out of respect for the embarrassing discovery Joe had made about the prearranged deal between Sam and Joel Levine and partly to process the tension of the unexpected events.

Lucas kept his eyes peeled on the rearview mirror, ever mindful of the parting threat the burly Bert had heaved their way. But nothing happened: No speeding cars appeared behind them; no roadblocks sprang up before them. Gradually, he relaxed as the pickup cruised along U.S. Highway 82, passing out of Dougherty County and easing through the town of Sylvester.

"Quite a day," Tom finally remarked as the truck idled at a traffic light.

Joe shrugged and continued to stare out the side window. "I'd say that's putten it mildly," he said dryly.

The light turned green and Lucas eased across the intersection, gaining speed as the truck cleared the city limit signs and headed once more for open road.

Though still fuming over the treachery of his grandfather, Joe decided to put aside his frustration rather than spoil the journey by pouting. "What in the heck happened back there anyway?" he inquired.

"A little accident," Tom suggested.

"It was kinda my fault," Lucas contended.

Tom shook his head. "Not really, Lucas. I saw the whole thing, and he wasn't watchen where he was goen anymore than you were."

Joe waved a hand to quiet his friends. "I still don't know what happened," he said.

"We were on our way to the truck," Lucas explained. "I heard Tom call my name, turned around to see what he wanted and the next thing I knew ran slam-bang, head-on into that short white man."

"That was Bert," Tom interjected, taking over the story. "He had just bought a cold drink, and he dropped it when they ran into each other. Coke and glass everywhere. Anyway, he got all huffed up and started cussen Lucas."

"Told him I was sorry, and I was," Lucas said apologetically. "But he didn't seem to care."

"Next thing you know, the tall one, Perry, was over there tellen Lucas to buy his friend another drink, maken all kinds of threats and asken where Lucas came from," Tom continued quickly. "That got Bert all the more excited. He started toward Lucas and then ...." Tom paused. "And then you came gallopen to the rescue, Joe."

"I wouldn't say I galloped," Joe replied with a modest smile.

"You were pretty impressive," Tom said respectfully.

"Shore enough was," Lucas agreed wholeheartedly. "That was some stand you made back there, Joe-Joe." He hesitated for a second. "But you best be careful 'bout taken up for a nigger, 'cause it usually means trouble."

Joe frowned. "It never crossed my mind that I was taken up for a Negro," he replied testily. "I thought I was just helpen out a friend."

"Well, whatever," Lucas said. "Those were some fine fighten words. You probably saved my butt, Joe-Joe, and I appreciate it."

Joe stared down into his lap. "Good grief, Lucas," he grumbled. "It wasn't that big a deal."

"Well, I thought it was," Tom persisted, "especially for a cripple with a crutch. There I was," he said excitedly, "scared to death and ready to pee in my pants. Then all of a sudden, here comes Joe, waven crutches every which way and tellen those overgrown apes they've got to go through him and me to get to Lucas." Tom sighed. "I do believe, Joe, that this beats all those stories about Grandpa and how he lost that eye. It's purely legendary, Joe, purely legendary."

He hesitated, glancing at Lucas. "Of course, Lucas," he added drolly, "I don't mind tellen you now that I feared for your life the whole time. Those boys were big and mean. And if they'd've taken a notion, I expect they could've wrapped those crutches around our necks."

"Nothen like a little two-edged flattery to keep me in my place," Joe commented, cocking an eyebrow at his younger friend. "Huh, Tom?"

"I'll keep that bit of information between the three of us," Tom promised. "After everybody hears about this, they'll think we're the Three Musketeers or somethen."

"Your daddy'll be proud of you, Joe," Lucas said sincerely. "Just like I was."

Joe acknowledged the compliments with a modest grin that changed almost instantly into a grimace. "Hey, boys," he said worriedly. "How 'bout we keep what happened to ourselves? Mama and Daddy find out about this, and I'm liable to be twenty-one before they let me out on my own again. Whataya say?"

Both Tom and Lucas frowned.

"I don't know Joe-Joe," Lucas fretted. "This ain't the kind of thing we should keep from your daddy and mama. They find out what happened, and they'll be plenty mad at me for keepen it from 'em."

"Come on, Lucas," Joe pleaded. "Nobody's gonna find out if we don't tell. There's no harm done. And besides, we'd just end up worryen Mama."

Lucas considered the request for several minutes. Too often these days he had to choose between responsibility and friendship when it came to Joe and Tom, and he detested such situations. He was nine years older than Joe, thirteen years younger than the boy's father, and, like his age, his loyalties belonged somewhere in the middle. He weighed the current situation, balancing Joe's request against Matt's expectations and came up with an answer. "It's against my better judgment, Joe-Joe, but I won't tell your daddy," he said reluctantly. "We should, though. I don't like keepen secrets from him."

"Thanks, Lucas," Joe replied.

Tom released a heavy sigh. "All I can say is it's the loss of a great story," he lamented, shaking his head from side to side. "Truly legendary and nobody's never gonna know it."

"Truly, Tom," Joe muttered, "it's a story the world can live without."

---

They arrived home in the shank of the afternoon to a busy household caught up in the throes of cooking, cleaning and chores. Tom and Lucas took one look at the commotion and fled to their respective homes, seeking a peaceful end to a hectic day.

Joe had no such opportunity, so he did the next best thing, volunteering for a solo performance of the evening milking and feeding-up duties he usually shared with his father. First though, the boy was obliged to tell everyone about his big day. Reluctantly, he delivered a terse description of the deal struck with Joel Levine and presented the check to his grandfather.

"That's a good deal you made, son," Matt told him when Joe had finished. "I'm proud of you."

Joe looked down at his feet, feeling foolish. "It was pretty much a sure shot, Daddy," he replied politely. He looked at his grandfather, who was standing beside the kitchen fireplace. "Actually, you could say it was a gimme, and to tell you the truth I don't feel right about taken the money. It really belongs to Grandpa."

Sam shook his head, disagreeing with his grandson. "Now why would you say that?" he asked cautiously. "We made a deal, Joe, and you kept your end of the bargain by taken care of business for me. That money in your pocket is my end of the deal."

Joe pulled the money from the pocket of his blue jeans, placing it on the kitchen table. "It's all there," he told Sam. "Except the seven dollars I paid Lucas."

"That money belongs to you, Joe," Sam persisted. "We made a deal."

"Maybe you made it too easy for me to keep my end of the deal, Grandpa," Joe hinted quietly, keenly aware of the curious eyes and ears of his family. He shrugged, disengaging himself from the conversation, put a cap on his head and laid aside the crutches. "I'm goen to feed up now," he announced, hobbling out the kitchen door.

"What was that all about?" Matt asked when the door closed behind his oldest son.

Sam bit the corner of his lip, suspecting Joe had learned about the preliminary discussions between him and Levine. "I have an idea," he replied reassuringly before finding his jacket, pocketing the money and following Joe out the door.

He found the boy in the barn. Joe was filling a tub with feed pellets and sweet hay, while uttering low throaty sounds of comfort to the cow, Brindy, who was impatient for her feeding and milking. Joe heard the approaching footsteps, glanced up to see Sam and returned to his work.

"I suppose Levine told you that I called him and said you'd be comen his way," Sam began straightforwardly.

"He did."

Sam cleared his throat. "There's no reason to be upset, Joe," he said. "I simply thought it was a good idea for him to be expecten you."

Joe laughed shortly. "Today meant a lot to me, Grandpa," he said seriously. "I believed you had the confidence in me to do a job and I wanted to prove myself."

"I do have confidence in you," Sam pointed out.

Joe shook his head. "Grandpa, everything said between me and Mr. Levine was nothing but lip service," Joe complained. "I thought I was sent to do a job for you; I thought I did a good job. Turns out I was just played for a fool." He shook his head again. "Maybe I shouldn't be upset, but the truth of the matter is I am. I'll get over it, though, so let's just drop the subject and get on with whatever's next."

Joe sat on the wooden stool and began milking the cow, refusing to look at his grandfather. Sam sighed, deciding the boy needed time to cool his temper. "Maybe I made a mistake, Joe," he admitted regretfully, "but my heart was in the right place. Regardless, this money belongs to you. I'm leaving it on the gate post, and you do whatever you want with it."

Joe listened to his grandfather's departing steps with mixed emotions and a heavy heart. Later, on his way out of the barn, he plucked the money off the gatepost and shoved it back into the pocket of his jeans.

———

Lying in bed that night in the room he shared with his two brothers, who were asleep in the double bed across from him, Joe was about to doze off when someone tapped on the door.

"It's Grandpa," a familiar voice said.

"Come on in," Joe replied quietly.

Sam entered the dark room and sat beside Joe on the edge of the bed. "Seems like we have unfinished business," he offered.

"I suppose so," Joe agreed.

"Apparently, for reasons we both thought best, neither one of us was as forthright as we should have been today," Sam said thoughtfully.

Joe sat up against the headboard, bringing blankets with him to ward off the chill. He looked questioningly at his grandfather.

"I hear you ran into some trouble at the warehouse," Sam answered.

"Oh, that," Joe replied tiredly. "Who told you?"

"Lucas mentioned it this afternoon. Said he promised not to tell your daddy and you'd be ticked at him for tellen me, but he thought somebody ought to know what happened just in case." Sam paused. "He's right, you know."

Joe sighed. "Seems like this is my day for be'en told one thing when people mean another," he said gravely. "But Grandpa, you could have told me that you already had a deal worked out with Mr. Levine. If I had known up front where I stood, I wouldn't have any reason to be disappointed. Now I truly feel like a fool and that's far worse than just feelen like a boy sent to do a man's job."

"I suppose it is," Sam agreed philosophically. "But the truth of the matter, Joe, is that you came home with two and half cents more per pound than the price Levine and I agreed on up front."

Joe sat up straight in the bed. "I did?" he said doubtfully.

"You did," Sam assured him. "I only made sure Joel understood that those pecans were worth at least twenty-nine cents a pound. You did the rest, and from what he told me, you did a good job of negotiaten. Fact is, he said if it had been me he was dealen with, he'd wouldn't have gone any higher than thirty-one cents. But he figured it was worth the extra half-penny just to see somebody cut a better deal than I do."

Joe smiled faintly in the darkness. "You're just tryen to make me feel better, Grandpa," he accused.

Sam nodded, pleading guilty. "Course, I am," he replied affably. "I wouldn't be much of a grandpa if I didn't, now would I?"

Joe smiled agreement.

"But I'm tellen you the truth when I say Levine told me you drove a hard bargain," Sam continued. "Though he was none too pleased when you threatened to drive off to Florida for a better deal."

Joe grinned. "I think that cinched it," he gloated. "Other customers were close by, and I don't think he wanted them to hear the argument."

"No, I don't reckon he did," Sam agreed carefully. "But what would you have done if he'd told you to dig off for Florida?"

Joe considered the question, a possibility he had not thought of seriously in his negotiations with Joel Levine. Finally, he grinned again. "I imagine I'd have stooped to beggen and taken his lowest offer."

Sam laughed heartily. "I tell you what, Joe," he remarked

amicably. "To make amends for my lack of complete forthright-ness, I'm gonna keep what happened with Lucas to myself. Mind you, I think we oughtta tell your daddy and I'm against these kinds of secrets. But you acted like a man in defenden Lucas, and you deserve to be respected accordingly. If you prefer to keep it secret, then so be it."

"Thanks, Grandpa."

"Do you really believe me?" Sam asked.

Joe stretched and cracked his knuckles. "Well," he replied with genuine cheerfulness. "Save a few tall tales about dragons and pi-rates and pretty maidens in distress, you've been pretty truthful with me. I don't imagine I'll lose any sleep worryen whether you'll keep your word."

Sam ruffed his head, then hugged the boy and kissed him on the cheek. "You're a good boy, Joe, and you're maken a fine man. But remember, son, it takes time and a few mistakes along the way, plus a little help every now and then. And if you follow true to form in the steps of us Baker men, you'll have plenty of each."

Sam rose from the bed, stretching and yawning. "Of course," he continued with overstated enthusiasm. "Age is the downside to becomen a man. You get old, your heart gets leaky, you get the rheumatism." He sighed. "Enjoy your youth, Joe, 'cause you really do only have it once."

Joe smiled soberly, the concern coming through in his eyes, re-sembling the worried watch he had kept over Sam during his recuperation from the heart attack.

"Well that's enough philosophy and ranten from an old man for one night," Sam said lightheartedly, bestowing a reassuring smile on his grandson. "I'm off to keep your grandma warm. Sleep well, Joe."

"You, too, Grandpa."

# CHAPTER 6

CHRISTMAS EVE DAWNED COLD and gray. The leaden sky teased of snow, but the TV weatherman promised only rain mixed with sleet.

Caroline and Matt woke early, then lingered in bed to celebrate the dawning of their nineteenth wedding anniversary. After their lovemaking was finished, he held her as they reminisced about the past and pondered the future. When at last talk turned to the time at hand, they left the warm bed and began the new day with a sense of purpose and fulfillment.

Christmas Eve fell on Saturday that year, which in itself meant nothing unusual around the Baker household. Like any other day, it was marked with routines, meals to be made and chores to get done. But it was also a day steeped in tradition and no sooner was the last morsel of breakfast eaten than the family began adhering to their Christmas Eve rituals.

Mainly, the morning traditions focused on the kitchen, so Sam, Matt and the boys did everything possible to stay out of eyesight and earshot of the womenfolk. None succeeded completely. Sam had the misfortune of bringing in the ham from the smokehouse, an occasion for which his wife also roped him into assisting John with the task of churning butter. Matt made the mistake of mentioning he was going down the road to see Paul Berrien, and Caroline promptly shoved a coconut cake in his arms for delivery to Slaton and Florence Castleberry, the elderly couple whose farm backed up to the west side of the Baker place. Summer hunted down Joe and Luke to pass along orders from their mother to pick a mess of turnips from the field across the road.

Summer, Carrie and Bonnie were assigned the household chores, making beds, cleaning the bathroom, dusting furniture, sweeping and vacuuming.

In the kitchen, Caroline and Rachel worked like greased bakery equipment. Caroline cooked up two iron skillets of cornbread and a batch of biscuits, which she promptly set aside to dry out over the course of the day to become the substance of her cornbread dressing. Rachel put the hen on to boil and began preparing the pear tarts that consistently won high praise at church dinners.

By mid-morning, the kitchen was running in top gear at full speed and the menfolk were vanished from the place. Celery, onions and bell pepper were sliced, diced and sautéed; turnip greens and roots were minced, spiced with boiling meat and put on the stove to simmer for hours; Rachel's pear tarts joined her fruit cake in the pie safe, their place in the oven taken by pecan, pumpkin and sweet potato pies. Eggs boiled on the stove, a loaf of pumpkin bread batter waited for its turn in the oven and the aroma of Christmas cooking watered mouths.

When they felt sufficient progress had been made on Christmas dinner, Caroline and Rachel prepared the noon meal for their starving family. On this day, it was sandwiches made from a freshly boiled ham and the last of the hogshead cheese from the most recent butchering. Everyone ate their fill and complimented the cooks, but all minds were on the best part of the busy Christmas Eve day still to come—the afternoon trip to Tifton for last-minute shopping and fantasizing.

The Christmas Eve shopping trip had become a family tradition sometime between Matt's homecoming from the war and Summer's birth. Caroline thought it had arisen from a need to do some last-minute Santa Claus shopping for Joe. Matt swore it started the year he bought Caroline the two tall, fluted candlesticks that graced the sides of the French doors between the living and dining rooms. Rachel and Sam insisted the trips had begun out of necessity, to allow them to do their Christmas shopping, which probably was closest to the real reason.

For whatever reasons, Christmas Eve shopping seemed as much a part of the family's holiday rituals as the Christmas tree itself, especially to the children. None of them could ever remember a December twenty-fourth passing without the traditional trip to town, save those odd years when the day fell on Sunday and the stores were closed.

Early that afternoon, the whole family—scrubbed and bundled in their warmest clothes—packed into the big sedan and embarked on the sixteen-mile trip to Tifton, a town considerably larger than Cookville, located in the neighboring county. It was not an overstatement to say they were packed in the car like sardines in a can. Matt drove and Sam sat in the front seat holding Luke on his lap with John between them. Caroline, Rachel, Summer and Joe sat in the back, with Carrie on her mother's lap and Bonnie stretched across her grandmother and brother.

The temperature hovered near the freezing point, and a steady rain fell as they drove, but the big car's heater purred softly, bathing them with warmth.

"It's a good thing none of us is fat," Summer commented sagely as the car eased along Highway 125.

"Why's that, honey?" Matt asked, glancing at his daughter in the rearview mirror.

"We'd never fit in the car," Summer replied smartly. "We can barely squeeze in now." She hesitated, then asked, "What happens if we grow any next year?"

"Somebody'll have to stay home, I guess," Joe suggested with mock pragmatism, drawing gasps of horror from his impressionable brothers and sisters. "We'll draw straws tonight to see who stays and who goes," he teased.

"I'm not stayen home," Summer declared to uproarious approval from her younger siblings. "It wouldn't be Christmas without goen to town on Christmas Eve. You can stay home, Joe."

"Your brother's just teasen," Caroline soothed her children. "We'll find a way to get us all to town, even if we have to pack everyone in the back of the pickup."

"Mama, we'd freeze to death riden in the back of a pickup in weather like this," John remarked, pointing out a potential problem with his mother's idea. "Out in the cold with the rain and the wind, and nothing to protect us."

"I promise we won't let y'all freeze to death," Matt said quickly. "Why don't we think about next year when we get to it? We've still got this Christmas to deal with, and I'd hate to miss it because we were so concerned about next year."

"None of us will be in town on Christmas Eve next year," Joe said smugly, refusing to let the subject drop. "It falls on Sunday. All the stores will be closed."

"Then we'll go Saturday, the twenty-third," Caroline replied before anyone could voice disappointment.

"What about Santa Claus?" Luke asked suddenly from his grandfather's lap, a worried frown creasing his face. "He's gonna be out in this weather tonight. He could freeze to death riden around in an open sleigh."

"He's got that red fur suit to keep him warm," Matt reminded Luke.

"And on top of that, he's got a special heater built right into his sleigh," Sam added. "Besides, Luke, Santa Claus lives in the North Pole. They have snow and ice year-round up there, so I imagine he's used to the cold."

"Are you sure, Grandpa?" Luke asked dubiously.

"Sure as I'm sitten here," Sam answered with unmistakable confidence, quelling the boy's concern.

They sang carols from then until the merry Christmas lights of Tifton heralded their arrival in town. The children marveled at the collection of bell-shaped wreaths and Santa Claus faces attached to every streetlight, along with the glittering trees and garland suspended above each intersection.

Cars lined the avenues, making parking spaces scarce, but Matt finally found an open slot on his fourth trip down Main Street. Once out of the car, all went their own way, except Luke and Bonnie, who were too young to traipse around town without someone to watch after them. The family scattered, each with a different mission and all with at least a dollar in their pockets to spend as they wished. Sam headed for The Big Store and a brightly colored scarf he figured would be a welcomed addition to his wife's collection; Rachel set out for Western Auto and the flashlight her husband had claimed to need for the past six months.

Caroline and Matt intended to spend the day watching their children enjoy the festivities as well as helping Sam and Rachel with their shopping. But first, they had to find the few gifts still on their shopping lists, which was why Caroline took off for Bishop's department store while Matt headed for the bookstore in the opposite direction.

"I've got just two places to go," Matt told Joe, putting his oldest son in charge of Luke and Bonnie.

"But Daddy," Joe protested, "I've got things to do myself. I don't have time to baby-sit."

"Just two things, son," Matt wheedled. "I'll be finished in a snap, then I'll find you and the rest of the day is yours to do whatever."

Joe put a hand on his hip, looking from side to side while considering the difficulty of Christmas shopping with a six- and four-year-old in tow. At last, he gave a short laugh and waved his father off to his errands. "Make it quick," he admonished.

"Thanks, son," Matt grinned. "I'm sure Santa will remember what a good sport you were about this."

Joe laughed again and watched his father walk away, conscious of the loose stride and light steps that carried Matt. Joe had walked the same way once, copying the gait of his daddy. Now, however, all he did was hobble, and he momentarily felt embarrassed by his crippled condition. Quickly though, he put aside the discomfort and surveyed the Christmas festivities.

On every corner, Salvation Army soldiers stood, their bells ringing a reminder that not everyone was as fortunate this holiday as the happy shoppers who strolled along the sidewalks.

Save for the grace of God, Joe acknowledged to himself, those bells could have tolled for the Bakers this year. He knew his daddy and mama were pinched for cash worse now than at any other time he could remember. To a degree, he was older and simply more aware of the family finances than in previous years, but Joe understood implicitly that the money troubles ran deeper than usual this year. Given the poor showing of the crops, it would have been a difficult year regardless of the unexpected expenses that popped up during the year. But the medical bills alone for Joe and his grandfather probably had scuttled the likelihood of even a meager profit.

Joe pushed aside his concerns. He fully expected his parents to provide for the family. The Bakers would get by somehow, and he refused to worry over the particulars of how. Still, Joe suspected there was little money left over for frivolities like Christmas, which explained why he was determined to buy presents for everyone in the family this year.

He had managed Christmas gifts for his parents for many years and for his grandparents for several years now. But mostly they had been cheap tokens with little thought or meaning. This year, besides expanding his shopping list to include his brothers and sisters, Joe had put thought into the presents and would spare no expense. He patted the wad of money in his pants pocket and was greeted by a tug on his arm.

Joe looked down into the upturned faces of his brother and sister. "We need help," Bonnie told him expectantly.

"What's wrong?" Joe asked.

"Nothen," Luke answered swiftly. "We just want to use our dollars to buy presents for Mama and Daddy."

Joe smiled, leaning down to pull the children into an embrace.

"Well now that's a swell idea," he praised, putting a finger on his chin to think. "You know," he continued thoughtfully, "I'm buyen gifts for Mama and Daddy myself. You guys could contribute a nickel or a dime each, and we could all three sign our names to it. That way you'd still have money left."

His suggestion met instant rejection from Bonnie and Luke, whose heads shook with vigorous disapproval. "No," Luke declared.

"We know what we want to get," Bonnie said quickly.

"But we need help picken it out," Luke added.

Joe nodded acceptance of their wishes. "Okay," he said patiently. "What kind of gifts do y'all have in mind?"

"Perfume for Mama," Bonnie answered.

"And aftershave lotion for Daddy," Luke finished.

Joe grinned slyly. "Do y'all have something against the way Mama and Daddy smell?"

"Noooo!" Bonnie laughed.

Luke shook his head in agreement. "I heard Mama say she was out of perfume one day," he explained to Joe. "And she's always kissen Daddy and tellen him how good he smells when he comes home from the barber shop. We figured Mama might kiss him a lot more if Daddy smelled good all the time."

Joe hugged the two children. "I can't argue with that," he smiled.

"It's a good idea, ain't it?" Bonnie asked.

"It's a great idea, honey," Joe confirmed tenderheartedly, running his fingers through the little girl's tresses.

"So where do we go to get it?" Luke inquired anxiously.

Joe stood, glancing up and down the street until his eyes settled on a pharmacy across the street beside the toy store. "I'd say the Rexall drugstore over yonder probably sells just about the best smellen perfume and aftershave in the entire town," he guaranteed them. "Whataya say we head over there to buy the presents. I bet they'll even wrap them for y'all. Then we'll check out the toy store."

He paused, then added, "We might even find Santa Claus there."

Bonnie clapped her hands in delight. "Let's go," Luke said.

Without another word, Joe took their hands and led his brother and sister across the busy street to the drugstore, pausing only to drop a five-dollar bill in the Salvation Army's red bucket. The bell was still ringing when he steered the children into the drugstore.

---

An hour later, Bonnie and Luke proudly carried bright packages for their parents and had combed over every marvelous inch of the toy store. Besides the happiness of his brother and sister, the excursion had proven beneficial to Joe as well. He purchased a tiny porcelain carousel music box for Carrie in the drugstore and a plastic silver tea set and box of miniature cars for Bonnie and Luke, respectively, from the toy store.

Without too much difficulty, he led the children from the toy store to a jewelry store one block down the street. He window-shopped briefly, eyeing the collection of ID bracelets on display in the front window while Luke and Bonnie complained about the cold. He ignored the children until they began tugging him toward the door.

"Okay, okay," Joe relented at last.

The doorbell jangled behind him and Joe turned to find himself eyeball-to-eyeball with his father.

Matt hastily stuffed something into the pocket of his denim jacket. "What are y'all doen here?" he asked with obvious surprise.

Joe responded with a curious smile at his father. "Luke and Bonnie were cold," he answered evasively. "We were looken for a warm place." He stared pointedly at the pocket of Matt's jacket. "What about you, Daddy? What's your excuse?"

"Just browsen," Matt answered too quickly, looking from Joe to Bonnie and Luke. "You kids ready to come with me for a while?"

"Yes, sir!" Luke said.

"Let's go to the toy store," Bonnie chimed in. "We've only gone there once today."

"The toy store it is," Matt agreed. "See you later, Joe."

"Have fun," Joe told them as they walked down the sidewalk. He watched until they crossed the next street, then went inside the jewelry store to buy the ID bracelet for Summer and a cigarette lighter for his father.

His pursuit of gifts next carried Joe to Western Auto, where he bought a basketball for John and an electric blanket for his grandparents, whose room served as a protective barrier between cold northern winds and the rest of the house. Before collecting his final gift, Joe obtained the car keys from his father and deposited the neatly wrapped presents in the trunk. Although tempted to borrow the car, his good sense convinced Joe otherwise and, after returning the keys, he set out on foot to cover the half-mile journey to the Sears catalog store to pick up the present for his mother.

The goal of this trek was a package of pink drapes with white sheers. Personally, Joe found the curtains, like most other things pink, only slightly more tolerable than nausea. The color reminded him of medicine. Nevertheless, he knew Caroline wanted those drapes in the worst way. She had spotted them in the Sears catalog and promptly declared her heart was set on them for the living room because they would match the furniture and the area rug with its brocaded burgundy and floral design. Over the course of fall as the family's financial woes worsened, Caroline had given up on the idea of the curtains. Still, her desire lingered and when Joe had come upon his mother staring at the catalog picture of the curtains like a child pining for the impossible, he had resolved to see that she got them.

Even practical women like his mother deserved moments of folly, Joe believed. For that matter, he reasoned, so did practical guys like himself.

———————

Caroline hunted for last-minute bargains in Bishop's while waiting for the store clerk to wrap the yellow satin dress for Summer. She browsed through the women's winter dresses, ruled out Sunday shoes for her husband and was considering an apron for Rachel when a clerk handed her the package. Caroline thanked the clerk, admiring the dark green wrapping paper as she made her way out of the store. She was still looking at the package, running through a mental list of things to do when she collided head-on with someone who obviously had waited until the last minute to do her Christmas shopping. Both women reeled from the impact, and an assortment of boxes, sacks and packages spilled in the doorway.

"I'm so sorry," Caroline apologized immediately, bending with the woman to retrieve the parcels. "I should have been looken where I was goen." She glanced up at the stranger, smiling warmly until she recognized the sallow-faced woman staring back at her.

Martha Taylor was a gawky, thin woman with a long face and pinched features. Her straight dishwater blonde hair was pulled back in a messy braid hanging down her back, and she wore a dowdy gray dress. The reproving look Martha received from

Caroline as they knelt there together on the department store floor had nothing to do with appearances, however, but rather with her relationship to Bobby Taylor.

Despite her Christian duty to forgiveness, Caroline still harbored ill will toward Bobby and the entire Taylor clan. They had brought shame, grief and heartache to the Bakers over the long summer recently passed, and Caroline's mood was short on tolerance and long on judgment.

In that long gaze between the two women, Martha undoubtedly saw the loathsome opinion Caroline held of the Taylor family. A flicker of understanding registered briefly in her dull eyes, dying like embers splashed with cold water before Martha broke the gaze. She gathered her packages without further acknowledgment of Caroline, then retreated to the rear of the store.

Caroline rose from the floor, confused by a sudden urge to reach out to the sad-faced woman and the inclination to forget this encounter. She scanned the far corners of the store for a glimpse of Martha, deciding eventually that she must appear nosy to anyone observing her actions. At last, she concluded, perhaps for all the wrong reasons, that the time was not yet right to attempt a reconciliation between the two families. Much unpleasantness had passed between them, and the memories were still too close to both sides.

In time, Caroline tried to tell herself, she could befriend Martha Taylor. But she knew such a friendship was unlikely to happen. She and Martha had been neighbors for years, and this Christmas Eve run-in amounted to the most significant moment in their relationship. Caroline accepted part of the blame due to her stubborn animosity toward Bobby Taylor. But the fact that Martha just wasn't neighborly also had to be considered. It was hard to start a friendship with someone who rarely set foot off her own property, shunning church and community activities.

This reasoning, however, did little to suppress Caroline's notion that she had missed a golden opportunity to right a wrong. Rather than offer the hand of friendship to Martha, she had responded with judgment. Caroline moved to the door, hesitating only to tighten the belt of her tweed coat before moving into the cold afternoon with a heavy heart.

She walked briskly along the sidewalk admiring the window displays of the various stores, but her thoughts stayed in Bishop's with Martha. Caroline did not know Martha well enough to understand her motives, but she'd heard enough rumor and gossip to make some educated guesses about the woman.

Although she hated to admit it, Caroline suspected Bobby had represented a single chance of happiness for Martha. And not only that, Caroline thought shamelessly, but Bobby likely had come across as some knight in shining armor to Martha. She could imagine Bobby sweeping a shy girl off her feet with false promises. While Caroline did not put much stock in appearances, Bobby was a handsome man compared with his wife. It was easy to imagine Martha bowled over by her luck at snaring a man like Bobby. But what sustained their relationship? The possibility of a shared hatred for colored people crossed her mind, but Caroline shuddered at that thought and promptly discarded the idea.

Accepting that Martha was a complete stranger for all practical purposes, Caroline forced her mind to quit its gossiping about the woman and focused instead on what she knew about the Taylor family.

She hardly considered the Taylors neighbors. They were simply people who lived down the road and kept mostly to themselves. In nineteen years of living on nearby farms, Caroline had set foot on Taylor property just once and then only out of ignorance.

Caroline had devoted the first days of her marriage to Matt and his preparations for entering the Army. He had joined up in January 1942 a few weeks after their wedding, and she had returned to Aunt Evelyn's home in Tifton to finish her final year of high school. When school ended that spring, Caroline had taken up permanent residence with the Bakers and readily set out to learn about the place she intended to call home for the rest of her life.

New River was a crossroads community located along Highway 125 beside a river and a railroad trestle. The town of Cookville lay south of the little community and Tifton to the north. Carter's Mercantile was the focal point of the crossroads, a rambling wooden structure that also served as the community post office before the government shut it down in the early 1950s. New River Elementary School lay north of the mercantile around a sharp curve, and the one-room voting precinct stood between those two structures.

Route 125 had been paved in the 1950s, but the winding path bisecting the community was a dirt road with washboard ruts and slippery ditches. The western flank of the dirt road was the more thickly populated side, with smaller farms and shorter distances between houses. The Holiness Baptist Church sat on the western flank of the road, which also eventually led to the snake-handling church where a man had died from a rattlesnake bite a few months earlier.

The Baker home lay about two miles off the main highway, on the sparsely settled eastern flank of the dirt road. Deep woods hemmed both sides of the road, broken only by the occasional field or dwelling place. Coming from the highway about a half-mile down the road, Benevolence Missionary Baptist Church and its cemetery stood on the left. On the right a short distance farther lay the Berrien pecan orchard and the private lane leading to their home. Like the church, the Baker house sat on the left side of the road, which cut a swath directly through the family's farm. A few more scattered farms and homes lay farther down the road.

As fascinated as she was with the lay of the land, Caroline was even more fond of the people who lived in her new community.

Dan and Amelia Carter were newlyweds themselves, although both several years older than Matt and Caroline. She found the Carters to be friendly shopkeepers with a willingness to lend a hand to their neighbors in times of need. They kept the mercantile in excellent shape, stocked it with all the necessities and made every effort possible to obtain any other items their customers requested.

Dan was an affable, easygoing man who more often than not deferred to the wishes of his wife, while Amelia was a strong-willed, prideful woman who spoke her mind on most occasions. Considering their personalities, Dan might have become a hen-pecked husband if not for two factors: He had the backbone to stand up to his wife when the situation warranted, and Amelia had the good sense to know when her husband was right. Caroline had come quickly to count the Carters among her best friends.

Her friendship with the Berriens had required more cultivation. Britt Berrien had been a stranger to Caroline, so much so that in some ways she understood the man better in death than when he had been alive. She had known and liked Paul before marrying, and the years since had deepened her respect for Matt's best friend. April and June were oddities. They had given Caroline a whirlwind tour of their stately mansion before the wedding, insisting that she and Matt use the small guest cottage for their honeymoon. But two years had lapsed before the sisters extended another invitation to their home. She saw them regularly at Sunday church services and

Wednesday prayer meetings but very few times in between. She was puzzled by their reclusive behavior until Rachel had explained the strange history behind it.

The Berrien sisters had remained friendly strangers through the war and up to their father's death, which, sad as it sounded, had imbued the women with the freedom to pursue life. They still largely preferred an existence behind the facade of the Berrien estate, but they ventured out often these days, using the family money to travel extensively and lead privileged lives. And, too, they gave back a little of themselves to the community. April taught piano lessons for a minimal charge and June was spearheading a county-wide effort to build a new library in Cookville.

The emergence of the sisters from the iron rule of their father compared with a graceful bird taking flight. They were two delicate creatures tapping into a rich vein of strength, and Caroline had grown to admire their courage. It was true that she found both women scatterbrained at times, but April and June exemplified the best of Southern gentility and graciousness and Caroline marveled at their fastidiousness. She counted them as true friends to her family.

Caroline was closest to the Berriens and the Carters, but she had formed lasting friendships with almost everyone else in the New River community over the years. The Taylor family was the notable exception.

Several miles down from the Baker place on the right of the dirt road was a second private lane that Caroline had traversed only once. Unlike the Berrien estate, where the vast pecan orchard and sugar maple-lined lane created a formidable aura demanding privacy, the Taylor place made a similar statement in blatant terms, with a series of "No Trespassing" signs posted on scraggly pine trees.

Caroline invaded the privacy of the Taylor place a few weeks after moving in with her in-laws in the summer of 1942 when she accompanied Sam to deliver a letter mistakenly left in the Baker mailbox. Some six months had passed since her rude introduction to Bobby Taylor, and Caroline had no idea who lived at the end of the rocky, washed-out path. Still, she'd felt a sense of foreboding as they drove past worn-out fields before arriving at a weather-beaten house almost swallowed up by a host of mature pecan trees.

The front door opened as soon as Sam stopped the truck, and Bobby Taylor stepped onto the sagging front porch. Caroline recognized him immediately as the bully who had mistreated the little colored boy on her wedding day. "Who's that?" she hissed through her teeth to Sam.

"That?" Sam repeated inquisitively. He looked at Bobby, then back to Caroline. "That is Bobby Taylor," he answered finally.

Caroline quickly eyeballed her father-in-law. "Pa," she said urgently as Bobby approached the truck, "I'd appreciate it if you spared me an introduction."

Although he had no time to acknowledge the request, Sam complied with Caroline's wishes. He passed the letter to Bobby through the truck window, inquired about the family and chatted briefly about the war and the crops before bidding goodbye to the boy.

"Now what was that all about?" he inquired of Caroline as they drove away from the Taylor house.

Caroline told him about her first encounter with Bobby on the drive home.

"Humph," Sam had snorted as she concluded the story. "Let me tell you what I know about the Taylors. Some of it is gossip, some rumor, some innuendo and some of it is fact. Very little is pleasant."

———————

Robert Taylor moved his wife, Josephine, and only son, Bobby, to the Cookville community in the spring of 1939, acquiring the farm outright from the Farmers and Citizens Bank of Cookville in exchange for paying fifteen years of back property taxes. It seemed a meager price for the amount of land but it was more than any local farmer would have been willing to pay for the small farm. The locals considered it a cursed place, barren land that would never earn a decent living for a man and his family.

"I don't rightly know how the place earned its reputation," Sam had told Caroline later that evening as they ate supper with Rachel. "It's fertile land. One field is rich bottom soil right by the river. Somebody oughtta be able to make a liven out there with plenty left over to enjoy the luxuries of life. But for whatever reasons, nobody was able to make a go of the place until Robert Taylor took it over."

A young man known as Henry Anderson had owned the place before the Taylors acquired it. Henry was a tireless worker with a young wife and four children. Unfortunately, his best efforts met consistently with failure, more often than not from things beyond his control. Flood, drought and insects made it difficult for Henry to take care of his family, much less pay the bills and meet his bank note, but it was the iron fist of Britt Berrien that finally crushed the young man.

"No one could ever figure out why Britt turned against the man," Sam told Caroline. "Henry was a fine worker. When the farm left him short on cash, he went out and found whatever work he could to feed the family. He worked a lot for Britt himself, gardenen and handyman stuff. Then out of the blue one day, Britt foreclosed on him. Henry and his family stole away in the middle of the night, and, to my knowledge, nobody's seen hide nor hair of 'em since."

"Henry was a handsome man, too," Rachel continued with unabashed admiration. "Dark, tall and broad-shouldered with the greenest eyes you ever saw." Rachel shook her head as if realizing how unlike herself she sounded, but she continued, unaffected by the fresh attitude. "He had that certain look," she said daringly. "Like he could have whatever he wanted, but would never take it because he was too nice. I sound like a school girl with a crush, but Henry had that kind of effect on people," Rachel concluded. "Everybody—men and women alike—were just naturally attracted to him. I can't imagine whatever happened to make a man like him just disappear into the night."

But Henry and his family had disappeared and, for fifteen years, the Anderson place lay fallow, virtually untouched by human contact. The house and barns fell into disrepair, weeds reclaimed the fields and time seemed to stop on the farm. Some locals claimed the place was still trying to reclaim those lost years, despite the best efforts of Robert Taylor and his family.

Robert was a stern man, whose penchant for hard work was overshadowed only by his desire for privacy. The Taylors made no effort to become part of the community. Rather, they shut out their neighbors, posting the land with "No Trespassing" signs and putting up a gate across the driveway to their house. Their actions effectively isolated the family, while providing fodder for the gossip mill and piquing the interest of the community.

Through the grapevine and a series of discreet inquiries, disturbing details emerged.

Robert and Josephine had once owned a farm in north Florida, selling it and relocating to the Cookville area following the death of their teenage daughter. Officially, the death was ruled suicide because the girl hung herself. Unofficially, everyone said she was driven to kill herself, and rumors sprouted like seed in spring, irrigated with innuendoes like incest and pregnancy. It was an ugly tale, lingering through the years without substantiation or repudiation.

While the past proved elusive to hang on the Taylors, the present unfolded in extremes.

Despite his curious ways, Robert earned the grudging respect of the New River community. He tamed the wretched piece of land straightaway, transforming patches of weed and bramble into thriving fields. Other farmers had better land, but none tended it more skillfully than Robert. Within a few years, his fields were the envy of the community.

"If I had half his know-how, I could turn this place into what Tara must have been before the War Between the States," Sam had admitted freely to Caroline. "Robert Taylor can get more out of nothen than anybody I know."

The first hint of trouble came during the family's third summer in Cookville. Until then, no one suspected the Taylors held colored people in such low regard.

The hubbub began on a hot day in July when Robert beat a black boy in his tobacco field. Robert claimed the boy had sassed him, asserting his refusal to tolerate back talk from a nigger. The black field workers swore out a warrant for his arrest, claiming the attack was excessive regardless of the provocation. The accused spent a night in jail before a judge dropped the charges for lack of evidence.

In a community where racism was largely passive, Robert had touched a nerve.

Colored people knew their place in Cookville in 1941. Most of them either respected white people or wisely kept contrary opinions to themselves. Likewise, whites showed a degree of respect for the colored community, reserving their acrimonious feelings for private moments. Both sides used each other, profiting from the arrangement, and only the rare extremist on either side voiced dissatisfaction with the situation.

With one angry outburst, Robert Taylor shattered the fragile peace, endangering the long-established truce between the community's black and white factions.

The white faction divided sharply over the decision to drop the assault charges against Robert. On one side were the people who felt Robert deserved punishment, considering the broken ribs suffered by his teenage victim as ample evidence of the crime. This group was lined up opposite of those who believed that white people had the authority as well as the moral obligation to enforce strict discipline over the black community as a whole and any rowdy, disrespectful teenager in particular. In between these two groups lay the majority, those apathetic souls whose opinions wavered with the wind.

Cookville's colored community had strong opinions about the incident as well and strangely enough those viewpoints were not homogenized. Nevertheless, they united on one front. While powerless against the wheels of justice, the colored folk controlled their destiny when it came to field labor and they chose not to work for Robert from that point forward.

Once he recognized their method of retaliation, Robert tried to make amends, humbling himself because he needed the blacks as a cheap source of labor. He promised higher wages, free lunches and vowed never to lay another hand on black skin. His overture met with firm rejection among the black farm workers, leaving Robert frustrated, bitter and humiliated for having stooped so low as to grovel for niggers. When the humiliation passed, he made another vow, promising no niggers would ever set foot in his fields again. Then, he went to work, doubling his efforts to make good on his claim.

No one could say for fact whether Robert Taylor's deep-seated hatred for Negroes existed prior to this incident or imbedded into his character in the aftermath of the trouble. Undoubtedly though, his bigotry became the dominating influence in the life of his only son.

"I have a theory about Bobby," Sam had told Caroline late one recent summer night when the startling events of the day naturally harkened them back to their original conversation about the Taylor family. "There's no doubt that Robert made the boy work—if you'll pardon the expression—like a field nigger. But it's also plain as the nose on his face that Bobby has a streak of laziness in him a mile wide. Well, when you put hard work and laziness together, nothen good is bound to come from it. I think that's what happened to Bobby. He's spent many a day under a blazen sun, worken his tail off and looken for somebody to blame for his predicament. Seems only natural that he would lay that blame at the feet of colored people. I'm willen to bet that once or twice the thought occurred to him that his life would be a lot easier if there were a few Negroes in the field worken with him."

Beyond their common hatred for niggers, Robert and Bobby shared little.

As much as his father preferred privacy, Bobby Taylor relished attention. Bobby was brash and crass, a combination that won over impressionable teenagers, made him several friends and charmed a few girls along the way. In high school, he became a beacon for those who shared his prejudices and a thorn in the side of those who opposed him.

From an early age, Bobby learned to pick his fights carefully, to measure the costs against the benefits and to stay away from no-win situations. It was this ability that helped him avoid service through most of World War II, plus his father's insistence to the draft board that Bobby best served the war effort by working on the farm to produce food for the country. In early 1945, however, the Army finally summoned Bobby to Fort Benning for basic training, and he went despite the pleadings of his father.

———————

As she walked down the city sidewalk, pausing to glance in the window of another department store, Caroline pondered how deceitful appearances were. At first glance, the father-son bond between Robert and Bobby might have appeared unbreakable. But somehow, she knew otherwise.

Robert might have been quick to defend the cause of his son, but his call to duty had not come from love. His heart was black, and Caroline suspected his actions had been guided by a spiteful desire to control Bobby rather than to help him. Still, despite her lack of respect for Robert, she could not help wondering whether Bobby appreciated his father's role in the Taylor family's well-being. She wondered where Bobby would be without his father's guidance. And she wondered whether there was sadness in the Taylor household this Christmas or whether the feelings about Robert's death a few weeks earlier had been tossed away like slop in a bucket.

This was Caroline's last thought on the Taylor family and then she pushed them from her mind, intent on focusing on the good-will of man and peace on earth.

# CHAPTER 7

LONG AFTER CAROLINE BAKER had left Bishop's, Martha Taylor stood in the back of the department store reflecting on the woman's presumptuous nature. Martha had seen the disapproval in Caroline's eyes, knowing instantly that she had been tried and convicted by association with Bobby. Martha could live with the accusations, but she resented the sympathetic nod Caroline had bestowed on her.

Women like Caroline made Martha sick to her stomach. They presumed to understand every little detail about things they had no business worrying over in the first place, passing judgments and exercising their God-given rights to act on the wisdom of their holier-than-thou attitudes. Martha half-expected Caroline to come calling with a cake one day soon, offering the hand of friendship and asking where the coffee cups were at the same time. Well, if she did, Martha would tell the woman where to go and what to do with her cake. And under no circumstances would Caroline Baker ever know where Martha kept her coffee cups.

Martha snorted at the idea, condemning Caroline as a busybody, and then shuffled over to the shoe department, taking a seat in an empty chair. She closed her eyes, wishing for peace and quiet to take away the maddening headache. Headaches plagued her more often than not these days. It was a dull pain for the most part, but commotion brought it to a full throb. And life had brought one commotion after another for the longest time now.

Christmas was the final straw. Martha was worn out with all its trappings and cheer. She hated the shopping, she despised the crowds, she wanted to disappear. But as bad as it seemed, if she could get through one more day, Martha knew she could rest for a while. There would be no elections, no funerals, no holidays.

Just the prospect of doing the same old thing day after day, and she relished the thought. Though not fond of cooking and cleaning, Martha had gained a new appreciation for the predictability of housekeeping and the privacy it afforded her. She was more grateful than ever to have a roof over her head and food on the table every night, which had been her main motivation to marry Bobby in the first place. If she had ever desired more from marriage, even fleetingly so, Martha now knew she would willingly settle for less. She hoped the same was true of her husband's ambition, but somehow doubted it.

Indeed, Martha had a troublesome notion that the coming years might bring new commotion, or at the very least more than she had bargained for on the day Bobby Taylor swaggered into her life.

---

Bobby and Martha met at a bar in Columbus, Georgia, early on in his Army training at Fort Benning. He could not recall the exact details of their first meeting, but Bobby remembered she was easy to seduce and he was drunk the first time they slept together in a dingy motel.

When he woke the next morning to find the shy, homely girl from Opelika, Alabama, in bed with him, Bobby promptly pushed himself on her another time. He expected Martha to disappear from his life, but she proved a strange temptation. She was putty in his hands, yielding to Bobby's every demand, doing whatever he wished, molding her desires to his needs.

Through her unwitting complaisance, Martha introduced Bobby to the heady feeling of power over other people. When he had sated his carnal desires, Bobby lay back in bed and explained the way of the world to Martha. In the process, he became a king, the master of everything in his realm, and she became his servant.

Over and over Bobby had tried to walk away from Martha. He considered her inferior, beneath his dignity. Yet, unable to find a suitable replacement for his bed or his ego, he returned to her repeatedly over the next few weeks.

She was pregnant within a month of meeting Bobby. He ordered her to get an abortion. Martha agreed without protest, readily locating someone who could perform the procedure. But when she went to Bobby to collect the money, he changed his mind, concluding fatherhood would add another dimension to his domain.

The choice was difficult to make even for Bobby, who was prone to rash decisions. In a rare moment of honest self-appraisal,

Bobby admitted Martha was not the woman he wanted to marry. She was plain and dull, yet she made him feel the exact opposite about himself.

They were married in early April. Martha miscarried on V-E Day.

The loss of the baby demoralized Bobby. He was not heartbroken by any means, knowing another chance of fatherhood would come his way one day. But he felt trapped in a worthless marriage, seeing Martha as dim-witted and empty-headed, wondering how he could have deluded himself into believing she could make a fitting wife.

He inquired about a divorce. Discovering he had neither the grounds nor the money to pursue one, Bobby did the next best thing he could think of. He sent Martha to live with his parents in Cookville while he re-enlisted in the Army and spent the next few years chasing women and living the good life.

Martha complied with his decisions because she had no choice and no reason for doing anything else.

Bobby returned to Cookville in 1950, promptly impregnated his wife and later in the year became father to a son, Wayne Robert. A second son, William Robert, was born three years later, and Bobby was apt to boast about other sons he would have if Martha was not as inclined to miscarry a pregnancy as she was to carry it to full term.

Under his father's guidance, Bobby developed into a respectable farmer, paying his bills and building a small nest egg over the years. But his contributions to prosperity around the Taylor household came grudgingly because Bobby preferred the idleness of the lazy to the industriousness of the hardworking. While Robert sweated willingly for every penny, Bobby hunted for the quick and easy way to riches. In the spring of 1960, he thought he found it.

Bobby's decision to seek political office came impulsively. On the day after Sheriff Marvin McClelland announced he would not seek re-election, Bobby became the first of seven candidates to seek the job, believing a base of friends from across the county and the support of several kindred spirits would propel him to victory. He campaigned doggedly, forsaking his duty to the farm for the quest of a greater bounty. Bobby canvassed the county door-to-door, regardless of the welcome mat. His message was unwavering, and even those who opposed him admitted the candidate remained true to his beliefs, never mincing words or ideas. Good law enforcement, according to Bobby, meant strict control and discipline of the colored population, and he promised to keep them on a tight rein.

"This county needs a sheriff who will stand up for what's right, someone who won't coddle criminals, but will earn their respect and, more importantly, their fear," Bobby repeated over and over again on any and every stump. "Our way of life is fallen down around our feet, and too many of us are just standen by watchen it happen.

"Niggers are risen up, getten too big for their britches because they want *c-evil* rights. Don't you believe it, folks! They want to marry our women and confuse our children. They want this country to look like one big Oreo cookie, and unless someone has the guts to stand up to them and their nigger-loven, white-trash supporters, they're goen to get just what they want.

"And then where will we be?

"A bunch of Oreo cuckoos runnen round and round, biten off chicken heads, stealen, rapen, killen—all because we've elected cowards who kowtow to the niggers and everyone else who wants to see our way of life destroyed.

"Now some of y'all may think I'm talken nonsense. But, folks, if you don't believe me, then your heads are covered up in the muck and your butts are sticken up high, tall and proud for all to see. Y'all can read about it in the newspaper, you can see it on TV and I'm here to tell you it's happening—city by city, town by town, school by school.

"We're among the lucky ones here in Cookville. We have our bad seeds, to be sure, but everybody knows their place. I want to make sure it stays that way. That's why I want to be sheriff of this county. It takes a strong man to stand up to niggers in this day and age, and it's goen to take one who's even stronger tomorrow and all the days after. Folks, I am strong. And I'll stand up to what's wrong."

It was a simple message, preying on hate and fear, delivered with the venom and passion of old-fashioned politics, and it became more popular than even Bobby's most ardent supporters could have imagined from the outset of the campaign.

On a sizzling day in July, Bobby Taylor finished first in the Democratic primary, but his failure to capture a majority of the vote pushed him into a runoff with Paul Berrien. Bobby was disappointed, especially with the overwhelming rejection from voters in New River, his home precinct. Still, a victory for Bobby seemed likely, and the entire county took notice.

The runoff campaign played out over the dog days of August and early September when the air was stagnant, the sun sweltering and the ground so soaked with heat that shoes were a necessity to avoid blistered feet. So stifling were those days that it seemed the only breezes came from swarming gnats and the hot air of politicians. None stirred a hotter breeze than Bobby, and no one campaigned with more vigor or purpose.

The race seemed to come down to a matter of style over substance. Bobby and Paul offered distinct messages, and a minority of voters would cast ballots based on strong agreement or disagreement with the opposing viewpoints. But the election's outcome would be decided by the majority of voters, whose opinions waffled with the wind and who cast ballots based on the appeal of the messenger rather than the message. Unfortunately, for the voters, choosing between the styles of Bobby and Paul was a difficult choice to make because their respective strengths played perfectly into their weaknesses. On one hand, Bobby came off as a fanatic for force, the perfect foil for Paul's even-handed respect for the law. On the other hand, Paul's wooden temper came across as a lack of commitment to the cause he wanted to serve, a sharp contrast to Bobby's passion to administer the law.

"They either one could be the best of sheriffs or the worst of sheriffs," a curmudgeon was overheard to say one day among a gathering of old men on the courthouse square. "It just depends on whether you want a sheriff who reacts to a crisis by retiren to the verandah to sip a mint julep and pontificate on the matter in question, or one who shoots everybody in sight first—and I do mean everybody—and asks questions later."

---

On the last Saturday in August, ten days before the runoff election, a large crowd gathered in the cavernous confines of the Planter's Tobacco Warehouse in Cookville. Farmers from across the county, indeed, from all over South Georgia, were waiting in long lines to have their tobacco weighed and tagged for the final sale of the season.

Joe sat in the cab of the pickup, inching the vehicle forward every few minutes as the convoy of trucks passed through the warehouse to have their valuable cargo unloaded. His father, grandfather and brothers were scattered among the groups of men clustered throughout the warehouse in deep discussion. Both Paul and Bobby were there as well, but their politicking played second fiddle to even bigger news—the death of Alvah Shanks, a forty-year-old farmer, husband and father of three who had died from a rattlesnake bite at the Wednesday night prayer meeting of the Holiness Church.

Approaching one of the groups to shake hands and seek support, Paul stopped short upon a lively discussion about the good and bad of handling snakes in churches. His eavesdropping persuaded Paul to go elsewhere in search of votes and he was on his way out the door when he spotted Lucas Bartholomew emerging from the warehouse office.

Lucas had returned recently from his travels up North and was working in the warehouse. "Hello, Lucas," Paul called, genuinely pleased to see the young man.

Lucas smiled broadly. "Afternoon, Mr. Paul," he returned. "I guess you're looken for votes."

"I was," Paul admitted. "Unfortunately, everybody's more interested in Alvah Shanks than the election."

"Everybody's talken 'bout it, for sure," Lucas agreed.

Paul bit his lip. "I can see why," he said. "Elections come around like clockwork, but it's not every day somebody gets bit by a rattlesnake in church and dies."

Both men laughed soberly and drifted into conversation about job prospects for Lucas and the places and things he had seen on his trip up north. Their camaraderie did not go unnoticed.

Robert Taylor observed the easy chatter between Paul and Lucas for several minutes before the idea came to his mind. Almost immediately, he searched out the crowd, found Bobby and pulled his son apart from the group of men.

"What do you want?" Bobby demanded angrily. "I'm tryen to win an election, Pa. I don't have time for talken."

Robert scowled, shaking his head in disgust, tempted to walk away from his son. Finally, he gestured toward Paul and Lucas, who were locked deep in conversation. "There might be a vote or two to win over there," he muttered gruffly. "If you play your cards right."

The advice came in a condescending tone, but Bobby over-looked it in pursuit of a plan to turn the situation to his advantage. An idea formed quickly and Bobby soon stood in the midst of his cronies, pointing out the cozy appearance of Paul and Lucas, im-plying they were in cahoots on something devious and detrimental to the well-being of Cookville and the county. "Everybody knows those two are buddy-buddy," Bobby said. "Paul Berrien wins this election, then this county might just have a black deputy sheriff."

His ranting and ridicule curried rousing approval among his most ardent supporters and garnered significant interest from cu-rious passersby, especially those inclined to distrust hobnobbing between colored folk and whites. Within minutes, with a crowd behind him, Bobby marched across the warehouse floor to Paul and Lucas, who were squatted on the floor, talking and smoking cigarettes.

Lucas noticed the advancing crowd first, and the frown creasing his forehead conveyed his concern to Paul.

Paul glanced over his shoulder, rising almost instantly to put himself between Lucas and Bobby. Until now, face-to-face encoun-ters between the candidates had been civil affairs, but Paul sensed Bobby was ready for a direct attack. His suspicions were confirmed in quick order.

"I've heard the rumors, Paul," Bobby began contemptuously, "but deep down I didn't want to believe them. Now I don't have any other choice. I have to believe it."

Paul examined the crowd gathered behind Bobby while deciding how to respond. "What are you talken about?" he replied finally.

"You can play your little word games, Paul," Bobby hissed. "But you're courten the nigger vote and there ain't any use tryen to deny it." Bobby paused, then pointed at Lucas. "Especially not when you've been caught red-handed."

Paul glanced back at Lucas, his quick eyes expressing regret over his friend's accidental role in the confrontation. He returned his gaze to the man standing before him. "What I'm doen, Bobby," he said stiffly, "is talken with a friend. If you have a problem with that, so be it. Frankly, my business and my friends are not your concern."

Bobby stepped closer, appraising Paul with a scornful glare. "I disagree," he challenged. "You can tell a lot about a man by the company he keeps." Bobby motioned to Lucas. "My daddy always taught me that you can't trust a nigger," he continued. "But worse than that is a white man who coddles to every whim and wish of a nigger. This county don't need a sheriff who's a nigger lover."

Bobby turned slightly, shifting his gaze between Paul and the growing crowd. "From the day I got in this election, I've warned people about these kinds of things," he said boldly. "We're fighten to preserve a way of life in this county. How can voters expect you to lead that fight, Paul, when you're cozyen up to the very people who are doing their damndest to tear apart everything we stand for?"

Bobby turned his back on Paul. "This county needs a sheriff who will uphold the law and respect the traditions that go with it," he appealed to the crowd. "That's what you'll get if you vote for me." He gestured to Paul and Lucas behind him. "Vote for Paul Berrien and you'll get exactly what you see there—a man in charge of the law who's in cahoots with the very same people who are trying to overturn our laws and bury our traditions."

Several onlookers whooped in support of Bobby, who fixed another damning glare on Paul.

Tension lines gathered on Paul's face. He glanced at Lucas, then searched the crowd for a friendly face while considering a response to the attack on his character. Seeing Matt and Sam edge near the front of the crowd, Paul made up his mind. He walked over to his accuser, squaring off eye-to-eye with Bobby until the other man flinched. Satisfied, Paul shifted his gaze to the crowd.

"You people know the kind of man I am," he said slowly without apologies. "I believe everybody deserves a fair shake with the law—colored or white, rich or poor—it doesn't matter to me. You've known that about me from the very beginnen of this campaign and so has Bobby. If you're bothered because I'd treat colored criminals the same way I'd treat white criminals, then vote for my opponent. But if you're interested in justice and fairness for *everyone*, then vote for me. I'm a law-abiden man, and I'll be a law-abiden sheriff. It's that simple."

"No, Paul! It's not that simple."

The voice, cracked and bitter, resonated through the hushed warehouse. People looked from side to side, searching for the speaker.

Robert Taylor strode forth, parting a path through the crowd as all eyes turned toward him. He stopped a few feet from Paul and Bobby. "It's not simple at all," he repeated knowingly to Paul, who stood motionless and speechless.

"What's goen on, Pa?" Bobby asked.

Robert ignored his son, keeping his eyes trained on Paul. "You said a mouthful just then, Paul Berrien," he said mysteriously. "You sounded almost like a preacher with all that talk about upholden the law and doen what's right, and maybe you meant it. But you're no law-abiden citizen."

Paul visibly blanched.

"When it suits your needs," Robert persisted, "you're willen to bend the law. Ain't you, Paul?"

Paul shot a hollow glance toward the crowd, and Robert followed his eyes to Matt Baker. The crowd numbered about ninety men, women and children, all spellbound by the drama playing out before their eyes.

Robert waited for Paul's answer, then shrugged, turning to the crowd. "Seven years ago, Paul Berrien covered up his daddy's death," he announced bluntly. "Everyone thought Britt Berrien died of a heart attack, but the truth is someone stuck a gun in his mouth and pulled the trigger." He hesitated, allowing ample time for the enthralled audience to draw its own conclusions, daring Paul to dispute the accusation.

Everyone else waited for a response from Paul as well, some praying for a denial, others hoping for a confession. In the end, the silence convicted Paul. He stood frozen, the color drained from his lean face and his green eyes glassed over with disbelief.

The moment seemed endless, like an unwanted portion of time.

Robert drew closer to Paul. "I was at the funeral home that night," he murmured harshly. "My Josephine was a corpse, and I wanted to be with her. To tell you the truth, Paul, I never thought much about what you did till just now when you got all high and mighty and preachy about abiden by the law."

He stepped away from Paul, whirling to face the stunned crowd. "I was at the funeral home the night they brought in Berrien's body," Robert repeated loudly for the benefit of the crowd. "They said it was suicide and maybe it was. I don't know about that. But I do know Britt Berrien didn't have no heart attack." He glared across the crowd, halting his gaze on Matt. "If y'all don't believe me, just ask two more of our respected, law-abiden citizens—Matt Baker and the good coroner, Arch Adams," Robert continued. "Matt helped Paul bring the body to the funeral home, and both of 'em persuaded Arch to lie about the cause of death."

Robert paused once more, allowing the confused onlookers to mumble among themselves.

"Is he tellen the truth, Paul?" asked Virgil Parrish at last. Virgil lived in the eastern part of the county. He was the community's most prosperous farmer and people paid attention when he asked questions or spouted off opinions.

The question jolted Paul, who willed a pair of trembling knees to stand solidly. He swallowed the rising panic in his throat and squared his shoulders. "It's true," he admitted quietly.

Bobby Taylor stepped cautiously to his father's side. He glanced at Robert, then fixed his attention on Paul. "You've got a lot of nerve asken the people of this county to trust you to enforce the law, Paul Berrien," he said carefully. "Specially when breaken it came so easy to you."

Paul eyed Bobby stiffly. "I had my reasons."

"You used your reputation to break the law," Bobby countered quickly in tones both condescending and reproachful. "You lied, you cheated and you abused the people of this county with dishonesty—then and now."

"Spare me your sermon, Bobby," Paul snapped. "I neither need nor want your judgments and opinions." He swept the crowd with a challenging gaze, making eye contact with Virgil Parrish, Robert Taylor and several others before his glare settled on Bobby. "Maybe I did do wrong," he continued stoutly. "But chances are I'd do it all over again if I had to make that same decision today. Regardless, I'm more than willen to face the consequences of my actions— before the law and the people of this county. Now if y'all excuse me, I have business to tend to."

And with that, Paul Berrien marched out of the warehouse and straight to the sheriff's office, where he confessed his wrongdoing.

---

On Election Day, Bobby Taylor woke in a foul mood, the result of another dream about the amazing revelation regarding Paul Berrien. He lay in the sticky bed for a long time, alternately cursing the early morning heat and the gilded fortune of his opponent.

Bobby figured the election should have been handed to him by now, on a silver platter by Paul himself. It was inconceivable that his opponent had not dropped out of the election altogether, indeed, why Paul was not in jail or at the very least facing criminal charges for covering up the cause of Britt Berrien's death. So why then, Bobby wondered, did he have so many misgivings about the election outcome?

He roused himself from bed and went outside on the back porch to relieve his bladder, ignoring the morning greeting from Martha as he passed the kitchen. Bobby, his father and the boys all peed off the back porch every morning, none willing to make the long walk to the outhouse. He made a silent promise to see about indoor plumbing as soon as the election was over, then returned inside the house to the kitchen.

"Where's breakfast?" he growled, sitting down at the table.

"On the stove keepen warm," Martha answered. "I'll fix your plate."

Bobby observed his wife dish up congealed scrambled eggs and overdone bacon. Martha's movements were sluggish and heavy despite her thin build, and Bobby shook his head in dismay as she set the plate before him and turned to fetch the coffee pot. He considered complaining about the eggs but decided it would be a waste of time. Martha's cooking, like most everything else about her, left a lot to be desired.

She set the coffee cup on the table, and they made eye contact. Bobby quickly looked away, nibbling around the burnt edges of a piece of bacon. "Your daddy said to find out what time we're goen to vote," Martha told him.

Bobby dropped the partially eaten bacon back on the plate. "Sometime this afternoon," he replied. He pushed the fork through the eggs but could not work up an appetite. Finally, he picked up the coffee, pushed away from the table and went back to bed.

He sat on the edge of the bed, drinking coffee, while his thoughts wandered back to Paul Berrien and the election. If anyone ever needed proof that the rich were different and above the law, then surely this situation provided it. The whole mess bewildered Bobby. Had he conspired to cover up the cause of someone's death, tried to pass off a suicide as a heart attack, the sheriff would have slapped a pair of handcuffs on him in a heartbeat and Bobby likely would have ended up buried under the jail. No one would have given him the benefit of the doubt. Paul Berrien, however, had done wrong and walked away from it smelling like roses. Paul had gotten off scot-free as far as the law was concerned. The whole world, it seemed, was ready and willing not only to exonerate Paul but to praise his good intentions to spare his older sisters the truth about their father's decision to blow his brains out of his head. Well, April and June knew the truth now and Bobby hoped they were wallowing in every miserable ounce of it.

Bobby felt a vindictive mood coming over him. Realizing he could ill afford a short temper on this of all days, he decided to nip his anger in the bud. He forced himself from bed, determined to concentrate on something else beside the election for the remainder of the morning, deciding a walk around the farm would ease his foul mood.

It did not.

By dinnertime, his mind was off the election and Bobby was furious. The crops were withered from lack of rain, choked full of weeds from neglect, and Bobby doubted anything could be salvaged from them. He scarcely believed what he saw. Bad times had visited the farm before, but never had his father tended the fields with such dereliction. Bobby considered the possibility that his mind was playing tricks on him, that the heat had afflicted him with sunstroke and he was imagining the worst. But Bobby was sound of mind and body for the moment, and these wasted fields were laid by with reality.

In this state of disbelief and anger, Bobby sought out his father. He found Robert by the water pump outside the back door, bent over by a fit of wheezing and coughing.

"Crops look like shit, Pa," Bobby bellowed. "Just what the hell have you been doen all summer? And how do you think we are goen to get by this comen year?"

Robert coughed up a mess of phlegm, spat and wiped his mouth on his shirtsleeve before looking at Bobby. "You get elected sheriff today, and you ought to get by fine this year and the three after it," he answered tiredly. "Besides, Bobby, you never worried much about the crops in the past. Why the sudden interest?"

"I never had reason to worry," Bobby replied impatiently, beginning to scrutinize his father. "What's been goen on around here this summer?" he demanded. "Why haven't you taken better care of the farm?"

"I did my best," Robert muttered defiantly.

For the second time that day, Bobby wondered if his eyes were deceiving him. He blinked twice, peered closer at Robert and discovered that his father, much like the fields on their farm, appeared withered and beaten. His pa was a tired old man, haggard and worn out, shriveled and used up.

He'd spent a lifetime thinking of his father as robust and impregnable, so it took a moment for Bobby to digest these appearances otherwise. He'd been hell-bent on a confrontation with Robert a moment ago, but his attitude softened with concern over his father's well-being. "You're not looken too good these days, Pa," Bobby frowned. "Are you feelen poorly?"

"I'm okay," Robert insisted.

"Maybe," Bobby agreed halfheartedly. "But maybe you ought to see the doctor."

Robert coughed again, a dry, hacking sound that made Bobby wince while his father struggled to breathe.

"I hope you win the election," Robert told his son when he had regained his composure. He fixed a stern look on Bobby. "You don't care much for hard work, and you've never impressed me as be'en none too bright."

Bobby went pale beneath the criticism.

"Of course," Robert continued, "you might not win the election, and that'll put you right back here on the farm. It's a decent farm. Bought and paid for. A man can earn a liven on it if he's willen to put forth the effort, which is about the best piece of advice I can or ever will offer you, boy."

Robert turned away and walked a few steps to the back porch, then stopped and looked back at his son. "You and me never were much alike," he said stiffly. "Except for one thing. I never cared too much about anything or anybody, and I guess you've cared even less about most everything and everybody. Don't go tryen to do me any favors, Bobby. I don't need your sympathy and I don't want it. I've seen a doctor. He says I got lung cancer and I'm dyen." Robert hesitated, glancing around the yard into the fields and back to Bobby. "It won't be no great loss," he shrugged. "Not to me, you or anybody else," he added, turning back toward the house and shuffling up the rickety porch steps.

Bobby never knew whether his father or Martha voted. He skipped dinner that day, choosing to take a long drive through the countryside. In the early afternoon, he stopped by the voting precinct to cast his ballot, then continued on to the Tip-Toe Inn, the only legitimate honky tonk in the county. He parked behind the sprawling building, spent the next two hours getting drunk on an empty stomach and finally set out for home to catch a quick nap. He woke shortly after the polls closed, with a vicious hangover and low spirits. Still, he showered and dressed neatly, piled his family into the pickup and drove to Cookville to wait on the election returns.

His home precinct of New River reported the first results, giving Paul Berrien an overwhelming majority of the vote. Bobby won six of the next nine districts reporting, but the voting margins were too small to overcome Paul's early lead. It was the closest vote in county history and Bobby came up on the short end of the count.

He watched the final tally go up on the tote board in front of *The Cookville Herald* office on the town square, shaking his head in disbelief, astonished by the thin difference in the vote, enraged by the miracle of Paul's victory.

"Bobby."

It took a moment for the sound to penetrate Bobby's consciousness. He turned around slowly, his mouth agape, to find Paul standing before him with a conciliatory smile plastered across his face.

"Bobby," Paul repeated, extending his hand. "You ran a hard campaign. The vote couldn't have been any closer." He hesitated. "I hope we can move past our differences."

Bobby, still shell-shocked by the defeat, shook his head. "You're gonna turn this county over to the niggers, Paul," he hissed loudly.

He shoved past a startled Paul, marched into the gathering crowd and stopped abruptly. "Those of you who voted for this man," Bobby exploded, gesturing to Paul. "Mark my words!" He glared out at the crowd with bloodshot eyes, venting rage and despair. "One day, you'll remember my warnen about Paul Berrien. Y'all will be sorry that you voted a lawbreaker and a rich daddy's boy into office, and you'll wish you had voted for me."

Bobby scanned the crowd, searching for enemies and the misguided, then leveled his seething gaze on Paul. "I'll be back, Paul Berrien," he sneered. "I'm gonna watch your every move like a hawk these next four years. And next time, I'll win. You can count on it."

His peace said, Bobby stormed into the darkness.

# CHAPTER 8

TWILIGHT WAS FADING WHEN the Bakers headed home from Tifton. Sleet fell, icing the road and forcing Matt to drive cautiously. But no one minded the slow going. The family was in a festive mood, dreaming aloud about Christmas wishes and thinking silently about preparations still to complete.

Matt was the first to realize the sleet had changed to snow. "Will you look at that?" he whistled softly.

"What's that?" Caroline asked from the backseat, where she was planning supper and making a mental list of the things she needed to do before bedtime, including baking a spice cake and wrapping gifts.

"It's snowen," Matt announced to the entire family.

The children greeted the news with shrieks and gasps. Snow fell rarely in these parts—Luke and Bonnie had never seen it—and they could hardly contain their anticipation. Faces pressed against the windows in search of the white stuff, and all six children pleaded for Matt to stop the car so that they could touch the snow. Matt considered honoring the request, but they were only a few minutes from home and he wanted to get there before the road conditions deteriorated. He continued driving, despite the disapproving groans.

The short delay merely heightened expectations and none too soon they were home. Car doors flew open and the children spilled out with yelps of happiness, crawling over parents, grandparents and each other in their eagerness to acquaint themselves with snow. They were a sight to behold, and parents and grandparents watched in wonder at their various reactions to the touch and feel of snow. Joe raised his head to the heavens, attempting to catch the tiny flakes with his mouth, while Summer and Luke ran to the front porch walkway, scraping up enough white powder to make their first snowballs. John and Carrie stood openmouthed, he staring as if afraid the white fleece would disappear with any sudden movement and she reaching tentatively out with her hands to catch a falling snowflake. Bonnie squealed in delight, shaking her head back and forth as snow landed on her hair.

The snow cast a magic spell that not even the adults were immune to. Matt gathered Caroline in a full embrace, and even Rachel permitted Sam to wrap his arms around her waist.

"Looks like we're goen to have another white Christmas," Caroline said happily.

"Twice in a lifetime," Rachel replied. "Who would have dreamed?"

They watched the frolicking children for a while longer and then, all too soon, the snow ended. It simply stopped, without warning, and a vague sense of disappointment filled the adults whose imaginations had drummed up expectations of a white Christmas similar to the one in 1941.

The children, unhampered by such expectancy, barely noticed the snow had stopped. A thin white blanket covered the frozen ground like dust and its beauty was priceless in their eyes. They had woken on many winter mornings to frost gathered more thickly on the ground, but the snow was special. They regarded it with a moment of passing reverence, then turned the yard into an ice-skating rink, slipping and sliding across the slick grass, falling down on the cold ground and soaking their clothes through and through.

Rachel opened her mouth, prepared to utter a stern warning about catching cold, flu or worse. But Caroline caught her eye beforehand. "They'll remember this night their whole lives, Ma. A cold, they'll forget. But we make them go inside now and they'll never let us live it down."

Rachel shrugged. "You're right," she agreed. "Maybe if there's a hot supper on the table and dry clothes waiten when they come inside, we can keep everybody well."

Almost an hour later, Caroline called her brood into the warm house. They straggled in one by one with red cheeks, runny noses and frozen hands, exhausted from the horseplay, soaked to the bone and glowing with high spirits. She made everyone change into dry bedclothes, then ushered them into the kitchen to a roaring fire.

Christmas Eve supper was traditional fare in the Baker household—fried pork brains, scrambled eggs, sausage, bacon, grits and biscuits sopped in cane syrup. Everyone ate a hearty meal and then focused like elves on their final preparations for Christmas Day.

Stockings went up by the kitchen fireplace, presents were wrapped and put under the tree and, finally, the children were hustled into bed for the nightly devotional.

The children rarely bedded down at nighttime without a devotional and prayer. Usually, Caroline or Rachel read several verses from the Bible before prayers were said and kisses given. On this night, Caroline asked Joe to read the Christmas story.

"And it came to pass in those days, that there went out a decree from Caesar Augustus, that all the world should be taxed. (And this taxing was first made when Cyrenius was governor of Syria.) And all went to be taxed, every one into his own city. And Joseph also went up from Galilee, out of the city of Nazareth, into Judaea, unto the city of David, which is called Bethlehem; (because he was of the house and lineage of David:) To be taxed with Mary his espoused wife, being great with child …."

Caroline stood in the doorway for a moment, listening to the wonderful story, the words ringing deep and true from Joe, and her heart beamed. Then, she made her way to the kitchen.

———

Caroline finished wrapping the presents shortly before midnight and, with Matt's help, arranged them under the Christmas tree. Next, they stuffed the stockings, filling them with oranges, grapefruit, tangerines and kumquats, almonds, walnuts, Brazil nuts and cashews, gumdrops, fudge, hard candy and chewing gum. There were trinkets and small toys, Crackerjacks and novelties—until at last the bulging stockings would hold no more.

When they were finished, Matt picked up the glass of milk and saucer of cookies left on the table by Luke and Bonnie and retired with his wife to the living room. The soft glow of Christmas lights provided the room's only illumination and they sat on the burgundy sofa, dunking cookies in milk, observing the tree and packages and relishing the peace of Christmas night.

"Are you tired?" Matt asked when Caroline laid her head on his shoulder.

"Not really," she answered softly. "Just contented."

"Me, too," Matt agreed.

He put a finger under Caroline's chin, tilted her face and kissed his wife fully on the lips, long and slow. The kiss was different from the ones they had shared nineteen years ago, absent of mystery and full of familiarity, but it kindled the same passion.

"Nineteen years is a long time," Caroline sighed, breaking the kiss. "But it's gone by so fast."

Matt nodded agreement, looked at the tree and then back to Caroline. "Sometimes, I feel like we've been married forever," he said gently, "and I can't remember a time when you weren't a part of my life."

Caroline gave him a frowning smile.

"It's a good feelen," he assured her. "A very good feelen. The time has flown, though. I remember getten married like it was yesterday. But it also seems like somethen that happened a lifetime ago. Sometimes I wonder if you married me or somebody who just happened to look like me."

"I know what you mean," Caroline admitted. "It's probably because we're different people now." She paused, gathering her thoughts. "I was just sixteen when we got married; you were eighteen. I was me and you were you. Now, I think we're *us*, and that makes us both different people."

She laughed. "Does that sound silly?"

Matt smiled. "Not to me." He kissed her again, then broke away with a boyish grin. "I know we decided not to give gifts this year, but I just couldn't let both our anniversary and Christmas pass without somethen to remember it by," he said cheerfully.

Caroline bowed her head, then peered up at him with guilty eyes. "We're worse than the children," she confessed. "I got you somethen, too."

Matt smiled again, mischievously. "If we give our gifts tonight, technically they count as anniversary presents," he suggested. "And if I remember right, we only agreed not to give Christmas presents."

Caroline rose from the sofa, grinning at her husband. "Yours is in the bedroom," she said, moving past him across the hall to their room. She returned shortly, carrying a tiny package wrapped in red tissue paper and sprouting a white bow bigger than the gift.

"I didn't wrap mine," Matt said hesitantly as she took her seat next to him on the sofa.

"It doesn't matter," Caroline replied, handing him the red package. "This isn't much, but I thought you'd appreciate it."

Matt tore off the bow, bringing the tissue paper with it, and found himself staring at a small cardboard box. He opened the box and pulled out a triple-bladed pocketknife. A wide grin split his face and he looked at Caroline. "Thanks, honey," he said, genuinely pleased.

"You lost your other one this summer," Caroline explained. "I kept thinken you'd get another one, but you didn't. No man should have to go around without a pocketknife."

Matt opened the three blades. "There must have been a hundred times over the last few months when a pocketknife would have come in handy," he said, examining the knife. "I kept reachen for mine, but it wasn't there." He closed the blades. "This is good," he added, slipping the gift into the front pocket of his corduroy pants.

He kissed her quickly, then pushed away, grinning broadly and saying, "Now it's your turn."

Caroline eyed his grin with a curious frown. "What is it?"

Matt shook his head. "Close your eyes."

Caroline obeyed and Matt reached into his pocket. "Okay, open them," he said.

Caroline opened her eyes to find a delicate ring box setting on the palm of her husband's hand. "Oh, Matt!" she exclaimed softly.

She took the bone-colored box gingerly, opened it and gasped. The white gold ring lay on a velvety green cushion, its cluster of diamonds sparkling in the glow of the Christmas tree lights.

"It's beautiful," Caroline remarked finally, looking from the ring to her husband with tears of joy in her eyes.

As far as Matt was concerned, the band was too thin and the cluster of diamond chips too tiny. But the ring was the only one affordable, and he had settled for it. Now, gazing into the adoring eyes of his wife, Matt forgot what the ring lacked in splendor. He lifted the ring from the velvet bed, then slipped it carefully onto Caroline's finger.

"We didn't have much time to be engaged, but I always wanted you to have a ring," he said. "Sorry you had to wait nineteen years for it."

Caroline placed her hands on his shoulders. "I'm not," she smiled into his eyes. "Nineteen years ago, you made me the happiest woman in the world, Matt; now you've gone and done it all over again. I love you."

Her devotion and affection brought a blush to Matt's face. He glanced down at the ring on her hand, then back to Caroline. "I loved you a lot back then, honey," he said. "But I love you that much more now."

Matt kissed Caroline tenderly, then gathered her in his arms, carried her to the bedroom and made love with his wife. At last, with both of them exhausted and sated, Caroline laid her head on Matt's chest and was locked in his embrace for the night. In silence, they drifted into the familiar, comfortable and satisfying slumber of old lovers.

A stillness settled over the home that night, its quietness broken only by the occasional rustling of bed covers and the constant tick of various clocks, while outside, cascades of snow swirled silently, softly. The small flakes danced to an uncommon beat on their downward journey, settling over ground, trees and rooftops. Snow blanketed the land again and again, creating a winter wonderland and magic for a lifetime.

---

On that same night, a young black woman lay sleeplessly on a worn double mattress that had been pushed into the corner of her rented, single-room shack. Her name was Beauty Salon, and the pedigree behind it was at the top of the jumble cluttering her head and keeping the woman awake.

Beauty's mother had been born and raised in Cookville, living there until the age of nineteen when she took a notion to leave and moved to New Orleans. Some fifteen years later, Goodie Wright returned home and reintroduced herself as Goodness Salon. She brought with her a ten-year-old daughter and a sad story about her husband drowning in the Mississippi River.

Everyone accepted her story at face value, which was fortunate since every word of it was true. However, both friends and relatives scoffed at the ridiculousness of naming a child Beauty Salon. Some even accused her of lying about the girl's name, but Goodness silenced those doubters by producing authentic copies of her marriage license to Jacque Salon, his death certificate and Beauty's birth certificate. Afterward, relatives and friends decided the name was clever, and Goodness and Beauty set up permanent residence in Cookville. Goodness earned their living styling hair in the black community and Beauty, when she was older and had quit school, worked as a maid for a number of well-to-do white families in the community.

Beauty herself grew to despise the name and longed for the day when she could change it. Perhaps if she were indeed beautiful, she would have enjoyed the name. But Beauty was an average-looking woman, an inch or so taller and, perhaps, longer-limbed, smaller-breasted and leaner-hipped than most. She was moon-faced, with wide, expressive dark eyes and slender facial contours that offset her broad features. Her hair, which was jet black and tended to straighten naturally, framed her face like a picture, falling shoulder length and flipping under at the ends.

There was reason for Beauty to consider her name on this night, and it was lying beside her in the long form of Lucas Bartholomew.

Lucas had asked Beauty to marry him earlier in the evening. The proposal had shocked Beauty, who had been simply curious and mildly thrilled when Lucas showed up at her front door earlier on this Christmas Eve.

"I have somethen to ask you," he had told her when Beauty opened the door to find him standing in the frigid darkness. "Can I come in?"

She motioned Lucas inside, gesturing for him to sit in the only chair in her home, but he declined politely. "We don't know each other all that well, Beauty, but I think highly of you," he said respectfully. "I'm hopen you will marry me."

Lucas apparently interpreted her stunned silence as wariness about the proposal. "I'm a hard worker," he assured her, "and I'll make a decent liven for us. I'm not much of a drinken man, I'll go to church with you and I'll never lay a hand on you unless you want me to."

Until that moment, Beauty had considered Lucas only a passing acquaintance. He was younger than her by two years, they had never run in the same circles and most of what she knew about him came by reputation and word of mouth. No one could question his work ethic, but the Lucas she remembered also possessed a wild streak. Lucas had drunk his share of liquor and known more than a few women in Cookville before he went traipsing off across the country. To his credit, though, Lucas had been discreet about his carryings-on and his reputation was earned solely through gossip as far as Beauty was concerned.

She first took notice of Lucas one Sunday morning while

singing in the choir of the Cookville African-Methodist-Episcopal Church. They were singing *I'll Fly Away* when Lucas snuck into the back pew of the church. Lucas had gone from the back pew to the altar in a few Sundays, and their first conversation had come when Beauty found the courage to welcome him into the Lord's flock.

Since then, they had spoken to each other regularly at Sunday church services and on frequent occasions in the Berrien home, where Beauty did housekeeping twice a week and Lucas often performed odd jobs.

At the age of twenty-five, Beauty had begun to think marriage was an unlikely prospect, which meant she would be stuck with her outrageous name for eternity. But it was neither her spinster status nor dislike of being called Beauty Salon that moved her to accept the marriage proposal from Lucas. It was his humbleness and sincerity.

Lucas made no pretense about loving her. He was fond of Beauty, as she was of him. Lucas wanted a companion, someone to make a home with, and the idea appealed to Beauty. There would be plenty of time for love once they were married and knew each other.

"Yes," she told him without batting an eye.

Lucas accepted her answer with equal dispassion. But it was only a moment before he flashed her a broad grin, and his obvious delight unfurled a timid smile from Beauty. They laughed quietly, like children flushed from the unexpected success of a mysterious adventure. Then unexpectedly, almost as if he had forgotten, Lucas reached inside his winter coat and produced a gift-wrapped package for Beauty.

Her smile widened, and she accepted it eagerly, tore open the wrapping and found a Bible.

"I noticed you don't have a Bible at church," Lucas said thoughtfully. "I figured you need one see'en how church is so important to you. And I thought it would be a good way of keepen track of our family."

Beauty fingered the cardboard binder, then thumbed through the pages. "I don't read very well," she murmured, embarrassed by the revelation.

"Then I'll teach you," Lucas vowed.

Beauty was a serious person, deliberate and thorough in her actions and manners. Religion and church were especially dear to her heart.

She could trace her Christian commitment to a hot summer day when she was fourteen and some lunatic had burst into the church screaming about religion, the masses and how it was a tool white people used to keep colored folk in their place. Beauty had not understood the man's ranting and likely would have forgotten him, except that had been the day she first felt the power of God.

It happened sometime after the mad man was escorted from church. They were singing strongly and the preacher called everyone to the altar. Usually, Beauty sat in the pew during altar calls but on this day, she heeded the preacher's advice to unburden herself. She never made it to the altar. Six steps from her destination, she passed out cold, sucker-punched by a power so strong that Beauty swore God had belted her so she would see the light.

Ever since, Beauty had been a devout churchgoer. She sang in the choir, a soulful alto who was particularly effective on slower hymns like *Amazing Grace*. She would have studied the Bible but her reading skills made the task difficult at best, so Beauty contented herself by trying to recall the scriptures read by the preacher each Sunday and applying the message to her life.

The offer from Lucas to teach her to read filled her heart with joy in a way that Beauty had experienced maybe once or twice before. "I'd be much obliged," she acknowledged warmly.

Lucas moved closer to Beauty, turning the pages of the Bible to the front to show where he had written her name as owner of the book, his name as its giver and the date it was given. "I took the liberty of fillen out all that information beforehand," he said apologetically. "Took it for granted you might say yes."

Beauty was plagued by an innate shyness, which often stopped her from voicing opinions or joining conversations. She was a natural listener, but with Lucas, she lost her inhibitions.

Lucas entertained her with tales about his travels around the country, visits to big cities like New York, Philadelphia and Detroit, people he had met and the things he had done. He told her about his family, a father who drank too much, a mother who endured ill health, and she told him about the feeling of always being overshadowed by her mother's gaudy style. They discovered they were both only children, although Beauty volunteered that she considered two cousins like sisters.

Beauty, who prepared a supper of boiled turnip greens, baked sweet potatoes and cornbread while talking and listening, surprised

herself and Lucas by asking suddenly over the meal, "Do you believe God is a white man?"

Lucas weighed the question in his mind, at last answering, "I
never thought about it much to be truthful. Why you ask?"

"I'm just curious."

"What do you think," he inquired. "Is God black or white?"

Beauty told him that she believed God was a white man, just like
Santa Claus. Colored people tried to convince themselves that Jesus
and Santa Claus were black men, but Beauty knew better. If Santa
Claus were black, she told Lucas, then he would not pass over her
house year after year without ever leaving anything.

For a long time, Lucas had simply stared at Beauty as if he
thought her crazy. And then Beauty laughed mischievously, shook
her head and explained she always had silly thoughts around Christ-
mastime. She assured Lucas that she knew Santa Claus did not exist,
not even for white children, but the idea was a lovely notion anyway
and one she would pass on to her children one day. For as far as
Beauty was concerned, if there was a Santa Claus, then he would
love colored and white children equally—just as God did.

They talked late into the night, agreeing to marry as soon as
possible and deciding to live in Beauty's rented shack until Lucas
could arrange for more comfortable accommodations.

When Lucas finally rose from his chair, Beauty supposed he was
going to leave. Instead, he walked to her and pushed a lock of hair
off her face. "I can go now or I could stay the night. The choice is
yours to make, Beauty."

Once again, Lucas caught her off guard with a proposal and this
time Beauty's stomach leapt into her throat. She swallowed as Lucas
laid the rough palm of his hand against her cheek.

"You can stay," she said nervously. "But I've never been with
anyone before."

Lucas merely nodded understanding, then pulled her from the
chair and led her to the mattress. He had kissed Beauty and then
bedded her, gently at first to overcome her reluctance and later
more frantically as her need became greater. Lucas had drifted off
to sleep soon afterward, cradling Beauty in his arms for a while
before falling away and turning his back to her.

Now Beauty touched his naked back, gingerly so as not to wake
him. His skin was cold, so she pulled the blanket over Lucas and
was stricken by the most intimate sensation of her life. She allowed

her hand to linger on his back, caressing its muscled cords and bony ridges, realizing this body would share her bed and her life for all the years to come.

Joy filled her heart, and Beauty experienced profound knowledge: Earlier this night she had agreed to take Lucas as her husband; now she took him to heart. What she felt was not yet love but the beginnings of it, stirring deep inside Beauty, swelling like baker's yeast, bubbling like fine wine. She could not contain it and she could not lie still.

Ignoring the urge to rouse Lucas from his sound sleep to tell him about this revelation, Beauty eased herself off the mattress, crossing the cold floor in bare feet to the single window in her one-room shack. Beneath the window was a worn footlocker, a hand-me-down from one of the families whose homes she cleaned. Inside the cardboard trunk were Beauty's treasures, an assortment of odds and ends collected over the years through the philanthropic gestures of various employers. Pots and pans, dinnerware and flat-ware, candles and candlesticks, linens and coverings, a medley of miscellany no longer wanted by well-to-do white women, a hoard of household treasures for Beauty.

Working quietly, she unhitched the trunk and eased up its squeaky lid. An ivory lace doily lay on top of the neatly stacked collection. A donation from the Berrien sisters, it was delicate and dainty, one of Beauty's most prized possessions. She closed her eyes, imagining a beautiful lamp resting on top of the lace, remembering June Berrien had suggested to her sister some months ago that they should rid themselves of an old hurricane lamp stuck away in one of the empty bedrooms of their home.

Beauty blushed at the wayward thought, knowing her covetous nature violated one of the Ten Commandments. She shook away both feelings and began rummaging through the trunk, smiling to herself at the thought of using these throwaways to make a home for Lucas.

When she had examined the entirety of contents in the trunk, Beauty returned every item to its rightful place, closed the lid and reattached the locks. A combination of the late hour and personal satisfaction was waning her enthusiasm, but Beauty was not yet ready to return to bed.

She rose from the floor, reached across the trunk to pull back the curtain and discovered a miracle. It was snowing again. A few flakes had dusted the ground earlier in the evening, but this time the white stuff was falling in earnest, piling up in mounds. There would be snow on the ground in the morning, maybe all through Christmas Day. Cookville would have a white Christmas and maybe she and Lucas would have a white wedding.

Stifling a yawn, Beauty glanced one final time out the window at the falling snow. She'd always heard Christmas was the season of miracles but until tonight, she'd never understood the meaning. Now she did. Tonight, Beauty felt part of a miracle. She understood the promise of Christmas, she believed in the spirit of Santa Claus, and she felt blessed by a sign from God.

She dropped the curtain back in place, tiptoeing across the room to retrieve the Bible Lucas had given her, cradling it with reverence. Lucas had said they would fill up the blank pages with history while the printed pages guided their way.

For a while, she contemplated their behavior earlier in the night, coming together as husband and wife without the blessing of a preacher. Certainly, the Bible did not condone adultery and fornication. But had they been wrong to celebrate their commitment to each other? Did a preacher's blessing of their union matter when they already had God's blessing?

A ponderous woman might have brooded over such concerns. But Beauty was a simple woman. She had protected her virtue for twenty-five years, yielding it only to the man who would share her bed for the remainder of their lives together. Whatever doubts she had about her decision vanished in a wave of drowsy contentment.

She pattered across the room once more, to the mattress on the floor and, lying carefully down, drawing the covers around her, stretched out beside her man. Lucas, feeling her press against him, rolled over onto his side, facing Beauty, and without waking, snuggled against her. She explored his chest, found his heartbeat with her hand and closed her eyes.

It was the season of miracles, the fulfillment of promise, and she, Beauty Salon, was living a dream. That was her last waking thought, except for one: In a day or so, for better or worse, she would become Beauty *Bartholomew*.

––––––––––

Lamplight cast a soft glow around the elegant front room, the more formal of two parlors in the Berrien mansion. A fire crackled in the marbled fireplace, its flickering lights throwing shadows, breaking the smooth planes of muted illumination, dancing to the melodies of Christmas music playing from a stereo console. The stereo was a present to themselves from the three Berrien siblings, a purposefully self-indulgent Christmas Eve purchase of celebration.

Paul stoked the fire with another log, poked it and, laying aside the soot-stained iron rod, crossed the ivory colored floor rug with Wedgwood borders of ribbons and intertwined flower sprigs to a Queen Anne side table. On the cherry table were a crystal ice bucket holding a chilled bottle of champagne and three matching glasses.

"On an impulse I walked straight into this fancy Atlanta restaurant and told the maître d' I wanted a bottle of his most ridiculously expensive champagne in a bag to go," Paul informed his sisters, explaining how he had acquired the sparkling white wine.

"And what did the maître d' do, pray tell?" laughed June.

"He didn't bat an eye, that's for sure," Paul grinned. "He simply said, 'One moment, sir,' vanished behind closed doors and returned in a couple of minutes with the bottle, replete with a brown bag. The man assured me it was vintage quality, imported from France. I took his word for it, he charged me a small fortune and I was on my way home."

"I declare," April exclaimed as Paul plucked the champagne from the ice bucket. "Whatever would the church members say if they knew we were drinken champagne? No doubt it would be scandalous."

"I dare say, April," reasoned June, the saltier of the two sisters. "Not even the Hard Shell Baptists would begrudge us a drink or two after the year we've had. And I'm almost willen to bet the kind folks at Benevolence Missionary Baptist Church would do the honors for us were they here tonight."

"Here, here," Paul agreed, giving the bottle a final twist as the cork popped free and the bubbling foam elicited delighted gasps and clapping from his sisters.

"We haven't had champagne in ages," June reflected.

"Not since Paul graduated from law school and came home," April remembered.

"As I recall, we were celebraten my engagement," Paul reminded them drolly. "Fleeten though it was."

"Oh, yes," June frowned. "Now I remember. Paul, whatever happened to Paige?"

"She married a very respected doctor in Atlanta. They had a couple of children last time I heard, which was several years ago."

"Well, good for her," April said.

"Yes," Paul concurred, filling the three glasses with champagne. "Good for her."

He passed glasses to April and June, then picked up the remaining one for himself, bestowing a catching smile on his sisters. "To us," he toasted.

"To us," chimed in April and June as the three of them touched glasses and sipped champagne.

"Delicious," purred June. "We really should do this more often."

"We should," April agreed whimsically. "But let's not tell the Baptists if we do."

Everyone laughed lightly, using the ensuing moment of silence to collect their thoughts and savor the champagne.

It was an unusual Christmas Eve night in the Berrien home. For many years, they had given little more than passing interest to Christmas Eve, preferring to celebrate casually on Christmas Day itself. But this year, by mutual agreement, they had turned Christmas Eve night into a formal affair, dressing up in finery, dining in the ballroom and now retiring to the front parlor for quiet talk and music.

In truth, the Christmas spirit had come late this year to April and June. They had bought presents for each other and Paul as usual, decorated a small pine tree with lights only and prepared for a simple dinner on Christmas Day when, unexpectedly, the invitation to Christmas dinner with the Baker family had come and, with it, the first stirrings of the holiday's good tidings. Then, this morning, Paul had proposed they share a late Christmas Eve supper in formal attire and surroundings and suddenly April and June were ripe with Christmas cheer and full of last-minute plans. They had cajoled Paul into taking them to Cookville, where they bought additional gifts for each other, their brother, the Baker family and Beauty Salon. Finally, on impulse, all three had looked at each other with daring and carried out a longstanding threat to buy the new stereo console.

Now their eyes shone with pleasure, and their faces expressed joy.

Paul reckoned it was the happiest Christmas his sisters had seen in many years. All three of them had grown to neglect this special season over the years, losing their belief in its promise of miracles, conceding its wonders to the young, hardening their hearts to its birth of expectations. Why was it, Paul reflected to himself, when the three of them could watch over each other every day of the year with gentle love and devotion, that they could not find a warm spot in their hearts for the Christmas season?

"I think next year we might prepare a little earlier for Christmas," June suggested aloud, as if reading his thoughts, breaking the momentary silence that had enveloped them. "At least put a few more decorations on the tree, although I am partial to just the lights."

April nodded in agreement. "That's exactly what I was thinken," she said. "We've neglected Christmas far too long 'round here. June, do you remember when we used to go greenen?"

She looked at Paul by way of explanation. "It was one of Mother's traditions," she continued. "Always one Saturday shortly after Thanksgiven and before Christmas, she'd haul us out into the woods with axes and saws, and we'd come back with loads of cedar, pine, holly and mistletoe."

"Mother would put greenery in every nook and cranny of the house," June remembered, closing her eyes to inhale a faraway fragrance. "There's nothen like the aroma of winter greens fillen up a house."

"Let's go greenen next year," April said. "We'll revive a grand and glorious tradition."

"Why wait till next year?" June suggested eagerly. "Let's do it the day after Christmas. We can take Beauty with us, maybe Lucas Bartholomew, too. We'll see the new year in with a house full of fresh fragrant greens. I can hardly wait."

"Mother decorated this room, didn't she," Paul asked suddenly, provoking a startled look from his sisters.

"She did," April confirmed. "Mother had impeccable taste."

"She was partial to the Queen Anne style," June supplied, glancing around at the various chairs, sofas, and tables, all made from cherry wood, upholstered in creamy white brocaded material with Wedgwood and rosewood floral trimmings. "Everything in here is Queen Anne, except for that," she continued, gesturing to the grandfather clock in the corner near the foyer. "Daddy purchased that particular clock when they went to Europe. When Mother re-decorated this room—the year before you were born, Paul—Daddy insisted she keep the clock. She did not protest as I recall."

"It's a beautiful room," April opined. "We really should use it more often."

June sipped from the champagne glass, changing the subject. "You're looken rather dashen tonight, Paul," she remarked. "Is that a new suit?"

"I treated myself in Atlanta," Paul confirmed, pulling on the sharp creases of the newly tailored black suit, fiddling with a red tie and the starched collar of his white shirt. "I probably won't have much need for it over the next four years, but I was in the mood for somethen new."

"Good for you," April saluted.

"I dare say, Paul," June asserted. "Practically every eligible woman between eight and eighty in these parts already has eyes on you. Once they see you cavorten in that handsome suit, they'll swarm like sharks to blood."

Paul laughed. "I'll be sure to wear my sheriff's uniform in public," he said. "Besides, I should say the same about you two. You're both looken especially lovely tonight."

Both women blushed from delight. April and June were pleasant looking, stylishly groomed and exquisitely mannered, but they lacked the fine qualities of beautiful people, and age was beginning to take a toll on their fair complexions.

"Thank you, darlen," said April, who was fine-boned and de-mure like her mother, with delicate features, faded blue eyes and long, soft white hair, which she gathered in a bun at the nape of her neck. Tonight, she had selected an ivory colored silk dress, ac-centing it with a red belt, red heels, pearl earrings and a cameo broach.

June, the taller and more flamboyant of the two sisters, bore a striking resemblance to April, with the exception of a prominent nose and stylishly coifed sandy red hair. She was wearing a forest green satin dress beneath a coverlet of mint green organdy, ac-cented with emerald earrings and a matching choker.

"At our age, brother dear, any and all compliments are appreci-ated," she said dryly. "We are particularly fond, however, of those sincere, so I double the gratitude expressed by April."

Paul cocked his head, smiled at his sisters and poured everyone another glass of champagne. "I have somethen to tell y'all," he announced.

"Pray tell," said June, moving to warm herself by the fire.

"I hired a private detective," Paul informed them. "To track down Henry Anderson."

"We figured as much," April commented.

"Henry was your biological father, Paul," June said supportively. "You have every reason to want to find him."

"Did you?" April inquired.

Paul nodded. "But he died a few years ago. Of a heart attack." He shrugged. "It's just as well I suppose."

"Did you learn anything else about him?" April asked.

Paul nodded again. "Actually, quite a lot," he replied. "He moved his family from here to Jeff Davis County, which is where he came from originally. He and his wife had five children. Their oldest boy died in the Korean War—drove a jeep onto a mine. The others—a boy and three girls—are scattered across the state now, all of them married with families of their own. Henry gave farmen another go in Jeff Davis County, until World War II came along. Then he sold off the family place and moved to Macon. He got a job in a factory and worked there until he had the heart attack. His wife—her name is Marjorie—is still liven."

"I always wondered what happened to the Andersons," June remarked, "even before we found out what we did about Mother and Henry. I only knew them in passen, but they left under such strange circumstances. I was curious. I asked Daddy. All he said was that Henry found somethen else to do."

"What was he like?" Paul inquired.

"I was away at school, so I never got to know him," April answered.

"He was a hard worker," June recalled, stepping from the fireplace to the love seat. "But honestly, Paul, what I remember most about Henry was how handsome he was. There's a strong resemblance between the two of you. I wouldn't have recognized it without knowen what I know now. But it's there, especially in the eyes. Your eyes are his eyes, Paul."

"If Daddy saw that resemblance, then it must have been difficult for him, raisen me as his own flesh and blood," Paul concluded. "Under the circumstances, I'd say he deserves praise for the effort. I wonder if I could have been as charitable."

"Daddy was a mean and manipulative man, Paul," April said harshly. "I cried myself to sleep the night I first realized that. And when I was finished cryen, I decided to believe he had done his best—by his wife and by his children. I will go to my grave believen that."

"What you describe as charity, Paul, probably was more a matter of saven face," June continued. "Or control. Our father wanted everything in this house under his thumb, includen his children. I still can't believe I allowed him to bulldoze me into taken back my maiden name when Calvin was killed." She hesitated. "But despite his considerable faults, I loved Daddy. He did not wish one moment of sorrow in our lives. And like April, I, too, choose to believe that his overbearen manner was his misguided way of protecten us."

Paul nodded agreement. "I suppose I feel the same way," he mumbled. "I always thought he resented me because Mother died as a result of my birth." He shrugged and sipped champagne. "It's almost a relief to find out after all these years that he did not hate me or blame me for her death."

"May we deduce then that you are happy to know the truth?" June asked.

"Yes," Paul nodded. "It answers a great many troublen questions." He smiled sheepishly. "Of course, if we ever open up those journals upstairs to the public, we'd probably better invoke censorship rights."

"Yes," April agreed. "They contain quite a tale about our ancestors."

"I suggest we keep them private as long as we're all liven and breathen," June proposed. "In fact, we should continue recorden our family history. And then, after we're all dead and gone, turn over the whole shebang to the library in Cookville."

"Perhaps," April nodded.

"Maybe," Paul shrugged.

"Do you plan to tell Matt that you know about his conversation with Daddy that night?" June asked.

"No," Paul said emphatically, receiving silent agreement from his sisters. "This family has sworn Matt to silence once too often. At this point, I see no reason to burden him with more of our secrets. He—or at least his reputation—has suffered far too much already for the protection of our family name and honor."

"Paul," April said after a moment. "Knowen what you know now, when Daddy died all those years ago ...." She hesitated, then inquired, "Would you have done the same thing all over again?"

"Probably," Paul answered quickly. "But I would not have involved Matt. And, I would have taken greater pains to see that I didn't get caught, to make sure there was no one lurken around the funeral home late at night. Of course ...."

He hesitated, anticipating his sisters' reaction to what he was about to suggest. "Of course, what I did back then helped me to win the election."

"How so?" April frowned.

"It was my opinion that it almost cost you the election," June suggested.

"It sounds ridiculous, I know," Paul explained. "But that day at the warehouse when Robert Taylor told everybody what Matt and I had done when Daddy died, I almost crumbled. I was ready to withdraw from the race."

He grinned suddenly. "Then Bobby got all preachy, putten his virtue on a pedestal, talken down to me like I was some kind of common criminal. He wound up putten a fire in my gut. And that's when I uttered those famous words: 'Spare me your sermon, Bobby.'

"I think people heard me say that and decided maybe I had backbone after all. People like a little passion mixed with their politics. Bobby had too much of it, and I didn't seem to have any. But that day, I showed everybody my passionate side. And while I'm sure some people voted for Bobby because they thought I did wrong by coveren up the cause of Daddy's death, some people respected my intentions and probably realized I was a reasonable man. And they voted for me based on that."

"Well I declare!" April exclaimed.

"You may be right," June murmured cautiously. "It sounds plausible. But I wonder if you're overestimaten the public's tolerance for people who put themselves above the law. A lot of people did not take kindly to what you did, however noble your intentions."

Paul regarded his sisters curiously for a moment. "You raise another question, June," he said finally. "One we've all conveniently overlooked for some time. What do you two think about my intentions? Were they noble or misguided?"

"Both," June answered quickly.

"June and I talked it over," April explained. "We both agreed. We were disappointed you thought us so fragile that we needed protection from the truth, however harsh it was."

"But we also decided you did exactly what Daddy would have done under the same circumstances," June took over. "You were only tryen to protect us. And your heart was in the right place, so we can't fault you for that. In the future, however, please do not shield us from the truth simply because you fear we cannot handle it. April and I are far more resilient than you might believe."

Paul nodded agreement. "I know that now," he assured them. "Y'all have changed, though—all of us have changed since Daddy died. But when it happened back then, I saw y'all through his eyes. You were more than sisters to me. You were the ones who had indulged and disciplined me over the years, who had played nursemaid, mother and teacher to me. And, I wanted to protect you."

"See, Paul," April pointed out. "You really are a Berrien, through and through."

"Yes," Paul sighed. "I am. And glad of it."

"I might add, Paul," June said, "that you would do well to remember just how resilient your two old sisters are. You're taken on a big challenge in the next few days when you become sheriff, and you'll likely need an ear or two to bounce off your ideas and frustrations over the next four years. Please don't hesitate to use ours."

"I'll remember that," Paul smiled. "I admit to be'en a bit wary about becomen sheriff. Under the best of circumstances, the job can be difficult. My hope is that the next four years will be quiet around here, like all the decades preceden it. Bar-en that, I hope to prove my salt. I don't care about leaven a legacy from my days in the office, but I would hope to earn the public's respect. I hope I'm up to the task."

"No doubt, you are," June declared. "You are a Berrien after all, and we are a family brimmen with success."

Suddenly, the grandfather clock struck midnight, filling the room with the deep, rich timbre of Westminster chimes.

"Merry Christmas," Paul said when the last echo of the twelfth chime faded.

"Merry Christmas," chorused June and April.

"Let's open our gifts now," April asserted impulsively, with daring glances at her sister and brother.

"But we've always opened presents on Christmas mornen," June protested. "It's a tradition."

"Oh, fiddlesticks to tradition," April groaned. "If we can drink champagne without worryen what the Baptists might think of us, we can jolly well open our Christmas presents right here and now."

"And it is Christmas mornen after all, June," Paul pointed out.

June sighed. "I suppose it would be okay," she relented as April began moving toward the tree. "It's just that Christmas day—except for openen gifts and sharen dinner—has always seemed to drag on forever. But we've got a full day tomorrow, so ...."

"This one's to you from Paul," April interrupted, holding up a large box wrapped in shimmering green foil.

"Let's do it," June decided, moving eagerly to accept the gift.

She ripped away the paper, pulled open the white box and parted white tissue paper to reveal a classically designed navy silk suit. "Oh, Paul, it's just beautiful," she whispered, pulling the new clothes from the box and measuring them against herself. "Wherever did you find somethen so exquisite?"

"At Rich's in Atlanta," Paul answered. "I simply described you to the saleslady and she made a couple of suggestions. I picked that one for you."

"The color's just perfect for you, June," April admired. "What was the sales lady's other suggestion?" she asked her brother.

Paul grinned broadly, bent under the tree and came up with an identical package wrapped in red tissue paper. He presented the gift to April, who shortly discovered the box contained a suit identical to June's, except for its red wine color.

Sometime later, when all the gifts had been opened and ogled over, appreciated and admired again, the trio picked up the scattered paper, returned their presents under the tree and finally collapsed onto the furniture.

"I'm tired," admitted April, stretching out on the love seat. "But this has been the most wonderful Christmas Eve I can remember for ages. It was a good idea, Paul. The Christmas spirit is a wonderful feelen when it gets deep inside a body."

Paul smiled at her from across the room in a wing back chair.

"Indeed, it is," sighed June, who was seated in a matching chair across the room with her feet propped on an ottoman.

April bolted upright. "Let's be daren," she suggested boldly, picking up her empty glass from the coffee table. "Let's have one last glass of champagne before we retire."

"Now there's an idea," June added brightly. "And perhaps you could make a Christmas toast, Paul."

Paul rose and retrieved the nearly empty bottle from the ice bucket. He poured champagne into all three glasses, half filling them, then returned the empty bottle to the ice bucket and joined his sisters by the fire.

"A Christmas toast to us," he mused aloud, while April and June waited.

"To family ties," he finally toasted, holding forth his glass. "To our past, our present and our future. May truth guide us and love bond us through it all."

April smiled warmly, June brushed away a single tear, and both women extended their glasses to Paul. The crystal pieces touched lightly, ringing in good tidings of Christmas and, for a while longer, two spinster-like sisters and their bachelor brother sipped champagne in a circle by the firelight.

---

Joe was the first person to wake in the Baker home on Christmas morning, pulled fully alert from a dreamy sleep by the sheer force of anticipation. He cherished Christmas, with all its time-honored traditions and unexpected magic, divine inspiration and childlike innocence, holy reverence and even its overblown commercialization. While he no longer honestly gazed skyward on Christmas Eve night in search of Santa Claus and his reindeer, Joe still chanced an occasional heavenward glance. He believed fervently in Father Christmas, the power of goodness to achieve the impossible, the triumph of human kindness, the hope of the heart.

A smile plastered itself across his face as Joe lay there in the predawn cold pondering the mysteries of the most wonderful day of the year. Shortly, he eased out of bed, wrapped himself in a blanket and tiptoed through the room he shared with his brothers, down the hall to the living room. Even in the darkness, he could see the pile of presents under the tree.

Resisting an impulse to rummage through the packages, he lit the gas space heater and warmed himself before returning to the bedroom to fetch his own pile of presents from under the bed. Joe

carried the packages to the living room and placed them inconspic-
uously among the presents already under the tree. Finally, after
warming once more by the heater, he trudged down the hall again
to wake his siblings.

"John, Luke," he said, tapping his brothers on the shoulder.
"Wake up, guys. Santa Claus has come and gone."

Luke sprang instantly awake. "Did you see him?" he gasped.

"Not even a glimpse," Joe sighed disappointedly, ruffling his
brother's head. "But the milk, cookies and candy corn are all gone."

"All of it?" Luke inquired incredulously.

"There's a few pieces of candy corn scattered on the rug," Joe
replied.

"I wonder which fireplace he came down," Luke said excitedly,
dropping from the bed to the floor.

"My guess is the one in the kitchen," Joe suggested.

"More likely the one in Mama and Daddy's room," John said
smugly, inviting a sharp glance from Joe.

"What makes you say that, John?" Joe asked carefully.

John glanced from his older brother to Luke, who was gaping
at him with wide-eyed wonder as if he expected his brother to reveal some astonishing insight. "It's just closer to the Christmas
tree," he replied at last. "That's all."

"I see," Joe remarked knowingly.

Luke frowned at the reasoning. "I don't know, John," he said
earnestly. "He would have made a big racket comen down the chimney with a bag of toys. It would've woken Mama and Daddy up for
sure. I bet he went down the chimney in the kitchen."

"Does it really matter, Luker?" Joe asked tactfully, using his personal nickname for his youngest brother. "I mean, the important
thing is that he came. Don't you think?"

Luke's eager face split into a grin. "Yeaaaaa!" he yelled, bound-
ing out of bed, running from the room, down the hall, shouting,
"He came! He came! Wake up everybody, wake up! Santa Claus has
come and there's presents for everyone."

John started anxiously after his younger brother, but Joe
caught him by the tail-end of his nightshirt. "Whoa, there," he
said. "Sometime today, John, remind me to tell you about Father
Christmas."

"Okay," John replied impatiently, tugging to free himself from
his brother's grasp.

Joe grinned. "Merry Christmas," he said, releasing him.

Laughing, already intoxicated by the joy of the day, Joe crossed the room and walked through the connecting closet between the boys' room and his sisters' room—on the unlikely chance that the girls still needed to be roused from sleep. He found Summer and Carrie already out of bed, wrapping themselves in housecoats, while Bonnie watched drowsily from beneath the covers. "Merry Christmas, girls," he greeted them, entering the room.

"Did he come, Joe?" Carrie asked anxiously.

"He sure did, honey," Joe replied, crossing the room to lie down on the bed beside Bonnie.

"Hurry, hurry," Summer urged. "Let's go see the presents." She tied the belt on her robe. "Did he leave stockens for us, Joe?"

"Why don't you find out for yourselves," Joe challenged, focusing his attention on his youngest sister. "Mornen, bright eyes," he smiled at Bonnie. "Merry Christmas."

"It's cold," Bonnie shivered. "Do you think Santa Claus brought me anything, Joe?"

"I tell you what, sweetie," Joe said. "You crawl under my blanket to keep warm, and we'll go find out whether he did."

Bonnie snuggled tightly in his arms, and Joe carried her to the living room, where their brothers and sisters, having already discovered socks bulging with goodies, were pillaging with Christmas zeal. Joe secured a spot on the rug by the Christmas tree for them and was awarded almost immediately by his little sister's sudden restlessness. Seduced by the temptation to discover treasure, Bonnie forgot the morning chill and plunged headlong into the task of emptying her stocking. Joe observed the happy scene and, then, his own resistance crumbling, reached eagerly for the stuffed sock offered to him by Summer.

In most ways, it was a typical Christmas morning at the Baker home. As always, the children rummaged through their stockings first, while waiting for their parents and grandparents to make their way to the living room. It was the one morning of the year when everyone gathered without first fully dressing for the day. They came wearing housecoats and pajamas, wrapped in blankets and quilts, and settled themselves around the Christmas tree in anticipation.

It was well after six o'clock when Sam and Rachel occupied their traditional posts on the Queen Anne sofa and Matt and Caroline took their positions on the Victorian sofa, but, in spite of their eagerness, nobody hurried.

Christmas morning was savored in the Baker home, swirled and sniffed like an exquisite nectar from God Himself, sampled for body and flavor and finally feasted upon in triumphal celebration of the season everyone had waited for all year long.

Their celebration began with a photograph of the tree itself and then more pictures of themselves gathered around the shapely cedar—until at last the moment arrived to begin the annual procession that thrilled them all.

Matt turned over the camera to Caroline, then reached under the tree to retrieve the first present, while everyone waited with clenched teeth to see who would be the recipient of the year's first gift.

Matt plucked a bright red package with a green bow from the pile, examined it, shook it and finally announced, "To Luke from Santa Claus."

A chorus of groans, ringing with happiness, excitement and good tidings, filled the room as Matt handed his youngest son the gift and stepped back to join Caroline on the sofa. Everyone opened gifts at their own pace, and no one tackled the job faster or more furiously than Luke. Seconds later, the paper lay in tatters, the green bow still intact, and Luke shrieked in delight at a blue dump truck with a hydraulic release mechanism.

In due time, Luke laid aside the truck and reached into the pile of gifts, pulling out a slender package wrapped in green foil. "To Carrie from Santa Claus," he announced, offering the present to his sister.

Carrie's style of opening gifts was methodical. She found each piece of tape and gently pried it loose until the last piece of paper revealed a white box. She lifted the lid, and her eyes widened like saucers. "A watch," she whispered with astonishment, looking first to Caroline, then to Matt and finally to Summer. "I never told anybody but you that I really wanted a watch for Christmas," she muttered wonderingly to her older sister. "How could Santa have known?"

No one answered as Carrie wrapped the band around her wrist and wound the stem, casting an inquiring gaze around the room.

"Santa Claus just knows, Carrie," Joe remarked finally. "That's the wonder of it."

Carrie admired the watch until John urged her gently, "Now come on. It's hard to be patient when you're the one waiten."

She sprang to her feet, reached into the pile of presents and emerged with a large gift wrapped clumsily in candy cane paper "To Mama from Joe," she said, carrying the gift to Caroline.

And so, the procession continued, until every present had been handed out, opened, examined, admired and appreciated by everyone. Almost two hours later, Sam delivered their Christmas prayer.

"Dear Lord," he began, filling the room with his rich baritone. "We stand humbly before you this hallowed mornen, thankful for these treasures you have sent our way, grateful for the many gifts you have given us all through the year. Father, we praise you for our prosperity, our good health, for the simple pleasure of gatheren 'round this tree this mornen to share in the birth of your Son and our Lord, Jesus Christ.

"Lord, we ask you to lead us through the comen year, to walk beside us and guide us on a path pleasen to you, to remind us daily to remember the joy and beauty and grace of the Christmas season and to keep its wonder and promise and peace in our hearts every day of the year, and to protect us from ourselves and those who would do us harm.

"Lord, we thank you for senden your Son to be born in a manger in Bethlehem all those years ago, given us a reason for the season of Christmas. We are grateful in our hearts that your Son came to Earth as a baby boy, lived and walked as a man and set a perfect example for us to follow, gave up his life willingly on the cross for our sins and finally rose from the grave, conquered death and ascended into Heaven. We pray that we will follow in his footsteps, walken and talken with you each day, dear Lord, and that you will have grace, mercy and compassion on our shortcomens.

"Dear Lord, we are most grateful for this wonderful piece of land you have entrusted to our care. We pray for your guidance in our efforts to be shepherds of the land. We give abundant thanks for the blessens of the land, and we ask your blessens on every liven creature that inhabits it.

"Lord, we are mindful, too, on this holy day of those less fortunate than ourselves, those who are sick of mind, body and heart. We pray that you touch them with your healen powers and make their lives whole again. We ask dear Lord that you would feed the starven, give shelter to the homeless and bring righteousness to the world.

"In all these things, Lord, we ask for your blessens and pray your will be done. Amen."

---

On Christmas morning, Caroline forewent her customary inspection of the house and proceeded directly to the kitchen to prepare breakfast. She buttoned her sweater upon entering the room, trying to ward off the early morning cold. The room was like ice, and she was grateful to hear the gurgling of running water from the kitchen sink. What a mess they would have found themselves in with frozen pipes and Christmas dinner to cook.

A gusting wind rattled the house, and the patter of rain sounded against the tin roof and windowpanes as Caroline made her way across the room to peer out the window. She parted the curtain and looked out across a sea of white. A hand flew up to her breast, and she blinked to see if her eyes were playing tricks.

A deep cover of snow lay undisturbed in the early morning, growing thicker with every passing moment as showers of the white fleece danced and frolicked on a whistling wind. Drifts stood several inches deep in places, icicles clung from the eaves, and snow covered everything in sight. It was a sight to behold, a vision of sheer beauty, an answer to an unspoken prayer.

"Matt! Children!" she shouted. "Grandpa, Ma! Y'all come and see how it snowed last night. We've been blessed with another white Christmas."

The children came racing to the kitchen, each clambering for a place in front of the two windows that flanked the kitchen fireplace. Only a few hours earlier they had seen snow for the first time, and the experience had proved exhilarating. With the memory of last night in mind, they were unprepared for the breathtaking beauty that lay in wait for them. Each of them had seen pictures of snowfalls in New England, blizzards in the Great Midwest. But those were faraway places, no more real than dots on a map, and their minds had neither the experience nor the imagination to ponder the possibility of a snow-covered world in their own backyard.

Yet, there it lay, the first honest-to-goodness snowfall of their young lives, piled like blankets on a bed, frosty white as far as the eye could see.

The children simply stared out the two windows, overwhelmed, marveling at the snow-crusted landscape.

"Well now," Matt said, gazing out the window over the tops of John, Carrie and Luke. "Who'd have thought we'd ever see this bunch of young'uns all quiet like this on Christmas mornen?"

"Look at it, Daddy," John instructed with pure reverence. "Did you ever see anything so beautiful?"

"Yes, son," Matt recalled. "As a matter of fact, I did. Around this time nineteen years ago on the day I married your mama."

"On Christmas Eve mornen," volunteered Caroline, who was sharing the other window with Joe, Summer and Bonnie. "I lived in Tifton with Aunt Evelyn. I woke up early and there was snow everywhere. I thought it was the most beautiful gift anyone could ever hope to have on their wedden day. I was so excited, so anxious. But then, Aunt Evelyn reminded me the roads were covered with snow. She was afraid we couldn't make the drive out here from Tifton."

Caroline looked at Matt. "I was beside myself with worry, but it kept right on snowen. There didn't seem like any way in the world we could ever get out here for the wedden, and I had no way of getten a message to your daddy."

"But I knew what she was thinken," Matt interrupted. "And I was intent on getten married that very day."

"Around eight o'clock that mornen, I was at my wits' end," Caroline continued. "It seemed like my wedden day was goen to be spoiled. And then out of the blue, there was a knock on the front door. I opened it up and who do you think was standen there?"

"Daddy!" sang a choir of voices.

"It was him all right," Caroline confirmed, smiling at her husband. "Standen there big as life with this lopsided grin on his face."

Matt took over the story: "She looked at me and said, 'Matt?'— like she was dreamen and wasn't sure whether I was real or not."

"Well, I wasn't," Caroline admitted. "At least not entirely." She laughed. "Your father seemed about as unsure as I did. We just stood there staren at each other and then finally he said, 'Roads are a mess. I figured you might need a ride out to the house.'"

"Which she did," Matt said.

"I thought it was supposed to be bad luck for the groom to see the bride before the wedden," Summer remarked with concern.

"Lucky for us," Caroline smiled, "neither your daddy nor I was superstitious."

Matt cleared his throat. "Are you kids gonna spend all day inside the house strollen down memory lane?" he asked. "Or are y'all gonna stroll outside and play in the snow?"

The children required no further encouragement. In the bat of an eye, they scattered through the house, pulling on clothes, socks, shoes and coats, and filed out the front door to the waiting snow.

It was a deep snow, suitable for romping and tumbling, snowmen and snowballs, and the children charged into it with rampant enthusiasm. They ran full speed, sliding and slipping, flying through the air and crashing to the snow-covered ground. They rolled in the snow, they tasted the white powder. But their vigor waned quickly in the face of the icy elements. The snow burned their hands, the cold froze their noses and ears and a whistling wind pelted their faces with the stinging flakes. All too soon, they retreated to the warmth of the house, where Caroline and Rachel had a hot breakfast waiting for them.

————————

After breakfast, Joe put on gloves and an old aviator's cap and returned outside to feed corn to the hogs and hay to the cows. He was in a cheerful mood, calling Christmas messages to the various animals. He spent a few minutes talking with his father while Matt milked the cow, then went inside.

Entering the house through the back porch, he arrived in time to hear Rachel fretting about the late hour she and Caroline had waited to put the turkey in the oven.

"We've got plenty of time," his mother assured Rachel, glancing at Joe with a smile. "Did you get everybody fed up?" she asked him.

"Yes, ma'am," Joe said, moving past her to stand by the fireplace, listening to the melody of his mother and grandmother at work while he shrugged off his denim jacket and warmed by the fire.

"I guess we do," Rachel remarked, more to herself than anyone else. "But the dressen has to go in the oven, too, and so do the sweet potatoes. It'll be three o'clock or later before we're ready to sit down and eat."

Caroline hummed *Silent Night*.

"Course, it don't matter much when we eat today," Rachel continued. "It's Christmas Day and I don't guess none of us has anything pressen to get done."

Caroline began crooning the first verse of *What Child Is This*, her lovely alto filling the room with the peace and serenity of the day, chasing away any misgivings Rachel might have had about Christmas dinner.

Joe stood there a while longer, eavesdropping on their harmony as his mother and grandmother went busily about a task they enjoyed. His departure from the kitchen went virtually unnoticed as he ambled through the house before finally reaching his bedroom. He picked up the Robert Frost book from the fireplace mantle and settled on the floor against the bed. He flipped through the first pages to the table of contents, then to *Stopping by the Woods on a Snowy Evening* and read the first stanza before his mind wandered and his eyes drifted from the page to the room around him.

Joe was tired of sharing this room with his two brothers. He wanted the privacy of a room of his own—nothing fancy—just four walls to himself with enough space for a bed and maybe a desk. As his father said, though, privacy was a rare commodity in the Baker household. Still, Joe had broached the topic in his short conversation with Matt this morning, casually mentioning that the room he shared with John and Luke could easily be partitioned off to form a small alcove in the far corner of the house. Matt had made a noncommittal remark, but Joe read his father well enough to see he was open to the idea.

Laying aside the book, he rose and measured the panhandle space. It would make for cramped quarters, but there was room enough for Joe. He leaned against the far wall, considering the best strategy for persuading his parents to accept the idea. He was still standing there a few minutes later when John burst through the closet door with Summer on his heels.

"Tell us about Father Christmas," he demanded of Joe.

Joe regarded his brother and sister with a bemused expression, trying to determine their knowledge and feelings on the matter at hand.

"There's not really a Santa Claus," John announced smartly. "It's just Mama and Daddy putten presents under the tree. Ain't it, Joe?"

At length, Joe nodded, confirming John's suspicions. "I suppose last night that Mama and Daddy did play Santa Claus for us, John," he said slowly. "But I still believe in the spirit of Santa Claus. Maybe he's not a jolly old man who flies through the sky at night with a sled full of toys and a herd of reindeer leaden the way, but Santa Claus is just as real as you and I are."

"I knew he was made-up," John remarked, his tone changed from know-it-all to doleful.

"I had my doubts, too," Summer agreed, completely crestfallen. "For the last two years, I've had a feelen Mama and Daddy were the ones who got our Christmas presents, but I was afraid to face the truth. It was too much fun thinken about Santa Claus and Mrs. Claus, the elves and the reindeer, worken and liven happily ever after in the North Pole. It's almost as if they were real people, and now they've died."

"Y'all aren't listenen to me," Joe interrupted strongly. "There's no reason for you to quit believen in the North Pole, Summer. And, John, I'm tellen you again that Santa Claus is as real as you and me."

"You aren't maken any sense, Joe," Summer said. "Are you tellen us the truth or not?"

"And who is this Father Christmas you mentioned?" John asked.

Joe climbed into the middle of his double bed, gesturing his brother and sister to join him. When John and Summer were perched on either side, he repeated a story their grandfather had told him several years earlier."

"Let me tell you first about Saint Nicholas, the patron saint of children," Joe began. "He *was* a real man, flesh and blood, who lived hundreds—more than a thousand—years ago, and he devoted his life to given good things to children. Except for Jesus Christ, possibly no better man ever walked this earth than Saint Nicholas. He brought magic to people's lives. He filled their needs. He gave them the power to hope and to believe that all things are possible. Like all mortal men, though, Saint Nicholas eventually grew old and died. But his spirit lived on and flourished throughout the world. We call the spirit of Saint Nicholas, Santa Claus, and it's our custom to believe he's a jolly man who wears a red suit, flies through the sky on Christmas Eve night with his reindeer and delivers presents to all the good boys and girls."

"Now that's a wonderful story," Summer remarked when he was finished. "To think that Santa Claus was once a real man who actually gave gifts to people. I like that idea as well as Santa Claus—

maybe even better. He must have had a powerful spirit to still live all these years later."

"A very powerful spirit," Joe agreed.

"How come we've never heard of this Saint Nicholas?" John inquired, still skeptical.

"I suppose because you've never needed to know about him until now," Joe replied smoothly. "I've come to think of the spirit of Saint Nicholas as Father Christmas. It is faith, hope and love, the spirit of goodness, kindness and generosity, the power of imagination, inspiration and the heart. Father Christmas is all things beautiful and magical, traditional and eternal. He can be found in the smells of walking through the woods on a winter day, of preparen for Christmas Day, in church on a December mornen, or around the Christmas tree. It's true, I suppose, that we tend to think most often of Father Christmas in December, but he's also the reason Daddy will pick a bushel of sweet corn, squash, tomatoes or some other vegetable in the dead of summer and deliver them to a neighbor down the road.

"Father Christmas is the reason I believe in Santa Claus," Joe continued. "It's the spirit—the Christmas spirit—that makes this time of year so special. And you know where we get that spirit, why we celebrate Christmas?"

"From Christ," John said.

"Because Jesus was born on Christmas Day," Summer added.

Joe nodded, then said, "The Bible defines the fruit of the spirit as love, joy, peace, patience, kindness, goodness, faithfulness, gentleness and self-control—all the essential elements of the Christmas spirit and Father Christmas. If we can believe that Christ was born almost two thousand years ago in a manger in Bethlehem—Summer, John—then surely we can find it in our hearts to believe in Santa Claus. It is our faith that makes us believe—in Christ, in Father Christmas, even in ourselves and in each other."

Joe paused, glancing at the shining faces of his oldest sister and brother, hoping he had filled a need with his Christmas story. "Let's none of us ever lose that faith," he added. "Okay?"

John nodded. "I could never not believe that story," he said a moment later, with pure worship in his voice.

"That is the most beautiful thing I've ever heard, Joe," Summer said. "I've memorized a lot of Bible verses, but I don't know that one. Where can I find it?"

"The fifth chapter of Galatians—the twenty-second and twenty-third verses," Joe answered with a guilty smile. "And it's one of the few too many verses that I have memorized, little sister."

"Faith is a wonderful thing," John surmised. "And so is Father Christmas."

"So are love and hope," Summer added. "I think I'll memorize that Bible verse today. I want somethen special to help me remember this day."

"I'll help you," Joe promised.

For a long moment, they were silent, each lost in their various thoughts of Father Christmas and this special day of the year.

"Thank you, Joe," John said abruptly, his eyes aglow with the twinkle of the Christmas spirit. "I'm gonna like this Father Christmas."

"We love you, brother of ours," Summer added with adoration. "It's neat haven someone old and wise to tell us all the answers."

Joe looked quickly at his brother and sister, then laughed joyously, hugging them both tightly in his arms.

"Y'all are too much," he said happily. "Whataya say that we get dressed in our warmest clothes and spend the rest of the day playen in the snow. Somethen tells me we're bound to feel Father Christmas outdoors on this white Christmas Day."

———

Shortly after noon, the children returned outside to play. New snow had stopped falling and the sun was trying to break through the clouds, but the temperature remained below freezing. This time they were prepared for the cold, with gloves, hats and scarves.

They had been outside only a few minutes when John noticed their Christmas visitors walking down the road. Joe put Bonnie on his shoulders and trooped down the snow-covered road with his siblings to meet the Berriens. The children were particularly fond of Paul, Miss April and Miss June, who tended to fuss over them and pay close attention to their every word.

Luke greeted the Berriens by launching a harmless snowball at Paul, who feigned surprise and swooped the boy onto his shoulders. The children filled much of the short walk home with tales of the treasures Santa Claus had left them, delighting their older audience with genuine appreciation of their Christmas gifts.

"What's in those bags y'all are carryen?" Luke asked Miss April and Miss June, boldly voicing the question on the minds of his brothers and sisters.

"I'm not for certain," April replied, "but I think Santa Claus may have accidentally left some of your presents at our house."

"I didn't think Santa Claus visited old people," Bonnie said doubtfully. "He didn't leave anything at our house for Mama or Daddy or Granny and Grandpa."

"Oh, she's just teasen," June assured Bonnie. She shook the bag in her hand. "These are from us to y'all. Just our little way of sayen how much we appreciate the opportunity to have Christmas dinner with you folks."

"You didn't get a single present?" Luke asked worriedly.

"We most assuredly did, Luke," June reassured him.

"Indeed yes," April continued. "We were paid a visit by Father Christmas himself last night." She looked from Luke to Paul and June. "We've had the most wonderful Christmas this year."

"Who is Father Christmas?" Bonnie inquired.

"He watches over those of us who are too old for Santa Claus to come and visit," April replied.

"How do you get too old for Santa Claus?" Luke inquired, perplexed by the idea.

"Y, y, you," April stammered, groping for a plausible answer.

She was rescued from further explanation by their timely arrival in the Baker yard and the appearance of Matt on the front porch. As the greetings began among the adults, Joe sent a snowball aimed in Luke's direction. The packed snow landed squarely on the boy's back and Luke's thoughts were transferred from curiosity to revenge. For another year at least, there would be no more questions about Santa Claus and Father Christmas.

In the afternoon, the children, Matt, Sam and Paul fought a war with snowballs and built matching snowmen on the two step walls flanking the front porch steps. The snow quit falling, the wind died down and the gray clouds cleared, drenching the day with cold sunshine. They played vigorously, whizzing snowballs back and forth, shouting at the tops of their lungs and running full speed. The snowmen stood guard by the house, with coal for eyes, spools of red thread for noses, crooked mouths and tree limbs for arms.

At last, everyone collapsed on the porch, feeling their first hunger pains since breakfast. They drifted quickly into silence, ready for a change of pace. As if on cue, the front door opened and Caroline appeared.

"Goodness gracious!" she exclaimed. "Y'all look plumb tuckered out."

"Some of us more than others," Sam replied wearily.

Caroline laughed. "Dinner's ready," she announced, walking down the porch steps to inspect the matching snowmen. "We're setten it on the table, so y'all come on in and wash your hands.

"Those are just the smartest-looken snowmen I've ever seen," she added a moment later before ushering everyone into the warmth of home and hearth, where Christmas dinner waited.

———————

Caroline remembered every Christmas by painting pictures in her mind, slice of life details that gave the day its own special flavor. This was a Christmas Day ripe with memories, not only of the snow but also for the character of her family and friends.

More than once, Caroline caught a questioning gaze on Joe as he studied the faces around the table: the yearning in Miss April's face for something lost forever, perhaps children of her own; the joy in Miss June's eyes as one who had made peace with the will of God. Once, Caroline even glanced up to find her oldest son's gaze fixed solidly on her, and both realized with startled looks that the other was aware of what they each were doing. Caroline glanced away but quickly looked back at Joe, smiling to herself, knowing the boy possessed some part of her.

Had Caroline been a painter, she would have captured on canvas the range of emotions expressed this day. She would have painted the tired face of Bonnie, propped on the table by her elbows with a tiny thumb resting against her lips; the simple satisfaction in Matt as he savored a piece of turkey in a moment of thoughtful silence; the dazed, slightly embarrassed expression of Paul as cranberry jelly slid off his fork just before reaching his opened mouth; the unfortunate attempt by Luke to reach across the table for a pear tart and the admonishment he received from Rachel for his lack of table manners.

Caroline could not paint on canvas but she did burn these images deeply in her mind. And later, when the lazy pace of the day had meandered them through dinner and dessert, and they had gathered outside to wish Merry Christmas to each other one last time, she found a few more lasting memories. She provoked one by tossing a snowball at Sam and catching the twinkle of affection in his good eye as he cast a sidelong glance toward her. She noted the graceful movement of Summer, the gentle happiness of Carrie as the two girls chased John, who had put snow down their backs, an out-of-character action for her most mild-mannered son and yet revealing of his occasional penchant for doing the unexpected.

In the fading daylight Caroline found one final Christmas memory for the year, again of Joe, standing on the edge of the field with his back turned to her, looking toward the magnificent red and gold horizon.

The filtered hues of that deep orange setting sun spellbound Caroline, filling her with such happiness and peace that she paused a moment to bask in its radiance. This glorious horizon—like the strange white Christmas—seemed to promise a grand future for them all, and Caroline allowed her memories of family and friends to drift through her mind. She wondered what surprises the coming years would bring them, but, more than anything, Caroline clung steadfastly to the belief that better days lay ahead for her family and the farm. Finally, she prayed to God for His blessings and His will be done.

When her prayer was finished, Caroline gazed once more at the darkening sky, streaked with variegated shades of amber gold, burnt orange and gathering purple clouds. In the dusky haze of twilight, she felt anew the promise of the horizon, something impalpable and imponderable, yet commanding her attention—until at last a chilling wind sent a shiver through her, and she turned to bid her friends goodbye and hurry her family into the waiting warmth of home.

# THE TRAIN

1961-1962

# CHAPTER 1

JOE AGREED WITH HIS father and grandfather's belief that the Cookville community offered everything a man needed. Any able-bodied man with a minimum of gumption and perseverance could make a decent life in this small farming community for himself and a family. A good life even, as demonstrated by his own father who was abler and possessed more gumption and perseverance than the ordinary man in these parts.

What bothered Joe about their viewpoint was his equally certain opinion that Cookville could never offer everything he wanted out of life. He suspected Matt and Sam would dismiss his confusion as unnecessary brooding over nothing more than semantics, but to Joe there was a big difference between needing and wanting. Whether Cookville fulfilled the wants of his father and grandfather, Joe did not know for sure. He made a mental note to clarify the issue on their next hunting trip or some other suitable occasion.

These thoughts came to Joe as he walked along a moonlit path, his destination a back field on the Bakers' rambling farm. Above him, millions of stars danced and the moon, a bright white orb, hung cold and distant, decorating the nighttime sky with ambiance, suggesting something special at hand. He dug his hands deeper into the pockets of a worn corduroy jacket for warmth and quickened his pace.

Joe should have been in bed on this, a school night, but he was preoccupied with a different obligation—a summons equally mysterious and compelling, issued a night earlier by the distant call of a train whistle. The summons had come from the Southern Railway's midnight run to Atlanta from Valdosta, weaving its way into Joe's dreams and luring him from an uneasy sleep. He had listened to the train coming closer, heard its hollow crossing of the New River trestle. And somewhere between the thunderous roar and fading echoes of steel on steel, Joe felt called to witness the next passing of the train.

Tonight, he was heeding the call only because his curiosity exceeded strong suspicions that he was being plumb silly. Nevertheless, he expected to view the train in a different light after tonight, as something other than an annoyance that woke him from a sound sleep and more important than vital transportation for the crops his family grew.

From the house, it was a brisk fifteen-minute walk to the railroad tracks, which served as the Baker farm's western border. Joe had waited until his family was sound asleep before sneaking out the window of the room he shared, reluctantly, with his two younger brothers. He covered the distance at a slower clip, still favoring his gimpy left leg two weeks into the new year. Nevertheless, unburdened of crutches, he felt a renewed sense of strength, and each step carried him closer and faster to wherever he was headed.

His thoughts were on a highfalutin course this night. In truth, they had followed the same ponderous path for months now. In the beginning, Joe had blamed their wanderlust ways on the circumstances caused by his broken leg, which left him with too much vacant time to fill. He had grown to hope this brooding preoccupation with destiny and history might simply be a phase he was going through, like puberty, which had been much easier to handle. But now, with grudging acknowledgment, he was willing to accept his fondness for deep thought.

Joe fancied himself a philosopher, yet deep down, knew he lacked the keen intellect necessary for sweeping profundity of human nature, despite the straight As on his report card. Scholars would never examine his writings for the meaning of life. Joe was unconcerned. He was far more interested in the events of life. He wanted to write the first draft of history, preserve moments in time and chronicle destinies. He wanted to be a journalist.

At times, he ached for the future. He sensed its nearness, tantalizingly close but still out of sight. Had he merely been passing time or locked into an unlimited future of weekly visits to town, Sunday newspapers and a rare trip to the State Farmers Market in Atlanta, Joe would have withered like a cornfield without water. But he was nourished, growing and mostly content to let the future arrive at its own pace.

He owed his patience to the nurturing of a wonderful family, and felt an enormous debt of gratitude for their love, care and example.

Joe had been born at home and had never strayed far from the paths of his father and grandfather or the apron strings of his mother and grandmother. These four people were giving Joe and his siblings rich lives, and material things had little to do with their treasures. Hard work and responsibility were virtues, although worthless without ample time for play and laughter. Both his parents and grandparents made sure there was plenty of everything to go around for everyone.

They were not perfect, of course. Matt avoided the church; Caroline battled pride; Sam possessed a lazy streak; and Rachel was prone to haughty stubbornness. But it was easy to overlook their faults, especially for Joe, who mistrusted perfection.

Arriving at the railroad tracks, Joe climbed over the fence and made his way across the rocky right-of-way. He stepped across the first rail to the center of a wooden tie and peered south in search of headlights from the oncoming locomotive. It was a futile gesture since he was bound to hear the train long before he saw any approaching lights. Turning south, he stared down the tracks with anticipation and was rewarded with the stillness of the night. Finally, he pulled a penny from his pocket, placed it on the rail and moved away from the tracks to claim a seat on the cold ground.

His thoughts returned to the family and the prospect of one day leaving them. Any doubts Joe had about going out into the world on his own had vanished in a single moment in another field when his father pointed Joe in a direction away from home. Matt had released Joe from family bonds. He had granted Joe impending freedom. But freedom came with a burden of responsibility, which explained why, even with his occasional impatience for the future to arrive, Joe was most happy to wait. There was time enough. It would come.

He heard the train then and rose stiffly from the ground, blowing quick puffs of frosty breath into the cold night. Retrieving a cigarette from the pack in his jeans, he lit it with a match and inhaled the smoke for warmth, then made a final check of the penny's position. Though not superstitious by nature, Joe saw no harm in having a good luck piece, especially if it served as a memento from an important moment.

The train's rumble drew closer, picking up speed, and a long whistle signaled its approach to the New River trestle. A short time later, the engine's bright headlight rounded a curve and the train was bearing down on Joe. He stepped away from the tracks and waited for the train to cover the distance. It was a short wait.

The engine roared, a long, unexpected whistle acknowledging that his dark attire had failed to conceal Joe's presence from the conductor. Joe saluted back, took a step closer to the train and was lost in the hypnotic shadows of car after car racing past him, the scrape of steel on steel drowning the noise of the night. He thought about the faraway places the cars were headed, knowing someday he would buy a ticket and ride that train across his family's land to the beckoning future.

The passing of the red caboose surprised him, coming so suddenly, leaving in its wake anxious anticipation. "It won't be long now," Joe said softly to the train's fading vibrations, watching it race away into the darkness.

When the train was gone, Joe walked over to the railroad track, collected his flattened penny and crammed the coin inside the front pocket of his blue jeans. He took one last lingering look ahead, then quickly put his mind back in the present. He snuggled deeper into the coat, stifled a yawn and began the walk home. A warm bed waited there, and Joe was eager to get to it.

---

It was one of those rare days when his patience ran thin. Along with his blood.

Winter was Joe's favorite time of year, but he had never lived through a winter like this one. And with more than half the season remaining, he wasn't entirely convinced he would make it through.

Two-thirds of January was gone, and the temperature had hovered near the freezing point since the unexpected white Christmas, rising only to melt the snow and then plunging with an icy vengeance. Joe had tired quickly of waking to frozen water pipes. He found it impossible to rid himself of the chill that grabbed him each morning when he struggled out of bed. On this, the coldest day by far, he wished for an early spring.

Spring seemed far away, however, in the midst of an ice storm and frigid cold. Rain had fallen the previous night, turning to ice in the early morning. The ice had cracked tree limbs, snapped power lines and burst water pipes. Rachel was boiling water in the fireplace for coffee, and Caroline was putting together sandwiches for a sparse supper. Everyone else huddled in the kitchen for warmth, except Matt and Joe. His father was feeding the stock and Joe was scouring the woods for a pregnant pig. It was a dismal time, made all the worse by the impending arrival of another Arctic blast.

Joe traversed a forest of bare hardwoods and an occasional green pine, aiming for a favorite rooting hole of the hogs. He was looking for Sooner, a gilt expected to deliver her first litter of pigs at any time.

He would have preferred to be somewhere else, but Sooner was the daughter of Yorkie, one of the Bakers' most prized sows for the large litters she delivered. Her smallest litter had been her first, eleven pigs, and the largest sixteen. The Yorkshire sow not only delivered large litters, she raised them, too. With eighteen teats, all capable of providing milk except for the two small buds high on her rump, Yorkie carried an ample food source for her brood.

Her merits were such that Matt and Joe tended to overlook her nasty habit of eating an offspring or two every now and then. Yorkie never ate any of the other sows' pigs. And even when she gobbled up one of her own, she still raised more pigs than any other sow on the Baker farm. Matt swore he would keep the Yorkshire mama until she started eating her neighbors.

Given her pedigree, the Bakers had great expectations of Sooner. First, though, Joe had to find the gilt and lead her to shelter. Whether she delivered one or a dozen pigs would matter little if she gave birth in these elements because the entire litter would freeze in a matter of minutes. Under the barn, newborn pigs would have a fighting chance.

As far as Joe was concerned, hogs stood at the pinnacle of the farming business. Modesty aside, he considered himself the equal of his father when it came to tending hogs. He cooked their sour mash, wormed them and tracked breeding cycles. When the time came, he castrated the young males, chose the gilts for breeding and packed off the shoats to the market. He monitored the farm markets for hog prices every week, and Matt rarely made an important decision about the stock without first consulting him.

The Bakers maintained a brood of almost two hundred pigs. Joe named a large number of them: the sows and gilts kept for breeding and the two males who serviced them. Sows carried names like Red, Sugar, Rose, Geraldine and, of course, Yorkie. Besides Sooner, there were gilts called Stripe and Friendly, while the males were named, appropriately, Big Male and Little Male.

As much as pigs could be pampered, Joe did. He treated them to overgrown vegetables like squash and sweet potatoes in the summer, turnips and other greens in the winter, which was not unusual in itself—except Joe, fed them by hand. He scratched behind their ears, petted and sweet-talked the critters. To his father and grandfather's amazement, Joe could lull a standing sow to a near stupor simply by scratching gently behind her ears and whispering sweet nothings. Some of the sows—Sugar, Rose and Geraldine, in particular—craved his attention to the point of jealousy of their swine sisters. If Joe lavished too much attention on one, then the others would push for their turn, squealing and butting in until they received a due share of notice.

"Pretty amazen," Tom Carter had acknowledged dryly one day last fall when a boastful Joe demonstrated the hogs' affection for their master. "But wouldn't you rather have a pretty girl swoonen at your feet instead of dirty old hogs?"

Joe had allowed the question to go unanswered, he recalled, as a broken limb blocked his path and he stopped to examine it. Still dangling from the tree, the limb was a casualty of the heavy ice clinging to its branches. Joe clasped the hanging piece of wood, twisted it sharply and stepped back to let the limb fall to the ground. He told himself to drag it back to the house for firewood later, then moved on toward the rooting hole.

Joe wanted girls to swoon at his feet. So far, however, Betty Beddingfield was the only girl anywhere close to swooning over Joe. Unfortunately, Betty had a heart condition, so he could never tell whether she was swooning or simply keeling over from exhaustion.

Her present infatuation with Joe excluded, Betty still occupied a prominent place in his memory.

Way back in fourth grade, Betty had been cast as Miss String Bean, a key role in the class play that required a tearful performance. In rehearsal after rehearsal, Betty failed to deliver the necessary blubbering. Everybody offered suggestions, but Betty maintained dry eyes and offered up only grunts when tears were needed.

With everyone convinced the play was doomed to failure unless Betty learned to cry, Joe took matters into his own hands. While his part in the play was minor, it cast Joe in a position behind Betty during the scene's critical moment. When the time came for Betty to shed tears during the play's final rehearsal, Joe poked her in the butt with a straight pin he had procured from Rachel's sewing box. It worked wonders.

A lusty wail erupted from Betty, both stunning and delighting her classmates and their teacher, Miss Masterson. Overcoming its initial surprise, the class quickly broke into a hardy round of applause and cheers for Betty.

"Why, Betty, dear," Miss Masterson beamed, swelling with pride for her favorite student. "That's wonderful. You sound so real."

Betty gulped for air, sniffled and launched into another round of bawling.

Until then, Joe had been clapping and cheering with his classmates. But the tone of Betty's high-pitched sobs pricked his instincts, reminding him of the Biblical passage about the wailing and gnashing of teeth. His grin disappeared as Miss Masterson started across the stage toward Betty.

"That's wonderful, Betty," Miss Masterson repeated, a smile plastered across her face, which Joe considered a perfect cross between a horse and a prune. "I just can't get over how convincen you sound." Her tone turned coaxing. "But that's enough for now, sweetie. Save some of those tears for tomorrow night."

Betty went right on sobbing, sniveling and sniffling at a torrid pace, alerting Miss Masterson that matters were amiss with the teacher's pet.

Miss Masterson rushed to Betty and wrapped the petite girl in her arms. "Betty, darlen," she consoled with soothing chirps. "What's wrong, dear?"

Betty looked up at the distressed teacher. "Somebody stuck a pin in my butt," she wailed. "And it hurts."

The class erupted into raucous laughter, but Joe hardly noticed. His attention was locked on the pair of cold, beady blue eyes glaring straight at him.

Of all his teachers, Miss Masterson was the only one Joe had ever disliked. They had bumped heads literally on the first day of the fourth grade, and that one moment of closeness had been the high point of their relationship.

Miss Masterson made no accusations, and Joe offered no defense. She grabbed him by the arm, dragged him off stage and whacked his backside with ten solid licks from a two-inch piece of oak. Worst of all, she sent him home from school with a note explaining what had happened and requiring his parents' signatures.

The paddling gave Joe newfound respect for Miss Masterson, whose waif-like appearance belied her power. The note to his parents, however, nullified any budding chance she might have had to earn his goodwill.

Caroline and Rachel were beside themselves over the incident, throwing up their hands in disbelief and reprimanding Joe repeatedly for his derelict behavior. His grandfather sat silently in the corner of the kitchen, shaking his head back and forth with downcast eyes.

"Son, what in the world made you stick a pin in the girl's rear?" Matt asked.

"I was tryen to help her cry," Joe replied hopefully, before explaining about the play and Betty's inability to perform in the crucial moment. By the time he finished the long-winded account, Joe himself was wondering what indeed he had been thinking when he plunged the pin into Betty's butt.

"Son," Matt frowned when Joe was finished. "There's not any good reason to stick a straight pin into somebody's backside." He pointed to the kitchen door and motioned Joe to it. "You and I need to talk outside for a while."

Matt had led his son to the barn, where Joe soon cried tears as real as the sobs of Betty Beddingfield. It was the last whipping Joe received from his father. There had been scant cause for another because Joe well remembered the last one.

Joe sidestepped a frozen mud puddle and thought again about Betty Beddingfield. The years since fourth grade had been unkind to her. Betty had developed the heart condition in the fourth grade and subsequently became the target of cruel jokes. Joe stood up for her, and his defense had stopped the bullying. Now Betty saw Joe as some knight in shining armor, all because he showed her a small amount of kindness. She had an obvious crush on him, batting her eyes and blushing whenever he spoke to her. Joe tolerated her silliness out of sympathy and because he knew her bad heart had already stolen Betty's first love. He remembered the way she played a piano, her hands flowing with grace and style over the piano keys, filling the New River auditorium with sweet melodies. Betty had been April Berrien's prized piano student, and Joe still recalled her passionate performance in the sixth-grade recital. It was her last performance before illness robbed Betty of music. The doctors had silenced her hands, fearing even the exertion of playing a piano would overburden her delicate heart.

Joe's arrival at the rooting hole chased away the bittersweet thoughts of Betty Beddingfield and sent his own heart racing.

Across the way, Sooner lay heavily on her side in a crude oval nest of sticks and leaves.

Joe moved slowly toward the hog, breathing easier as he came closer and saw she still possessed a rounded stomach. If he could lead her to the barn, he would. If not, he would take the pigs when they were born and feed them with a bottle at home.

Reaching the white hog, he nudged her gently with his foot. "Get up girl," he urged. "It's too cold for you to be haven babies out here."

The hog snorted loudly, grunting her displeasure, but she rose awkwardly from the nest. As Joe shooed her away, one of the hog's feet pierced a layer of ice across the top of the nest. His curiosity piqued, Joe bent to examine the nest and recoiled. A newborn pig lay frozen in the ice, its head crushed where Sooner's foot had broken through the top layer.

Joe turned away to regain his equilibrium, taking time to observe Sooner. Her belly had lost hardly any of its pre-birth roundness. Even now, she appeared pregnant. "Sorry, girl," he called. "Your time came a little too soon."

Pained by a mixture of regret and disgust, Joe returned to the nest. He pulled the dead pig from the ice and discovered three others in a half-frozen gelatinous soup of slush and birthing gook. His stomach turned unexpectedly, forcing Joe to take a deep breath of the cold air to clear the nausea.

He waited half-a-minute, then resumed the grizzly task, prying the other dead pigs from the ice and removing the congealed glob of birthing fluids. Even in a frozen state, it was a gooey mess and required a light touch as Joe carried it to the edge of the small clearing. There, he dropped to his knees, dug a shallow hole with his hands and buried the glop. He used a wad of decaying leaves to clean his hands, then returned to the birthing place and grabbed the four frozen pigs by their tails. He would bury them somewhere else, where the carcasses would stay hidden from the other hogs.

A dispirited grunt from the mother halted his departure from the rooting hole.

Sooner was standing ten yards away, eyeing Joe suspiciously with a cocked head. She was a pretty sow, with a long body and a healthy pinkish glow, and Joe expected better results from her second try at motherhood. Of course, if the hog delivered another small litter, anything less than eight pigs, then she would accompany her brood to the market when the time came. But given her potentially fragile mental state at the time, Joe opted for encouragement rather than pressure with his farewell.

"Better luck next time, old girl," he muttered en route to a nearby field.

By spring, the unfortunate critters would be fertilizer, he told himself, perhaps providing nutrients and minerals for a field of corn that would feed their mother and the other hogs come the next winter.

---

The memory of the frozen pigs lingered for several days, until one morning when a matter of more importance forced Joe to speak his mind at the breakfast table. "I need a room of my own," he announced to his family between a bite of toast and a sip of orange juice.

"You do," Sam said vaguely, leaving everyone to guess whether he was agreeing with Joe or questioning his grandson."

"I do," Joe repeated brashly.

"What about your brothers, Joe?" Caroline asked. "It's hardly fair to push them out of their room." She smiled teasingly. "And it's a little cold for anybody to be sleepen on the porch."

"John and Luke can keep the room," Joe replied quickly. "At least most of it."

Matt cleared his throat and intervened. "Joe's got a good idea," he said. "All he wants to do is wall up that panhandle in the boy's room."

"That wouldn't be much of a room," Caroline frowned, finally giving the idea serious merit. "You couldn't get much more than a bed in it. A single one at that."

"A bed, a desk and maybe a chest of drawers," Joe informed her. "I measured it all out, and there's more space than you think. Anyway, I don't need much room. Just a little privacy every now and then."

Caroline smiled with understanding and considered the request. "It's a good idea," Matt opined. "Joe's older than the other kids, and he needs a retreating place." He observed Caroline watching him and sweetened the idea with a new proposal. "In fact," he continued, "I thought we might do some work in the bathroom, too. Maybe put up one of those shower rings around the tub and brighten it up in there a little bit."

"What about the cost?" Caroline asked, again frowning.

"Hardly anything," Matt said dismissively. "A few two-by-fours and plywood. Nails and paint. Things are slow around here right now, so Joe and I can do the work. We probably could knock out both jobs in two or three days." He hesitated, allowing his wife to consider the idea, watching the wheels of worry turn over in her head. "It's not gonna to send us to the poor house, Caroline," he told her finally.

This extra reassurance brightened Caroline. "Then I don't see why not," she agreed. "As long as it's okay with Ma and Pa."

Rachel and Sam had no objections, so Matt installed the shower ring and new plumbing the very next day. Two days later, he and Joe began work on the room. They put up the studs and braces, framed the door and dangled a light from the ceiling. Next, they added an electrical outlet, then walled in the room and hung the door. While his father painted the two rooms, Joe used the lumber scraps to build a makeshift closet.

Armed with a meager amount of money but plenty of bargaining prowess, Caroline went shopping for furnishings and struck gold at the salvage store in Tifton. She returned home with a wrought-iron single bed frame, a sturdy mattress and a ten-dollar desk. A coat of black enamel transformed the bed frame into something presentable, while a mahogany stain covered up the blemishes and added a stately quality to the desk.

On moving day, Joe transferred the furniture to his room, along with an old ladder-back chair that he had refurbished with a new cowhide seat. Rachel provided him a desk lamp, and the children arranged his clothes and other belongings in neat piles on the closet shelves.

In the shank of the evening, Joe bade the family an early goodnight and retired to the room to enjoy his newly acquired privacy. Sometime later, a nightmare woke Luke and the frightened youngster stole into his older brother's new room.

"I'm scared," Luke explained as he crawled into bed with Joe. "Can I sleep with you?"

Joe mumbled mild protest but slid over to give his little brother room. Just before drifting off, the thought occurred to him that he'd better not plan on getting too familiar with the idea of privacy.

———

It was another cold day, in the middle of February, when Sam set fire to a huge pile of wood, vines and other debris. Several other mounds of scrap dotted the newly cleared section of woods, and Matt was on the tractor harrowing a fire line around each one. They had cut the timber the previous year and now were preparing the land for its first crops.

Joe was working alongside his brothers, sisters, Lucas Bartholomew and Tom Carter, picking up roots and other obstacles that could snag a harrow or turning plow. He stretched his back for a moment and watched the fire erupt, belching gray smoke and giving off red heat, even as Sam torched a second mound in the distance.

The new field would be a welcomed addition to the farm. It was rich dirt, nurtured by years of decaying leaves, and the extra thirty acres would yield a significant boost to the farm's annual income. Come late spring, when green shoots of corn stood knee high, or early fall when the field lay brown and ripe for harvest, Joe would remember fondly these hours spent stooped over the land, tugging at entrenched roots and sweating against the cold. Right now, however, his back ached and he wanted the job finished.

He eyed the smoke a second longer, then returned to work, twisting furiously at a stubborn root and finally yanking it from the packed ground. Cursing the wood silently, he picked up another root and tossed both pieces into a nearby trailer.

"What's wrong?" his brother John inquired.

Joe glanced across the trailer, where his brother stood with a concerned frown on his face. "Nothen," he answered shortly. "Go back to work and stop yakken."

Turning away quickly, dismayed by his short temper, Joe asked himself the same question and came up with few answers. There were good days and bad days, for sure, but peace of mind was usually a consistent quality in his life. Despite his restlessness, his impatience for the future, Joe followed a familiar course of contentment, dodging obstacles with the security of knowing that each day carried him forward. As of late, however, peace of mind eluded him. Little things bothered him and stayed on his mind. He was distracted and preoccupied, all over nothing it seemed. And he needed something, yet had no idea what it might be.

This lack of focus, these bouts of moodiness and the sudden attachment to self-centeredness disturbed Joe. His inability to understand, to make sense out of the mess, irritated him. And left him with nothing else to do but take his own advice and get back to work, allowing the monotony of repetition to numb his thoughts.

In another fifteen minutes, he had cleared a stretch to the edge of the woods and was working his way back to the middle of the field when the smell of smoke penetrated the thin accumulation of cobwebs in his head.

He paused long enough to glance around the field. Smoke now rolled across the cleared land in waves, rising from the various fires that crackled ferociously with leaping flames and sizzling hisses. The first mound had been reduced to embers, but nearly a dozen others were at full blaze.

Joe was considering whether the veil of haze provided enough cover to conceal a cigarette when his sweeping gaze landed on a strange protrusion from the ground. He stared at the reddish-brown object, realizing at length that it was a rock of some kind. His curiosity aroused, Joe hurried to the rock and dropped to his knees to examine it.

The rock was imbedded in the ground, with two smaller pieces at its side. All three pieces were rough and jagged, the color of burnt ocher, scarred with streaks of carbon black and tiny porous craters.

Joe rubbed his hands across the larger piece, guessing that he had found a meteorite. He picked up the smaller rocks, examined each and estimated their weight between three and four pounds. Carefully laying them aside, he studied the larger rock and discovered a hairline fracture running down the middle of its largest outcropping. Joe braced one hand against the rock for leverage and used the other to jiggle the broken piece, enlarging the fissure. Wedging his fingers in the small cleft, he gave a swift jerk and the flat outcropping broke away from the main piece. Joe glanced quickly at the broken rock and laid it beside the two other small pieces.

He had thought perhaps the fissure would reveal a closer look at the core of the meteorite, but the fracture merely changed its shape. Joe tested the rock's sturdiness and saw it was lodged loosely in the ground. Rising to his feet, he bent over the rock, grabbed both sides at the bottom and tugged the meteorite from its landing place. It came out easily.

Joe estimated the rock weighed about twenty-five to thirty pounds. He placed the shapeless blob of space matter on the ground and studied it from all angles, flipping it from side to side, caressing the rough texture and tracing each streak of carbon black with his fingers. His senses roared with excitement over the discovery. He laughed in disbelief and gaped at the heavens with awe and appreciation.

Along with English and history, science was Joe's favorite subject, especially the study of the stars. He found the subject of astronomy as limitless as the universe itself and, now, standing here with a meteorite at his feet, he was reminded of the only cross words he'd ever had with his grandmother.

Joe was prone to speculate about the possibility of life in outer space. At the Sunday dinner table recently, he had voiced some of those conjectures. His grandmother scoffed at such ideas, believing steadfastly God had given the capability of life only to Earth and would destroy it and the rest of the universe when Jesus returned to claim his flock on Judgment Day.

"I agree, Granny," Joe had told her when Rachel objected to his speculations and voiced her beliefs. "All I'm sayen is that the universe is vast." He sent Rachel a placating smile. "It's quite possible the Almighty could have put another flock on another planet," he added a bit too blithely. "Don't you think?"

"Rubbish!" Rachel seethed. "Blasphemous rubbish."

Mealy-mouthed was an impossible description of Rachel by any stretch of the imagination. Her words were often hard-edged, but her tone rarely venomous as it suddenly had become with Joe. She slammed her fork against the table and pointed a finger at her grandson. "I will not tolerate Christian disrespect in this house, Joe," she told him in harsh tones, befitting of a fire-and-brimstone preacher. "There is one God and He made one world and one man in His own image."

"Granny!" Joe interrupted. "I wasn't questionen the creation. I was just suggesten ...."

"Enough!" Rachel shouted. "Your suggestions are not welcome at this table, young man. Or in this house. And neither are you if you intend to keep spouting off blasphemy. If you were my young'un, I'd put a belt across your backside and teach you proper respect for the good Lord and his Word. Be that as it may, I suggest you sit there and keep your mouth shut. Or leave."

Sufficiently chastised, Joe had heeded his grandmother's warning. He would keep his speculations about the cosmos to himself. But the meteorite was proof positive of the comings and goings in the vast universe, and, as far as Joe was concerned, the meteorite could be a gift from the good Lord Himself.

"The things you must have seen," Joe whistled softly to the chunk of dead matter, pondering with awe the vast gulf of space the meteor might have traveled to reach this landing point. "The places you must have been."

Shaking his head in amazement, Joe stacked the three broken pieces atop the larger portion of the meteorite and set off across the field to show the prize to his family and friends.

"What you got?" Sam called out as Joe lumbered closer with the rocks in his arms.

"A fallen star, I believe," Joe answered quietly. "Make a wish," he suggested. "I've already made mine."

# CHAPTER 2

TOM CARTER MADE, IF not a wish, a request. "I become a teenager this week," he informed Joe following church services the day after the discovery of the meteorite.

"Yeah, well, congratulations," Joe muttered. "It's not all it's cracked up to be."

"Yeah, yeah," Tom shrugged. "I've heard. That's why I've got plans to celebrate the occasion. In a big way."

Joe drew a circle in the sand with his shoe. "How's that?" he asked finally, succumbing to curiosity and his friend's patience with the details.

"I thought maybe you and I would go campen by the New Pond," Tom announced. "Do a little fishen, maybe set a trot line." He paused before adding nonchalantly, "Drink a beer or two."

Joe's head flew up as he scanned the church grounds for prying ears, and Tom knew he had hooked the older boy's attention. "Whataya think?" Tom asked.

"Campen and fishen sound good," Joe replied warily. "I've tasted beer once in my life, and it wasn't that good." He hesitated. "But I'm game to give it another try ... if we can get the beer. Just how do you plan to do that, hotshot? We're not exactly twenty-one."

"Bribe Lucas," Tom shot back. "A six-pack for him, a six-pack for us."

Joe glanced around the churchyard, considering the proposition. "It might work," he determined aloud. "It just might work. I've known Lucas to drink a beer or two in his time."

The two boys approached Lucas the following Friday afternoon.

Lucas and his new wife, Beauty, had moved into a one-room barn on the Baker farm shortly after the new year arrived. The barn sat far off the main road on the southeastern corner of the farm and was hidden by deep woods where the hogs roamed. It was a tightly built structure high off the ground with wooden walls, a tin roof and a porch across the front. The Bakers stored tobacco in the barn during the summer. Matt had offered the structure to Lucas as part of his payment to help on the farm when the working season arrived.

Lucas and Beauty were overjoyed with their new home. Although shy and reserved, Beauty had beamed while showing Joe the way she had fixed up the room a few days after the newlyweds settled in the barn. Dishes and food were stacked neatly in a ramshackle cupboard in a back corner, opposite a mattress on the floor that was made up pretty with a worn chintz cover. A clothes chest occupied one of the front corners, while a wood stove sat across the room. Two chairs stood in front of the stove, with a table and a hurricane oil lamp between them.

Her obvious pride had embarrassed Joe, who took conveniences such as electricity and indoor plumbing for granted, although he had been born at a time when neither existed in his own home. He was still uncomfortable about the situation, even after realizing the barn was relatively comfortable compared with the squalor of dirt floors, tarpaper walls and a leaky roof. More troublesome to him, however, was the knowledge that once summer arrived, the barn's rightful owner would reclaim it, leaving Beauty's home to play second fiddle to the Bakers' tobacco. Beauty and Lucas, of course, were prepared to share space with the tobacco, but Joe found little peace of mind in their expectancy.

These thoughts crossed his mind as Joe approached the barn with Tom. Lucas was outside, with his head stuck under the hood of his worn-out truck, while Beauty was perched on the porch in a small rocker.

"Afternoon, Beauty," Joe called, his greeting echoed by Tom as they emerged from the concealing confines of the narrow lane that led to the main road. "You, too, Lucas. What are y'all up to?"

"Hello, Joe," Beauty returned. "Same to you, Tom."

"I'm tryen to get this heap of junk runnen again," Lucas told them by way of greeting. "The battery froze up on me last night."

He blew on the battery cable for luck, retired a screwdriver to his pants pocket and closed the hood. "I was just about to take a little drive to warm it up. Y'all wanna come with me."

Joe and Tom glanced at each other, then at Beauty and back to Lucas, conspiracy gleaming in their eyes at the perfect opening presented to them. "Sure," Joe said.

"Might as well," Tom shrugged. "We've got nothen better to do."

Beauty snorted at their false sincerity. "Those boys got somethen on their mind, Lucas," she concluded. "They're up to no good, and they're wanten you to help."

Lucas eyed them suspiciously for a long moment. "Y'all do look awful bright-eyed and bushy-tailed," he surmised. "What's on your mind?"

"Nothen," Joe lied, feigning innocence.

"Humph!" Beauty sniffed. "I smell trouble."

"You swear?" Lucas asked.

Joe rolled his eyes. "Come on, Lucas," he urged in his most believable tone, crossing his arms for emphasis. "You know I don't swear to nothen."

"What about you, Tom?" Lucas inquired.

"We were just out for a walk, passen time," Tom replied quickly, sticking his hands behind his back and crossing his fingers. "Honest, Lucas. That's all."

Lucas looked at his wife. "I don't believe either one of 'em," he announced. "But if they go along with me, then I can keep my eye on 'em. What you think?"

Beauty smiled behind a disapproving frown. "I smell trouble," she repeated emphatically. "But go ahead and go. Me, I got supper to cook. You boys make sure my husband is home on time to eat it or there'll be the devil to pay."

"I won't be late," Lucas assured her. "I'm just gonna ride around a little bit to build up the battery."

"He won't be late," Joe promised, nodding his understanding.

"We'll make sure he's home on time," vowed Tom, who was already at the door of the pickup.

The three of them waved goodbye to Beauty as the truck eased out of the yard and down the narrow lane toward the main road. "I guess you'll be glad when the weather warms up," Joe said to Lucas. "For the battery," he added by way of explanation.

Lucas gave them a long glance. "You boys *are* up to somethen," he decided as they approached the dirt road and Joe jumped out of the cab to open the metal gate.

"Yesterday was my birthday," Tom announced as Lucas drove the truck through the opening and they waited for Joe to shut the gate and rejoin them. "I was thirteen."

"Congratulations," Lucas replied hesitantly. "I hope you're not expecten a birthday present from me."

"Nah," Tom remarked as Joe climbed into the cab and shut the door.

"Did you tell him?" Joe asked Tom almost immediately.

"Tell me what?" Lucas demanded to know.

"About his birthday," Joe answered quickly.

"I told him," Tom said.

"Oh," Lucas mumbled with relief, at last applying his foot to the accelerator and guiding the truck away from the farm.

They rode in silence along the dirt road, past the Berrien estate and the church, until the mercantile came into view. "Mama and Daddy gave me a sleepen bag for my birthday," Tom said. "Joe and me are goen campen by the pond tomorrow night."

"Which one?" Lucas wanted to know.

"The New Pond," Joe answered. "I'll be usen blankets and quilts for a sleepen bag."

"Wouldn't it be better to wait until the weather warms up?" Lucas asked. "It's cold and damp enough to make a body shore enough sick." He paused. "I'm surprised your mamas are letten y'all go."

Lucas brought the truck to a complete stop at the highway, and the boys held their breath while he looked left and right. Finally, after lengthy consideration, he eased their minds with a right-hand turn toward the county line liquor store. Their relief was almost audible.

"We're gonna build a fire, cook out and maybe do a little fishen tomorrow night," Joe told Lucas when the mercantile was out of sight.

"Try to scare each other with ghost stories," Tom continued. "Maybe drink a little beer."

"That so," Lucas said tonelessly.

Joe leaned forward and looked directly at his older friend. "We were kind of hopen you might buy it for us," he proposed quickly. "See'en as we're not exactly twenty-one and can't do it ourselves."

"You were hopen," Lucas repeated him.

Tom continued the pleading. "We've got the money," he said, producing a rumpled five-dollar bill from his pocket. "All we want is a six-pack. And you can buy one for yourself while you're at it. Our treat!"

"No way!" Lucas exploded. "You two boys are gonna be the death of me yet, with all your cajolen and favors. We're goen straight home."

"Come on, Lucas," Joe coaxed. "A cold beer sure would taste good goen down. It might cool you off some after all that hard work you did to get the truck runnen."

"It's forty degrees outside, Joe-Joe, and the heater ain't worken in this truck," replied Lucas, unmoved by their appeals. "We're cool enough. Besides, y'all's mamas and daddies are raisen their children to be good churchgoers."

"I don't think a beer or two is gonna send us down the road to wickedness," Joe declared, sensing a chink in his friend's resistance. "You know, Lucas, there's a lot of debate in the Baptist church about whether drinken beer is sinful at all."

"Don't get highfalutin with me, Joe-Joe," Lucas barked. "I don't know and I don't care what the Baptists believe. But I do know your mama and daddy—and Mr. Dan and Mrs. Amelia—don't want their boys drinken. And that's that."

"What's the harm?" Joe persisted. "You drink it occasionally. In fact, you're the one who gave me my first taste of beer." He paused, seemingly remembering the occasion. "Frankly, I didn't like it," he continued, changing his course of persuasion. "But Tom's never tried it at all, and he needs convincen that it tastes rotten. A guy only turns thirteen once in his life, and it's supposed to be a big deal."

Joe hesitated, allowing Lucas to mull over the idea. "I tell you what, Lucas," he continued at length. "Buy one six-pack for yourself and one for us, and we'll make sure you get whatever we don't drink. How's that for a deal?"

Completely ridiculous and out of the question, Lucas thought to himself, deliberating at length over the boys' request. His head urged Lucas to turn the truck around and head for home. But a soft spot in his heart for youthful rambunctiousness kept the truck on course for the county line.

"Lordamercy!" he finally relented. "I'll do it this one time, boys. But if you ever ask me to again, I'll tell your mamas and daddies the whole story."

"We won't ask," Tom promised. "Heck, I probably won't even like the stuff."

"Fair enough," Joe agreed.

———————

Saturday turned out cold and cloudless, perfect conditions for camping, even without a tent. Joe and Tom set up their sparse campsite on the east bank of the New Pond late in the day. It was quick work, spreading blankets on the grassy bank, setting out grocery bags of food and drink and gathering wood for a fire when night fell. Within minutes, they were finished and in the small rowboat paddling toward the far side of the pond to set a trotline for fishing.

The New Pond was deliberately inhospitable to humans. Accessible only from its long eastern bank and a tiny portion of its southern flank, the pond was a large body of water, carved from a mature grove of cypress, pine and water oaks. The eastern edge was clear and deep, but farther out, the pond turned swampy, with hundreds of jagged stumps and waterlogged trees breaking the surface. The pond eventually merged with a swamp known as Bear Bay on neighboring land owned by a cantankerous widow.

Matt and Sam had built the pond during the drought of 1954, the worst dry spell anyone could remember in these parts. They had financed the construction with the timber harvest necessary to clear the land, and both men claimed every ragged trunk and waterlogged tree on the premises were part of their master plan to create the perfect habitat for a fisherman's paradise. The pond was stocked with bass, bream, catfish and perch among others. Giant bullfrogs, turtles, water moccasins and at least one alligator had taken up residence on their own accord. Beavers occasionally tried to establish a colony on the banks but were promptly shot and their dams destroyed, as was the only otter ever seen on the place. Sam said beavers and otters would fish the pond clean if left unattended.

Joe shared the pond's history with Tom as he navigated the treacherous water. "We dug the pond in 1954, but it was bone-dry that year, and it took till the next spring before there was any water in it," he recalled. "We had a lot of rain in the winter of '56. That's when it filled up and we put the first fish in here. Grandpa didn't let a hook near the place for two years. Now there's some genuine monsters in here."

"What's the biggest one you've caught?" Tom asked.

"A four-pound channel cat in this pond," Joe replied. "But I nabbed a nine-pound bass from the Old Pond. That's the biggest fish I've ever caught." He gestured with an oar to the nearest field, which was hidden from view by a stretch of woods. "Grandpa says there's even bigger catfish in that little water hole in the middle of that field over yonder," he pointed out. "He's probably right. The place is so snaky that nobody ever fishes it."

"That hole makes my skin crawl," Tom said.

"Granny once sat on a moccasin there," Joe commented. "She wasn't payen attention and sat down on an old stump. Nobody noticed the snake till she got up. And there it was, all rolled up and ready to strike. I don't know how in the world she didn't get bit."

An involuntary tremor ran through Tom, who despised snakes. "She was lucky," he guessed. "Let's not talk about snakes out here."

Under normal circumstances, Joe would have honored his friend's request. But this was a special occasion, and he decided to strike with the night's first scary story.

"You'd better make sure you zip that sleepen bag real tight tonight," he advised Tom.

"I will," Tom replied. "It's getten downright chilly out here. We need our heavy jackets."

Joe shrugged agreement. "Yeah, but that's not what I'm talken about," he explained. "You know what they say about snakes and sleepen bags. I've heard stories about a rattlesnake crawlen in a sleepen bag while somebody was asleep inside it. Crawled all the way to the bottom and then bit the guy when he woke up." His tone became increasingly dramatic. "I even heard about one man who woke up with a rattlesnake curled up right beside him. Woke up and found himself face-to-face with it. Can you imagine waken up to find a rattlesnake—or a moccasin—looken you right between the eyes." He shivered his shoulders on purpose and restrained himself from a backward glance to see the horrified frown on Tom's face.

"Gee, Joe," Tom sighed. "Don't go talken that way. You know I hate snakes. I won't sleep a minute tonight from worryen."

Joe smiled to himself and picked out a stump, which would make a good tie-end for the trotline. He rowed toward it, slicing the single oar through the water with smooth strokes. At last, when he could stand it no longer, Joe pulled up the oar and turned around to face his friend. "You know what would be worse than waken up to find a snake staren you in the face?" he asked.

Tom shook his head violently. "No! And I don't want to, either."

"Waken up to find one all coiled up against your pecker," Joe told him anyway.

"Dang, Joe!"

"And if it bit you down there, imagine what big balls you'd have," Joe continued blithely, barely able to conceal his mirth as the boat bumped against a stump. "Of course, I don't guess a pair of big balls would do a guy much good if he was dead."

Tom suddenly turned a ghastly shade of white, and Joe nearly fell out of the boat with a chortle of uncontrollable glee.

"Joe!" Tom emphasized with a quiet forcefulness that failed to penetrate the older boy's rolling laughter. "Joe!" he repeated more loudly the second time."

Still shaking with smiles, Joe finally looked up, and Tom pointed past him. "Don't turn around, Joe," he ordered, "and give me the oar."

The sincerity of his tone brought Joe's laughter under control but failed to wipe away the silly grin from his face. Joe shook his head, pointedly dismissing Tom's attempt to feign attention away from his own fearful gullibility with such a feeble display of caution. "Nice try, partner," he gloated. "But I got you."

Joe made a leisurely about-face and almost fainted dead on the spot. A few feet away, two mammoth moccasins lay piled on top of each other in a stump hollow, and they were stirring, awakened from their late afternoon sunbath by the boat, which had butted against the broken tree trunk.

"J-e-s-u-s," Joe moaned unintentionally, stretching out every sound and syllable. "Let's get out of here, Tom," he whispered after what seemed like an eternity later. "Fast."

"I need the paddle," Tom said.

"Use your hands," Joe hissed. "If they get in this boat, I'm dead and you're next in line."

Tom peered cautiously over both sides of the boat, fearful his hands were about to become an inviting target for the snakes' children. Or worse, their brothers and sisters. Seeing nothing beneath the dark surface, he eased his hands into the water and began paddling. When the boat made its first slight movement, Joe slid the oar deftly across the stern and pushed hard against the stump, hurdling the small craft along with himself and Tom back several feet to safety. Seconds later, the moccasins slid off the stump into the water and slithered away from the boys.

"Dang!" Tom murmured later, when they were able to breathe freely again and the snakes had disappeared into the far reaches of the pond.

"No more snake stories from me," Joe vowed.

"Ain't beer supposed to calm your nerves?" Tom asked hopefully.

"I hope so," Joe muttered. "Let's set the trot line and find out."

Joe rowed the boat back toward the middle of the pond, and they swiftly finished the task. The line stretched forty feet between stumps, with baited hooks dangling in three-foot intervals. They planned to check the line in about three hours and put out new bait. With luck, they would catch Sunday dinner for their families.

---

The last light of day was dimming when the boys reached shore, and both felt as if a lifetime had passed on the water. Joe built a fire, while Tom fetched the beer from its hiding place.

They had wound up with both six-packs for themselves when Lucas ordered them from his truck, ranting and raving about the situations the boys put him in with their shenanigans and declaring he hoped the beer made them sick as dogs. In his agitation, Lucas had forgotten to retrieve his own six-pack. All day, Joe had expected the man to come looking for the beer, which explained why he had made himself scarce around the house as much as possible.

Joe was reposed on the blankets, smoking a Winston cigarette, when Tom returned with the beer. The brown bottles were chilled and dewy from the dampness of the night, and the boys immediately twisted off the tops and tested the brew.

"The Pilgrims drank beer," Tom remarked, primarily to assuage the trepidation he was feeling about the wrongful deed they were doing. "They called it ale," he went on seriously. "But it was nothing more than beer."

"And Jesus made wine," Joe added, amused by his friend, perhaps feeling a trifle guilty himself for partaking from the cup of sin, which was the way Preacher Cook had described drinking during a communion service in church one time. "He probably drank it, too," Joe continued. "But the Baptists are convinced it was nothen more than grape juice."

Joe tilted the bottle back and took a long swallow. "Whataya think?" he asked Tom when the amber liquid had slid down his throat and settled in his empty stomach. "Is it what you expected?"

"I'm not sure," Tom replied, matching Joe drink for drink. "But I don't think God's gonna send us to Hell for drinken a beer or two. Do you?"

"Probably not," Joe agreed.

"Of course," Tom said with uncertainty. "Now that I'm thirteen, I suppose I've reached the age of accountability. Is that right?"

"I'm not sure to tell you the truth," Joe answered. "Everybody's always talken about the age of accountability, but nobody ever tells you exactly what it is. Personally, I figure it's when you have a clear sense of what's right and what's wrong."

"But a person knows the difference between right and wrong when he's a little fellow," Tom interjected. "Surely God doesn't send a kid to Hell for breaken a few rules every now and then."

"You didn't let me finish," Joe grumbled. "Knowen right from wrong is only part of it. I think you also have to understand the consequences of doen wrong and be capable of taken full responsibility for your actions. And, too, I think people come to a point in life when they just automatically know whether they've reached the age of accountability. If you're old enough to worry about it, then I'm guessen you've reached that age."

"Wow!" Tom murmured. "I've just reached the age of accountability." He looked down at the nearly empty beer bottle in his hand. "I'm not off to a very good start at liven right, am I?"

Joe chuckled, which was easier than answering the question.

In these calming moments after their scare on the water, the boys forgot supper. They had planned to fry fish but had never gotten around to catching them. Now, neither was interested. But they were hungry, so Tom rummaged through the grocery sack and produced a bag of potato chips, while Joe added another log to the fire. They opened their second beers, put the chips between them and settled back on the blankets, contemplating the nighttime sky.

"It's pitch black," Tom remarked. "What we need is a full moon?"

"Moonlit nights are fine," Joe said, "but you can see the sky better on a night like this."

He pointed out Mars, various constellations and the Milky Way for Tom, and they speculated about the meteorite: Where it might have come from, how far it had traveled, what kind of star it might have been?

"Who knows," Tom pondered. "Maybe you actually saw it in the sky before it fell."

Joe gave a negative nod in the darkness. "Nah," he said. "From what I gather, it takes a fallen star years and years to reach Earth. If that meteorite was indeed a star at one time, then it began fallen a long time before you or I was even born."

"Still, it's kind of strange that it wound up here, and you found it," Tom suggested. "Maybe it was a sign or somethen."

"Maybe," Joe concurred. "But of what?"

There was no answer and for a while, they sat in silence, lost in their respective thoughts. Joe surveyed the heavens and contemplated the journey of the meteorite, of which one of the smaller pieces was sitting on the desk in his new room. He had given another chunk to Tom, while the larger section was displayed on the front porch of the Baker home, making for excellent conversation with anyone who happened to stop by the house.

"Joe?" Tom said sometime later when they were well into their third beer each and beginning to feel lightheaded from so much alcohol on empty stomachs.

"Yeah, Tom."

"Are you sure we're not goen to Hell for this?" Tom asked.

Joe knew there was a concerned frown on his friend's face without even looking at him. "Not for drinken beer, I don't think," he answered sincerely.

"Then I don't guess a cigarette would hurt too much, would it?" Tom supposed.

Joe snickered and offered his friend a cigarette, lighting it with the red tip of his own smoke.

"Now that we're pretty much sure we're not goen to Hell for drinken and smoken, I've got another question for you," Tom began again when he had inhaled deeply from the cigarette and chased it with a long gulp of beer. "If you died now, where would you go? Heaven? Or Hell?"

Joe sat up and crossed his legs Indian style to peer closely at his friend. "You're a bulldog tonight," he said. "What's this fixation with Heaven and Hell? Frankly, I'm plannen to stay earthbound for a long time to come. I figure—at least I hope—I have a few years to prepare for the hereafter."

"You never know," Tom said, snapping his fingers. He hesitated, then persisted, "So which is it? Heaven? Or Hell?"

Joe shifted his gaze across the blackness of the pond and mulled over the question. There was not a pat answer at hand. And since he was being pressed for a serious commitment, he wanted to give Tom a thoughtful response rather than a brush-off.

Religion baffled Joe. On the surface, it seemed easy to figure out what God expected of Christians. But scratching the surface was akin to opening a can of worms. God's expectations were complex, and while Joe considered himself a good person, he feared whether he could measure up to Christian standards. It seemed to boil down to a matter of good or good enough, and there was a thin line of distinction between the two. Of course, he knew, too, that a person must be prepared to meet his Maker as if every breath was the last. At the same time, though, he wondered whether God expected a person to remember that every move might be the last and preface it as such. Frankly, he doubted even monks could be so single-minded. And he was positive that he could not be. None of which provided him the elusive answer.

"That's a hard question," he answered at length, "and, honestly, I haven't given it much thought. But since you ask, I figure I have fairly good credentials for Heaven." He took a deep breath. "Still, when you come right down to it, I suppose I'd have to say Hell at this point in time."

An incredulous expression graced Tom. "Are you serious?" he asked gravely.

"I've felt saved a few times," Joe explained seriously. "But the Bible says you have to accept Christ publicly and be baptized, and I haven't felt called enough, or good enough, to do that. Since it's one of the key points laid out by Jesus for salvation, then I'd say my bid for Heaven is flawed right now. It all goes back to what I said earlier about right and wrong and understanden the consequences and taken responsibility. The Bible pretty much lays out the plan for salvation and if you reject it and realize you're rejecten it, then I'd say you're probably doomed to Hell."

Joe paused, then added quickly, "At least I'd say that about myself. Of course, as the Bible also says, I try not to judge others."

"We're goen to Hell," Tom murmured with the slow comprehension of a new idea.

"No, we're not," Joe assured him, laughing. "We've got time to do the right thing, Tom, and when the right time comes, we'll do it. Now let's change the subject."

There was no more talk of religion, but the conversation flowed smoothly. The more beer went into their mouths, the more nonsense flowed out of them. They were at once boisterous and boastful, crass and courageous, thoughtless and thoughtful. They discussed girls and school, girls and themselves, girls and sports, girls and sex.

Both of them were virgins, lamentably so. At fifteen, Joe was particularly worried about his lack of experience, especially when other boys his age boasted of sexual conquests.

"They're lyen," Tom said.

"Probably," Joe agreed. "But town people seem to do everything faster than we do out in the country. Maybe they're more sophisticated about sex. Maybe the girls in town are more willen."

He stood and staggered over to retrieve more beers for them. "Hell, I've got all the tools for maken love," he boasted. "Plenty of it, if I say so myself. I got the prowess for it. And Lord knows, I got the interest. But I'm still a cherry, and I don't even stand a chance out here. The only girls I ever see around here are my sisters or those who come to church. And I try not to think about girls at church."

"You think you've got problems," Tom said, having heard enough. "What about me? I'm still waiten for a good bulge in my blue jeans."

"You'll get it," Joe shrugged. "I got most of mine in the last year. You just wake up one mornen and it's there, ready and willen to conquer the world. Then you spend all your time worryen it's gonna spring into action at the worst possible time and everybody's gonna see you with a hard-on."

Such was the stuff of the evening. By midnight, the pair had consumed ten bottles of beer and were staggering drunk when they reached for the last two.

"This stuff grows on you," Tom remarked, holding out the beer bottle for an examination. "It tasted horrible at first, but it gets better with each sip."

Joe belched, long and loud, and swigged down another ounce or two.

That was when they remembered the trotline, which should have been checked hours ago and plied with new bait. Falling all over themselves, they climbed into the boat and rowed a ragged course toward the trotline.

"This is one spooky place at night," Tom commented as the boat glided across the water, occasionally bouncing off a shadowy stump. "It's dark as sin."

"Do you remember where we set it?" Joe asked, straining to see in the darkness when he was certain they had rowed past the trotline. "I can't figure out where we are."

Tom stumbled to his feet and made a sweeping gaze around the pond, teetering on the edge before finally pointing to his right and collapsing back into the seat. The boat rocked precariously, and Tom burst into giggles.

Joe laughed, too, and shook his head. "You're drunk," he accused good-naturedly.

"Sho, nuff," Tom replied. "But I found the trot line, mister, so you must be drunker than me."

"Whatever," Joe shrugged. "But you'd better keep your butt sitten down so the boat doesn't tip over. It's too cold for swimmen."

"There ain't no way I'm goen swimmen in this snake hole," Tom shivered. "You'd either end up full of snake holes or some ornery alligator would bite off your balls for a late-night snack."

"Yours might make a snack," Joe deadpanned. "Mine would be a full-course meal."

"Either way," Tom continued. "I think I'll keep my butt sitten down."

"You do that," Joe urged. "And be quiet while you're at it."

Tom took the advice and was dozing by the time the boat reached the trotline, which was nowhere in the vicinity of the direction he had pointed. Noticing his friend slumped on his side, Joe promptly jabbed Tom in the gut with the oar. "Wake up!" he ordered. "We've got fish to haul in."

Tom sprang instantly alert. "What a night," he remarked. "Guess I picked the right place after all."

"Close enough," Joe lied.

The first four hooks netted two perch, a small bream that Tom tossed back, and a good-sized channel catfish that finned Joe and was dropped inadvertently into the water. The next two hooks were empty, which was when Tom noticed the heavy sag in the line.

"Jesus, Joe," he shouted. "We must have caught a shark or somethen. The whole line's under water at this end."

Joe was rubbing his palm and cursing his clumsiness with the catfish. "We don't have sharks," he muttered, picking up the paddle and rowing them closer to the sagging line. "Pull it up," he instructed. "Let's see what's on the other end."

"Dang, it's heavy," Tom said, tugging on the line. "I need help."

Joe dropped the oar and lifted the trotline with both hands, while Tom leaned over the edge, grabbed the hook line and began reeling in the catch. Neither one of them had an idea about what had been snagged on the line, but at that moment, their catch began fighting for its freedom. The sudden thrashing in the water caught Tom off guard, and he lost his hold on the hook line.

Joe roared with amusement, while straining to pull the main line higher out of the water. He stood on shaky legs to gain leverage. "Grab the line and pull it up, Tom," he shouted. "Whatever the thing is, it can't hurt you with a hook in the mouth."

"I ain't so sure about that," Tom yelled back before cautiously gripping the line once more. This time his grip was tight and, ignoring the thrashing water, he made steady progress in reeling the catch to the surface.

"I've got it!" he cried.

Then the water exploded.

Tom sensed rather than saw the oblong object lunge at him with powerful snapping jaws. He screamed, dropped the line and tried to scramble away as the hard-shelled monster landed in the boat.

"A snappen turtle!" Joe hollered, laughing. "Watch out!"

Tom yelled again and hurled himself away from the turtle, jumping over the snapping jaws of the long neck protruding from the wide-bodied shell.

Overweighted on one side, the boat flipped before the boys even comprehended the danger. Joe, whose balance had been in jeopardy all along while trying to stand on the bottom of the boat, pitched headlong into the water, scraping his back against a jagged edge of an underwater stump as he sank into the murky depths of the pond. It was the single most-terrifying moment of his young life, complete with a hallucination of hundreds of water moccasins, snapping turtles and hungry alligators, all lurking about their rightful abode and eager to attack any unlawful intruder.

Surrounded by total blackness, out of air, Joe decided against a watery grave. He righted himself beneath the water, kicked to the surface and received, along with a greedy gulp of air, the second, single-most terrifying moment of his life: a stillness and silence over the pond that made its black depths far more ominous than they had ever been.

Fear seized his heart, and Joe uttered a single word, softly at first and then in a long scream.

"Tom!"

_____

Tom felt the boat capsizing and was all at once grateful for escaping the snapping jaws and fearful the turtle might follow him into the water. By his own reckoning, the turtle had missed Tom's flesh by a hair's breadth and he figured to have nightmares about those powerful jaws for years to come.

He landed in the water on his shoulder and went under off balance. But Tom made an immediate recovery. He turned a quick somersault, kicked up toward the surface and was promptly snagged by one of the trotline hooks.

The hook snared him by the nape of the neck, imbedding deep in the flesh. Wrought with pain, Tom involuntarily opened his mouth to yell and was choked with a gullet full of water. He floundered to the top of the pond, coughing and gasping for air, aware of someone screaming his name.

He grasped his neck, yelled for help and went under once more with another long swallow of water, most of which he inhaled.

Joe was treading water ten feet away when Tom emerged. His mind cleared instantly, and two sturdy swim strokes covered the distance in seconds flat. Joe took a deep breath, dove underwater and slammed into Tom, who was coming up a second time for air. They untangled themselves and pushed to the surface, where Joe grabbed Tom by the arm and pulled him through the water to the sturdy anchor of a waterlogged cypress stump.

"I've got a fish hook in my neck," Tom moaned, coughing up water at the same time and clinging to the ragged stump with both arms. "It's killen me," he wailed.

"You're okay," Joe said in his calmest voice. "Just keep holden on to this stump, and you'll be fine."

"Try to get it out, Joe," Tom cried. "Please."

It was impossible to see in the darkness, and Joe lacked the dexterity to keep himself afloat while performing minor surgery at the same time. Still, he examined Tom and discovered the hook was buried deep in his neck, with only a tiny portion of the straight end sticking out of the flesh. Seeing the hook was still attached to the main line, he realized the tension was adding to Tom's torment. He fished his pocketknife from his jeans and cut the line.

"Is that better?"

"Some," Tom moaned.

Joe looked around to get his bearings, trying to readjust his eyes for night vision. It was pitch black. The boat was nowhere in sight, and the oar had floated to some hidden place. He tried to remember the path they had followed in the daylight, seeming to recall they had set the line somewhere near the middle of the pond. It was a long way to shore, he realized. Whichever way it was.

---

The ice-cold water was chilling his imbibed mind to a numbing soberness, and Joe was worried.

Tom was hugging the cypress stump for dear life, moaning occasionally about his neck and shivering in violent fits.

If they stayed in the water much longer, exposure would kill them—if the snakes and alligators did not get them first.

Joe gazed heavenward for divine intervention and was rewarded with a clear nighttime sky. He sighted the North Star and the two dippers and knew immediately the pond bank lay somewhere to the right.

"I don't know about you, buddy," he told Tom, "but I don't want to be fish food or gator bait. We have to get out of here, or we're gonna freeze to death."

"I'm not sure I can make it," Tom said meekly without lifting his head from the stump. "My neck's on fire."

"You'll make it," Joe declared. "I promise. We'll swim from stump to stump and rest whenever we need to. I'll be right beside you the whole way, so there's no need to worry."

"Okay," Tom exhaled.

Joe pointed in the darkness. "The bank's that way," he said. "Are you ready?"

Tom shook his head, and they began, swimming side-by-side from stump to stump. They moved through the water in virtual silence, except for an occasional word of encouragement from Joe and a groan from Tom.

It was an agonizingly slow journey for Joe and even more so for Tom. Every stump held the potential to harbor a bed of moccasins and the worst ones were those unseen beneath the surface. His heart beat faster every time Joe touched one of the waterlogged remnants of some cypress or oak tree, and he prayed silently that it might be the last one they came across.

In a way, Tom might have been lucky to have that fishhook in his neck. His agony was all too real to dwell on anything else.

After what seemed like hours of trading one stump for another, the distance between the broken tree trunks became longer and more taxing to cover. At last, they came to a hollow stump resembling an arch, and Joe knew the pond bank lay about a hundred yards before them. They took this final opportunity to rest, each clinging to one of the thick tendrils that had once supported a massive water oak.

Joe peered closely at the pale face of Tom, who was obviously fatigued, his weakness exacerbated by the pain in his neck and the excessive alcohol in his blood.

"Are you okay?" Joe asked the younger boy for the second time that night.

"Just tired," Tom answered.

"How's the neck?"

"It hurts, but not as much," Tom said. "Maybe I'm getten used to it." He paused. "Heck, maybe I'll keep it."

Joe smiled for what seemed like the first time in ages. "The latest in fashion neckwear," he said drolly. "Who knows, Tom? You might be starten the latest, greatest fad."

Tom smiled tiredly. "We were awful stupid, weren't we?" he said.

"We were lucky," Joe agreed. "But we've still got a way to go before we're out of the woods." He hesitated. "Or should I say out of the water. Are you up to it?"

Tom looked off in the darkness. "It's a pretty long way," he surmised.

"Yeah, but you could swim it underwater if you wanted," Joe encouraged. "You go first. I'll follow, and if you get tired, I'll be right there to help. We'll make it, Tom. We've come too far not to."

"Piece of cake," Tom smiled, then suddenly surged free of the oaken anchor and began swimming strongly toward the shore.

Joe spotted him ten yards and followed at a slower pace.

Minutes later, Tom found the bottom of the pond with his feet and staggered up the bank with Joe on his heels. They collapsed face down on the grassy shore, breathing heavily and catching their breath while the tension melted in waves of weary relief.

"When's the last time you had a tetanus shot?" Joe inquired when their breathing had returned to normal.

"I don't remember," Tom answered, his words muffled against the ground.

Joe pushed himself off the grassy bed to a sitting position. "You'll need to get one, you know," he said.

"I need to see a doctor," Tom suggested, rising slowly. "I've got to get this thing out of my neck. And soon!"

"But you can't go tonight," Joe informed him with sympathy.

"No, I guess not," Tom agreed. "Everybody'd know we'd been up to no good."

"And if they found out where we got the beer, Lucas would wind up in a lot worse shape," Joe said. "We've got to keep this to ourselves, at least until we're sober and presentable."

Tom nodded in agreement. "Okay," he said, touching the back of his neck. "But we've got to get this hook out. I can't hurt like this all night."

"I can do it," Joe grimaced. "It'll hurt like the devil, though."

"I know," Tom conceded with a determined frown. "But at least there'll be some relief when you're finished. Let's go ahead and get it over with."

"Okay," Joe replied. "Let me look at it."

The hook was sunk fully into Tom's neck. Blood trickled from the ragged tear in the skin. There was only one way Joe knew to remove a fishhook, and that was to push it through the skin. Pulling the hook out would cause worse pain and rip more flesh. "I'll be back in a second," he told Tom after examining the wound.

Joe walked back to their campsite and procured a small pair of pliers with wire cutters from his tackle box, then scoured the pond bank for a stout stick. A short time later, they were ready to begin.

"Here," Joe said, offering the stick to Tom. "Put it in your mouth and bite down if the pain gets to be more than you can bear. I've heard it helps."

Tom took the stick and gazed at the pliers.

"Lie down on your stomach," Joe instructed him after a

moment's hesitation. "I'm goen to sit on your back to keep you still. Try not to make any sudden movements."

"Easy for you to say," Tom muttered as he moved into a prone position on the grass. "Just make it quick. That's all I ask."

Joe kneeled beside him and studied the angle of the hook. Using his thumb and index finger, he pressed against Tom's neck to measure the depth of the imbedded angle. Tom squirmed under the pressure, and Joe withdrew his hand.

"It's deep in there," he explained. "I'll have to push it down a tiny bit and then up and through to get it out. Are you ready?"

Tom nodded.

"Remember to bite down on the stick if it hurts more than you can bear," Joe advised.

Tom nodded again and buried his face against the grass as Joe pressed against the injured area with one hand and gripped the straight end of the hook with the other. "Take a deep breath," he ordered.

Joe worked quickly and efficiently. In one sweeping motion, he pushed down on the skin and up with the hook. The curved end of the hook tore through the flesh, along with a heavy flow of blood. Using his weight to keep Tom penned to the ground, Joe used the wire cutter on the pliers to clip the end of the hook. From there, he pulled both metal ends from the wound and jumped away from Tom.

Though the whole process took less than twenty seconds, the pain was excruciating. His neck screamed for relief and Tom bounded to his feet the instant he felt Joe release his hold on him. He took three blind steps forward and promptly provided a vocal outlet for the pain. It was a yell, loud but blessedly short. A spasm of delirious laughter mixed with cries shook Tom next and then he was spent.

He collapsed and allowed Joe to wash away the blood and press a cold rag against the wound. Ten minutes later, most of the bleeding had stopped and Tom was able to drift off to sleep.

Joe built a roaring fire beside his friend and stripped out of his own wet clothes to dry them. He wrapped himself in a blanket, then gathered up the beer bottles and threw them far out into the pond rather than risk their discovery.

A thousand thoughts raced through his mind, most of them disturbing as Joe huddled by the fire waiting for his clothes to dry.

He contemplated how their plans had gone awry, what might have happened to him or Tom, with each realization more chilling than the previous, leaving him colder from fright than the brisk night air.

Shortly before dawn, with his mind at last numb and his clothes dry, Joe finally dozed, secure in the knowledge that he was, at the very least, older and wiser for this perilous night.

———————

The boys dragged themselves home shortly before noon and gave everyone their carefully distorted version of the previous night. To listen to them tell it, their camping trip had been unremarkable, except for a freakish boating mishap. And even the accident had been uneventful, they maintained, except, perhaps, for some minor pain to Tom.

There were a few questions to answer for their fathers and some assurances to provide their mothers, but, largely, the story won easy acceptance. Tom got his tetanus shot, which had been due anyway, and Joe caught the devil from Lucas, who was angry the boys had taken both six-packs. The entire incident might have passed without note, but for one significant milestone in its aftermath.

On the next Sunday, which was Big Meeting at church, Joe and Tom made their public professions of Christ, admitted they were sinners and asked for forgiveness and baptism. Remarkably, they insisted on baptism that very day, even though it was late February and the waters of New River were cold and running swiftly.

Preacher Adam Cook honored their request with gladness in his heart, and the boys were buried in the cleansing water of New River. A few days later, Joe came down with a miserable cold, while Tom was put to bed with a nasty case of flu.

It was worth being sick, they told each other. One never knew when a baptism might come in handy.

# CHAPTER 3

GERUNDS, PARTICIPLES AND INFINITIVES were the topic of the hour, and Mrs. Elizabeth Gaskins had the propensity to make them interesting. Normally, Joe would have given his undivided attention to the feisty, redheaded woman. But on this day, he spent the entire second period conjugating Spanish verbs, completing a neglected homework assignment from the previous day. He finished the task as the bell rang and reviewed his work while his classmates collected books and filed out of the room to their next class.

Stuffing the paper in his notebook, he clasped his hands behind his back and stretched. Mrs. Gaskins was staring at him when Joe looked up from his desk. He smiled easily, sobering just as quickly when he detected the piercing gaze the English teacher reserved for severe reprimands. Her eyebrows were arched, her nostrils flared and her lips pursed.

"My time is as valuable as yours, Mr. Baker," she said frostily, "and my class is not intended to serve as a study hall for someone else's homework. I do not appreciate your lack of sensitivity."

"I'm sorry, Mrs. Gaskins," Joe apologized, bestowing his most winning smile. "I forgot my Spanish homework last night, and it's due next period."

"Nevertheless, I am disappointed, Joseph."

Mrs. Gaskins was his favorite teacher and a friend as well. She taught grammar and literature with flair and panache. Once, while studying *Beowulf*, she had ordered students to bring fried chicken to class and made them ravage the food with their bare hands while reading portions of the old English epic. She viewed the grease stains on the pages of her literature books as medals of honor.

Joe worshipped the woman. Once he had dreamed about having a love affair with her in Paris or London. But she had introduced him to her husband at a basketball game one night, beginning with, "This is Joe Baker. He thinks he's my favorite student."

Her husband had smiled brightly, extended his hand and said, "I'll tell you a secret, Joe. You *are* her favorite student."

Joe genuinely liked the guy, so he now confined his thoughts about the teacher to friendship and her work.

As much as she brought passion to the classroom, Elizabeth Gaskins also ruled with a firm hand. She required good behavior and those who acted otherwise felt the full weight of her wrath. She also demanded excellence in everything, expected thoughtful answers and urged her students to search for meaning beyond the words. She wanted students to learn but she also asked them to think, and from her, Joe had discerned the importance of distinguishing between those two tasks.

Outside his family, Elizabeth Gaskins was the most influential person in his life and, right now, she was ticked with him.

Joe honored her with his most contrite expression, casting brown eyes downward to indicate his unworthiness. He mumbled another apology, then raised his eyes and inquired slyly, "Does this mean I'm not your favorite student anymore?"

"You're in the doghouse, buster, but I'll let it pass this time," she replied testily. "If you promise not to let it happen again."

"I promise."

Joe eased out of the desk and gathered his books, while Mrs. Gaskins shuffled papers. "Here!" she said abruptly, waving a folded set of papers to him.

"What is it?" Joe asked.

"Your last writing assignment," she answered with interest. "When I ask my students to write an essay defenden somethen unusual, I expect some strange responses. Your choice of subject was most interesten."

"Oh," Joe muttered cautiously.

"I gave it an A-plus," she continued. "It was written superbly; your logic was excellent and your examples honest. Although I suspect some college professor might make mincemeat of it, I was intrigued. Without doubt, Joe, you are the first and very likely will be my only student to write an essay defenden clichés. Frankly, I'm not sure whether to applaud your originality or worry about your psyche."

"I suppose you noticed there are no clichés in it," he boasted.

"Most certainly," the teacher assured him. "I read it twice to make sure. It's fortunate that you refrained. Just one, and I would have given you an A-minus at best, and your grade would have fallen proportionately with each cliché."

"Thank you," Joe smiled sheepishly as Mrs. Gaskins handed the paper to him. Written neatly in red and circled, the A+ appealed to his ego. Joe grinned appreciatively at his teacher. She immediately stifled his moment of glory.

"I had planned today's lesson around your paper," she said sternly. "But, of course, your attention was elsewhere." She unleashed another withering frown on Joe and added a touch of sarcasm to her voice. "And far be it for me, a mere teacher, to interfere with your busy schedule. So, I decided it better to wait until tomorrow before throwen your genius to the wolves. We have some bright students in this class, Joe, and they'll show you no mercy. I warn you in advance to come prepared to defend yourself, as well as explain why you chose to make a spirited defense of clichés of all things. Are we clear?"

"Yes, ma'am."

"Very well, then," she dismissed him. "You may go."

"Yes, ma'am."

He almost made it to the door before Elizabeth Gaskins halted him once more. "And Joe," she called as his hand grasped the doorknob. He glanced backward and found her smiling warmly. "Well done," she saluted.

"Yes, ma'am," he grinned. "Thank you."

---

At Cookville High School, the town students set the style and the country folk did their best keep up with it. The differences between the two groups were hardly distinguishable, although some of the snootier town students cast their country counterparts in the role of bumpkins, while the rougher elements from the farms were quick to pick a fight with so-called Cookville snobs. In general, though, the two sides mixed and mingled in peace. The town students simply navigated the hallways with a little more finesse, while the country kids carried a few more calluses.

Perhaps it was the smooth way they operated that allowed the town students to dominate most high school activities. Most likely, though, it was who you were that made the difference. All qualifications aside, participation in everything from sports to the annual spring play was virtually assured if your father was a doctor or a law-yer, owned his own business or was a politician. The children of the prominent were most often the students who received the cheers at the pep rallies, on fields of play and during most every other high school assembly. And almost exclusively, they lived in town.

With a few notable exceptions, students like Joe, who passed their first eight grades in the country at New River Elementary and other outlying community schools, trolled relatively unnoticed through four years of high school. Two of Joe's elementary school classmates had found their way into the inner circle of the privi-leged. Their success was to be expected. Amy Shaw was too beautiful to overlook, and Greg Mathis too funny to ignore.

Joe belonged to the supporting cast, that great bulk of students who seemed to exist so that a chosen few could feel all the more privileged about their run of the place. Even among the supporting cast, there were distinctions. There were those, mostly girls, who talked too much, overdressed and tried too hard to become mem-bers of the inner circle. Then there were the ruffians, and the group that managed to remain virtually invisible through all four years of high school. And, of course, there were a very few whose ugliness, simple-mindedness or other grotesque distinction prevented them from slipping unnoticed through those hallowed, harrowing halls of high school.

Joe existed on the fringe, among those people who were liked by almost everyone and occasionally earned recognition for some minor talent, deed or happenstance. One of those occasions oc-curred soon after the reprimand from Mrs. Gaskins, and Joe owed his sudden notoriety to the English teacher.

As promised, she threw Joe to the wolves and made his defense of clichés a topic for discussion in her class. It generated a spirited debate. Joe defended himself admirably in his own estimation, simply stating that clichés deserved respect because they emerged from years of truth and satisfied the human need for familiarity and comfort.

"Like an old pair of slippers on tired feet," he offered.

Not everyone agreed, with the protest led most notably by Rich-ard Golden. One of the more snobbish town students, Richard was the potential heir to a growing grocery store chain. He wrote the disjointed "School Happenings" column in *The Cookville Herald* and fancied himself a writer of unrivaled talent.

"Anyone who knows anything about language understands that clichés have no merit," Richard argued airily while sneering at Joe. "Clichés are nothen more than crutches for those who are unwillen, or unable, to think of a more suitable phrase to express themselves."

Dismissing Joe with upturned nostrils, Richard turned to the teacher for confirmation. "Isn't that right, Mrs. Gaskins?"

"In your opinion, Richard," she answered noncommittally. "And in the opinion of many others as well. But remember that we are talken strictly about opinions here. Joe is entitled to his, whether you, I or anyone else agrees with him. In this case, his opinion is no righter—or wrong—than yours."

As Richard's mouth fell open, the discussion took an unexpected twist, courtesy of Karen Baxter, another town student who occupied the desk behind Joe in the alphabetized seating arrangement required by their English teacher. "I happen to disagree with Joe," Karen announced.

Joe turned around in his seat to look her in the eye and was captivated by a pair of emerald green orbs.

"Both on the use of clichés and that dribble about familiarity and comfort," Karen continued. She smiled regretfully at Joe, then set a disparaging gaze on Richard Golden. "But regardless, Richard," she began smartly. "You'd do well to heed your own advice. I wade through that column you write every week, and it's positively rife with clichés." She paused, then added sweetly, "Perhaps, Richard, you're unwillen to express yourself more eloquently." She hesitated, then asked politely, "Or are you just unable?"

Joe detected thinly veiled sarcasm in her inquiry, recalling briefly that Karen and Richard had dated once. But it was a mindless thought, forgotten as quickly as it was dredged up from the inner recesses of his mind.

He had more important things to consider—like being struck dead center by Cupid's arrow.

———

Karen Baxter belonged to the exclusive inner circle of privileged high school students. She was a cheerleader, an honor student and prized catch for a date. In short, she was off limits to Joe, although rarely out of his thoughts during these dreary winter days of their junior year at Cookville High School.

There were prettier girls in school than Karen and one or two who made superior grades. But her aura was unmatched. She radiated innocence and fragility, bewitching and enchanting with a tilt of her head, a shift of the eyes or slender fingers combed gently through her soft chestnut brown hair. At her core, however, was cool strength, which could transform those sparkling emerald eyes into cold orbs of malevolent green, evoke a tart tongue and give rise to a guileless smile of polished steel.

Karen was a girl of winter, no doubt, and her brittle side attracted Joe. His protective instincts sharpened around her, and his hormones went haywire.

Her chestnut brown hair hung shoulder length, framing a delicate, heart-shaped face. She was petite, about five inches shorter than Joe, with a waist so tiny he felt certain his splayed fingers could clasp around it. Her figure was a perfect fit for her small frame, and her face was angelic with the dazzling emerald eyes and full, pouting lips. Her complexion was pure ivory, a sharp contrast to the swarthiness of Joe, who was consumed by this comparison when a voice interrupted his thoughts at lunch on the day of his sterling defense of clichés.

"Richard's just jealous of the way you have with words."

Joe peered up from his plate to find Karen regarding him with an amused expression. "May I join you?" she asked, setting her cafeteria tray opposite him.

"Sure," Joe said, taking a sip of milk to calm his racing thoughts, while savoring the soft lilt of her voice and ravishing her with his eyes.

Karen caught his admiring gaze, flashing a smile of pure innocence, and Joe dropped his eyes to the hamburger and French fries on his plate.

"That was quite a paper you wrote," she said. "Richard Golden would sell his mother to have an original idea like that."

Joe shrugged. "Defender of clichés," he remarked dryly. "Somehow I don't think that's gonna get me very far."

Karen laughed lightly. "Everyone has to start somewhere," she offered. "Anyway, you're farther along than most everyone else around here, especially the Richard Goldens of our class."

"Richard's not so bad," Joe suggested. "He just tries too hard."

"Richard's full of himself," Karen shot back. "He's arrogant, snobbish and thinks he's God's gift to the world. Unfortunately, he suffers from visions of grandeur when, in truth, he has neither the vision nor the talent to do but one thing in life."

"Which is?" Joe inquired with understated curiosity.

"To draw a fat paycheck from his father's grocery stores and live comfortably and safely right here in good old Cookville," she answered. "Richard will have a pleasant life."

"Interesten," Joe mused.

"Which is exactly what Richard's life will not be," Karen said sweetly.

Joe shrugged, took a bite of his hamburger and washed it down with milk. "I take it Richard's not one of your favorite people?" he inferred.

"Perceptive, aren't you?" Karen remarked with droll sarcasm.

"Y'all used to date, didn't you?" Joe pushed.

"We went out a few times," she replied, shrugging her shoulders. "He wasn't up to my standards, if you know what I mean?"

Since he had no clue, Joe allowed this last remark to pass without comment, returning to his food while Karen did the same.

"What about you?" she asked after a minute of companionable silence.

Joe glanced up, his face expressionless. "What about me?" he countered.

"Do you intend to live comfortably and safely here in Cookville?" she challenged. "Or are you looken for somethen more interesten?"

Joe matched her intense gaze while pondering his reply. "What do you think?"

"It's a mystery to me, Joe," Karen said. "You're not exactly forthcomen and open about yourself."

Joe nodded. "Actually, I think some people have everything you're talken about right here in Cookville," he replied. "Comfort, safety, interesten lives. My parents do. And my grandparents, too."

He paused, then informed her without fanfare, "I want to be a journalist. I figure I'll wind up some place besides Cookville."

"Ambitious, aren't you," Karen remarked quickly. "I should have figured. You're too smart to waste away your whole life on a backwoods farm."

Joe started to defend the farmer's way of life, but Karen cut him off with another question. "How come I know so little about you?"

"We don't exactly run in the same circles," Joe answered bluntly.

"We could," Karen suggested. "It's not a closed circle." She tilted her head, flicked her hair and unleashed an alluring smile that turned Joe's hormones inside out.

"I'm gonna keep my eye on you, Joe Baker," she purred. "And if you ever decide to venture off that farm to go someplace other than school, let me know." She smiled knowingly. "I have a feelen you and I might be ... two birds of the same feather."

---

Karen drifted into the daily habit of eating lunch with Joe in the high school cafeteria. She was a quick-witted, challenging conversationalist, who tossed out a new idea with almost every flick of her hair and every bat of her eyelids. She was coy and seductive, reserved and overwhelming, attentive and calculating. Joe was forced to stay on his toes to keep pace with her changing moods. She stimulated him as no other girl had done, both physically and mentally.

Joe considered it quite possible that he was in love, but he kept those thoughts strictly to himself, rebuffing even the curious inquiries of Tom Carter, who suspected something afoot between his best friend and this privileged girl. Had he been more certain about Karen's intentions toward him, Joe would have been more forthcoming with Tom about the status of the relationship. Of course, he reminded himself often, Karen might very well find the whole idea of a relationship between herself and Joe preposterous. It was possible that he was nothing more than her current, favorite lunching partner.

Despite her keen mind and spirited tongue, Karen suffered from flights of fancy. She thrived on inconsistency, and her appetite was fed by a carefully disguised rebellious streak. For instance, she criticized the notion of stereotypes, yet constantly categorized people under neat labels. She downplayed her popularity, while basking in the glow of the spotlight and keeping attention focused squarely on her shoulders. Her charm was ingratiating, its effect insidious.

Karen was between boyfriends, she often reminded Joe. In the fall, she had dated the quarterback of the football team, dropping him the week before the season ended. She had broken up with her latest boyfriend, the captain of the basketball team, in the middle of the season.

"He was an athlete," she explained to Joe. "Nice looken but all wrapped up in himself. And not exactly a conversationalist, either. I mean grunts and groans have their place in a relationship, but a steady diet of them is deadly dull. Don't you agree?"

"I suppose," Joe grunted.

Karen smiled. "I sound pretentious."

"Yeah," Joe nodded. "You do."

Her eyes narrowed and the smile changed instantly to a cold glare. "I have high standards," she said flatly, rising from the table and collecting her lunch tray. "And no time for those who don't, can't or won't meet my expectations."

For two days, Karen deserted him at lunch, leaving Joe to sneak quick glances her way whenever they were in class or close contact. He thought all was lost until Mrs. Gaskins came to the rescue, elevating him once again with sudden notoriety.

The vehicle was a short story assignment. Joe wrote about two brothers who discovered a secret stairway in their room. The stairway led to an underground world, and the brothers eventually abandoned their old lives for the newfound utopia.

Mrs. Gaskins flattered Joe with praise for the story, spending an entire class period analyzing it. Embarrassed by her enthusiasm, Joe nevertheless paid close attention to the teacher's theories about his intentions and nodded dutiful agreement at every request for verification of her interpretation. In actuality, her theories stunned Joe. But he did not have the heart to tell the woman he had given little thought to the story's deeper meaning, especially when it was much easier to sit back and have his ego stroked with her noble praise and dreamy gazes from Karen.

"You're brilliant, Joe," Karen told him when she returned to their table to share lunch later that day. "You've bedazzled me."

Bedazzled seemed a rather strong reaction to Joe, but he kept this thought to himself, along with many others he might have had. Just like Mrs. Gaskins, Karen maintained a constant chatter about the story, reanalyzing his intentions and spouting off her own endless theories with repeated requests for his confirmation. Joe merely nodded and gazed at length across the table.

"Do you really believe there's a world better than this one—someplace besides Heaven?" Karen asked abruptly.

Completely smitten, Joe barely heard the question, much less paid attention to it. "I do," he sighed before the significance of the admission penetrated his consciousness.

He realized his mistake almost immediately, with alarming concern, especially should word of such blasphemy ever get back to Caroline and Rachel.

"Well, no, Karen," he stammered, regaining equilibrium of his thoughts. "I most definitely believe in Heaven. And Hell, too." He hesitated, then continued in almost dreadful, yet determined, tones. "It's just a story, Karen. I wrote it for fun, and I'd rather not make more of it than it is. It's like trying to make somethen sophisticated out of plain homespun. Can we talk about somethen else?"

A pout crossed her face, and Joe feared he had made a fatal mistake. But abruptly, Karen tossed her hair and flashed him a warm smile. "Let's talk," she agreed.

Joe relaxed, then wondered what in the world he would say to her.

———————

On the next Monday, Karen brought sensational news to school. She and her younger sister, Nancy, had spent the previous weekend with their grandparents, who lived on a farm in the southeastern corner of the county. At supper Saturday night, Nancy told her family of seeing a big cat pacing near the edge of the woods.

"Nancy said it looked like a female lion," Karen explained in English class. "We ignored her. Everyone figured she had seen a big bobcat. It's not unusual to see them around the farm."

A piercing scream in the middle of the night and the discovery of a cow's mutilated carcass the next morning convinced Karen and her grandparents that Nancy had seen a big cat, indeed. "It was the worst kind of scream you could imagine," Karen recalled. "My papa says it sounded like a panther, but we don't know for sure."

She shuddered, dramatically and sincerely. "Whatever it was, that poor cow was torn to pieces. I hope she died quickly."

At lunch, Joe pestered Karen for more details until she finally took his lead from her own nettling about his short story and pleaded for a new subject. Joe complied with her request, but his thoughts rarely strayed from the cat. He discussed the situation thoroughly with Tom on the bus ride to New River from Cookville, and they swapped tales of panthers prowling their community in days of yore.

In his excitement to share the story with the family, Joe covered the distance between the mercantile, where the high school bus deposited him, and home at a faster pace than usual. He barged into the kitchen telling the story, and Caroline and Rachel were beset instantly with worry. Joe left them to it, racing from the house to relay the news to his father and grandfather.

Matt and Sam were in the pecan orchard behind the syrup house and smokehouse, changing a worn tire on the tractor.

"Guess what!" Joe said eagerly as he emerged from the shelter attached to the smokehouse side of the dual-purpose outbuilding.

Sam eyed the boy closely, while Matt gave his son a sidelong glance from the hydraulic jack. "I don't know," Sam chuckled, "but you look like you're gonna burst wide open if we don't figure it out soon. Go ahead; spit it out and save us all the trouble of guessen."

"A girl in my class, Karen Baxter, says a panther killed a cow on her grandfather's farm Saturday night," Joe revealed as he approached the men.

"That so?" Matt said with interest.

"A panther, you say," Sam added with skepticism. "Are they sure? I don't think there are any panthers left in these parts."

Joe quickly relayed the details of the story. "Karen said the cow was ripped to pieces," he concluded. "And they were woke up in the middle of the night by a scream of some kind. Her little sister saw a big cat just before supper. She said it looked like a female lion, but her grandpa figured it was only a bobcat."

"Is that Phil Baxter you're talken about?" Matt asked.

"Yes, sir, I think so," Joe answered. "Karen said her grandpa wasn't certain it was a panther," he continued, to appease Sam. "He claims panthers don't usually kill somethen and leave it out in the open. He says they usually hide whatever they kill."

"Uhm," Sam mused, while Joe went to help his father raise the heavy tire to the rim of the tractor wheel. "That's true."

"You must have water in this," Joe grunted, straining to align the tire with the hub bolts.

"Yeah," Matt affirmed. "Heavy, ain't it?"

"That doesn't sound like a panther at all," Sam said, his contribution to the task at hand forgotten. "The girl must have seen a wildcat. There hasn't been a panther 'round these parts since I was a boy. And even then, it was a rare sight to see."

"You're probably right, Pa," Matt said. "But regardless, don't say anything to your mama or granny, son. They'll get scared and start worryen over nothen."

"Uh-oh," Joe gulped, tossing a rueful grin toward Matt. "Too late. I already told them." He paused, then added cheerfully, "And you're right. They're worryen."

"Way to go, Joe," Matt said dryly, a teasing frown on his face. He shook his head, picked up the tire iron and began tightening the nuts to the hub bolts on the tractor.

"Maybe Grandpa can tell them there aren't any panthers around here," Joe suggested. "At supper tonight. That should ease their minds."

"I'll give it a shot," Sam volunteered, "but I wouldn't count on it helpen much. Those women are natural born worriers and once they get somethen on their mind, it stays there."

---

As soon as Rachel blessed supper that night, Joe repeated his story about the big cat and the mutilated cow, sparing none of the details. Caroline and Rachel renewed their worrying and were soon fretting over whether to allow the children outside by themselves. When the women were worked up sufficiently, Joe asked his grandfather's opinion about the potential danger of the situation.

It was an old tactic used by Joe and Sam when they had something up their sleeves, and the crafty plotting brought a smile to Matt, who himself had been suckered on a few occasions by the innocent scheming of his father and son. He attacked his supper, enjoying his father's tale, confident Sam would ease the women's worries.

"The panther is a mysterious creature," Sam began with an educator's tone. "A cousin of the African cats if I'm not mistaken. Panthers are loners. They go out of their way to avoid people and, in this day and age, it's a rare man who can honestly say he's laid eyes on one."

"Have you ever seen a panther, Grandpa?" Carrie interrupted.

Interruptions came frequently in Sam's stories, and he welcomed them. "Have I ever seen a panther?" he repeated, his lecture scuttled for an adventure. "What do you think?"

"I don't know," Carrie said.

"When I was a little boy like Luke there, plenty of panthers roamed these parts," Sam said. "How do you think I came to wear this eye patch?"

"A panther scratched out your eye?" Bonnie squealed.

"It did, indeed," Sam replied, snapping the black patch over his scarred eye. "I made the mistake of goen hunten by my lonesome in Bear Bay—one of the thickest, wickedest swamps you'll likely find anywhere. You see, children, panthers like swampy places, where it's dark and they can hide in the shadows. They prefer to ambush their prey rather than face it head-on."

"Grandpa?" Luke interrupted doubtfully. "I thought you said a dragon breathed fire on you and burnt out that eye."

"That's the trouble with you, Luke," Sam said haughtily. "You think too much, 'cept when you're in school. Then, you don't do enough of it."

"We believe you, Grandpa," John interjected, affirming shared faith in Sam. "Go ahead. Finish tellen how that panther scratched out your eye."

"Yes, please do," Rachel muttered aside. "I want to hear all about it."

His dignity salvaged by John, Sam ignored the quip from his wife. "Well, now," he continued. "As I said, I was hunten and had sighted a deer, a twelve-pointer as sure as I'm sitten here. Anyway, I was tryen to be real quiet like, so I could get a good shot. I aimed my shotgun and was just about to pull the trigger when all of a sudden, there was the most piercen, the most caterwaulen scream you can imagine." He hesitated, then added bluntly, "Sounded even worse than your grandma when she's all worked up and carryen on because things ain't gone her way."

The children came through with obligatory laughter, which they cut short out of respect for Rachel. "That scream, though," Sam continued. "It scared the daylights out of me. I froze right there in my tracks. And that's where I made my mistake. You see, a panther counts on that terrifyen scream to paralyze its prey. Then it lunges and snaps the neck of the hapless victim. A panther has some of the most powerful jaws in the world. It can kill quick as lightnen."

Sam leaned back in his chair and crossed his arms. "Fortunately, I was quicker than lightnen," he boasted. "I ducked in the nick of time. When that old cat hit me, he just did miss sinken his teeth right into my neck, which he surely would have snapped like a toothpick." His arms uncrossed, and Sam laced his fingers behind his neck. "Unfortunately," he continued, "the bugger swatted me across the face with one of his big paws. Tore my eye right out of the socket. Then the coward ran off into the shadows. I never saw hide or hair of him again."

"Is that true, Grandpa?" Bonnie questioned in a long drawl, her face mingled with excitement and fright.

"It is," Sam declared. "But don't you go fretten about it, darlen. There hasn't been a panther 'round these parts since I was about your size, and that was several years ago. Most panthers in this country live out west. They're called mountain lions. There's probably a few in Florida, too."

"Florida's only about fifty miles from here," Summer said excitedly. "Maybe one of those panthers crossed the state line without realizen it."

Sam bit back a smile. "Not likely," he assured her. "I think they mostly live in south Florida. Besides, we have too many fields and open spaces around here. Panthers prefer dark places, where they can keep to themselves and hide when necessary."

"But, Grandpa," John protested. "We got a swamp right here on the farm. The river's close by, and there's woods every which way you turn. Not to mention Bear Bay, where that old panther got hold of you. A panther could hide almost anywhere he wanted to around here."

"The simple truth is there are few panthers left, here or anywhere else," Sam proclaimed. "But people like to think otherwise because there's somethen wild and mysterious about the panther. I've heard grown men spin tales of panthers screamen in the night and big cats loiteren by streams and creak beds. But all they're doen is tellen tall tales and repeaten legends."

He paused a second, spooning mashed potatoes and gravy onto his plate. "No, sirree," he concluded. "There're no panthers around here. But ...."

The slight hesitation brought absolute stillness and silence to the table, leaving forks and spoons stranded midway between plates and mouths, glasses poised on the edge of lips and knives halted halfway through pieces of meat. "But just in case I'm wrong," Sam continued in dramatically hushed tones, "I'll tell you the one unmistakable way to know when a panther is near."

He pitched his voice lower. "If you're ever in the woods near sunset and leaves rustle like a whisper, then there's probably a panther very close by, with eyes only for you."

The children gave a collective gasp of anxiousness. "What should we do if that happens?" Luke almost whispered.

Sam was enjoying his tale, and his pleasure eased Rachel and Caroline's worries. Noticing the relaxed attitudes of the two women, Matt and Joe exchanged knowing smiles across the table.

"Well, Luke," Sam answered diplomatically after taking time to swallow a bite of his supper. "If it was me, I'd run for safety as fast as my legs would carry me. Panthers are close-up hunters, you see, and they're quick to tire in a chase. If you don't freeze in your tracks when they let go with that scream, then you might just live to see another day."

So ended the tale of the panther.

# CHAPTER 4

ON A SATURDAY EVENING near the middle of February, Joe found himself with Lucas Bartholomew in the wooded acreage on the farm's southeast end. They were putting the finishing touches on a new fence, working amid a section of mature hardwoods so thick that only slivers of sunlight filtered through the stands of oak, sassafras, sycamore, poplar and the occasional pine tree. The job had brought them to an outlying corner of the farm, two hundred yards from the house where Lucas lived with Beauty, and an even greater distance from the Baker home. Usually, hogs roamed these woods, but they were penned now on the other side of the road until the new fence was in place.

The fence, which separated the Baker farm from the Berrien estate, had been mended year after year for as long as Joe could remember. It was rusted, broken, falling down in places and—in this winter of 1962, Matt at long last conceded—beyond repair. The task of replacing it fell to Joe and Lucas, and they had worked the better part of two weeks at the job. Joe thought his back would break if he dug one more hole for a fence post.

His aching back contributed to the litany of complaint that Joe was reciting for Lucas as they neared the end of the task. They had worked alongside each other in virtual silence for the better part of the two weeks, except for these moments of idle chatter when their words tended to magnify the humor of the situation. A sense of humor was necessary to spare them from the boredom of the hard work, Joe supposed, but he was disappointed by their inability to talk on a deeper level.

Joe had anticipated the fencing job as an opportunity to get inside the head of Lucas, to gain a better understanding of what made his black friend tick. But regretfully to Joe, they had failed to approach this delicate subject on even a superficial level. They would leave these woods as they had entered them, linked through a bond of friendship and separated by shackles of mutual ignorance.

It occurred to Joe that he might pursue answers to some questions in the remaining hours of the job, but the idea was discarded before the thought ran completely through his head. Instead, he continued his good-natured verbal assault on the great burden placed on him by the demands of the farm. "I've had my driver's license for almost two months now and a lot of good it's done me," he complained. "I haven't had a single date. And here I am again, spenden another Saturday night with you, planten fence posts and stringen wire. I tell you, Lucas, it's more than a body should have to stand."

Lucas laughed at the lamentations. "You sayen that spenden Saturday night out here in the woods with me ain't your idea of a good time," he chaffed. "I'm hurt, Joe-Joe, deeply hurt. I thought we were friends."

"No offense, Lucas," Joe replied dryly. "But frankly, I'd rather be in the woods with Karen Baxter. Be'en a married man and all, you should be able to understand that."

"Oh, I see," Lucas droned with exaggerated sincerity. "Now we cut to the quick of it. You're feelen frisky and ready to sew some wild oats."

Joe scratched his head. "I wouldn't exactly call it frisky," he remarked finally. "But Lord knows I'm ready and willen."

"I bet you are," Lucas said.

A million questions crossed Joe's mind and Lucas might have answered them, but the two companions lapsed once more into silence. Lucas thought about Beauty and the coming night, while Joe resolved, again, to ask Karen for a date.

An hour later, with night falling over them, Joe hammered the last staple nail into the corner fence post and checked the wire to make sure it was secure. The line was taut and built stoutly.

Joe glanced up at Lucas. "I think it'll be here a lot longer than you and I," he predicted.

"It's a job well done," Lucas nodded. "Your daddy'll be real pleased. If he wants, we can bring those hogs back over to this side of the road on Monday."

"I think I might actually miss menden this fence from time to time," Joe remarked as he rose from his knees and dusted off his blue jeans. "It's somethen I've come to expect to do, maybe even look forward to."

Lucas shook his head in dismay. "Joe-Joe, only you'd come up with a fool idea like that. Don't fret too much, though. There's plenty more fence 'round this place that's ready to fall down. I'm sure Mr. Matt will let you fix fence till your heart's content."

"True," Joe shrugged philosophically.

"You're a strange one, Joe-Joe," Lucas smiled. "Sometimes I'm not quite sure what to make of you, but you're a good man to have around in a pinch. Now, though, I'm gonna walk this fence one last time to make sure we didn't leave any tools on the ground."

"Okeydokey," Joe grinned. "I'll get our stuff together and meet you back at the house." He pointed to an old twelve-gauge shotgun on the ground near them. "You wanna take that?" he asked.

"Nah, it's too dark," Lucas answered. "I brought it 'cause Beauty wanted me to try and get a squirrel or rabbit. I told her there wouldn't be any runnen this time of year." He rolled his eyes. "You know how womenfolk are."

Joe gave his friend an understanding nod. "Some of it," he volunteered. "But I'd like to know a whole lot more."

"You will," Lucas promised, talking over his shoulder as he started the walk along the fencerow. "But you won't ever know it all. That's what makes it exciten and keeps things cooken."

Joe smiled to himself, his eyes following Lucas' progress along the fencerow, watching him test the sturdiness of their work at regular intervals. Finally, Lucas disappeared in the dark distance, and Joe began gathering their tools and reflecting on the day.

It was an important day, one of those moments in time when there was substantial cause for reflection. While Joe and Lucas had finished their fence, the United States government had released convicted Soviet spy Rudolf Abel in exchange for Francis Gary Powers, the U-2 pilot shot down by the Russians during a reconnaissance mission nearly two years earlier. Joe had followed every twist and turn in the plight of Powers and was heartened by the man's freedom. He wondered, though, how Powers himself felt. Was he focused on his newly gained freedom or on the two years stolen from his life? Was he prepared to savor the days to come or would he dwell on the agonizing slowness of two years in captivity?

Joe himself was an astute time tracker and, depending on your state of mind, two years could seem either like a lifetime or two days.

A year ago, as he recovered from his football injury, the pace of life seemed inordinately slow to Joe. He had become impatient, aggravated, melancholy and moody, a stranger to himself and those around him. Now, the days passed in a blur. Joe was mindful of the swift, sweet passage of time and determined to preserve it with memories that he could savor on a day when he was far away from here and now, empty and longing for a taste of his past. Such a day would come, and Joe would remember affectionately his endearment to a past that had prepared him for the future he wanted so badly.

These days, more than ever, Joe felt comfortable with his burgeoning manhood. And even if the vagaries of life and women remained a mystery to him, his personal antenna was tuned on dreams and goals. He was making plans and sharing his vision with those close to him. College waited in the offing, and nobody expected Joe to lay down roots in Cookville. The plans were fluid, but his commitment was etched in stone.

He inhaled a head-cleansing breath of cold air, picked up the tools, the gun and started toward the house.

A minute or so later, he was compelled to honor nature's call. He emptied his hands, relieved his bladder and had just finished zipping his blue jeans when he sensed a presence.

Dead leaves crackled to his right and Joe froze with dreadful expectation of an eerie shriek to come. Instead, he heard a low guttural groan and saw an amber silhouette. A moment later, the big cat moved directly into his line of vision.

Man and creature glared eyeball to eyeball with stark intensity, separated by nothing more than a few yards and the dangling branches of barren trees. Their eyes flashed confusion and distrust, yet both seemed strangely unperturbed.

It was a desperate bluff on Joe's part. And yet, even in his inner panic, he admired the panther's beauty. The cat's tawny brown coat glimmered in the dying daylight, turning white as eggshells at the breast line of its stomach. Shiny brown eyes glowed in a pear-shaped face, with the white fur on its chin, lips and lower cheeks contrasting sharply with the black sides of its snout.

The panther hissed and stepped toward Joe, who took a deep breath and made up his mind to lunge for the nearby shotgun.

But abruptly, the big cat hesitated, cooed a soft purr and gazed intently into Joe's eyes. The panther took one more step forward, then turned away and slipped into the black shadows of the woods.

His legs buckled and Joe collapsed to his knees, releasing a stale breath of air, reaching for the shotgun. His hands shook violently, the gun jerking back and forth while he sought to calm the shock waves jolting his instincts. A minute passed and then another as he listened for the animal and regained his senses.

He came slowly alert but it was when his hands steadied enough to take careful aim with the shotgun that Joe remembered Lucas was walking the fencerow. And the panther had disappeared in that direction.

Joe was on his feet instantly, ready with the shotgun, stalking quickly, cautiously through the woods.

---

Merrilee Bartholomew was a proud woman who had maintained her dignity until the end of a long struggle with the consumption. Her influence on Lucas had been tremendous.

His mother had been a no-nonsense woman who instilled sound principles and laid a solid foundation for her only child. She had taught Lucas that substance mattered more than style, that honesty and responsibility were virtues, and that independence, above everything else, provided freedom.

Under her firm guidance, Lucas had matured into an unassuming, unpretentious man, who saw the value of dutiful, respectful and polite behavior. What he lacked in daring and intelligence was more than offset by his competency and reliability.

"There's nothen wrong with be'en called dependable," Merrilee had reminded her son repeatedly.

Her conviction had helped Lucas grit his teeth on more than one occasion and look the other way when one would-be master conveyed to another that third-person, bargaining-tone reference: "He's dependable."

Fortunately, Lucas had earned a reputation that afforded him the opportunity to steer his services away from the masters of the world. He treated those fools with courtesy and regard for their position. But nowadays, Lucas worked for men who understood that respect was a two-way street.

Like his mother before him, Lucas suffered no delusions about the place of colored people in a white man's world. His conscience maintained a strict awareness of black and white, the way some men carried pocket combs. But Lucas had no chip on his shoulder.

Everyone had his lot in life. The burden was what a body chose to make of it, and Lucas was choosing to make the most of every opportunity.

Lucas considered himself the most capable colored man in Cookville. Others were more successful, but none extracted the amount of marrow from a bone that Lucas did. He could squeeze blood from a turnip, which was what his father had said often of his mother.

Lucas was a junior, and the name was the father's major influence on the son. The elder Lucas had died when his son was fifteen. Lucas remembered him with affection. His father was a happy-go-lucky, harmless man, whose penchant for strong drink sent him to an early grave. At one time, Lucas had resented the man's untimely demise because it denied him an opportunity to finish high school. But his forgiving nature prevented Lucas from holding a grudge, and his preoccupation with the present allowed him to forget missed opportunities.

Merrilee had adored her husband, despite his weaknesses. When he'd stagger home drunk, with half his paycheck spent on beer, booze and gambling, she'd shrug her shoulders and accept the capricious nature of her husband as inevitable.

Few ill words passed between them. Merrilee never criticized her husband, and the senior Lucas always came through with the necessities. When he died, Merrilee, sickly herself for several long years by then, had grieved deeply.

It was not until her final days that Merrilee afforded Lucas the privilege of her insight about his father. And then it was only because she saw one final opportunity to exercise influence and provide guidance for her son.

The memory of that day never strayed far from Lucas, and it was clearly on his mind as he trod along the fencerow in the gathering darkness.

The consumption, chief among many ailments, had withered Merrilee to a shell of her former self. She looked more dead than alive, shriveled and shrunken like a carcass hung out to dry. It seemed as if the decay had set in before the body was completely dead, and the buzzards were circling.

In those final weeks, Lucas had stayed with his mother day and night, keeping her parched lips moist, offering soup and playing nursemaid to her every need. Despite all its repulsive moments, her process of dying had seemed the most natural thing in the world to Lucas.

When nothing else about his mother seemed real any longer, her voice remained the one consonant of her faculties, smooth, silky and possessed with wisdom of the ages.

"Lucas, Lucas," she called, awaking from a sound sleep. "We need to talk."

"Yes, Mama. I'm right here," Lucas informed her, leaning forward in his chair beside her deathbed.

"There's somethen you need to know," she said, pulling onto her side.

"What is it, Mama?"

"It's not the most pleasant thing you'll ever hear me say, but it's probably the most important," the frail woman said. "There are exceptional people in this world, Lucas, and there are lucky people. Your daddy wasn't either one of those things, exceptional or lucky. And neither are you, son."

She searched his face for a reaction, but Lucas remained impassive, having discerned long ago that his mother had only his best interests at heart.

Merrilee Bartholomew smiled at his deferral to her judgment and settled back into a comfortable position on the bed. "Men," she continued. "Most men have the best of intentions, Lucas. But they're gullible and easily led astray by senseless things like drinken and any pretty woman who happens to shake her tail in their direction. Booze and women have been the downfall of many a man I've known in my time. It takes hold when they're young like you, and some of 'em never get over it. Your daddy was one of those who didn't. He'd have been a lost man without me by his side."

Merrilee eased onto her side again to impress her next remarks on Lucas. "Now you're a young man," she said bluntly. "You've got a thirst in your gullet for alcohol and an itch in your pants for women, and you're gonna drink your fill and chase anything that wiggles in a skirt over the next few years.

"But Lucas," she intoned sternly. "Watch out for pretty women. They'll use you, son. They'll dish it up for any man who can give more than what they've got. And to tell you the truth, despite how that tail wiggles and shakes on the outside, it's pretty much the same thing on the inside."

She fell back on the pillow and took a haggard breath. "Now, boy, I want you to have your good times," she continued. "But when you've played around and made a fool of yourself, it'll be time for settlen down. Don't make the mistake of fallen for some fancy pants, Lucas, 'cause you're never gonna have what it takes to satisfy them kind, and you'll make yourself miserable tryen.

"When you get ready to settle down, find yourself a woman who's a churchgoer and doesn't care much about getten herself a husband. A man needs a companion, boy. Someone who'll stand beside him and take care of him come hell or high water and not pass judgment while she does it. You find somebody hungry for a either a good man or no man at all, and you'll make your own luck in this world, Lucas. You fall hard for some Miss Fancy Pants, you'll spend the rest of your life wishen you'd've listened to your dyen mama."

Merrilee sat up in bed, her face full of fire and determination. "Do you understand what I'm sayen, boy?"

"Yes, ma'am."

"Will you grant your mama's dyen wish?"

"Yes, ma'am."

She glared hard and long at Lucas, memorizing this moment, impressing him with her concern, then slowly nodded her head and reached across the bed to pat his hand. "You know, Lucas," she whispered. "I believe you will."

A week later, Merrilee died quietly with Lucas at her side. His last words to her had been uttered with quiet conviction. "I promise, Mama."

Lucas was reflecting on his mother's wisdom and the promise he had made when a scream shattered the night.

———

It was a shriek, deadly shrill and bloodcurdling. Joe felt it in his veins.

The panther's scream froze him in midstride, about thirty-five yards behind Lucas. From this vantage point, Joe saw with his own eyes the incarnation of scared stiff.

Lucas froze in his tracks, paralyzed with incomprehension, stiff-necked from premonition. On his back flank was the panther, heavily muscled, slunk low to the ground and crouched for attack.

Time played out in fractions of seconds, and Joe began running forward at the same moment the big cat lunged toward Lucas.

The panther slammed into the right side of Lucas, its powerful jaws clamping down into the top of his shoulder. The force of impact was crushing, ripping an agonized scream from Lucas as man and beast crashed to the ground in a twisted, hissing heap.

Lucas landed on his back, with the big cat on top of him, its teeth tearing deeper into his shoulder. He round-housed his free arm to swat the panther in the head. Growling, the cat reared back, slapping Lucas with his paws and raking razor-sharp claws across the man's neck. Lucas landed a forearm against the panther's jaw, warding off another strike at his neck, and wedged booted feet beneath the cat's belly as the animal snapped again at his mangled shoulder. Calling on every reserve of strength, Lucas kicked hard, flinging the panther away while struggling to gain a favorable fighting position.

Momentarily surprised by his human opponent's powerful thrust, the supple cat retreated an inch, crouched and loosed another rattling growl, low-pitched this time but equally menacing.

Joe was stopped, with the gun aimed dead center before the panther sprang its attack. The shot exploded in the darkness, finding its mark in the middle of the cat's leap. Crimson spurted midway up the animal's white breast, and the panther collapsed on top of Lucas.

For a moment, the silence was deafening. Joe was frozen, with the gun still aimed, waiting to see if the danger was gone. Almost immediately, he was aware of the quiet moans of his friend. Dropping the gun, he rushed to Lucas.

"I can't breathe," Lucas gasped. "Get if off me, Joe-Joe."

Wordlessly, Joe responded. The panther was heavy, but the weight no match for Joe's adrenaline. In seconds, he dragged the dead cat away and was on his knees examining Lucas' wounds.

Blood poured from the mangled shoulder, but Joe saw no danger signs of spurting vessels among the mess of exposed muscle and raw meat. The crimson seeped at a slower pace from Lucas' neck, but the rapid loss of blood worried Joe, as did the pallor of his face and the glassy look in his eyes.

"You're gonna be okay, Lucas," Joe said firmly. "Just keep your mind on me. If you're hurten, forget it and concentrate on what I do and what I say."

Lucas lay trembling. "Easy for you to say," he mumbled, allowing his eyes to close.

"Don't do that!" Joe ordered, slapping Lucas on the cheek.

Lucas blinked and stared at Joe.

"I'm not dyen, Joe-Joe," he said. "I promise. So, I'd appreciate it if you didn't hit me in the face."

Joe examined him again, closely from head to toe. "You sure you're not dyen?"

"I'm sure."

"Well, you don't look so good," Joe remarked with dry excitement. "There's blood everywhere."

Lucas closed his eyes again and rested his head against the carpet of dead leaves. Joe stripped off his own red flannel shirt and undershirt, using the white cotton garment as a tourniquet to bandage the hurt shoulder. Lucas lay still, his breathing shallow, groaning softly as Joe tended to his wounds.

"We have to get you to a doctor," Joe said when the bandage was secured. "The house is not far from here. Can you walk?"

Lucas opened his eyes. "I think so. If you'll help me get to my feet."

"We'll take it slow and easy," Joe replied, pushing Lucas to a sitting position.

Lucas draped his good arm around Joe's neck for support, and they struggled to their feet, then rested for a moment.

"Let's go," Lucas said at last.

It was a long walk home as they stumbled through the dark woods. Conversation was rare, except for the occasional groan from Lucas and encouraging words from Joe. At last, they came to the edge of the field and the lights of the house beckoned across the way. Joe stopped their progress and lowered Lucas to the ground.

"Stay here," he ordered. "We'll bring the truck across for you."

Lucas nodded weary agreement.

"I'll be right back," Joe promised. "We'll have you to the hospital in no time."

"Send somebody after Beauty," Lucas said softly. "I want her with me."

Joe nodded and sprinted across the field toward home.

———

It was an unhurried night in the Baker house. Rachel and Caroline were finishing the supper dishes, with a plate warming in the oven for Joe. The television hummed in the living room, and the few not watching it were preoccupied with quiet pursuits. This relaxed atmosphere came to an abrupt halt the moment Joe tore open the screen door, bursting into the living room with fresh blood caked on his bare chest and matted on his face and in his hair.

Carrie screamed loudest at his sudden appearance and the room turned topsy-turvy before Joe calmed the commotion with a finger pressed to his lips. "Daddy, you've got to come quick with the truck," he said. "Lucas is hurt real bad."

"Oh, dear Lord!" Caroline cried as she stepped through the French doors into the living room. "I heard the gun go off. Is he shot?"

"No, ma'am," Joe said. "I shot a panther! It jumped Lucas. He's bleeden everywhere. We've got to get him to the hospital."

Joe pointed across the road. "He's at the edge of the woods over yonder. I told him we'd bring the truck for him."

Matt took control of the situation with quiet authority, issuing orders and directions in seconds flat. Almost instantly, he, Sam and Joe were in the truck, while Caroline gathered bandages and John raced down the road to tell Beauty what had happened.

---

Lucas was unconscious when they reached him and, for an awful moment, Matt, Sam and Joe feared he was dead. But Lucas came to when Matt pressed a finger on his throat, checking for his pulse.

"I'm okay, Matt," he said softly.

"We brought the truck," Matt informed the injured man. "We're gonna put you in the back, Lucas, and get you to the hospital."

Lucas shook his head. "I think I got some broke ribs," he said groggily. "That cat was a heavy sonofagun, and it landed hard on my chest. It hurts to breathe." He closed his eyes, then asked, "Joe, did you get word to Beauty?"

"John went to tell her," Joe answered. "She'll be waiten for us."

"Good," Lucas sighed.

They loaded Lucas gently into the bed of the pickup, with Joe using his lap as a pillow for the injured man's head. It was a bumpy ride across the field, which Lucas tolerated with clinched teeth and closed eyes. Caroline was waiting with clean rags and blankets when they arrived at the house, along with a shaking Beauty Bartholomew, who took her rightful place beside her husband. Taking the rags from Caroline, Beauty quickly dabbed at the bloodiest parts of her husband's injuries, while Caroline and Matt covered him with blankets.

Ten minutes later, the pickup arrived at the Cookville hospital.

Caroline rushed into the emergency room to seek help, and two nurses dressed in starchy white uniforms sprang into action. One called for a doctor, while the other grabbed a wheelchair and raced outside to the truck where she helped Matt and Joe seat the sluggish Lucas.

"What in the world happened?" the nurse asked as she examined the mauled arm.

"A panther got hold of him," Matt informed her. "He's lucky to be alive."

The nurse was a stout woman, whom Joe recognized but could not put a name with the face. She was blunt-spoken.

"We've gotta do somethen about all this bleeden, or his luck is fixen to run out," she said. "Follow me," she ordered Matt, who pushed the wheelchair up a concrete ramp through a swinging door with Beauty and Joe in tow.

The antiseptic odor of the hospital reassured Joe, who had grown wary of all the blood gushing from Lucas. Anything that smelled this clean had to have healing powers, he reasoned.

"You two help him up on this gurney," the nurse barked to Matt and Joe, while pulling a curtain around them to create an island of privacy in the spacious emergency room. She looked at Lucas. "I'll be back in a second," she told him. "I'm goen to get some scissors so we can cut off what's left of that shirt."

Lucas acknowledged her with a nod. "Can my wife come in here with me?" he asked.

The nurse nodded curtly. "Yes, she can," she replied, pointing a short, stubby finger at Matt and Joe. "But I want you two out of here as soon as you get him settled on that gurney," she added sternly. "Y'all can wait with your wife, Mr. Baker."

"By the way," she hesitated. "What's the patient's name?"

"Lucas Bartholomew," Matt told her.

When the nurse had gone, Matt and Joe settled Lucas on the gurney, then turned him over to the care of his nervous wife and followed their orders to wait outside with Caroline. Almost half an hour later, Dr. Ned Turner ambled through the emergency room door.

A portly man, Ned Turner was shiny bald with a droopy blond mustache and a tightly drawn round face. He wore the thick brown glasses of a scholar and carried himself with the grace and manners of an aristocrat. His regal posture, however, failed to hide the heavy paunch hanging over his dark slacks.

The doctor lived in a gabled and turreted brownstone mansion right off the square in Cookville. The house was beautiful, but Ned had a well-deserved reputation as overbearing and arrogant. He considered himself one of the privileged few and held in contempt the majority of those less fortunate.

"Good evenen, Matt," the doctor said, strolling across the polished tile floor. "Is some of your family hurt?"

"A friend of the family, doc," Matt replied, gesturing behind the curtains. "He helps me on the farm. Believe it or not, a panther got hold of him tonight." He nodded to Joe. "My boy shot it, but the cat tore up Lucas pretty bad, especially his arm and shoulder. He's bleeden a lot."

"A panther!" the doctor exclaimed. "Well I'll be damned. I'd heard they'd spotted one around here, but I figured people were just see'en ghosts." He slapped his thigh. "This I got to see," he continued, walking toward the curtain.

Dr. Turner peeled back the plastic shield, peeked inside and pulled back immediately. He dropped the curtain and glared from Matt to the young nurse who had called him to the hospital. "Matt, you should know I don't treat colored people," he bristled before venting his anger in a stream of cursing and berating aimed at the young nurse, whose name was Linda.

"I didn't know it was a Negro," Linda almost whispered. She was on her heels. "I called you back as soon as I found out, but nobody answered."

"I don't want excuses, Linda," Dr. Turner raged. "Just show some competency next time. Go call Maddox or someone else to come. I'm goen back home. And I would prefer not to be disturbed again."

The young nurse took one step backward and was on the verge of fleeing the room when Joe bounded from his chair, advancing on the doctor. "Good god!" he roared incredulously. "Are you an idiot? There's a man over there bleeden to death and you're worried about the color of his skin. Well, I got news for you, doc. That's red blood comen from his veins; it's the only color you need to concern yourself with. How 'bout getten your fat ass in there and doen what you're supposed to instead of bellyachen?"

Ned Turner scowled at Joe, turning beet red.

"Pipe down, son!" Matt ordered, stepping between Joe and the doctor.

"But Daddy!" Joe persisted before Matt eyeballed him into submission.

Dr. Turner took a single step toward Joe, then stopped and shook a pointed finger at him. "Now see here, hotshot," he lectured. "I don't have to answer to you. I have a right to treat whomever I want, and I choose not to treat coloreds. Are we clear on that?"

"No, Ned, we're not clear on it," Matt remarked abruptly, the hard edge evident in his words, despite the even tone of his voice. "We're not clear at all, but let me set you straight. My friend over there is hurt, and he needs a doctor. You're the only doctor here, and it's your responsibility to treat him. If you're offended by the color of his skin, that's tough luck. I suggest you get your ass over there and take care of the man. Or you'll have *me* to answer to."

Matt looked the doctor straight in the eyes. "Are we clear on that?"

Ned glared at Matt, but it was a face-saving gesture while he studied his options. There were not many in the angry face of Matt Baker. Or in the fiery eyes of his son, who stood behind Matt like a raging bull, pawing at the ground for his long-awaited chance at the matador. Even Caroline, whom the doctor looked to for sympathy, regarded him with a determined expression. But it was the stout nurse—her name, Joe now recalled, was Bobbi Jean Tucker—who pulled the final straw for the doctor.

"Dr. Turner," she called loudly, poking her head through the curtain. "I know you have principles, but you're gonna have to bend them tonight. This man is cut up bad, and he's lost a lot of blood. He needs a doctor. Now!"

Ned raised his chin and flared his nostrils. "Oh, all right," he relented. "I'll make an exception since I'm already here. But this is the first and only time. I expect everybody to understand that."

Matt visibly relaxed his jaw. "Understood," he replied, stepping aside to allow the doctor passage across the room to where Lucas and Beauty waited behind the curtain.

The first thing Dr. Turner did was order Beauty from the make-shift room. Thirty minutes later, he emerged from behind the drapes, having cleaned the wounds, stitched the deeper cuts and confirmed that Lucas suffered two cracked ribs.

"Thirty-two stitches," the doctor told them. "Six in his neck, five on his face and the rest in his arm. For his sake, he'd better be right-handed because that left arm suffered some serious damage. It'll take time to heal.

"Those cracked ribs will be sore for a while, too, but, all in all, I'd say he's lucky to have come through with nothen more serious," the doctor concluded. "A few inches deeper and that panther might have ripped open his throat. We could keep him overnight for ob-servation. It costs money to stay in the hospital, though, and I'm not sure it's worth the expense."

"I'll take care of the bill," Matt said clearly.

"Suit yourself," Dr. Turner replied without concern. "I'd still take him home. There's really nothen else that can be done for him tonight, although he should see his own doctor in a couple of days or so."

He turned to Beauty, who had followed him out of the make-shift room. "I've ordered three prescriptions," he addressed her specifically. "One is to fight infection. Another is a salve, and the third is for pain. He'll have plenty of that. I'd call Glen Adams over at the pharmacy and ask him to fill it for you tonight.

"Make sure you keep clean bandages on those wounds," he con-tinued, "and wash your hands before applyen the salve. If that shoulder gets infected, there could be serious consequences."

"He'll be okay, though?" Beauty inquired nervously, seeking re-assurance.

"Yes," the doctor sighed, glancing impatiently at his watch. "That's what I just finished tellen you."

He turned to Matt. "If it really was a panther, you ought to have it checked for rabies," he suggested. "And proceed accordingly."

"We'll do that," Matt said.

"Then I'll be on my way," Dr. Turner said. "Unless Matt," he added sanctimoniously, "you feel the urge to apologize for yours and your son's rude behavior?"

Matt smiled coldly at the doctor. "My family and I make it a policy not to apologize to pompous asses, doc," he replied without missing a beat. "So if I were you, I'd proceed accordingly."

Caroline moved quickly to her husband's side, cupping his elbow with her palm in a calming gesture. "Let's just pay the bill and leave," she urged.

Matt looked at her and smiled disarmingly. "You have the checkbook," he reminded before turning to the stout nurse. "Thanks for your help, Bobbi Jean. How much do we owe?"

Dr. Turner snorted his indignity, but was roundly ignored by everyone except Joe, who glared momentarily at the doctor, then shook his head in dismay and went to help Lucas to the truck.

No one bothered to notice as the good doctor made his grand exit, stomping from the room.

———————

Sometime later that night—when the bill had been paid and Lucas ensconced in bed with instructions for Beauty to call on them if she needed help—the Baker family sat on the front porch, recounting the entire episode. Joe provided all the details about the panther and answered every question directed at him, then sat back hunched against the wall while his parents filled in the story with everything that had happened at the hospital.

"I was right proud of you both," Caroline told her husband and son when the story seemed exhausted. "You stood up for what was right."

"I lost my temper," Matt reminded his wife.

"I felt a bit ruffled myself," Caroline said. "And frankly," she laughed, "we'd still be there if you'd tried to kill the doctor with kindness."

"Some things shouldn't be tolerated," Sam declared.

"No, Pa," Matt agreed. "They shouldn't."

It was a cold night for sitting on the porch, but everyone was huddled beneath blankets and warm in their bedclothes and jackets. The night was quiet, except for the soft squeaks of rocking chairs, the glider and the porch swing.

"Joe," Matt said, "You've been quiet for a while. What's on your mind?"

"I'm a little amazed, I suppose," Joe replied. "That people think the way they do. That people who should know better don't." He rose and crossed his arms against the cold. "It's one thing to be aware of somebody's color. I'm as guilty as the next person of doen that. Even with Lucas, I tend to think of him as a black friend of mine or maybe even as the colored man who helps us on the farm. But to hate someone—or refuse to help someone in need—just because of the color of their skin ... I don't understand that."

"It's a complicated subject, no doubt," Sam remarked.

"But it shouldn't be," Joe maintained.

"No," Matt agreed. "But it is."

Joe walked across the porch to stand on the step wall and gaze into the nighttime sky. "Will things ever change?" he asked.

"Gradually, they will," Caroline answered. "But it will take patience and understanden from everybody."

"Things are bound to change," Sam agreed. "But the Ned Turners of the world will always be around to make you stop and think about what's wrong with the way things are."

"You know," Joe remarked, turning to face his family. "I've read about sit-in demonstrations, freedom marches, the Montgomery bus boycott, and I've thought all along stuff like that was the wrong way to go. Now, though, I'm beginnen to wonder if maybe those people have the right idea after all." He looked at Caroline. "Mama, I agree change will come gradually. But how patient and understanden can you expect people to be when things like what happened tonight keep happenen?"

Joe paused more out of courtesy than expectancy of an answer. "Until tonight," he continued, "I didn't really understand prejudice. Now, I have a good idea. And even though tonight had nothen to do with me personally, I felt like I had been slapped in the face by that doctor." He hesitated again before adding, "Maybe it wasn't my place to shoot off my mouth the way I did. But sometimes you can't look the other way. You can't always turn the other cheek."

He looked squarely at his father. "And to tell you the truth, Daddy, I'm glad you didn't ask me to apologize to that man, because I don't think I could have done that."

"No, son," Matt acknowledged. "I doubt you would have either. And for what it's worth, Joe, I'm glad you couldn't look the other way tonight. It makes me think that maybe you've been raised right."

"Indeed," Sam agreed. "And, Joe, you just may be right about a few other things, too. I've never set much store by all those demon-strations and shenanigans, especially when it seems like nothen more than a bunch of outsiders comen in to stir up trouble. But maybe that's what it takes. People need challenges to prod their conscience and bring out their character."

Joe treasured nights like this when his family gathered on the front porch and idled away an evening with meandering talk. But now he felt the need to bring a little levity to the moment. "Daddy?" he said to Matt. "Do you think we prodded the good doctor's conscience tonight?"

"We jarred it for sure," came the wry reply from Matt.

Laughter stirred a chilly breeze on this still night of another waning winter, and Caroline was mindful of sleepy children all around her. It was well after midnight, hours past their bedtime. She rose from the porch swing, stretched and yawned, a signal for her family to follow suit. No one objected; indeed, they were eager for an excuse to find their beds, crawl under the blankets and close their eyes.

"We'll all sleep well tonight," Rachel said as everyone crowded toward the door.

"I hope so," Caroline agreed. "Tomorrow's a church Sunday, and I'd like to carry this good feelen with us."

The brood trooped into the house until only Caroline and Joe remained. Caroline crossed over to where her son leaned against one of the porch's four brick piers that supported tapered wooden columns. "You've had quite an evenen," she suggested.

Joe shrugged. "It's been eventful. No doubt about that."

Caroline sighed. "Consideren everything that's happened to-night, Joe—and especially how proud of you I am—I hesitate to bring this up," she said softly, taking his hands. "But I'm a mother after all, and I'd be remiss to let it pass without mention."

Joe smiled at his mother, reading her thoughts. "It was the heat of the moment," he explained. "I've got my faults, Mama, but I usually keep a civil tongue about me. And I know it's best to keep the Lord's name out of arguments, unless, of course, they concern Him directly."

Caroline rolled her eyes, put a hand in his hair and embraced her son. "Like I said," she reaffirmed, "I hesitated to bring it up. But ...."

"But you're my mother," Joe interrupted, finishing the sentence for her. "And I'd have been disappointed if you had done anything else."

"You're getten too big for your britches," Caroline muttered, hugging him again, then noticing he had grown as tall as she was. She pulled away from Joe and measured the top of her head against his. "When did this happen?" she asked.

"Gradually," Joe answered. "Recently, I think."

Caroline looked him over for another moment, from head to toe and back again to his face. "Yes, I suppose you're right. But it seems sudden to me. Before long, I'll have to look up to see your face?"

Joe smiled shyly. "Probably so."

Caroline kissed him on the cheek and hugged him once more. "Are you comen in?"

"I'll be along soon," he told her. "Goodnight, Mama."

# CHAPTER 5

"SO HOW DOES IT feel to be a legend in your own time?"

It was the Monday morning after Joe had shot the panther. Tales of his exploit were rampant. The story had been embellished and exaggerated by everyone but Joe. It was growing taller by the minute, and he felt compelled to lend a little perspective to the situation.

"To tell you the truth, ma'am," he said to Mrs. Gaskins in English class, "mainly, I feel lucky. Lucky that Lucas brought his gun along; lucky even that his wife wanted rabbit for supper. Otherwise, Lucas might have been supper for that panther."

"Were you scared?" the teacher asked.

"A couple of times," Joe nodded. "The first time I saw the panther, it seemed like he was comen right at me. And then, he turned and walked off into the woods. My legs turned to jelly. The second time was after I shot the cat and pulled it off Lucas. There was blood everywhere. He was hurt real bad, and I thought he might die. That scared the daylights out of me, but I tried not to let on to Lucas. I figured he had enough on his mind without known I was worried he was gonna bleed to death right out there in the woods."

"What will you remember most about all this, Joe?" Mrs. Gaskins persisted. "And did you learn anything about yourself from it?"

Joe gave her a long look. "I'm not sure I should answer that, Mrs. Gaskins," he said at last. "The answer probably would surprise you, and it might offend some people."

The teacher cast her infamous glare around the class, daring anyone to raise an objection. "Class," she challenged. "Does anyone mind be'en offended by one of their own?"

A quick glance around the room indicated no one minded. Indeed, his classmates were curious and encouraged Joe to provide them his uncensored version of the story.

"Go ahead, Joe," Mrs. Gaskins urged. "You have the floor."

He gave them a searing account of how events had transpired

at the hospital. When he was finished, none of his classmates had any mistaken impressions about his opinion of Dr. Ned Turner. And, Joe had stepped across the safety line of invisibility. He had reached the perilous point of definition from which he would be judged forevermore. His passion impressed a few of his classmates, amazed others, embarrassed some and annoyed several.

"I don't see what all the fuss is about," remarked Richard Golden, who was one of those annoyed by Joe's frank indictment of the doctor. "I know Dr. Turner very well, and I don't think you're be'en fair to him with all these malicious accusations. He's a doctor, a pillar of our community. It's his prerogative to choose whether or not he wants to treat Negroes."

Joe stared coldly at the red-haired, freckle-faced boy. "Somehow, Richard, it doesn't surprise me you're the first one to defend Ned Turner. It's exactly what I'd expect from someone who makes a point week after week to remind everyone that his newspaper column is for white schools only."

"Nobody cares what's goen on in the colored schools," Richard said.

"You're wrong," Joe countered smoothly. "You may not care, Richard. For that matter, I may not care. But somebody does, and one day their caren may make a difference in the way things are."

"You sound like a nigger lover, Joe Baker," Richard accused.

"There are worse things," Joe replied calmly. "I could be like your friend, the good doctor, who doesn't have a heart. But I'm who I am, and I don't care to see one man do another man wrong. Ned Turner turned up his pompous nose at a man who needed help, simply because that man had colored skin. I can't understand that. In fact, I refuse even to try. There are differences between colored people and white people, I'm sure, but sometimes you have to look beyond the color to do what's right. The good doctor may seem like a pillar of the community to you, Richard, but as far as I'm concerned, he's nothen more than an ass. And if you share his opinions, then so are you."

Sensing trouble at hand, Mrs. Gaskins seized control of the class once more, steering the discussion to a smoother path. But the battle lines were drawn, and Joe's reputation was cast in stone. There were a few snickers heard throughout the day, and once or twice, Joe thought he detected rumblings of retribution. But Richard Golden knew better than to pick a fight he would lose, and his snobbishness had offended almost everyone at some time, so no one was eager to pick up the gauntlet for him. And then, too, people respected Joe. He might have surprised some people who simply took his and everyone else's attitudes for granted, but the majority applauded his bravery and courage, both for the deed he had done and the stand he had taken.

For Joe, the day's most memorable moment came at lunch when Karen Baxter gushed over him. Twice, she reached across the table and strummed her fingers along the length of his arm. It was a hair-raising experience and unsettled Joe until, finally, Karen looked at him, smiled, batted her eyes and announced, "I don't have a date Friday night. I wish I did."

"Would you like to go see a movie?" Joe blurted out.

Karen gave him one of her shy, coquettish smiles, glancing down and picking at the food on her plate, while Joe waited breathlessly for an answer. With his attention fixed squarely on her downturned face, Joe failed to notice Karen slide her hand across the table until it came suddenly to rest on the top of his hand. His eyes dropped to the table, then focused upward again to find Karen regarding him. She tilted her head, tossed her hair and branded Joe with the most sensual of gazes, all while raking the tips of her fingers gently down the top of his hand until they were intertwined with his splayed fingers.

Joe heated up like lightning, and they gazed intently at each other for a long moment. "Yes, Joe," Karen answered finally. "I look forward to it. You and I are goen to enjoy each other's company." She tilted her head once more. "Very much so."

---

Joe reckoned it was one of the finest days life could offer, and he wanted to savor every moment, especially those with Karen. But he was stuck on the back of the school bus later that afternoon, answering one question after another from Tom Carter and the other boys who crowded around their seat.

"He was a beautiful animal, no doubt," Joe told them. "I'm sorry he had to be killed. But it was the panther or Lucas."

"My daddy says that's the one mistake you made, Joe, not letten that panther kill a nigger before you shot it."

The comment came from Wayne Taylor, who looked and

sounded like a carbon copy of Bobby. "Daddy wondered if you meant to hit the spook but missed and got the panther instead," he added with a grin.

Had he listened closely, Joe would have realized the hollow tone of those remarks from Wayne. He would have grasped the question originated from the sheer curiosity of a twelve-year-old rather than from spite. But Joe was fed up with the opinions, spoken and unspoken, of those who believed he should have spared the panther and killed the nigger. In the back of his mind, too, he still held a grudge against Wayne for killing Stonewall Jackson several summers ago. Perhaps he had ill feelings for the entire Taylor clan and their gospel of hate.

These thoughts passed through his mind, and none put Joe in a forgiving mood. He planted a cruel gaze on the Taylor boy. "You tell your daddy that I hit what I aimed for," he said with contempt. "And you tell him, too, that the likes of Bobby Taylor better hope I never have to make a life-saven choice between him and anybody else. Because he'd come out the loser every time, Wayne. And so would you."

Wayne went pale.

"Can you remember to tell him that, Wayne?" Joe asked. "Every bit of it?"

The boy gulped, impaled by the ridicule, and turned away from Joe.

As for the other boys on the back of the bus, they were stunned, too. They had known Joe for most of their lives, considering him someone willing to go that extra mile to be friendly and diplomatic in unpleasant situations. Now they backed off, lapsing into such silence that everyone in the front of the bus turned around to see what had gone wrong.

Joe felt like a bully. He was on the verge of offering Wayne an apology when Tom jolted him back to reality.

"It needed to be said, Joe," his friend remarked quietly as the hum of conversation rose around them once more. "Wayne's poison, and everybody knows it."

"Maybe," Joe hesitated, staring straight ahead. "But he's just a kid. A dumb kid who's only repeaten the filth he heard his daddy say."

"Yeah, but you still did the right thing," Tom tried again to reassure him.

But Joe was not at all sure about that.

For a moment, Wayne thought he would cry. But he pinched the inside of his arm and turned embarrassment into anger. He had taken worse crap from his own daddy and walked away without tears. He'd be damned before he let the sorry likes of Joe Baker get the best of him.

His pride intact, Wayne raised his chin in defiance and turned his thoughts to revenge. He was uncertain how to go about it, but one day Wayne would make Joe pay for talking down to him.

"One day," he whispered to himself. "One day, you'll get yours, Joe."

The car windows were steamed, and Joe and Karen were wrapped around each other on the backseat. A full moon shown down on the car, casting the young lovers in a pale glow.

Karen was a vision of milky white, intertwined like lace with the swarthiness of Joe. They seemed more disheveled than undressed. Karen had discarded her blouse and bra. Her panties lay in the floorboard, and her skirt was pushed up around her waist. Joe's shirt was torn open, and he had managed to get one leg out of his pants. The other pants leg was caught on his foot but out of the way nonetheless.

Joe had wondered for years about this moment. He was too impatient to savor it.

Karen was impatient, too. This was her third date with Joe and she was ready to have him. She broke a heated kiss, running her tongue down his chin and neck, pushed back his shirt and seared the top of his chest with a passion mark. It was her calling card and when she had left it, Karen lifted her eyes to Joe and demanded softly, "Now."

Breathing heavily, fumbling for a tighter embrace, they fell against the back seat.

On their first date, Joe had taken Karen to a movie at the Majestic Theater. It was an old Burt Lancaster flick on its first run in

Cookville, but Joe barely noticed. He was too busy cuddling with Karen. After the movie, he treated her to a hamburger and a milkshake at the Dairy Queen. They ate in the car, talking like old friends. It was Karen who brought up the idea of parking when they had finished their food.

"Why don't we go somewhere quiet and talk for a while?" she suggested.

"Any place in particular?" Joe asked.

"That's your department," Karen said boldly, sliding across the car seat next to him.

Joe knew the perfect spot. It was a deserted road off the main highway between Cookville and Tifton. The road cut through the Berrien estate before coming to a dead end at an old block house that was presently unoccupied. Joe figured it was one of the most private, secluded places in the county.

Karen snuggled closer as he drove carefully along the sandy lane, which was covered by a canopy of trees. "It's dark back here," she said. "Are you gonna try to scare me with stories about men with hook arms."

Joe laughed dryly. "Hardly. I doubt even a maniac could find this place."

As they rounded a sharp curve, Joe slowed the car and turned onto a secluded field road hidden from view by a wild growth of vines, weeds and trees. He maneuvered the car a short distance down the lane, then cut the lights and switched off the engine.

"This is nice," Karen purred in the darkness, and Joe knew she was looking at his face, expecting him to make the next move. He slipped his arm around her shoulders, kissing her lightly on the lips with wonderment. But even his wildest imagination left Joe unprepared for what happened next.

Karen placed her hands on his face, drew Joe toward her and kissed him hard. The passionate assault sent shock waves through him. Her tongue pried his lips apart, wrapping around him and exploring every inch of his mouth. Joe was at first amazed, then aghast as he realized his own tongue lay dead in her mouth. He quit thinking then and kissed her back with equal fervor.

He touched her breast by accident the first time. But Karen moaned in response, pressing tighter against his hand, so Joe kept right on touching, cupping her through the clothes, then slipping his hand under her blouse and bra.

A short time later, Karen placed her delicate hand high on the inside of his thigh and Joe hardened like a rock. Karen purred in admiration, stroking lightly across his blue jeans until Joe moaned with unfulfilled pleasure. In a while, Karen broke their kiss and pulled Joe to her breast, willing him to lift her blouse and bra. He stared hungrily at her for a moment, then lowered his head and took first one and then the second breast into his mouth, capturing the nipples gingerly with his teeth, then filling himself with her.

Karen groaned, opening her legs and grinding against Joe. He was ready to explode inside his jeans when Karen gasped, relaxed and fell away from him.

Joe was panting, with a hard ache in his groin, as Karen smiled lazily at him.

"I didn't expect that to happen," she murmured, lowering her eyes. "I hope you don't think I'm a bad girl," she worried. "I'm not." She paused, then leveled Joe with a pouting smile. "It's just that you make me dizzy, Joe. And you do terrible things to my self-control."

Joe figured he would have robbed a bank for her at that moment. He reached across the seat, pulled her against him and kissed her deeply. She broke away quickly, dropping her head so that his face was filled with the intoxicating scent of her hair.

"It's late, Joe, and I have to be home by eleven," Karen whispered against his throat.

"Yeah," Joe agreed reluctantly. "Do you have any plans for next Friday?"

"No," she nodded against his neck. "And none on Saturday, either."

"Is seven o'clock okay for both nights?"

Karen nodded again. "And, Joe?"

"Yeah?"

"Movies take an awful long time to see," Karen said. "We could skip it if you wanted to."

———

On their second date, they paused long enough to buy a milkshake at the Dairy Queen, then headed to the privacy of the woods. This time, they were more daring, discarding clothes and making new discoveries with their hands and mouths, but the result was the same. The night ended with Karen exhausted and fulfilled and Joe stranded just short of the brink.

Joe sat back against the front seat, taking deep breaths to calm his hormones. He glanced over at Karen and found her smiling sympathetically. "Eleven o'clock is the only thing my parents are really strict about, Joe," she apologized.

He smiled back at her. "Does this mean we're in love?"

Karen raised her eyes, almost frowning. "Not hardly," she laughed shortly. "But it's a good way to pass the time, isn't it?"

Her answer settled like lead in the pit of his stomach. Joe forced himself to look straight ahead out the front windshield and swallowed the lump in his throat.

Karen handed him his shirt, hooking her bra while Joe slipped on the pullover. "Well, isn't it?" she repeated.

"Sure," Joe answered, zipping his pants.

Karen smiled, adjusted her skirt and slipped into a silk blouse. "Besides, Joe," she said. "We've got our sights set on bigger things and better times than these. Love is the last thing we need."

Joe started to protest, but she cut him off.

"Face it, Joe," Karen argued. "You're like me. Ambition is the love of your life. You and I are destined to spend our lives cutten ties. We'd be lousy at love even if we wanted it. And I don't think either one of us could stand the thought of be'en lousy at anything. Do you?"

Joe kept his thoughts to himself for two reasons. First, he wasn't sure what to say. And furthermore, he feared Karen might have struck too close to the truth.

---

On their third date, they headed straight for the woods and, at her suggestion, moved their lovemaking to the backseat. In the darkness, Karen reminded Joe of a sheet of pure white chocolate, and he was ready to devour her when she whispered the word.

"Now."

It was a frantic coupling, fueled by groans and moans as their bodies meshed. And it was over quickly, as Joe blew like a high-pressured rocket.

Karen screamed a moment later, an anguished cry of outrage. "Damn it, Joe!" she scolded, pushing up against his chest, forcing him to withdraw long before he was ready. "It's not a race." She clinched her fist and struck him in the chest. "And you didn't use anything."

Joe sat back against the door, gaping in disbelief as hopes for a repeat performance were dashed. "What?" he asked, dismayed.

Karen punched him again, harder. "A rubber! You dumb-ass!" she yelled. "That's why I waited until tonight. So you would come prepared."

"I'm sorry," Joe mumbled.

"You will be if I wind up pregnant with your baby, hotshot," she hissed.

Joe choked visibly. "That won't happen," he suggested naively.

Karen scowled. "You'd just better hope it doesn't, big boy," she said sharply. "Because there'll be hell to pay and there's no way I'm haven a baby."

———

Karen was home well before her curfew that night. Joe made it home shortly after eleven, letting himself in through the back porch in hopes of not disturbing the family. He eased open the door, stepped into the kitchen and found the embers of a dying fire waiting for him.

Feeling chilled, he lit a cigarette and stood there smoking it, contemplating the night. Despite everything, the wrath of Karen, the fear of an unintended pregnancy, he smiled. He wasn't a cherry anymore. Few things compared, and Joe considered the possibility that perhaps Karen was right after all. Love complicated matters and the feelings that came with it obviously were not necessary for making love. It was a hollow thought, but believable.

He was lighting his second cigarette when the dining room door opened and his daddy entered the kitchen.

Matt regarded his son with a bemused expression. The match was burning down quickly, and Joe looked like a deer caught in the headlights of a car.

"You best light up, son, or you're gonna get burned," he suggested, crossing the floor to the kitchen light and flipping the switch. "The fact that you smoke is not exactly a secret, Joe, but this is the first time I've flat out caught you. I probably should give you a lecture, but experience tells me I'd be wasten my breath. So instead, I'll bum a smoke off you and we'll keep this our secret. Fair enough?"

Joe smiled stiffly as Matt came toward him.

"I was almost asleep," Matt informed him, "and remembered the fire. I thought I'd better check it."

Matt accepted the cigarette and was about to ask for a light when he noticed Joe's rumpled clothing, along with the boy's meshed hair and skittish behavior. He stepped back, making a hasty appraisal of the situation but keeping any conclusions to himself. He picked up a box of matches from the mantle and lit the cigarette.

"You're looken kind of rough, son," he remarked.

"It was a long night," Joe shrugged, easing away from the fire.

Matt took a long drag on the cigarette, allowing Joe to reach safety before looking again at the boy. "I have a feelen you and I should have a heart-to-heart talk, Joe," he said a moment later. "Man to man." He saw Joe swallow, then added quickly, "But everyone deserves privacy, and there are some things a man has to find out for himself."

He paused long enough to inhale on the cigarette once more, then tossed the unfinished portion into the embers. "I guess I'm luckier than most men, Joe," he continued at length. "I discovered what I was looken for when I was not much older than you are now, and it's made all the difference in the world to me. You think about that, son, from time to time. Will you?"

"Yes, sir," Joe promised with a cracked voice.

Matt nodded and walked past him, out of the kitchen to the room he shared with his wife.

# CHAPTER 6

HIS LEGENDARY STATUS FADED quickly enough. Karen sat at a different table in the high school cafeteria and ignored Joe, except to hand him a brief note in their homeroom class one morning. "You were lucky, hot shot," was all it said.

Joe read it once, crumpled the paper and dropped it in the trashcan on his way to first period.

He might have dwelled on these happenings, but work kept him too busy.

Spring rains replaced the winter cold and preparing the fields for planting took top priority. Joe woke early every day, helped with chores and went to school. In the afternoon, he returned home, ate a snack and then spent long hours on the tractor, guiding harrows, plows and planters through the fields. The hard work wore him out. He rested easy at night.

The tobacco was set and they were halfway through planting the corn when three days of heavy rain bogged the fields and halted the spring work.

Joe was grateful for the respite and made time for a late-night walk to the railroad tracks. These midnight sojourns had dwindled considerably over the past year, but the train remained a treasured symbol. In the middle of the day, when he was doubled over in some distant field with the sun beating down on his back, Joe would hear the train whistle and the work would become lighter. At night, he would wake abruptly, realizing the train had just passed, and he would take comfort knowing the wheels of his own life were turning with the same regularity, carrying him closer to his destination.

A late evening shower had brought warmth to this cool, damp spring day, shrouding the land with thick fog and hiding the heavens. As usual, upon reaching the railroad tracks, Joe searched for signs of the oncoming train, peering through the pea soup for the headlamp and straining to hear the first faint rumblings. It was a brief search, his typical exercise in futility but a harmless habit all the same on nights when Joe arrived early at the tracks.

His gaze swept down the far edge of the tracks and was coming back up the other side when a shadow snagged his eyes. His heartbeat accelerated and Joe stood still in the darkness. He looked again, his senses alert, and made out the form of a man standing thirty yards down the track.

Joe was intrigued more than unnerved by this stranger trespassing on the Baker place. He figured the fellow was an acquaintance of the family. Strangers rarely made it to Cookville without attracting attention and even less so in the New River community. Something in him wanted to leave the man to his privacy, but curiosity got the best of Joe. What kind of desperate soul would venture out on a night like this?

Picking his way along the tracks, Joe halved the distance between himself and the stranger before pausing to get his bearings and take a second look at the shadow. The dense fog continued to work against him, so he crept closer, straining his eyes in the darkness when the stranger lit a match. Blue light sprang to life, turned brownish yellow and flickered to its death, leaving behind the red glow of a cigarette tip and revealing the man's identity.

Lucas Bartholomew was no stranger. But he was a mystery to Joe.

A few centuries ago, Joe thought, Lucas might have been a loyal African tribesman, distinguished by his courage on the battlefield and quiet determination off it. Although not necessarily the first one called, he would have been a member of every great hunting expedition, leading by example and fading into the background as others stepped into to claim the glory of the kill.

It was easy to imagine, too, that slave traders would have desired his stock, while American buyers would have fought over him on the auction block. Lucas was tall and rangy, muscled and armed with the stamina for day after day of backbreaking work. His skin was smooth and colored like a milk chocolate candy bar. He wore a serious expression for almost every occasion, the wide flat features of his face seemingly cast in granite, varying only by a few degrees when he smiled or frowned. His cheekbones were prominent, and his dark brown eyes clear and alert.

As far back as Joe could remember, Lucas had been clean-shaven with a close-cropped head of hair. As of late, however, he grew a mustache from time to time and wore his hair longer and fuller, though still cropped neatly above the ears.

The change in Lucas' appearance bothered people. Amelia Carter, for one, had mentioned his longer hair to Caroline recently, and his mother had shrugged off the remark, saying people needed to change things about themselves from time to time. Joe had remained mum on the matter, concluding it best not to point out that Amelia changed the color of her hair, to some extent, nearly every other time she visited the beauty parlor.

As far as Joe was concerned, Lucas had earned the right to be taken at face value, and these veiled suspicions other people had about him were wrong. More troubling to Joe, however—though he hated to admit it—was his own curiosity about this sudden change in Lucas.

Joe regarded Lucas with great affection. Lucas had been a regular fixture around the Baker household for most of Joe's life. Some of his fondest memories were of hunting expeditions with Matt, Sam, Lucas and Paul Berrien.

Hunting relaxed Lucas, loosened his tongue and revealed a different side of him. He showed off a dry sense of humor, amusing his white companions with clever stories about the town's colored people. The stories were full of insight, regardless of whether he poked fun at someone's shenanigans or portrayed the inner strength of another's simplicity.

While Lucas was closemouthed about his personal life, his actions revealed a man who sought a fair shake in life and nothing more. He had little time or regard for those who waited on handouts. Although he might not understand the concept, Joe thought, Lucas was guided by the principles Emerson termed self-reliance. A few men such as Matt, Sam and Paul Berrien recognized the black man's able attitude. Others were slow to see it, and some would never acknowledge it.

Joe knew people had taken advantage of Lucas when he went door-to-door looking for work after his father's death. He had heard various farmers boast about the deal they worked with Lucas, the work they received for a poor man's wages. When he had been younger, Joe had asked his daddy why these men took advantage of Lucas. Matt had been at a loss for words, but Joe noticed afterward his father made the extra effort to see that Lucas worked for him or some other fair man. Now Lucas had a yeoman's reputation, which allowed him to pick his employers. That he worked primarily for Matt was a testament to his appreciation and loyalty.

Lucas was nine years older than Joe and shared more in common with Matt, Sam and Paul. But Lucas and Joe were kindred spirits and had kindled a friendship from years of working side by side. Joe confided in Lucas on occasion, the most recent being the tale of his torrid, short-lived romance with Karen Baxter, always certain what he revealed would stay between them. Lucas listened to his musings without offering advice, which suited Joe, who preferred to sort out things for himself. In fact, it was his own penchant for privacy that kept Joe from prying during those times when he wished Lucas would divulge his own thoughts and feelings.

The cigarette burned bright red as Lucas inhaled, and Joe watched in continued silence, wondering what his friend was thinking and why he was standing by the railroad tracks at this time of night. Perhaps he had an argument with Beauty, Joe considered, or was worried over something. Or like himself, Joe concluded, it was altogether possible that Lucas had ventured out to these railroad tracks this night in search of perspective.

Joe gazed up at the heavens, mindful that a world of difference separated the perspectives of a white boy and a colored man. Despite their shared experiences, proximity and genuine interest in the well-being of each other, he and Lucas were miles apart, separated by the gulf between black and white.

Joe had encountered bigotry and demonstrated his sympathy with the emerging civil rights movement. Yet, he found it difficult to reconcile the prejudice in Cookville with the ugly likes of Selma and Montgomery, Alabama. Those places seemed far away from Cookville. But were they? Joe wondered, recalling the ugly climate of the sheriff's race between Paul Berrien and Bobby Taylor two years earlier.

Bobby and his cronies were exceptions in the Cookville community, where the majority of people, white and colored alike, treated each other with fairness and respect. Harmony was the trademark of relations between the races in the community, but Joe suspected it was a fragile peace.

Blacks did not complain about the separate water fountains and bathrooms in Cookville, where they had free run of the entire town, except for the churches and the schools. Brown versus the Board of Education meant nothing in Cookville. Joe had never attended school with a colored person and probably never would. This idea was so foreign that Joe rarely had given it a thought until lately. The colored students had their own school, their own football and basketball teams, and no one ever grumbled about the situation. Two years ago, the county had built a new high school and moved the Negro students into the old building. In an election year when even the few black votes mattered, community leaders nearly had broken their arms while patting themselves on the back as if to say, "Look at us. We treat our colored folk real good. We've given them a fine new school."

Joe willingly conceded that blacks seemed to have a decent life in Cookville, as good as could be expected anyway. True, most of them were poor, extremely poor. Almost all of them lived on the wrong side of the tracks in a collection of tarpaper shacks, kindling wood frame houses and block buildings with dirt floors. A few lucky ones had running water and indoor plumbing. Most used outhouses.

The poverty disturbed Joe, but he could rationalize it. Poor white people lived in the same squalid conditions, on both the wrong and the right sides of the tracks, as well as in other parts of the county, including right here in New River.

It was easy, maybe even understandable, for Joe to assume colored people might find life harsher in places other than Cookville. No one had ever challenged segregation in the community. If everyone, both black and white, was contented with the way things were, then the system must be working. Still, Joe could not help wondering what the outcome would be if someone challenged the system. But those were lofty issues to weigh, better left to someone with a vested interest. For the moment, Joe was more concerned with matters closer to home.

If he had been outraged by the shameful behavior of Dr. Turner, then how had Lucas felt? In fact, how did Lucas feel about separate bathrooms, water fountains, schools and theater seats? Could Joe understand those feelings?

Atticus Finch, a fictional hero of Joe's, seemed to think you had to walk in someone's shoes to find answers to these kinds of questions. Since that was near to impossible, Joe settled for the next best thing.

Lucas was learning to love Beauty.

His wife was like a newborn filly, finding her colt's legs and gaining confidence with each new step along the way. He was teaching her to read and write, and Beauty was an excellent student. When she set her mind to something, which she rarely did, Beauty was a bulldog, persistent and determined all the way. At the moment, her mind was set on reading the Bible for herself and bedtime stories for the children they would have one day.

With hunger pains gnawing at his stomach, Lucas hoped that one day soon Beauty would add cooking to her list of pursuits. As it was, though, his wife was more concerned with making sure the table was set properly than with the preparation of the meal itself. On some days, Lucas half expected to come home to find the table set with fine china, silverware, linens and fresh flowers, only to discover that Beauty had forgotten to cook supper. On other days, he wished that was the case.

About the best thing he could say for Beauty's cooking was that it was filling, and sometimes even that stretched a compliment. Still, Lucas refused to complain about the meals Beauty prepared and was determined to encourage her to experiment and try different things. Until then, he would try to figure out ways to wind up at the Bakers or the Berriens around mealtimes. On principle, Lucas was opposed to charity. But he was learning fast that a man could starve on principles.

Lucas smiled to himself and inhaled on his cigarette. He considered himself a lucky man, despite his wife's shortcomings at the stove. Merrilee Bartholomew would have approved his choice of a wife.

The Bible said women were to be helpmates for their men, and Beauty was that and more to Lucas. She honored any request, supported every endeavor and treated him like a king. She was a willing lover, a trusting partner and his best friend. Beauty allowed Lucas to be the man of the house. And he wanted to make her proud.

Lucas had gone to church that Sunday two years ago for the sole purpose of finding a wife. He'd had a vague recollection of Beauty even before setting foot in the church, and was determined to wed her from the first time she approached him to offer congratulations on his acceptance into the church.

Beauty sang in the choir and, while Lucas had some qualms with organized religion, her voice was reason enough for him to attend church every Sunday. Beauty could lead a man to God with her voice. It was melodious, pitched low and soulful, and Lucas liked nothing better than coming home to a house filled to the rafters with the spiritual croonings of his wife.

Lucas stretched and yawned, glancing skyward and then lowering his gaze once more to the ground in front of him.

They were making a home, Beauty and him, and they were on the verge of something special. He had joined with Beauty to create the miracle of life. Now was the time to hurry up and wait.

Lucas was caught in this last thought when a voice in the dark startled him. His heart missed a beat; he stumbled backward, searching the fog for the intruder. He heard the voice again, calling his name this time, and he relaxed, recognizing the familiar ring.

---

"Lucas?" Joe called as he approached. "Is that you?"

Lucas groped in the darkness, trying to recognize the voice as Joe drew closer.

"Lucas," he repeated. "It's me."

Joe stepped into his line of vision, and Lucas relaxed with visible relief. "Goshamighty, Joe-Joe," he grumbled. "You scared the mess out of me."

"Sorry about that," Joe laughed lightly. "I was on my way home when I saw you standen over here. What's got you out on a night like this?"

"I was doen some thinken," Lucas replied, casting a reproachful eye on Joe at the same time. "I could ask you the same thing. I bet Mr. Matt and Mrs. Caroline don't know you're out here traipsen around in the dead of night."

"Nope, they don't," Joe confirmed. "But I don't think they'd mind too much. A guy needs a place where he can think without be'en interrupted every now and then, and there aren't too many places like that in our house."

Lucas nodded understanding. "I guess not. I'm in the same boat with Beauty. Four walls can get awful close around two people."

Joe glanced off in the darkness, then deliberately changed the subject. "We had quite a night the last time we were off by ourselves," he said. "I don't suppose you brought a gun along tonight—in case some wild animal shows up and tries to make a meal of you?"

"Not this time," Lucas smiled, rotating his shoulder to show it was healing. "I don't think we oughtta worry too much about anything else like that happenen. It was one shot in a million." He paused, then added, "By the way, I never thanked you properly for saven my life, Joe-Joe, but I'm much obliged."

Joe shrugged modestly. "It was the least I could do," he grinned. "I'd call it the shot of a lifetime."

Lucas smiled again, and Joe asked him for a cigarette.

"What's on your mind?" Joe asked boldly as he lit the Camel.

Lucas dropped his own cigarette to the ground, stared briefly at the red glow and then ground it into the earth with the soul of his boot. "Well, Joe," he began hesitantly. "You might say congratulations is in store for Beauty and me. She told me tonight at supper that she's gonna have a baby." He glanced up at Joe. "I came out here tonight to think about be'en a daddy and how I can make my baby's life better than mine."

"Congratulations!" Joe exclaimed, extending his hand to Lucas and pumping the handshake vigorously as the excitement registered on his friend's poker face. "You're bloated with pride, Lucas. No doubt, you figure to get a son."

Lucas shook his head from side to side. "I don't care nary a bit. I just want a healthy, happy baby."

Joe smiled in agreement. "Give my best to Beauty," he said. "Can I tell the family?"

"Might as well," Lucas answered. "Near as we can tell, she'll be looken like she's expecten before too much longer."

"I'm proud for you, Lucas," Joe said. "You'll make a good daddy." He paused, then added with feigned indifference, "I guess every parent wants to make the world better for their children. I know Mama and Daddy do."

"They should," Lucas suggested. He hunched his shoulders, looking Joe squarely in the eye. "But don't hem and haw with me, Joe," he said with conviction. "Your mama and daddy have the world on their side. But me? I've got to try harder."

"Yeah," Joe agreed with sincerity. "I know what you mean, Lucas, and it's funny because that's been on my mind a lot lately. Fate must have meant us to meet here tonight. I have a feelen we've both had a lot of the same things on our minds lately."

"Like what it's like to be colored?" Lucas supposed.

Joe nodded. "For you in particular."

Silence ensued, and Joe worried he had stepped beyond the bounds of friendship.

"Why you wanna know?" Lucas asked finally.

"Who's playen games now?" Joe shot back.

Lucas shrugged indifferently.

"You and I have known each other for as long as I can remember," Joe said, "but over the last few months especially, we've had an opportunity to get closer. I've grown to trust you, Lucas, and I hope you can say the same for me. I've got some questions on my mind—questions about you because you're my friend."

"You're worth a million in questions, Joe-Joe," Lucas said, "but you're always a dime short on answers. I still wanna know why you're so interested in wanten to know what makes a colored man tick."

"I like to know what other people think," Joe responded. "And things have happened lately that caused me to think as well. Quite honestly, Lucas, a few people have given me the feelen they'd have rather I shot you than the panther. That boggles my brain. And then there was the good Dr. Turner. He didn't want to treat you just because you're colored. That ticked me off. I've wondered how it made you feel. You've never said the first word about it."

Lucas hunched his shoulders again. "To tell you the truth, Joe, I don't remember much about that night, 'cept for the hurten. But I'm glad you were ticked off. I would have been, too, if somethen like that happened to you. As for those feelens you've been getten from other people, I'm not surprised. Some people figure the world would be a better place with one less nigger. Believe me, there's been times when I thought the world would be a whole sight better with a few less white masters.

"Does that surprise you?" Lucas asked a pregnant moment later. "Does it scare you?"

"It surprises me some," Joe answered, smiling. "But it doesn't scare me. I know you pretty well, Lucas. You're fairly mild-mannered." He hesitated, then inquired, "When you think about me, Lucas, what do you think first? Am I Joe? Or am I white?"

"First, you answer that question about me," Lucas challenged.

"Okay," Joe relented. "I think of Lucas ... my black friend. But I don't associate any of your peculiarities as having to do anything with be'en black. Actually, I think of you and me as kindred spirits to some extent. We like our privacy, you even more than me."

"Agreed," Lucas said. "When I see you, I think, 'There's Joe. He's white. He's different.'" Lucas smiled. "But eventually, I get 'round to rememberen that I'd count on you with my life."

"I can say the same for you, Lucas," Joe told him. He shifted his stance, then asked, "Is it hard to be colored?"

Lucas scratched his jaw and rubbed his nose. "Sometimes," he answered at length. "In a white man's world, it is. Most of the time, though, I don't think of myself as colored. I don't have the time to dwell on what all that means. Besides that, I figure I'm doen okay for myself. I got plenty of work to keep me busy, a place to stay and a good woman beside me all the way. Now I got a baby on the way, too. A man can't ask for much more than that, no matter whether he's a colored man or a white man."

"That sounds like my daddy and my grandpa talken," Joe commented.

"Some of it is," Lucas admitted. "I can't deny Mr. Matt and Mr. Sam have influenced my thinken more than a little. Maybe that's why I don't think of myself as colored very often. They've pretty much treated me as plain old Lucas for 'bout as long as I can remember."

Joe finished his cigarette, rubbing it out in the ground. "You ever wish you were white, Lucas?" he asked.

"When I was little, I did," Lucas confessed. "It would've made life a whole heap easier."

"And now?" Joe pushed.

Lucas crossed his arms. "There's some people who think that about me," he conceded. "I live among white people more than colored people these days. I look at your daddy and your granddaddy and Mr. Paul Berrien and what they've accomplished, and I see myself tryen to do what they've done. So on one hand, I have to admit that white men more than black men have given direction to my life. But on the other hand, my mama was a smart woman and she taught her boy well. She's the one, Joe-Joe. She's the reason I do what I do. She made me."

He unfolded his arms and rubbed his palms against his pants legs. "That's a roundabout answer to your question," he continued a moment later. "Directly speaken, though, I don't have any desire to be a white man. Not anymore. I wouldn't want to change who I am, Joe." He shook his head. "Maybe change the world, but not me."

Joe glanced at the ground, then quickly back to his friend. "I'm glad to hear that, Lucas."

Lucas nodded appreciatively, adding, "Well, I'm glad to tell you, Joe-Joe."

Joe tilted his head, sheepishly casting another curious glance at Lucas. "When did you decide you no longer wanted to be white?" he asked slyly.

"Probably when my mama was dyen," Lucas replied patiently. "But I was in Detroit when I realized it once and for all." He closed his eyes. "That's why I went North. I thought life might be easier up there. But it wasn't—least not for me."

"What about that trip?" Joe pushed again. "You've never said much about it."

"That's right. I haven't," Lucas remarked, fishing a crumpled pack of Camels and a box of matches from his shirt pocket.

Taking his last cigarette from the pack, he stuffed the empty paper into the front pocket of his worn brown trousers and struck the match. He lit the cigarette, inhaled deeply and returned the matchbox to his shirt pocket, leaving Joe to wonder once again whether he had pried beyond the boundaries of their friendship.

"I trust you, Joe," Lucas said at last, staring off into the distance. "I know what's said here tonight will stay by these railroad tracks."

"It will," Joe guaranteed him.

"When I was your age," Lucas began, "I used to lie in my bed at night and think about leaven this place and never comen back. My daddy was dead by then, and Mama and me lived in Cookville. I'd hear that train roll through town on some nights, and it was all I could do to keep from runnen after it. I wanted to hop a ride in the baddest sort of way. I didn't care where it was goen. I just wanted to leave.

"But I couldn't," he continued. "Mama was bad sick, and she needed me. Still, I started saven up for a day when there wouldn't be nothen to keep me here. Every job I worked, every heavy load I lifted, brought me one step closer to somethen better. I was sure of it. I'd find some place where I could be somethen and someone I'd never be here in Cookville."

Lucas leveled his gaze at Joe.

"Now I know better," he said, and his story began in earnest.

It was a journey of two thousand miles, traveled in a third- or fourth-hand pickup, and the first stop was Sweet Auburn Avenue in Atlanta. Lucas stayed in the city for three months. He heard Martin Luther King Jr. preach civil rights and the gospel at Ebenezer Baptist Church, and he listened to politics and protest at Paschal's Motor Inn. He respected the passions and admired the battle plans for integration. But selfish reasons kept Lucas from joining the Movement. He bid Atlanta goodbye and moved on to Raleigh, to Richmond, to Washington, D.C., picking tobacco along the way and doing any other odd job to keep cash in his pocket.

"The towns were bigger, but the life didn't seem much different from what I'd left in Cookville," Lucas told Joe. "Face it. Croppen baccer is croppen baccer, whether you do it in Cookville, Georgia, or outside Raleigh, North Carolina. I did wash dishes at a restaurant in Washington for a few weeks. That was enough time to know I needed to find somethen else to do."

Lucas spent two months in the City of Brotherly Love, Philadelphia, and landed next in New York City, where he stayed for eleven months. He found a job moving boxes at a grocery warehouse in Harlem, rented a room in a boarding house and took his meals at a nearby restaurant on 135th Street.

Food flavored his fondest memories of the city. The natives called it "soul food" in Harlem, but Lucas thought of those meals simply as good Southern cooking. He kept his belly full, feasting day after day on chicken, fish and pork chops, all deep-fried in fat; pig feet, pig tails and chitlins served with collards, turnips, mustard greens and pot liquor. There were mouth-melting corn dodgers, fatback, sweet potatoes, okra, peas and, inevitably, a delicious sweet to top off each meal.

The hardy fare filled out Lucas' rangy form, and the warehouse work hardened his muscles. It was a glorious time, and Lucas dared to believe he had found his place in life. He might have convinced himself completely if not for the grim reality of the city.

Each day, he saw dope pushers and drug addicts turn deals in back alleys, drunkards stumble from row upon row of liquor stores and bars, prostitutes turning tricks on every street corner. He stared at these people in disbelief, wondering which broken-down building the poor creatures claimed for home and thanking the Almighty for his own good fortune.

Lucas loved Harlem and he hated it at times. But in the end, when he almost died on its mean streets, Lucas was driven from it.

He discovered the party life in Harlem and took it to heart. Wine and women became the song of life, and Lucas played it like a troubadour.

His favorite nightspot was a bar on 116th Street, and one summer night there, Lucas was pointed in a direction that would lead home to Cookville. "It was on a Friday," he recalled for Joe. "The place was jam-packed. The women were easy, and I was looken for somethen sweet."

Lucas found a beauty queen, with cherry red lips and sparkling white teeth. He slid onto an empty bar stool beside the woman, ordered a beer for himself and whiskey for her. They chatted for a few minutes, then danced and Lucas figured he was on his way to getting lucky. Finishing the last of several dances, they found a table and were becoming cozy when his luck turned sour.

Lucas had just leaned close to her face when the back of his skull exploded. Although he did not realize it at the time, the woman's boyfriend had belted him with a set of brass knuckles. Struggling to remain conscious, Lucas was spun around and witnessed firsthand the driving force of another ringed fist into his face. The blow shattered his nose, and Lucas had vague memories of his laundered white shirt turning crimson as the man dragged him from the bar to one of Harlem's feared alleys.

"You pay for messing with my woman," the man told Lucas, then plunged a bowie knife into his abdomen. He was unconscious before the knife was removed from body.

When he woke, Lucas was outside an emergency clinic. He stumbled to his feet, staggered through the door and gasped for help before passing out a second time.

A young white woman was hovering over him when he next woke. Lucas was lying on a gurney, and the female doctor proclaimed him lucky to be alive.

"That knife missed your liver by a hair and a whole lot of other stuff you need as well," she told him sternly. "How did you manage to get here?"

"I don't know," Lucas answered truthfully. "One minute I was talken to a pretty woman. The next, somebody was beaten me in the head and sticken a knife in my gut."

The doctor shook her head in dismay. "I don't understand you people," she told Lucas. "You cut somebody up, then drop him off at the hospital for stitches like it's the most normal thing in the world to do. It makes no sense."

"I don't understand it, either," Lucas mused half-heartedly. "Back where I come from, people ain't so mean to each other."

"Then I suggest you go back to that place while you still can," the doctor recommended.

Instead, Lucas took off for Boston. He saw the autumn colors in New England, motored through Pittsburgh and Cleveland and spent a Christmas, New Year's and winter in the frigid cold of Chicago before moving north to Detroit.

In Detroit, Lucas attended his first honest-to-goodness civil rights demonstration. It was a peaceful rally to show support for sit-in protests at a Woolworth's lunch counter in Greensboro, North Carolina. Lucas lent his voice to the demonstration, chanting slogans for justice and equality, singing familiar freedom songs. But his heart was heavy.

Speaker after speaker condemned the poverty, inadequate education and second-class citizenship of Negroes in the South. They claimed the white man was a universal enemy in the South. They threatened to invade the region, vowing to free their Southern brothers from the final bonds of white oppression and slavery.

As they spoke, Lucas looked around and considered the plight of the people gathered around him. Perhaps many of them were better educated and wealthier than their colored counterparts in the South. But the very same problems they expounded so passionately about in the South were festering in their own backyards as well. He thought about the slums in Harlem and other cities he had seen. The white man was not the enemy in Harlem, Lucas believed. The enemy was a system that destroyed hope and swallowed up young souls into a destiny of misery and squalor.

"Colored people got more than their share of problems down here," Lucas commented, explaining his feelings to Joe. "Maybe we do need outsiders comen in to shake up people. But I don't put much store in people who set out to save the world without first taken care of their own."

At his first civil rights demonstration, Lucas decided it was time to go home. It would take him two months to get there, and he would arrive by way of St. Louis and New Orleans. But Lucas was sure of his destiny. In Cookville, his enemies were familiar and

Lucas believed they would soften over time. It was slender trust, perhaps, but the first glimmer of hope that Lucas had seen in a long time.

———————

"This is home," Lucas stated simply to Joe. "It's where I belong."

"But is it everything you want?" Joe asked.

"It's everything I need," Lucas replied with firm conviction. "What you want is not always what you need, Joe-Joe. But the way I figure it, if a man can get what he needs, he's bound to have enough of everything and maybe a little extra in the long run."

"You're sounden like Daddy again," Joe remarked.

"Yeah, well," Lucas arched his eyebrows. "That's not so bad, is it?"

"No," Joe agreed. "Not at all."

Lucas finished another cigarette. "Did I answer some of those questions for you?" he asked in time.

"A few. But I've got more."

"Why ain't I surprised?" Lucas laughed. "Joe-Joe, you obviously never heard that curiosity killed the cat."

"I ain't no cat," Joe declared.

"You're a tomcat for shore," Lucas teased. "I can see it in your eyes."

"What you see is cat-scratch fever," Joe countered smartly. "But seriously, Lucas, can you stand another question or two?"

Lucas made an off-handed remark about the train's tardiness, then allowed for another question.

"Do things like separate bathrooms and water fountains bother you?" Joe inquired. "Have you ever considered standen up against stuff like that?"

"Have you ever considered it?" Lucas parried.

"It's not my place to," Joe suggested.

"Who says," Lucas shot back. "I don't suspect you'd be welcome in a bathroom marked for colored people any more than I'd be in one for whites."

Joe was confused. "I hadn't thought of it that way."

"No, I didn't figure you had," Lucas said. He shrugged, then added, "I don't care about those things, Joe," he admitted. "They'll work themselves out eventually, maybe one day when somebody gets tired of keepen all those bathrooms clean. When I pick a battle to fight, it's gonna be over somethen really important, somethen that matters to me."

"Such as?"

"Opportunity," Lucas replied fiercely. "I can make a good life for myself. My needs will be met. But what's good for me won't be good enough for my children. They'll need more than I do. I want them to have opportunities that I didn't have. I want more for them than what comes with be'en grateful that a few white people are able to see beyond the color of your skin."

Lucas paused, scrutinizing Joe for reaction, finding a blank expression on his face. "I'll pick a fight one day, Joe," he continued passionately. "I'll fight to make sure my children get the same education that you're getten, to make sure they're not treated as second-class in second-rate schools. And I'll win that fight. Because the law of the land is on my side, even if it's ignored 'round here."

"Do you agree?" he asked after a slight pause. "Do you think I'll win?"

Joe glanced deliberately past Lucas, uncertain of the answer. Civil rights were a vague concept to Joe, but he understood the plainly stated goal of his black friend and appreciated the fierce determination to succeed. "I hope so," he answered finally, returning his gaze to Lucas. "I suppose we'll have to wait and see."

"Wait and see!" Lucas rolled his eyes and shook his head in exasperation. "It's always wait and see," he said angrily. "That's everybody's answer for anything unpleasant today that can be put off until tomorrow. Your daddy's said that same thing to me more times than you'd imagine. And your granddaddy was sayen the same thing to my daddy way back when."

"Well, what the heck are we supposed to say, Lucas?" Joe retorted sharply. "You're not exactly marchen off to battle yourself."

In the blink of an eye, tension came unexpectedly and thick between them. It seemed to Joe they had stepped on different sides of the same track. Lucas realized their guns were drawn as well and pulled back his attack.

"I'm talken big, Joe-Joe," he allowed. "Sounden high and mighty, too."

"It's nothen, Lucas," Joe shrugged.

"Maybe," Lucas nodded. "But I got no right asken you or

anyone else to do my fighten for me, especially when I'm not ready or willen to do it myself."

"When will that be?" Joe inquired.

"When I've got a reason, too," Lucas said quickly. "When my children are ready for it."

"Why not now?" Joe asked.

"Because it's not my fight right now," Lucas answered frankly. "Because I'm selfish. Because I'm comfortable with the way things are. There's any number of reasons. Take your pick. The way I look at it, I'll do my part when the time comes. I'll make a stand. I'll fight a battle. I'll do what I can to change things. But my first commitment is to my family, now and always. I won't sacrifice them for a cause.

"It's all about needs," he added. "I'll do what's necessary to meet the needs of my family. And if there's anything extra, then so be it."

"For what it's worth, Lucas," Joe said, "I'd fight with you."

"I don't doubt it," Lucas grinned, clapping him on the shoulder. "Joe-Joe, you'll be there with guns a-blazen."

In the distance then, they heard the train, rushing toward the trestle at the New River crossroads.

Joe glanced eagerly down the track, searching the fog for the first sign of the approaching locomotive. "I'm glad you figured out what you needed, Lucas," he said sincerely, eyes still glued to the steel tracks. "I'm glad you came home. And happy we had this talk tonight."

Joe broke his long look down the tracks and faced Lucas. "Do you realize how envious I am of you? You've done exactly what I want to do. You've gone to places I want to go. Maybe sometime you can tell me more about those places—Boston, New York, Philadelphia, Chicago, New Orleans. I'd give anything in the world to stand on top of the Empire State building or to eat crawfish and jambalaya in New Orleans."

Joe shook his head as the train reached the trestle, its whistle blasting the night, the heavy vibrations echoing through the countryside. He heeded the call instinctively, peeling his eyes once more down the track as the engine headlight loomed into view.

"Lucas, you mentioned the train earlier tonight, and I knew exactly what you were talken about," he said. "It calls out to you, and sometimes a body just has to answer. That's why I came down here tonight. One day, I'm gonna hop a ride on it, Lucas, and go far away from here. There's a whole world out there, and I think I'm gonna like it better than Cookville."

"Wait and see," Lucas suggested, smiling as Joe looked at him. "Cookville might look a whole lot better to you when you're a thousand miles away from it, especially when it seems more like you're a thousand miles from nowhere."

"Oh, I don't doubt that," Joe agreed quickly. "This place, this time—it might just be the best there is. But like you said, Lucas, it's all about needs." He smiled, almost reluctantly. "And as good as it is here, it's not enough for me."

The train was on them then, approaching fast with two long whistle blasts, and they stepped away from the steel rails in unison. As the train streaked past them, unaware that Lucas was watching him with undisguised interest, Joe reached down and grabbed a handful of the hard earth. He sifted it through his fingers, gritted his teeth and tossed the dirt at the passing cars, wondering what unknown destination awaited that little piece of earth.

Joe turned around to find Lucas regarding him with an amused expression.

"It's always too fast," Joe complained, raising his voice loud enough to be heard over the fading racket of grinding steel. "It's here one moment, then before you know it, it's passed you by again. I have to keep reminden myself that another one will come along in due time."

"Uhm," Lucas mused. "Well, I best be getten home," he said. "But Joe: Best you always remember that for every train goen away from here, another one comes back."

Joe smiled at the sage advice as the late-night companions ended their unexpected sojourn. He gazed down the tracks once more, watching the train lights disappear in the fog, closing his eyes as the last faint thunder echoed in his head.

Turning toward home, Joe thought: The train may run both ways, Lucas, but I want a one-way ticket.

# QUESTIONS FOR DISCUSSION

*Warning: Questions contain spoilers*

1) In the book's opening, a young Joe is clearly conflicted by his personal desires and ambitions versus his loyalty and responsibility to his family? After Matt tells his son to follow his own dreams, Joe concludes that life means "freeing yourself from one set of chains in order to be yoked to even tighter bonds." Do you agree or disagree with this viewpoint and why?

2) When we're introduced to Paul Berrien, one of the first things we learn about him is that he convinced the county coroner to cover up his father's suicide. Yet, despite his actions, voters are willing to forgive and forget and he gets elected sheriff. Even Bobby Taylor is dismayed by Paul's ability to succeed, wondering why his aristocratic opponent hasn't been jailed, much less remains a viable candidate. What does Paul's gilded fortune suggest about the idea of privilege and how does that relate to the world we live in today?

3) The Bakers had several Christmas traditions, including a shopping trip and pork brains and breakfast food for their supper on Christmas Eve. What's one of your favorite Christmas traditions?

4) In the episode, "The Train," Joe notes there's a big differe4nce between "want" and "need," and he wonders whether the Cookville community and family farm provide his father and grandfather "everything they want." How would Sam and Matt answer that question? Do your current circumstances provide everything you want in life?

5) In an English class, Joe becomes known as "the defender of clichés," and argues that clichés deserve respect because they emerge from years of truth and satisfy a human need for familiarity and comfort. Do you agree or disagree and why?

6) Lucas Bartholomew traveled the country to find out if a black man stood a better chance in life in some place other than Cookville. Why do you think he ultimately returned to Cookville?

# Book One
# The White Christmas and The Train
## 1960-1962

It's December 1960, and a cold wind is blowing a rare white Christmas toward the Baker farm in South Georgia. Joe Baker, an intense young man hell-bent on achievement and responsibility, finds himself torn between his own desire and ambition and his loyalty and responsibility to his family. Joe can't shake the notion that he is destined to remain solid and will never soar as long as he remains on the family farm.

Thus begins *Plowed Fields*, setting the stage for a conflict that will nag at Joe for the next decade as he tries to reconcile his own desire and ambition with loyalty and responsibility to his family.

"The White Christmas" sets the stage, introducing Joe and his family, along with a host of friends and acquaintances who will shape their fates during the next decade. They include Lucas Bartholomew, a black farm laborer, and Bobby Taylor, the spitting image of a civil rights-minded Yankees' vision of a racist. Tensions erupt between the Bakers and the Taylors, sparked by a senseless act and fueled by Bobby campaigns for the sheriff's job against Matt Baker's best friend, the aristocratic and troubled Paul Berrien.

In "The Train," Joe confronts racial prejudice in his school and community and feels the strain of taking an unpopular stand. A girl claims his heart and a heroic deed plants a seed of hate that will fester as the decade unfolds.

# Book Two
# Angels Sing, The Garden,
# <u>Faith and Grace, and The Fire</u>
## 1963-1967

As the decade progresses, Joe Baker and his family see their fortunes rise and fall, beginning with an illness that shakes the family at its very core. Prosperity comes calling when it's least expected, but a harrowing ordeal forces a reckoning with faith that nearly shatters the family.

Book Two of the *Plowed Fields* trilogy offers an intimate portrayal of the farming life. The Bakers also encounter more unexpected turmoil with their friends and neighbors, including Lucas Bartholomew, Bobby Taylor and Sheriff Paul Berrien, stoking the conflict that will bring the family face-to-face with fire and famine, war and peace, good and evil.

Amid a severe drought, Book Two builds to an exciting climax as one violent act leads Joe to mete out his own vicious brand of retribution. Ultimately, the Bakers need an act of daring and courage to save them from utter ruin.

The family's journey—from innocence to sin, from good to evil, from despair to triumph—sets the stage for the riveting conclusion of the *Plowed Fields* saga.

# Book Three
# The War, The Dream and
# Horn of Plenty
## 1968-1970

When we first met Joe Baker and his family, it was December 1960, and a rare white Christmas was blowing toward their farm in South Georgia. As the decade unfolded, they faced fire and famine, war and peace, good and evil. But those weighty issues served only as the backdrop for hardships encountered by a large farming family more concerned with making ends meet than saving the world.

In Book Three, the Bakers and their friends and neighbors move from the tobacco field to the battlefield, from main street to city lights, from the church door to the gates of Hell.

Tom Carter, Joe's best friend and his sister's fiancé, finds himself slogging through the muck and mud in Vietnam, while an old flame entices Joe to participate in an antiwar demonstration. The resulting firestorm consumes the community, their friends and the Bakers themselves.

As the tumultuous year of 1968 gives way to the final year of the Sixties, Joe fulfills his dream of becoming a newspaper reporter and immerses himself in the South's last stand against school integration. The ensuing battle pits old adversaries like Lucas Bartholomew and Bobby Taylor, as long-simmering animosity unleashes the unthinkable and wields devastating consequences.

# PLOWED FIELDS
## TRILOGY EDITION

Get a head start on the next book in the *Plowed Fields* Trilogy:

# BOOK TWO
# ANGELS SING

"DAMN!"

Summer was on a warpath on this last afternoon of 1962, battling the angst of youth and forced domesticity. New Year's Eve had been uneventful thus far on the Baker place, especially for Summer, who heretofore had washed windows, ironed clothes, vacuumed floors and presently was polishing furniture in her younger brothers' room. It was unfair the twelve-year-old girl had told Joe a moment ago in his room next door to John and Luke's.

"I could just scream," Summer railed even as Joe gave her a reprieve on orders from their mother to make his bed. "The men around here never have to lift a finger in this house. Y'all are doing exactly what you want to do today, and I'm stuck cleanen up after you. I'm tellen you, it ain't right."

"Do you hear me, Joe?" she yelled a moment later when he failed to acknowledge her tirade. "It ain't right."

Glancing up from his desk where he was writing an essay—a holiday homework assignment in senior English from Mrs. Gaskins—Joe shot his sister a disinterested look. "I heard you, all right. Listen, Summer, I'm busy here, and I told you not to worry about my bed. What more do you want?"

His sister bristled, hands flying to her hips in outrage as Joe's casual dismissal of her tirade became apparent. A quick retort appeared on the edge of her tongue, then disappeared. "I could still scream," she muttered before leaving his room.

Instead of screaming, Summer apparently had decided to utter every profanity in her vocabulary. Listening to his sister's ranting, Joe smiled and sympathized with her plight. In a few years, she would learn to control these outbursts, but now the desire to vent her anger blotted out twelve years of training in good manners and responsibility.

"Damn!" Summer growled for the fourth time and loudly

enough that Joe thought it wise to advise his sister against foolhardy conduct.

"Damn!" she said again, even as Joe leaned back in his chair and saw her admiring the shine on the fireplace mantle in John and Luke's room.

"WHAT did you say, young lady?" Rachel said unexpectedly, sternly.

The question rang with accusation and startled Summer. Gaping, she withered under the glaring eyes of their grandmother and started to apologize. Something stopped her though. It might have been indignation, but Joe figured it was more a mixture of stubbornness, frustration and plain stupidity.

"I said damn, Granny, and I meant it," Summer said, her tone sassy, her expression defiant. "It's not fair that we have to stay inside and do this durned old housework, while the men around here have a good old time doen whatever the heck they please." She crossed her arms, then declared, "I resent it."

Rachel stepped fully into the room, coming into Joe's range of observation. He approximated her temper at a slow boil as she considered an appropriate response to this willful display of temper by her granddaughter.

Like the season for which she was named, Summer was strong-willed, feisty and unrelenting on occasion. Rachel was the same way. As Joe saw it, his oldest sister and grandmother were two different patterns cut from same bolt of cloth. They shared common interests, particularly sewing and needlework, but their perspectives contrasted as sharply as the difference between a summer shower and a hurricane. Fortunately, Summer and Rachel rarely butted heads, but when they did, their sameness and differences clashed like stripes and polka dots. Joe sensed such a fashion faux pas at hand.

"Fair or not, young lady, that's the way it is," Rachel admonished her granddaughter. "And you'd better get used to it cause you're a young woman and young women are responsible for keepen a clean house." She paused, no doubt, Joe figured, to let her good advice sink into Summer's hard head. "Now you finish up your dusten. Then go copy ten Bible verses, and I won't tell your Mama what you said. But between us, you should be ashamed of yourself, Summer."

Joe smiled, thinking his sister was getting off lucky for the transgression. He Bible up his mind to show Summer ten of the shorter verses in the Bible as he waited expectantly for her contrite acceptance of the punishment. The girl fooled him.

"Granny, I don't think I should have to write down any old Bible verses. I've got a right to be mad. And besides, Daddy says damn all the time. If you weren't so ignorant about the ways of the world, you'd probably damn all this housework, too. There's more to life than just housework, and I'm sick and tired of all this cooken, cleanen, ironen and sewen."

Summer regretted the words as soon as they spewed from her mouth. Joe saw the remorse in her expression, as surely as he saw disappointment flash in his grandmother's eyes. For a split second, Rachel and Summer were bewildered, torn by desire to make amends and conviction in their beliefs.

Joe considered intervening to restore the peace, but the sudden appearance of his mother in the doorway doomed the prospect before it fully evolved.

"Summer!"

Their mother swept into the room on a wave of carefully controlled anger, obviously appalled by the situation. "In this house, young lady," Caroline Baker exhorted her daughter, "you do not talk to anyone that way, especially your elders. Tell your grandmother you're sorry this very instant; then go to the kitchen and wait there until I decide an appropriate punishment."

"I'm sorry," Summer spat, her indignation rising to another level.

"Say it and mean it, Summer," Caroline ordered.

Summer stared at her mother, then at Rachel and back to Caroline. "Mama," she replied. "That's the best I can do right now."

His sister's insolence stunned Joe. Summer always spoke her mind, but she was never deliberately spiteful. Yet, in one fell swoop, she had committed treason against her grandmother and declared open rebellion on her mother. Joe settled back and waited for her impertinence to be quashed.

More and more these days, he found himself witness to the travails of his sisters and brothers as they plodded through rough spots in the road to becoming young men and women. He deemed such observations as a due of his birthright, an act of passage that signified his coming of age and heralded a season of coming-out parties for the long line of siblings who trailed him. Joe had traversed the path of adolescence, and the road ahead—while certain to contain a few rocky places—looked relatively smooth to him. For the moment, he was intrigued more by the idea of stepping aside as his brothers and sisters took their turns as Johnny-come-lately. He considered it an obligation and a pleasure.

In some imprecise way, his salad days had passed and Joe felt as if he were between seasons. But Summer, John, Carrie, Luke and Bonnie were chomping at their bits with impatience, and Joe looked forward to watching the performance from the shadows. That was another privilege of his birthright, a position that brought huge responsibility but endowed him with the unique perspective of having been there. Joe was young enough to sympathize with the fervency of his brothers and sisters, yet old enough to understand the wisdom of his parents and grandparents.

Indeed, when he thought about it, Joe enjoyed his domain as the oldest child. It was the perfect vista, affording him the distance of deep shadows while extending leeway around the edges, providing a jumping-off place, yet allowing him to come rushing in to the rescue at a moment's notice, of his own volition or at the beck and call of someone else.

He was on the verge of plundering this last thought with more thoroughness when Caroline abruptly ended her dressing-down of Summer.

"You've disappointed me, Summer, not to mention your shabby disrespect of your grandmother," Caroline said gravely. "Nevertheless, it's your decision to be satisfied with your feeble apology and if you are, so be it. I, however, am not satisfied. Go to the kitchen."

"Yes, ma'am," Summer answered, her comedown so low that Joe leaned back once more in his chair to observe the goings-on through the doorway.

"I don't know what gets into that girl sometimes," Caroline remarked to Rachel when Summer had fled the room. This was not the first time Caroline had played mediatrix between her daughter and mother-in-law. She paused, expecting Rachel to give her version of the situation.

Instead, the older woman picked up the dust rag abandoned by Summer and used it to wipe away an invisible spot on the fireplace mantle.

"You two are so much alike that I guess there's always goen to be an occasional wrangle," Caroline prodded. "What started this one? Why was she so disrespectful?"

"Punish her for swearen, Caroline," Rachel said, looking her daughter-in-law in the eye. "But not for her insolence. It will pass, and Summer and I will work out our differences in due time."

Caroline considered the request for a moment, then nodded her agreement before casting her suspicions on Joe. "Son, did you hear your sister cursen?"

"She was haven a bad day," Joe suggested glibly.

"Well, that's no excuse!" Caroline retorted.

"No, it's not," Rachel agreed quickly. "And Joe, you should have told her so. You're a Christian, and you shouldn't condone such behavior."

Joe started to protest the rebuke, then changed his mind and smiled penitently. "You're right," he agreed. "Sorry, Mama. Sorry, Granny."

Seeing the two women sufficiently appeased, it occurred to Joe that while his sisters and brothers were coming into their own and taking center stage, he still had a few lessons to learn himself and would—of his own volition and heeding the beck and call of others—stay close in the wings as this drama unfolded. Joe shrugged his shoulders and told himself it was not a bad feeling at all to have such an important role.

# ABOUT THE AUTHOR

Jim Barber grew up in South Georgia, helping his family raise hogs and working on his uncles' tobacco farms while pursuing his dream to become a newspaper reporter. His first "public" job came at age sixteen, covering sports for his county newspaper, *The Berrien Press.* Jim spent the bulk of his newspaper career with United Press International's Atlanta bureau before a short stint with the *New York Daily News* led him to transfer to the world of corporate journalism and a twenty-five-year career with Georgia Power and Southern Company, one of the nation's largest utilities.

A state and national award winner for his writing, Jim previously co-edited three published books: *Atlanta Women Speak,* a collection of speeches from notable women such as Jane Fonda, Atlanta Mayor Shirley Franklin and author Pearl Cleage, as well as *Journey of Faith* and *Art from our Hearts,* both church histories.

While his work on the family farms is a distant memory, Jim does enjoy raising gardens in his backyard, especially tomatoes for his wife of nearly thirty-five years. Jim doesn't eat tomatoes, but he does play a lot of tennis and works part-time as the administrator of his church. He and Becky live in Atlanta near Stone Mountain, which he climbs faithfully almost every day. They have three grown daughters, one son-in-law (soon to be two), and three grand dogs.

Visit the author's website at www.jimbarber.me.

# A CONVERSATION WITH JIM BARBER

**Q. What inspired you to write Plowed Fields?**
A. As a young reporter, I covered the resignation of a bedridden sheriff who had been paralyzed by a stroke a year earlier. This individual had a reputation for being extremely harsh to black citizens in the county. Prior to the resignation, I had covered demonstrations for and against the sheriff. As I was driving home on the day of his resignation, I was intrigued by the rage and helplessness felt by both sides—the sheriff's supporters and his opponents. But it was the idea of people caught in the middle of something beyond their control that planted the seed for *Plowed Fields*.

**Q. What research was required to write the book?**
A. It was fairly extensive. Fortunately, I have always loved history, so I naturally knew about most of the historical events that made it into the book. I did some limited research on those aspects to confirm I had the correct dates and authentic details. The heavy research came to ensure I understood the time and setting of the story. The main character, Joe Baker, is fifteen years older than me, so he had a difference frame of reference. And while I grew up on a farm in South Georgia, I had to make sure I had the details right. I read through countless issues of my hometown newspapers from 1960 to 1970. I also relied on interviews with my daddy and my uncles to ensure I got the farming details right for the period, as my personal farm knowledge was limited to the 1970s.

**Q. Obviously, *Plowed Fields* is a work of fiction, but what is real in the novel and what is based on your own experiences?**
A. The historical references are certainly real. That part of the South did elect a woman to Congress in the late 1950s and I personally knew of two people who died from rattlesnake bites in a snake-handling church. The Baker family's farm and house were modeled almost exclusively after my paternal grandparents' farm (my mama lives there now), although I did expand the size significantly and throw in landscape features that make the book's farm more intriguing. Beyond that, it's mostly my imagination. No doubt, my life experiences are reflected in the book, but I think they're reflected in the attitudes and values portrayed and not so much in the actual events in the story. I can count on two hands the actual

events that occurred in my life and made it into the book. But with one exception, those life events simply provided a nugget that could be expanded and embellished into something much more interesting than the real event. The one exception involves something that happened to me and a friend when we were camping at his pond. I drew enormously on that real-life experience to write that particular scene. But even the scene is embellished. I want to assure my mama that my friend Jerry and I did not drink any beer that night when we camped out!

**Q. What do you want readers to take away from reading *Plowed Fields*?**
A. Beyond being entertained, I hope they come away with a true sense of the time and place where the book is set. It's a special time and place in my mind, and I wanted to preserve it in some way when I wrote *Plowed Fields*. I also hope the book challenges their faith as well. I believe the story is a journey of faith in many ways—sometimes in very blatant terms and sometimes just hovering in the background. I hope readers will consider their own faith in light of what happens to the characters in the book and end up in a very positive place.

**Q. What do you like most about the book?**
A. Oh, gosh, that may be the toughest question anyone has asked me. I like the detail and what I hope is the deep exploration of the characters. I think you get to know the people—even the minor characters—inside and out in many ways. Beyond that, I love the portrayal of a farming family's life, especially in that day and age. The story does a credible job of helping understand what it's like to own and work on a farm, especially the joys and the hardships that come with it.

Made in the USA
Columbia, SC
06 December 2019